D1569706

THE
CONSTANT
TRAVELLERS

THE
CONSTANT
TRAVELLERS

GORDON ALLEN BASICHIS

G. P. Putnam's Sons, New York

Copyright © 1978 by Gordon Allen Basichis

All rights reserved. This book, or parts thereof, may not be reproduced
without permission from the publisher. Printed simultaneously in Canada
by Longman Canada Limited, Toronto.

SBN: 399-12109-9

Library of Congress Cataloging in Publication Data

Basichis, Gordon Allen.
    The constant travellers.

    I. Title.
PZ4.B2988Co   [PS3552.A812]   813'.5'4   77-17432

PRINTED IN THE UNITED STATES OF AMERICA

For Marcia . . .
. . . for everything.

THE
CONSTANT
TRAVELLERS

Chapter 1

Shelby Lopez burped and stared in the general direction of his campfire. He watched the flames die, unable to restore themselves upon the meager bits of wood he had held in reserve. Poor Lopez, he was much too tired from his travels to stumble around in the darkness in search of more fuel. For his efforts he'd probably be bitten by a snake, or shot down by some nameless figure hidden in the shadows. Lopez saw himself clearly, an arrow in his back, dying as the different creatures of the desert rejoiced at the prospect of another human meal.

Things had not gone well for Shelby Lopez. Not well at all. Ever since the Civil War, his once promising life had dwindled into fatelessness. Little that was promising appeared before him, and what was in the past was best left forgotten. His former potential, his business reputation, had been exchanged for the primitive instincts of his ancestors. These ancients, berobed and bearded, in the meager light of the fire stood before him, as if they were guided through

9

some vicious animal cycle. They seemed amused by his frustrations, found laughter in his hopelessness. How Shelby wished they'd mention their names or offer advice. If not, then at least offer their daughters as a momentary consolation. But as suddenly as they appeared, these ancient figures disappeared from view, their images yielding to the encroachments of the desert chill and footsteps plodding through the sand.

Lopez trembled slightly and listened to the sound. He hoped to pinpoint the location of the footsteps before he moved away from the fire which offered him up as an easy target. His hand slipped back to his .45. Cautiously, he cocked the hammer and crawled deeper into the shadows. He prayed he was not backing off into the wrong direction, toward the approach of the assailant. Almost afraid to look, he glanced over his shoulder. Nothing. Above him the moon was shining, illuminating the desert plain. For just an instant Shelby thought himself on a different planet. Again he was reminded just how far from home he had travelled.

Lopez slipped between the rocks and aimed his revolver toward the approaching footsteps. A horse, he thought, for no other desert animal could make that noise. Shelby felt his chest and his heart pounding from within his rib cage. This was really happening, he told himself. Really taking place.

Thunderbird Hawkins allowed the light from the distant campsite to direct his travel. He too had come a long way since the break of day, and it was time to rest. To Thunderbird, what could be better on the desert than to meet with another human being? To laze about a campfire and exchange stories. To bullshit and lie to his heart's content. For there was little chance he'd ever see the other person again. And if he did, or if the other person caught him in a lie, so what? In the midst of the Great Massive Desert what else should they exchange? Facts? Facts were always so boring. Even he, the poorly educated Thunderbird

Hawkins, knew man lusted toward that which was beyond his means.

Shelby was startled at first by Thunderbird Hawkins. He had anticipated a cat and mouse game, with each man chasing the other about the eerie night. He had envisioned sporadic gunfire, mutterings and a hail of chastisement. He had half expected, before it was over, for the two men to be locked in mortal combat, his knife thrust toward the other's throat. Which would've been an unfortunate condition, since Shelby's blade was nowhere to be found. But here was this Indian walking right down the center of a clearing, just as calmly as he pleased. Behind him came his horse, following obediently, free of rein.

Thunderbird Hawkins was hardly the most formidable figure to be seen cutting through the desert landscape. A short, squat man, he was wrapped inside an Indian blanket. A battered high hat was pulled down around his ears, shadowing his dark eyes. Leather pants, with silver conchos running down both legs, jutted from beneath his wrap. Several strands of silver and turquoise hung down from his neck. He carried a shotgun in one hand, clutched by the barrel. He didn't appear ready for violent action.

Shelby cautiously stepped from the shadows and pointed his pistol at the Indian's belly. He searched for a threatening statement, but none reached his mind. So he stood his ground, feigning ferocity.

Upon seeing Lopez, the Indian pulled up sharply. He said nothing, though his eyes were fixed on the pistol Shelby clutched in his hand. The combined apprehension and disdain added new wrinkles to Hawkins' weathered face. He furrowed his prodigious brow and assessed the situation. Some dumb sonofabitch is gonna kill me, he realized, cause I happened in his direction.

"What's the matter, don't you like Indians?" Thunderbird asked after the passing of several awkward moments.

11

Shelby was taken aback. He was sure this solitary Indian had been a guise to trick him into dropping his guard. Certainly more Indians were waiting in ambush behind the rocks. At a given signal they'd spring forth and slay the lonely Shelby. After which they'd celebrate, before relieving his corpse of his guns, his horse and his knife, if they could find it. Also they would take his hair, adding his rusty wire to their collections of flax and auburn. He didn't like it. For his ancestors to have fled from one nation to another. For them to have travelled thousands of miles across the ocean to a land they weren't sure even existed. And then for their youngest descendant to trek another few thousand miles across hostile wilderness simply so his hair could hang at the end of an Indian's trophy stick was ridiculous. Totally insane.

"May I come forward?" Thunderbird asked in deep and even tones. "Could I sit down?"

When Shelby failed to reply, Thunderbird cautiously seated himself on the far side of the campfire and rearranged the kindling. "You call this a fire?" he challenged the young stranger. "This couldn't even keep the spirits warm. And they have no bones, no blood, no flesh. Nothing to worry about."

Shelby clucked his tongue against the roof of his mouth and considered his reply. His teeth chattered when he tried to part his lips in order to form words.

"Have any coffee?" Thunderbird wondered aloud. His eyes were still focused on the gun in Shelby's hand.

"Coffee?"

"Coffee," Hawkins repeated, drawing his arms over his shoulders to indicate he was suffering from the midnight chill.

"Oh." Shelby sidestepped to where his saddlebags were lying. He pulled back the flap and dove in with one hand; the other still trained the gun on Thunderbird Hawkins.

12

The Indian accepted the coffee can which was tossed by Shelby. "Are you expecting a bandit?" He nodded toward the gun.

"You're a stranger," explained Shelby. "Out here."

Hawkins looked around him, his stocky body twisting from its squatting position to take in the four directions of the Earth.

"Anyone coming off the desert would be a stranger," mused the Indian as he reached for the coffeepot.

Still apprehensive, Shelby approached the Indian, affording the older man his first real glimpse of Lopez. In silence Thunderbird noted the abundant red curls squashed beneath the floppy Western hat, the wrinkled muslin shirt, the ratty old jeans that were stained by a careless pair of hands. Slowly, the Indian shook his head. "Should I make more coffee for you?" he asked, the coffeepot brandished in the firelight.

"Not too strong," Shelby warned him. "I have a long way to go before I can buy more grounds."

Hawkins smiled. "Certainly." He regarded Shelby's broad shoulders and the chest sloping down into a narrow waist. Tall, thought Hawkins, approximating Shelby to stand a good foot above the Indian. But despite his man-size stature there was still much of the boy in his appearance. Something awkward. Something vulnerable.

Hawkins stood up and moved toward his horse. "I'm getting my things," he explained, hauling a huge leather sack from the back of his horse. With surprisingly little effort he lugged the sack back to the campfire and dropped it to the ground. The bag served as a comfortable mattress for Hawkins, and, after performing a brief wiggling ceremony, he settled into its folds.

Shelby tried to conceal his amazement at the man's apparent calm. All this time a .45 revolver had been trained on his chest, and he chose to ignore it.

"I could shoot you," Lopez proposed suddenly.

After first showing a trace of alarm, Hawkins settled back into his usual nonchalance. "What for?"

"To be sure you won't harm me."

Thunderbird sighed in disgust. He had decided he liked the young man with the curly red hair, but his recent behavior was becoming difficult to overlook. "You're sure already," he insisted, "otherwise you would've shot me when I walked into your camp."

Lopez brushed his nose with the back of his hand and considered Hawkins' point of view. "What about the others?" he asked, feeling stupid as the words left his mouth.

Hawkins looked around him once again. "What others?"

Shelby belched again, before cursing the beans that had messed with his digestion. Hiccups followed in rapid succession. Each was painful to Shelby's insides.

"Hold your breath and strike yourself here," directed Hawkins, his fist indicating the solar plexus. "Go ahead."

Reluctantly Shelby used the top of his fist to strike himself in the solar plexus. Nothing happened. His second blow was launched with more enthusiasm. It found its mark, eliciting a resounding belch that echoed through the darkness. All around him the different forms of desert life responded. Some chattered, while others croaked. A few merely fled from the scene, the phantom whisper of their footsteps proving their existence. But the hiccups had also disappeared. Shelby smiled in satisfaction.

"You've beaten the spirit."

"What?"

"He had climbed inside you and pushed against your chest. By striking here, you hit him squarely, and he was forced to run away. It happens all the time. Now, would you please put that gun away?"

After a moment of hesitation, Shelby returned his gun to its holster. He squatted by the fire, eyeing the old Indian

14

suspiciously. He was unsure of his interaction with an Indian.

Hawkins paid no attention to the white man's discomfort. The coffee was ready, and the aroma spewed from the fresh pot, delighting his senses. All day he had longed for the brew.

After savoring a few swallows, Thunderbird returned to Lopez. "How do they call you?"

"Shelby. Shelby Lopez."

Hawkins narrowed his eyes incredulously and poured for the younger man. "Are you of Mexican descent?"

"No. I'm not of Mexican descent."

Thunderbird wouldn't leave it alone. His face twisted and he wrinkled his mouth. "Lopez ... and you're not of Mexican descent?"

"No."

A wash of silence passed between them. Shelby, through the years, had grown tired of people asking what a person of his appearance was doing with a name like Lopez. At one time Shelby even considered changing his name. To Logan. But he could never get used to its sound. He often wished people would dub him with a nickname. Call him Reds, or Kid. But he was not the type.

"It's Jewish," Shelby finally proclaimed.

"You're a Hebrew? So am I."

Lopez viewed the Indian suspiciously before he searched for the joke. Hawkins was being sincere, almost boastful.

"You're what?"

"A Hebrew. At least part of me. On my mother's side."

Shelby cast a long look about him. His head bobbed as he twisted it to regard the space. At last he returned to Thunderbird Hawkins. His thickset face was beaming from beneath his ragged high hat and dark, braided hair.

"How could you possibly be Jewish?" asked Lopez.

"A Hebrew," Thunderbird corrected. "From the lost

15

tribes who wandered into this continent many years ago. I read about it many times, in many places. I am a descendant of Abraham, the father of Isaac and Jacob. I've spent many years, many different lifetimes, on many different deserts. I am a constant traveller, a wanderer whose roots journey through the source of my consciousness."

Even though he had finished speaking, Thunderbird's index finger still indicated a point existing just above his eyes in the center of his forehead. His eyes widened, as if the finger had energized certain faculties, as if he was entranced by its power. His expression grew blank and remained so for several minutes. At last he returned, his eyes blinking as he studied Shelby's reaction.

"I don't know. I was never told. . . ."

"How could you know?"

"All right," laughed Shelby. "You can be Jewish."

"Hebrew!"

With that settled the two men concentrated on the taste of their coffee. They sipped slowly, savoring each ounce of flavor. The Indian was pleased, and he often sighed as the hot liquid slipped down his throat. With the first cup out of the way, he poured himself a second. After drinking half, he rested the cup between his legs while he reached into his sack, extracting a small pouch, which was also made of leather. Intricate beadwork decorated its exterior. With this on his lap Hawkins then removed a foot-long deerhorn pipe from his large pouch and set it down. His thick fingers dipped into the smaller bag and extracted some of its contents. This he rolled between his fingers, crumbling the contents into the bowl.

"Tobacco?" wondered Shelby.

Hawkins smiled. He shook his head and persuaded Lopez to smoke it. He pulled a flaming twig from the fire. "It's used much on the desert," he explained.

Shelby took his first pull and allowed the smoke to enter

16

his lungs. He coughed at first but became more accustomed to the sensation with each passing draw.

Hawkins patted his solar plexus indicating contentment. "It lets the spirit know you're happy with its presence."

Soon there was no more need for the smoke. The deerhorn pipe and its leafy contents had done their work. The two men, with faces flushed, sat staring into the brilliant firelight. They had not moved for several hours, Thunderbird because he was comfortable, and Shelby because he feared the slightest move on his part would cause the top of his head to fall off. An odd way to scalp someone, noted Lopez, between spectacular digressions. He glanced over to Hawkins, noting the contented look on the older man's face. He liked Thunderbird. He was relieved he had come along.

"Where do you come from?" asked Hawkins, as if his question had stemmed from an hour's worth of contemplation.

"Back East," pointed Shelby.

"And now?"

Lopez shrugged it off. He gestured to the bags and his horse. "This is it. The whole business."

"You could always wish for more."

Shelby was compelled to snicker. "No, I couldn't."

"Why?"

"It would never fit on my horse," he answered, before erupting into fits of laughter.

Thunderbird had seen the humor also. The two men rolled about the campsite, clutching their sides. They laughed until they ached, and then they laughed some more. Somewhere in the distance a lone coyote howled its sentiments, and nearby a snake slithered through the night. But the rattler had few evil intentions, especially toward men who found humor in the midst of the desert.

17

Chapter 2

The morning sun had just cleared the eastern mountains when Shelby was roused from sleep. He awakened suddenly. Creeping fear gnawed at his insides as he searched the landscape through bloodshot eyes. He expected the crazy Indian to have long been gone with everything Shelby possessed. He was wrong. Instead, the inimitable Thunderbird Hawkins was crouched by the fire, preparing morning coffee. It struck Shelby that the Indian might not have moved all night, but remained squatted, drinking endless quantities of coffee.

"Want some?" asked Hawkins.

Lopez peeled off his blankets and nodded his head. "Yeah. After all, it's my coffee."

Thunderbird regarded Lopez with mild derision, his black liquid eyes widening momentarily before reverting to their normal drowsy appearance. He decided against reprimanding the young man, since it was too early in the morning.

Again, he turned his head for a better look at Shelby and found that much of what he first ascertained about the young man's appearance held true in the light of day. The only difference in Lopez was his hat. It was no longer a western cowboy hat, but an easterner's hat worn with the brim turned down. Crushed down upon his red curls it made Lopez seem all the more comical. Hawkins grunted and returned to his coffee.

Lopez yawned and stretched his muscles. "I still can't sleep on the hard, bare ground. It hurts like hell in the morning."

"I'll tell the spirits, and perhaps they'll soften the ground for you," Thunderbird said with a wink.

Shelby accepted the cup of coffee from Hawkins and gazed about him. He gave every direction equal attention, pausing now and then to squint at points of particular interest. East and west were the mountains, sweeping across the plains from the north and south. All that seemed to prevent the two different mountain ranges from joining into a circle were undisrupted passages vanishing beyond the horizon.

Lopez shook his head, more alarmed than awed. "Christ, it's like we're in the middle of nowhere, surrounded by more of the same. Strange. I never thought it'd happen to me."

Hawkins followed the path of Shelby's vision. He too noted the mountains looming so far away. He regarded the countless shrubs, the cactus and the mesquite, the mesas and the arroyos. He watched an eagle dive from the clouds and a lizard streak across the sand.

"Yeah, in the middle of nowhere," Shelby repeated.

"A person is always in the middle of nowhere," intoned the Indian.

"Why's 'at?"

Thunderbird paused to sip his coffee. "We're lost where we stand. We must travel, must find new places, new voices of the spirit. No discoveries are made by standing in

19

emptiness. We must journey to seek what we will. To find ourselves."

Lopez stared incredulously, pausing after a while to transfer his eyes to the Indian's odd physique. In the daylight Thunderbird Hawkins seemed more like a cannonball mounted on a bed of concrete. His arms and legs were like short bands of steel, his fingers like railroad spikes. Though he only stood to Shelby's chin, the younger man was assured the Indian would be one tough customer if he so chose.

Hawkins watched in silence while the young man scrutinized him. He smiled at the glint of surprise in Shelby's expression. Satisfied he had made the right impression, Thunderbird packed and saddled his horse.

Lopez swayed behind him, his arms awkwardly set at his sides. Unsure of his next move, Lopez glanced across the desert and grew frightened. He never assumed anything, except the sea, was quite as big. He wished Hawkins would indicate that Shelby could follow, even discreetly to the rear. At last Hawkins nodded his head. Breathing a sigh of relief, Shelby mounted his horse. He looked around him once again, shivering at the awesome space he dwelled in. It all seemed so strange. He was overwhelmed by its vastness, by its silence.

"How far is it exactly to the next town?" Lopez asked Hawkins after they had travelled some ways.

Thunderbird **indicated the** direction with the point of his chin.

Shelby peered after but saw nothing. He frowned and ran his tongue across his lips, which were already dry and cracking. "Yeah, but how far?"

This time Hawkins indicated the direction with his hand. His steel digit pointed to a spot just off from the southern mountain range. It was there the mountains ended. At least they appeared to end. From their distance it was still very hard to determine.

20

Shelby was even more puzzled than before. "I still don't know how far it is we have to go," he insisted.

Hawkins shrugged and began to ride away. Shelby followed, begging the Indian's pardon.

"It doesn't matter how far," Hawkins explained after they'd ridden some distance. "You're either going or you're not going. That's all that matters. The length of the journey should make no difference."

A little further along the trail Hawkins extracted another leather pouch from beneath his Indian blanket. From this he removed several cuttings of dried mushrooms. Without a word of explanation he popped several cuttings into his mouth and passed the rest to Shelby. "It'll occupy your thoughts," he explained as Shelby reluctantly accepted the mushrooms.

The mushrooms were tough and ugly, like dead, dried toads in miniature. Lopez stared at them with apprehension before he finally dropped them inside his mouth. The terrible taste of the cuttings overwhelmed his tongue. Quickly he swallowed them and turned to the Indian for further explanation. "What the hell are those things?" he asked of his companion.

"Mushrooms," Hawkins said easily.

"God! They taste awful!"

"You're not eating them for their taste, but for their substance."

"Hell, I should hope so. Hey, what's your name anyway?" he asked, remembering it hadn't been discussed the night before.

"Thunderbird Hawkins."

"Thunderbird Hawkins? You know you're the first Indian I've ever spoken to."

"I'm overwhelmed with gratitude."

"No. I mean, I've not had much chance to come into contact with Indians. Are there many named Thunderbird?"

"Some."

21

"Hawkins. What about Hawkins?"

Thunderbird shook his head. "No. Not many. None other that I know of."

"How did you get to be named then?"

"My father was a strange man."

"Yeah, so was mine. More dull than anything else. Funny, in all the years I've known him, he never once told me what he wanted out of life. All the time he'd give me lectures on what he expected from me, what he predicted I'd be, if I do this and that. But he never did get to the bottom of it all. He never said what it was that got him up every morning."

Thunderbird removed his hat and used his hand to brush back his hair. "Maybe he didn't know himself."

Shelby pondered aloud. "You think so, huh? You think a man can live for fifty-odd years and never know what causes him to rise every morning. That's awfully hard to believe."

"Did he talk of other things?"

"Yeah. Sure. Occasionally."

"Did he take the time to explain them?"

"When he thought it necessary. Or if the store wasn't busy. He never had time when his store was busy. Customers! His one great pleasure was serving his customers."

"And you never asked why he awakened every morning?"

"No. He wasn't the type you asked such a question. Straight answers were never his best means of explanation."

"Then maybe he really didn't know."

"I guess."

An hour passed before their conversation came abruptly to a halt. The sun was extremely strong now, and the mushrooms had begun to inflict their passion. Shelby felt it in his cheeks and at the back of his neck. He found his head growing lighter, and for a few terrible moments he believed it would sail clear away. Just twist from his neck and fly off into the sun. Shelby's fingers were numb, as were his toes. A hollow was carved in the pit of his stomach. Atop his horse he swayed indifferently with each passing step, as if his travels were bringing him no closer to the point just west of the southern mountain range.

Thunderbird showed no clear sign of change except that his eyelids had fallen over his eyeballs. Like silk over marble, the lids dropped free of wrinkles or tension. Unafraid of external threats, he kept his eyes closed, his concentration focused on his insides. Before long Shelby discovered Thunderbird was sleeping. It was not apparent until the Indian snored. Each snore boomed like thunder in the canyon, and Hawkins' lip dangled so spittle escaped to his chin. His head bobbed and weaved in rhythm to his horse's motion, and his hands rested on his saddle.

After much staring at Hawkins, Shelby blinked, and the magic in his eyes caused Thunderbird's face to transform into that of Shelby's aged and missing Aunt Belle. Her cheeks were red with rouge and a bright floral bandanna was wrapped around her head. Thick, gold hoops dangled from her ears, and vibrant red lipstick stained her mouth. She was laughing, roaring in her peculiar manner, the type unacceptable for ladylike behavior.

"You know what you can do with ladylike behavior," she once challenged Sarah, Shelby's troubled and serious mother and the younger sister of Aunt Belle. "It wasn't etiquette I was born from, but from copulation," Belle rambled. Her deep, magnificent voice bellowed forth another round, while timid Sarah squirmed with dismay.

Later that night, Aunt Belle was taken from Shelby's house and escorted to Poor Yussel's Home for the Insane Aged, better known as Poor Yussel's to all who feared and resented its presence.

"She'll be happy there," his father, Leonard Lopez, had insisted. "She'll meet others like herself, and she'll get along just fine."

Poor Sarah couldn't answer. She was too busy crying.

"She will be happy!" commanded Leonard.

But Sarah was not convinced. Throughout the evening

she pleaded with her husband to relent on his convictions and prevent Belle's incarceration at Poor Yussel's. But Leonard's heart was hardened. Years of the woman's outbursts had caused Lopez senior to harbor little more than disdain for the woman. It was Belle who constantly mocked all Leonard held sacred.

"And my sister's not so hot either," Belle suggested to all the members of the family who had gathered together to celebrate the holidays. "She can be a stinker at times. Not as bad as her husband, of course, but she's so ashamed of her side of the family, of the pirate spirit that dwells among us. She believes her brother Shmuel, and my younger twin, was no better than a common thief. Which is untrue, since in no way is Shmuel common at all. Not to mention the years he supported her royal highness, as well as our dear and dead mother.

"And all this scorn for Shmuel's dishonesty while her own husband grifts pennies and dimes from the senile old fools who shop his store. Imagine!"

The family did. With their jaws agape. Occasionally they ventured a look at one another, but mutual embarrassment forced them to divert their eyes.

"I think it's time you went to bed now," put in Sarah, hoping the attendants from Poor Yussel's would soon arrive and end the ordeal. "You need your sleep."

"That's the last thing I need at my age. One day I'll close my eyes and fail to open them. And then where will I be? No one knows. Which reminds me ... so what good does prayer do you?"

No one in the family seemed to have an answer, or cared to express it.

"Dinner's ready now," Sarah interrupted. She wished the appetites accumulated during the recent fast would cause her family and friends to ignore Belle's ravings.

Belle followed them into the dining room where a huge spread lay waiting for the fast-breakers. She smiled to one and all and began eating.

"Not yet," warned Leonard Lopez, checking the watch he'd been given on his last birthday. "Love—the Family," was written on the back. "Now!" he shouted when the final minute had elapsed. "Eat, everyone. Eat!"

Shelby stood in the doorway and watched friends and family break the fast. They were all there, that's for sure, except for Uncle Shmuel, who had been excluded long ago by Shelby's father. The exclusion, over the years, had become somewhat of a ritual in itself. Young Lopez considered Shmuel on the eve of the end of the holiday. He, if he was at all true to character, couldn't care less if the holiday existed. Only to satisfy his political position would the holiday be any concern of his. Quietly, in the bedroom of his well-appointed house, Shmuel would be seated with his latest favorite hooker. Dressed in his expensively tailored suits, he'd reveal signs of fatigue. His rounds on the holidays were always exhausting. Still his position, his stature in the community, was better regarded than the thief he formerly was. A damn good thief too. It was said that he could steal anything in his time.

"Don't you ever visit your Uncle Shmuel!" Leonard always threatened. "If I catch you over there I'll beat you within an inch of your life."

But what excitement did Leonard hold for his son in the face of Shmuel's dramatic involvements? Besides, it wasn't the inch of his life that Shelby was concerned with, but the six inches that hung below his belt line. And it was Shmuel, not his father, who could take care of that.

Ever since he had reached his teens Shelby always visited Shmuel for advice on sexual matters. Though he laughed good-naturedly at the serious expressions on his nephew's face, the gray and wiry-headed Shmuel always responded with a straight answer. Problems of adolescence always seemed to be in Shmuel's domain. He was the only one to turn to.

For constantly Shelby searched for love and emotional involvement. He peeked in windows, under dress lines and in the park. He asked, he taunted, he suggested, but all the nice young ladies on the block recoiled with horror. Soon Shelby was branded a smartass by his elders and was prevented from visiting with any of their daughters. So, in desperation, he crossed the lines and turned to the *goyim*. But they weren't much good either. At first, at the very sight of Shelby, they'd surround him and hope to kick in his silly ass. Usually they couldn't catch him. And when he grew older, he also grew tougher, and few dared take him on.

But Shelby was soon to learn, after a truce was finally arrived at, that the goyim held no great sexual advantages. Likewise, they had strange and silly customs that forbade just about everything that was fun. Even jerking off would bring God's wrath down upon one's dirty little neck. Death and insanity were probable, if not certain. And, if by some miracle they were circumvented, there was always Disgrace. Disgrace was a big deal where Shelby lived. Since little could be done to the dead or insane, Disgrace was the only recourse left to punish the guilty. To be Disgraced meant finding another place to live, as well as someone to fix your meals. Even your own mother wouldn't dare risk touching your food.

And then of course, if all else failed, there was Complete Disgrace. Complete Disgrace was sometimes followed by a period of mourning, during which one's family donned black. Collectively they would bemoan the death of their precocious child.

With the threat of Complete Disgrace looming before him, Shelby had only Shmuel to turn to. It wasn't a bad choice since Shmuel, being well connected in politics, had his fingers in a good many operations. On his sixteenth birthday young Lopez was presented by his uncle with the use of a pretty young hooker. Unfortunately, Shelby was so nervous that he came as soon as he removed his pants. Try as she might, the young woman could do little to revive Shmuel's nephew.

"It's no use," she proclaimed with harsh finality. "I could do better with a celery stalk."

Shmuel nodded his head and tipped the hooker ten bucks. "That's okay," he said. "We'll try some other time."

"It's your father," Shmuel explained to his nephew, after the girl had departed. "His influence. It's bad for you, as it is for anyone with common sense. Don't go limp in life every time you brush against a bare ass. It could cause your downfall."

Worried over his downfall, Shelby left Shmuel's and returned to his house, vowing a life of celibacy all the way. He ate little for supper and went directly to his bedroom after the meal. He tried to sleep but was too filled with anguish. He had just about given up when there came a knocking at the front door. Shelby jumped out of bed and ran to the top of the stairs, just in time to hear his mother shrieking. His father cursed and otherwise expressed his agony.

"What is it?" called Shelby from the top of the stairs.

"Nothing," replied his mother.

But his father was much too angry to display the tact of concealment. "Your damned Aunt Belle just escaped from Poor Yussel's. She knocked a guard over the head and jumped out a window. They chased her but she disappeared."

Shelby could barely contain himself. "Oh," he cried, more in exhilaration than surprise. Belle escaped. Dear, dear Belle. Taking her pirate spirit with her. Certainly there was hope for Shelby, after all.

Chapter 3

As a buffer against the sun, Thunderbird Hawkins erected a wide-brimmed parasol which he mounted in the socket he had fastened to his saddle. The parasol's colors were vibrant, especially when contrasted by the singularity of the clear blue sky. Oranges, yellows, reds and greens flashed about, struggling for dominance on the rugged canvas. A white fringe hung down from the circumference, and one small tear in the fabric allowed a spot of light to embrace Hawkins' cheek.

The smug display of satisfaction on the Indian's face only reminded Shelby of his own discomfort. He was a city boy, born and bred in the moisture of the north, and the dryness of the desert caused his skin to itch. Compounded with his shirt scraping against his sunburn, every movement became a barbed tongue, licking at his arms, back, and abdomen. His head ached from the heat, and from the weight of his old hat. Both hatband and crown were drenched with sweat, and beads of perspiration poured down Shelby's face. In notes he would jot down on pages he'd lose, Shelby contended he had had a miserable time with the desert heat.

In contempt for its ferocity Shelby glanced upward to the pale orange sphere he had grown to detest. Wasn't there ever a cloudy day on the desert? Never, back East, did it ever seem this hot. Not even in Tennessee, or Georgia, or the places visited during Sherman's March to the Sea. It wasn't Sherman marching, but Shelby. As he thought of the war, blue soldiers appeared in his field of vision, suddenly turning purple and vanishing in swirls that traversed the sun. Lopez recalled the battles, the rushing up and down hillsides, the peekaboo death games played from behind trees, rock formations and stranded cattle. He saw a pool of blood, stretching across the breadth of the valley he and Hawkins were approaching. Men shrieked until yellow discs surrounded their words and sped them off into the mountains. Everywhere there were dead men, lying about in a multiplicity of contortions. What a haven for souvenirs, Shelby had thought as he chased across the fields, trying not to step on the dead men's faces. Someday, someone will make a bundle.

His concentration suddenly ended, Lopez blinked his eyes before resuming his surveillance of the distant valley. No blood this time. Only sand and scrub and assorted cacti. And a strange movement, attracting his attention, forcing spasms in his soul. He turned to Thunderbird, who showed no signs of surprise, before turning back toward the valley. Once again Shelby glimpsed a movement. Something larger, much bigger than life, was moving around down there. Lopez blinked his eyes and took a sip of water, thinking it would do him some good. No sooner had he replaced his canteen than he saw it again. Another flash, illusions playing hide 'n' seek with his consciousness. He dared not find it, although he couldn't bear to avert his eyes from that spot in the valley.

Lopez turned to Hawkins, but Thunderbird revealed no

sign that he had been attentive to Shelby's hallucinations. He appeared most comfortable beneath the shade of his parasol. Hesitantly, Shelby attempted to ask the Indian if he had observed anything strange, but the restrictions of logic blighted his tongue.

Lopez glanced at the Indian with due suspicion. He frowned at Hawkins and considered what tricks the older man was playing on his eyes.

"What was in those mushrooms, anyway?"

"Just something from the desert."

Lopez brought his focus on Lana Culvane, whom he desperately hoped had not married her fiancé, Lloyd De-Pugh—that his pride had prevented him from taking Culvane's daughter's hand in marriage. DePugh, one of the nation's leaders in beef processing, could have built a virtual livestock empire with the assistance of Doug Culvane. Together they could've dominated—DePugh with his cattle, Culvane with his hogs and sheep. But the vision of his fiancée embracing Shelby in a modified sixty-nine was more than the young magnate could bear. Disgusted was he, when he walked unannounced into Lana's hotel room, the bellboy and his lackey by his side.

"Never have I seen such a thing!" he wailed, interrupting Shelby and Lana at the height of passion.

"It's good that you told me," said Lana, not bothering to cover up her naked body. "For this is one of the things I like to do best."

"Call the police!" the enraged DePugh demanded. "Call her father!"

DePugh wouldn't listen to reason. He fumbled for his gun while Shelby raced to dress. With his shirt still unbuttoned, Lopez reached the bedroom window just as DePugh cocked the hammer of his gun. Fortunately for Shelby, his paramour was a better aim than DePugh. From inside the night table drawer, Lana had extracted the King James Bible, which she hurled at Lloyd, forcing him to miss his shot. By the time the young meat broker had recovered, Shelby had escaped through the window.

And now where was she, this woman Shelby had come to love? Where was she hidden? Where did she go? A tear fell from his eye when he considered Lana being forced to uphold her family obligations. Many times Lopez had considered writing a letter to DePugh's residence in hopes Lana would receive it. But logic ruled, for he was only too well aware that upon receipt of the letter, DePugh would whisk his gunmen to the city indicated by the postmark.

Lana was especially beautiful. Her flaxen hair was streaked with silver, and her blue eyes glistened like the pools of a grand mirage. Her favorite brown shawl hung casually from her shoulders, and a pretty lace dress was crimped at the waist. She loomed tall, but was slight in build. Her legs were as long as Shelby's, and her trunk was lithe, limber like that of a baby willow tree. Her breasts were small, and hardly noticeable when embroiled by the passion which burned inside her. On the desert, or anywhere else, Lana Culvane was a remarkable woman.

When their horses tired, the companions dismounted and walked toward the point lying just west of the southern mountains. Shelby, like his horse, was covered with sweat, and panting. His jeans and shirt were soaked, his feet ached, and perspiration burned his eyes as it slipped from his forehead. Endlessly Shelby dabbed himself with his bandanna. It was useless.

"How is it you never sweat?" he asked in envy of the Indian, who plodded through the sand like a man just beginning his day.

Thunderbird cocked his head to note the strain on Shelby's face. He could see the young man's arms and legs growing numb. Their trek was exhaustive, there was no doubt about it. Yet there was little Hawkins could do to assist Lopez. He must bear the burden or satisfy none of his wishes. Unable to bear his burden, he would die where he stood, rotting like an abandoned mule.

"You must evict the spirit of pain," warned Hawkins. "You can't let him know you're afraid of his power."

Shelby ran his swelled tongue over his lips and mulled it over. "Is that what you do?"

Thunderbird removed his hat and brushed off the dust on the sleeve of his poncho. "I do many things. Staying dry is only one of them."

For support Shelby tightened his grip around his horse's rein and gazed past the Indian to the gnarled and tortured landscape. In the distance clouds had gathered in vast formations. A strange menagerie of godheads and mythical beasts appeared rich and nascent. Shelby spotted them one by one as they passed above. He wished momentarily to be among them, at the mercy of the wind, free of all decisions. So what if they lasted but a moment, just a different moment, gauged by different eyes?

"It would be easier to become a cloud," admitted Hawkins, as if he read Shelby's thoughts. "If you were a cloud, you'd not be here, stuck on the desert. And then again, if you were a cloud, you wouldn't be here tomorrow."

"I'm not sure I care either way," muttered Shelby, more for his own benefit than for Hawkins'.

Thunderbird shrugged, his eyes filled with understanding. "I used to think like you, a long time ago. I was younger, little more than half your age."

"Who changed your mind?"

"I did."

A strange consideration disturbed Shelby. He had seen Hawkins before. Perhaps on the Jersey beaches, the deserts of the East. Maybe his recollection was just another dream, a mere glimpse of Thunderbird Hawkins' most distinctive

32

face. The heavy, round face, the black, piercing eyes ... he had seen them before! Shelby was certain. He had witnessed the same mug among a crowd of faces, faces whose characteristics had faded to a blur. All except Hawkins'. Misshapen, distorted and frightening, the other faces had appeared before Shelby with a savage presence before yielding to that of Thunderbird Hawkins.

"Where are you from?" he asked Thunderbird, just as they parted from the valley and began to climb uphill.

Hawkins toyed with the feathers that were attached to the golden hoop hanging from his left ear. He wound them around each other, and then, as if he sensed the feathers couldn't be twisted anymore, he let go, giving his answer at the same time. He smiled. "I'm from the desert."

"You were born out here?"

Thunderbird glanced around him, taking in the different scenery. "No. Not out here. Somewhere else."

"A place like this?"

"No place is just like this."

Shelby wished to avoid the significance in the Indian's answer. He'd already determined the Indian was filled with too many riddles to go chasing after every one. Since he had first met Hawkins, Shelby found that the Indian's brand of confusion provided relief for some of the grief he had been feeling. A strange but certain satisfaction was derived from his companionship. Shelby laughed, believing in the future. He'd recall Hawkins as a decent companion with whom he had travelled during his time of need. But for now, as the heat burned down, piercing his skull and draining his brain, as the dryness cracked his skin and creased his bones, Shelby ignored most of what the Indian was saying.

"Did you enjoy growing up in the desert?"

Thunderbird shook his head. "I moved around much. My father was a strange and restless man."

"What'd he do for a living?"

"A breeder. Of horses, goats and. . . ."

33

"And what?" Shelby was anxious to pursue.

"Trouble," whispered Hawkins, suddenly drifting off into thoughts of his own. "Any force to which he attached himself seemed to betray him. He was brave, strong and intelligent. But he could never master the forces around him. He was a victim of his own chemistry."

"Did you like him?"

Thunderbird rubbed his nose with the back of his hand and considered Shelby's question. "I barely knew him," he said, recalling the image of his father. That it had dulled with the passage of time came as no surprise to him. But now the image was more vivid than it had been for years. Perhaps the light was right, or the winds were favorable. Or the mushrooms had created new dimensions within Thunderbird's perceptions. For there was Burning Bush, as bold and as vivid as you please. His thick, dark hair clung to his shoulders. Teeth of different animals, and of the men he'd slain in battle, hung from his neck. An odd, but beautiful, necklace draped over his chest. Apparent was the beadwork, the feathers, and the assorted elements that went into the making of the necklace. Gold and silver were the most apparent metals. Others were also included among the different pieces, upon which there were symbols for all the natural forces. The sun, wind, fire and earth were emblazoned upon the metals. Multicolored and dazzling in the sunshine, the Necklace could arouse even the dullest of imaginations. It was said to contain magical powers and was Burning Bush's most prized possession. He would've lost all else without blinking an eye, but would've died first before surrendering the Necklace.

The Necklace had been presented to Burning Bush by Sacred Heart, the dying medicine man, who had looked after the medicinal and spiritual needs of his tribe for many generations. No one actually recalled the true age of Sacred Heart, or even cared. His posterity and personal dignity had

34

garnered too much respect from the tribesmen for any to be concerned with the years he had lived.

"Sacred Heart has given the Necklace to Burning Bush," the tribal chieftains exclaimed with surprise. Many protested, thought Burning Bush unwise and undeserving to receive such a coveted gift. They had all been summoned by Sacred Heart's daughter, Elk Angel. She had sensed her father was dying and called them all around her father so the medicine man could pass his judgment. Most expected the Great Necklace to be passed down to Chief Sour Broth's oldest son, Long Deer, the husband of Elk Angel. The counselors gathered and waited for Sacred Heart to make his move. At last, with trembling hands and much suffering, Sacred Heart removed the Necklace from around his head. In one desperate attempt he extended the magnificent piece to Chief Sour Broth, who immediately assumed it was meant for him. But the great medicine man grew sullen and shook his head with exasperation. He denied what Sour Broth was thinking.

"For Burning Bush," hissed the ancient medicine man, his voice threatening and scornful. He then relinquished his sense of this world for that of another mood and texture.

"What?" asked Sour Broth, who leaned over in surprise. Unsure of what his next move should be, the chief looked about him, reviewing the different expressions on the faces of his tribal counselors. They too were most surprised at Sacred Heart's decision. Some were ready to obey without question, believing the medicine man's wisdom had always prevailed. Besides, it had been Burning Bush's mother, Fair Rainbow, who had, years before, undertaken a most perilous journey to retrieve the Great Necklace. Still, others couldn't see where Burning Bush deserved the Great Necklace.

However, being true to the customs of their tribe, and rigid in their disciplines, and dreadfully afraid of the tone of voice invoked by Sacred Heart before he departed, the tribal

35

counselors at last agreed to give the Necklace to Burning Bush.

As usual, luck was not with Burning Bush that day. While the counselors debated, Burning Bush was occupied with Swan Lake, the third wife of Sour Broth's second son. Having no real influence, except in times of war, when his brilliant spirit showed itself, Burning Bush had removed himself from Sacred Heart's deathbed, believing it was best that the old man should die in peace. By the river he had found Swan Lake.

That day when the tribal council appeared before Burning Bush's tent, they heard torrential sounds of ecstasy. Curious, the men leaned forward and peered through the cracks in the teepee. One by one their eyes found Burning Bush and Swan Lake engaged in the act of passion.

"Take a look at this," Sour Broth angrily commanded of his second, youngest son, Gopher Tracks. "Once again you've made an ass out of me." The chief pulled the covers on Burning Bush's tent for all to see.

"What is the meaning of this?" cried Gopher Tracks.

"The meaning lies in your ignorance of affection," Swan Lake answered.

"I'm just filling in for you," added Burning Bush. Turning to the chief, he asked, "Can I help it if your boy goes limp at the sight of his third wife? She, being so fair and capable, while he remains aloof, a goatherd frightened of his flock. Look at her! What man in his right mind would not attempt to satisfy her?"

Neither Sour Broth nor Gopher Tracks were in the mood for any sort of logical explanation, especially one that came from the fast-talking Burning Bush.

"Get up!" ordered Gopher Tracks. "We will fight to the death!"

"All right, motherfucker, you're gonna get what's coming to you. Still, I don't see what it'll satisfy."

Although Gopher Tracks was a giant of a man, Burning

36

Bush was no slouch either. He had many times distinguished himself in battle, winning the coveted black feather for two years in a row. He had a great command of poise and fighting style, and many of the tribal youngers attempted to emulate his style. When the two men met in the ring of death, Gopher Tracks was only slightly favored to win this duel of honor.

Swan Lake was forced to watch the battle. Defying all convention, she cheered openly for Burning Bush. "C'mon, Burning Bush," she clapped with glee. "Whip the fool's ass."

If the members of the tribe disliked Burning Bush, they held even more disdain for Swan Lake. For it was she who openly flaunted her womanly virtues before the other women of the tribe. Bare-breasted, she did her laundry by the riverbank, leaving ample portions of her skin to be colored by the sun. It was also no secret among the women that Swan Lake had experienced other men in her time. They hadn't believed the blood on the ceremonial robe for one minute. Even the peddler, who used to frequent the Indian camp, had exchanged his goods for her favors. Little did they know that the one-armed peddler had fallen for Swan Lake and wanted to take her away to exotic lands and strange places. But she refused, alluding to her sense of duty. Still the peddler visited, telling her of other peoples. He claimed he had once been a sailor and had roamed the seven seas.

When he took her, it was quite simple and without protest. Swan Lake didn't even pretend to resist. Their affair continued for several years, their passions occurring in the bushes, across the river and even in the peddler's wagon. And then one day he came no more.

For months after, the tribal women taunted Swan Lake. They swore she was abused and left as old cloth, to be swept by the wind.

"You can all go to hell," she told them. "At least I don't have to beg, or wait my turn."

37

Animosity prevailed and carried through the years until the moment of the duel. All the other tribal women wished Gopher Tracks would slay Burning Bush, if only to teach Swan Lake a lesson. And it appeared it would happen that way, since Burning Bush was weakened by his intercourse with Swan Lake, and Gopher Tracks' desire to impress his father had given him the upper hand. Around the ring of death the two men scrambled, with Gopher Tracks swearing and kicking all the way. It appeared he'd never tire. But at last a great kick missed its target, and Burning Bush, quick to take advantage of the opportunity, ducked under the flailing Gopher Tracks and drove his knife deep into his back, running it up his spine until the chief's son moved no more.

"You've done well," Sour Broth angrily informed the killer of his son.

While Burning Bush caught his breath and pondered his chief's next move, Sour Broth summoned Swan Lake to him. With great speed he cut her throat, leaving her to die at the feet of Burning Bush.

Sour Broth gestured to his son. "That's how it started, and this is the end. Because Sacred Heart gave you the Great Necklace, I will not kill you. But you will leave this tribe forever, to roam in exile, a nomad in the land of emptiness. Gather your belongings and leave by sundown."

"First I'll bury Swan Lake," Burning Bush said bravely.

"No! I will bury Swan Lake. By the side of Gopher Tracks."

Not wishing to carry it further, Burning Bush gathered his few possessions and headed west. He travelled for many miles, across varied terrain, all of which appeared very strange to him. At last he came to the desert. He was frightened and overjoyed at the same time.

"Here I am, at last!" he shouted into the empty landscape. He grew nervous when no one answered.

Chapter 4

The day passed and the sun shifted from east to west, changing the color and texture of the landscape. No longer were the vast surroundings dry and faded, but were instead so rich and deep in color that any creature, lizard or king, would stand in awe of their magnificence. Gradually the moon appeared over the southern horizon, modifying the impact of the shadows against the eye. Gnarled shrubs, dwarf trees, animals and mountains assumed a life filled with even greater mystery than that of the day.

The temperature also dropped substantially, and Shelby was forced to wrap his sheepskin jacket around his sunburned skin. Feeling chilled and hot at the same time, young Lopez reconciled himself to a night filled with shivers and fitful sleep. For a moment he wished he had never attempted to cross the desert but had remained in the East where life was said to be more civilized. He thought of the fine restaurants, the clubs and the young couples promenading up and down the gaslit streets, enjoying what nightlife held in store. Unwittingly they mingled with hookers, pick-pockets, swindlers and thieves, who welcomed the darkness.

Thunderbird Hawkins sensed his companion was suffering from the cold and bid Lopez to seek a good campsite.

"It appears all the same to me," snickered Lopez, after he searched the constant landscape.

"We should camp by water," said Hawkins. "Judging by my canteen, we have barely enough for a decent cup of coffee."

Shelby regarded his own thirst and looked at the Indian with mild consternation. "I think it's gone to your head, Thunderbird. Cause there's no water in sight."

Thunderbird grunted and sniffed the air. He gazed up to the moon and with both hands made what appeared to be the double sign of the cross. Vague utterances grumbled from his rib cage. He then repeated the sign with his hands and bleated like a sheep in heat. Suddenly, he clapped his hands twice and pointed just north of the trail on which they travelled.

"There is water," he nodded toward his dubious companion. "About a half mile from where we're standing."

Shelby could hardly conceal his disbelief. He stared for a long time at his Indian companion. He shook his head, blinked his eyes and hoped the lapse of time would cause the Indian to reveal his joke. But Hawkins wasn't laughing, not even making the slightest sign that he was only kidding. And they did need water. With necessity as his motive, Shelby found himself half wanting to believe in Thunderbird.

"I guess you should know," he admitted finally, but his incredulity could still be traced in his words.

Thunderbird nodded his head and muttered something under his breath. He kicked at his horse's flanks and bounded forward. The horse, tired from the day's journey, loped along aimlessly. After a few moments had lapsed, Shelby followed behind. By the time he reached Thunder-

40

bird, he was on his hands and knees, sniffing at the sand. In the moonlight Hawkins resembled an overfed house dog searching for his favorite shitting spot. Shelby recalled his own dog, a mongrel compelled to sniff at every piece of trash that lay in his path.

Hawkins raised his hand, signaling the water's location. Shelby jumped from his horse and stared down at the spot Thunderbird had indicated. It seemed like any other spot in the desert, only a little darker, and the darkness could've been caused by the shadow of a nearby dwarf juniper. Before he could determine its cause as moisture or a shadow, Thunderbird had dug down with his hands, throwing the dirt behind him. At last he paused, eyeing Shelby, extending a fistful of mud.

"I could feel there was water here."

Lopez was truly amazed. Nothing he had ever experienced seemed as odd as this crazy Indian finding water in the middle of the desert. At night yet. Intimidated by the process, Shelby reluctantly grabbed for the fistful of mud Hawkins was presenting him. He felt it squish between his fingers, and he pressed his nose against its moisture.

"I don't believe it," he laughed delightedly. "I just don't believe it. Thunderbird, you're amazing."

Hawkins returned to his digging. Before long a small pool of water formed beneath him. With each additional handful of sand the Indian cleared away, the pool expanded until the hole was wide enough for the two men to easily dip their canteens into the water.

"That's enough," said Shelby after he had only filled one canteen. "Tomorrow I can fill the others with fresh, cold water."

Thunderbird disapproved. He shook his head and pointed down at the pool of water. He reached down, retrieving his elliptical, animalskin waterbag. "Tomorrow there will be no more. Tonight you must take what you wish."

Lopez squelched his desire to ask further questions. He

41

had insulted his companion enough as it was. Obediently he filled his remaining canteens and joined the Indian in slurping up his fair share of water.

"That's awfully good," remarked Shelby, after he had had his fill.

"It comes directly from the spirit. A good brand."

"But how did you know it was here?"

"I smelled it. I felt it."

"Some trick."

"No trick. Unless one finds the knowledge of his necessities amusing."

"I'm sorry. I didn't mean it that way."

"I understand. You're confused. It's only natural."

"I just never thought I'd end up in a place like this. I guess you never know."

"You know no distractions can hide your fear. That's part of what scares you. Your insides are bared to yourself, with no barriers to keep away the pain of living. It is bad, but it is also good. Through pain comes understanding. Understanding brings destiny. You are fortunate, since it seems the spirit is drawing you toward your destiny like an arrow to the heart of its prey. You are lucky that you may yet have a destiny."

"But what about you? Where are you going? What are you doing out here?"

Thunderbird tossed back his head and rolled fresh water around the insides of his cheeks. "There's no other place for me to be." Before he could be asked any more questions, Hawkins was on his feet, searching about for firewood. After much exploration, he returned with a few twigs and some dried shrubs. Carefully he arranged the woodpile and then touched a match to his kindling. In short order a fire burned intensely, its flames rising against the black light of the sky.

Shelby had removed the coffee and a few pieces of jerky from his pouch. He extracted a can of beans which he weighed in his hand. Eating the beans would leave them nothing to eat the following night.

"Should I make the beans?" he asked.

"I have something for us to eat," advised Hawkins. He displayed a handful of dried beans which would swell to their full size after they'd been boiled in water. As they cooked they'd make their own sauce. "They're very good with vegetables," Thunderbird told his companion. "What a shame we don't have an assortment of nice, fresh vegetables."

"Don't even remind me," warned Shelby. "It's been a shame about too many things. Everything in which I become involved turns into a shame. Seems every time I sit down, it's atop a bomb."

"Then you've known love," remarked Thunderbird, preparing his deerhorn pipe for an evening's worth of smoking.

"What's that have to do with it?"

"Love awakens all the senses, even those of anger and despair. It is fulfilling," he claimed, grasping a handful of sand, and yet ..." he allowed the sand to sift through his fingers.

Lopez observed in silence until all of the sand had escaped from the Indian's hand. "Dammit, I'm so stiff and sore. If there was only another way around this place."

"Then what would be the use of the desert?" Hawkins added to his smoke a white powder, and then a brown powder, which he claimed would relieve Shelby of some of his aches and pains. He handed the mixture to Shelby.

Lopez narrowed his eyes at the brown and white powder. "I've never seen anything like that before. Not even in the Army."

Thunderbird laughed aloud. He snorted and grunted and clutched at his belly. "The Army? The Army would never heal a soul if it didn't need his body. I've also been in the Army. Ridiculous. Bored and lonely men opposing other bored and lonely men on ruined farmland."

"I didn't like the war. The fighting was certainly nothing like I'd expected. It scared me shitless. Then one day, as if by magic, I just got over being scared. I didn't care no more.

43

Didn't care if I lived or died. To care either way seemed ridiculous."

"You killed many men?"

"A few," replied Shelby, handing the pipe to Hawkins.

Moments later the powder and smoke had taken their effect. Shelby propped himself against his saddle and stared into the campfire. Occasionally he sipped his coffee, or turned to Hawkins. But mostly his attention was taken with the events of his past. They rose above him, imposing themselves in the orange light of the fire. One by one, episodes in Shelby's life peeled over like pages in a book. Hawkins all the while appeared not to notice. He too seemed deeply under the influence of the powder and smoke.

The temperature dropped, and the coffee's warmth was amply appreciated. The hot liquid seemed to be the one unifying force in Shelby's constitution. With a warm spot in the middle of his gut, and Thunderbird at his side, Lopez felt secure against the eerie silence of the desert evening. His defenses gave way to concentration upon the events of the past. He imagined the battles and remembered the look on his father's face when he announced he was running away to join the Army.

"We never join the Army," replied his father. "We support it."

But that's not true, thought Shelby when he was reminded of his Great-Uncle Yonkel who had fought so valiantly as a privateer in the Continental Navy. Likenesses of him adorned the albums and scrapbooks maintained by Belle Gluntz. It was she who first revealed Yonkel to Shelby. The pirate spirit she called it, referring to Yonkel's lust for adventure. He was a fierce fighter, a restless creature who bred the likes of herself and Uncle Shmuel. And Shelby too, if he so chose. If he could break the restrictions imposed by Leonard Lopez and, instead of minding the store, go out in the world, as his Great-Uncle Yonkel had done before him.

Belle's frequent discussions had built a lasting impression

44

in her nephew's mind. She had claimed that Yonkel and his brother Leon had arrived in the colonies not long before the outbreak of the War of Independence.

Through the force of Belle's imagination, Yonkel the Pirate grew to become an awesome figure. He was the sole brother of Leon Attias, the patriarchal grandfather of Belle, Shmuel and Sarah. Unlike his brother Leon, Yonkel lusted for adventure. He swore he'd get his share once the yoke of persecution was cast from his shoulders. It was later a different form of persecution that did lift his head, high above the crowds who attended the mass hanging of Yonkel the Pirate and his loyal crew. It occurred once the war had ended, and the privateer was no longer beheld as a symbol of righteousness and freedom.

A smuggler by trade, Yonkel had been quick to learn the mechanics of the ship. Although, at the outset, he knew nothing of sailing, he befriended John Mayes, a Scotch-Irishman, and he instructed Yonkel in the ways of ships at sea. The two soon formed a partnership, and they rose to positions of influence among the smugglers. As Yonkel learned more about ships and naval warfare, he reciprocated by teaching John Mayes and others the principles of good business procedure. Business flourished for all, and much of the profits was redistributed to revolutionary activities.

Despite brother Leon's refusal to take an active part in the revolutionary activities, he was not against accepting his share of smuggled molasses. This he converted into some of the finest whiskey available, with the aid of his assistant, a Jamaican he had found roaming the streets in search of menial work. Gradually he dissolved the import business and concentrated on whiskey production. The few odds and ends he kept in his store, the bric-a-brac, cloth and such served mainly as a front to conceal his more clandestine activity.

With the revolution imminent, John Mayes wished to be at its front, despite the protestations of his wife, Lyla. He

45

saw himself as a designer wishing to cover the bare colonies with the fabric of his own military expertise. Adventure was just at hand, and he didn't want to be kept from its grasp.

Convinced that her husband John preferred adventure to herself, Lyla Mayes took up with another man. Together they plotted her husband's downfall. The man, a William Schmidt, was a closet Tory, who concealed his true beliefs beneath a barrage of patriotic rhetoric.

Throughout the course of the war, Schmidt, with the assistance of Lyla, plotted the ruination of John Mayes and his partner Yonkel. In their desire to wrest assets from the two partners, Lyla and Schmidt asserted that Mayes and Yonkel were cruel opportunists who were only involved in the revolution for their own glorification. Schmidt passed rumors from colony to colony until the conspiracy manufactured by Lyla and Schmidt unfolded with gruesome detail. Papers were forged and informers were bribed in order to denigrate the characters of Yonkel and John Mayes. While the privateers were winning major sea battles, Schmidt and Lyla continued their plotting, leaving the two partners unaware as to what lay in store for them.

Yonkel and John had been having great success on the high seas. Many British ships of war, including a frigate or two, were laid to waste by the privateers and their gallant crews. Severely outnumbered, outgunned and outclassed, they fought for the lust of adventure and managed to defeat several of England's capable sea captains. Much of their plunder was then expropriated by the Continental Congress in order to purchase badly needed war supplies.

Oddly enough, it was Mayes himself who predicted his doom. "They'll get me yet," he assured his longtime companion. "Sooner or later, I'll go down with my ship, but I fear, dear friend, a fate much worse lies in wait for you."

"If you do pass before me," assured Yonkel, "I'll keep Lyla in the comforts to which she's accustomed."

"Fuck Lyla!" the usually reticent Mayes declared. "I hope to see them both rot in hell."

46

Unfortunately Mayes never had the chance. His premonition came into fact when a stray twelve-pounder caught him flush in the chest while he stood on the bridge of his ship. He died instantly, and was buried at sea, further clearing the path for Lyla and her beau to discredit her late husband and his partner.

As the war neared its end and victory seemed assured, Yonkel prepared himself for a life of leisure. He promised he'd sail no more, but retire to the country with Culuvara Ulmstead, his Eurasian mistress. Together they'd share the fruits of his life as a privateer. He'd write his memoirs and pose in dignity when receiving the laurels he felt sure were to be bestowed upon him. However, when he at last returned to port, he found Lyla, Schmidt, several government officials and a battalion of constables waiting to arrest himself and crew. Before they could resist, the constables were upon them. In the melee only one man escaped, a ship's mate named Elijah Hawkins. Wisely, he took refuge with Culuvara Ulmstead, who hid him in her cellar.

Only the day before did Culuvara and Hawkins learn that Yonkel and his entire crew were sentenced to be executed. To bear the anguish of this gross injustice, the ship's mate and Yonkel's mistress took shelter in each other's arms. Overwhelmed with grief, they made love *in memoriam* to their beloved Yonkel. Somehow their burden of remorse was lightened when they found refuge in solemn fornication.

Meanwhile, in the dampness of his cell, Yonkel nibbled at his last meal and wrote a letter of apology to his brother Leon. He claimed he was sorry for not being closer to his brother and wished him all the luck and health in the world. Yonkel added he had no regrets for what he'd done, and knew in his youth he was doomed to die a gallows death. He was sure that sometime in the future he'd be exonerated.

What Yonkel didn't say was that his mistress Culuvara was with child. So it came as a surprise to Leon when Culuvara Ulmstead appeared at his door some ten months later with a baby girl wrapped in her arms.

"Take it!" she begged of Leon. "I could never be the mother it deserves."

Leon, who had always wanted a child, but for some reason could never manage it with his wife, Adele, was overcome by the offer. Being a timid man, Leon had never asked his wife or himself about the problem that seemed to exist between them. His same reticence prevented him from asking Culuvara any further questions. That the child had gray eyes and not brown like either Yonkel or Culuvara didn't seem to matter. That Yonkel had made no mention of her pregnancy in his final letter was of little significance. A child was born, was alive and healthy, that's all that really mattered.

Graciously, Leon accepted the child from Culuvara Ulmstead. He and Adele raised the child as their own. They called her Ida. Later she was to marry Mad Gerson Gluntz and bear three children—Belle, Shmuel and Sarah. Although in her youth Ida was to provide the aging Leon with much comfort, at times the sight of her reminded him of his unfortunate brother Yonkel. He was forced to recall the bitter day they hanged the notorious privateer. At the head of the procession, they led him to the gallows, his crew in solemn march behind him. He climbed the gallows steps, revealing no emotion as he faced the crowd. With much pomp and ceremony the military and several public officials took a few brief moments to remind the crowd of Yonkel's valor. They praised his devotion to the revolutionary cause and cited his brilliance as a military strategist. In detail they recounted his scourge of the British naval forces. And then they hanged him.

Six years later, Yonkel the Pirate was exonerated of all charges placed against him. He was decreed a hero by order of the President, and his body was exhumed to be interred in the Memorial Cemetery. He was buried again with full military honors.

For his part in the conspiracy William Schmidt was sentenced to life imprisonment. He died in his cell, a few years after his incarceration. As for Lyla, she had taken another love and found protection from justice in the man's influence with governmental figures. But unfortunately for Lyla, she had the ill manners to quarrel with her lover the night of the Grand Ball. She left in a huff, vowing she'd never speak to her suitor again. She kept her word.

On her way home she was nabbed from her carriage. After three days of searching, her body was discovered. The pirates' skull and crossbones was wrapped around her neck.

Several days after their meeting, Hawkins and Lopez were overtaken by a terrible sandstorm. It came suddenly, beginning as a gentle breeze, but soon increasing in velocity so sand, twigs and brush whipped against their faces. Desperately they clung to their horses' reins, their bodies leaning well over the necks of their animals. Often the horses themselves were nearly knocked from their feet.

Shelby felt the sand beat against his body and swirl before him. He was frightened. Never before had he witnessed such a violent display of nature. The sand felt like a hundred strands of barbed wire as it lashed against his face. It felt like his nose and cheeks were being rubbed against the concrete sidewalk by some vicious bully. At once he was helpless, but ashamed of himself for being caught in such a situation. For a moment he considered blaming Hawkins for his troubles, but he soon realized the stupidity of the suggestion. He looked to Thunderbird, who was clinging to his horse's neck. The Indian's hat was squashed down over his forehead. A muffler enshrouded his face, and his blanket was pulled tightly around him.

Despite the sudden chill and the fierce winds that ripped against him, perspiration slid from Shelby's armpits. The familiar knot tightened in his gut, and he winced as more sand particles peppered his cheeks. He was assured that when it was all over, if he wasn't quite dead, he'd be scarred for life. So stupid, he thought, that he once believed sand was harmless.

"What's happening? When's it gonna let up?" he hailed at Thunderbird. Hawkins showed no signs of hearing him. He started to cry out again, but thought against it. He huddled even closer to his horse.

For what seemed like an eternity they plodded on. The horses staggered, and the men swayed from side to side. It seemed as if any moment either horse or rider would lose their equilibrium and tumble to the ground. In moments they'd be buried by the sand.

In the midst of the whirl and the howl of the storm, Shelby heard the cries of thousands of men storming through Georgia and Tennessee. He witnessed death all around him, bodies crumpled in a multitude of grotesque positions. They were strewn like placards left after a rally, no longer cared for, discarded as solemn evidence that belief and sacrifice had once existed. And as the cannons boomed in between his ears, the image of Rebecca Maltesin flashed before him. She was lovely, shy and smiling beneath the autumn light of her native Georgia. She was naked and gentle, her skin shimmering white in her lamplit bedroom.

"I'd like to visit up North sometimes," she was saying. "Once this mess is over."

"It'll be over soon," Lopez was quick to assure her. "The end is now in sight."

"That's what they say in the midst of every war," she frowned. "I doubt if this one's any different. All it's done is destroy everything I've ever known."

Shelby rubbed his face and gazed through her window, across the plantation to the cluster of shacks where the blacks were huddled in sundown positions. Men and women of all ages were gathered together, waiting for the time to

50

pass. They were free, Shelby's commander had told them, but what difference did it make if there was nowhere else to go?

A quick glance by a white man assured him that all was the same, that the darkies remained oblivious to the goings-on of the white folks at the top of the hill. Each day the freed slaves went through their usual routine, cleaning what was left of the plantation, planting seeds and hoping food crops would grow in the desolate soil. Everyone had to eat. Neither freedom or slavery could change that fact. So they sat by themselves and waited for the war to end. They talked and they sang and told stories among themselves. When a white man passed, they fell silent, wishing only to be left alone.

But few of the conquering soldiers could resist looking at the women who huddled in the squalid shacks. They loved the poontang nestled beneath the gunny sacks. Often they sought its favor with tobacco and candy. Others, including many of the commanding officers, eschewed such appeasements and considered the darkies as spoils of war. However, after months of provocation, the blacks retaliated. Many Union soldiers who ventured into "niggertown" simply didn't return. Naturally this raised quite a stink among the Yankees. In desperation they turned to the remaining brood of white southern ladies, a group whom they had originally promised not to molest or torment. Being few in number, however, most of these women fell prey to the officers. An even greater stink was raised about town when it was learned the boys in blue were chasing after the womenfolk.

Young Shelby had never entertained the intention of raping Rebecca. At first sight he had fallen in love with her and preferred her conversation to greed and desire. She too was aroused by their meeting. She recalled a vision she had had once in the rain, just before an autumn harvest. It was his face, receding in the wheat fields, unable to be touched. Despite her intentions to remain aloof from the Yankee soldiers, Rebecca found herself talking easily with Billy Brick, which was what Shelby called himself throughout the war.

"My father always urged me to be my own person," she confided after several meetings. "Don't be like the other ladies around here. Don't do a thing but sit on their asses and fan themselves, lest any signs of work would ruin their delicate skins. An' don't you go takin' up with no mama's boy. It wouldn't become you. Yeah, that's what he used to say to me."

She had trusted her father's words, and set out to become the first renaissance woman of Muldoon County, Georgia. She took up painting. Brisk and proud, she strode past the townfolk on her way to her favorite pasture. There she'd sit and paint for hours, undisturbed by thought or ill intention. And then the war came. Its promise of violence broke the heart of Valery Maltesin, Becky's mother. She died soon after Fort Sumter.

Her father was prompted to pursue his legal practice with intensified zeal. He espoused his share of unpopular causes and defended in court the most difficult cases to arise in Muldoon and neighboring Winslow and Detwiler counties. He defended blacks, poor white farmers and other indigents who chose to place themselves against the domineering plantation owners.

"He was never a popular man," said Becky. "Most folks hated him around these parts. The Hacketts, who used to own this plantation, called my father the 'will of the motley devil'. Hardly a name to do the man justice. Very hard on his legal practice."

"Where is he now?" asked Billy Brick.

"Off to war. Like everyone else. Joined the Confederacy, he did."

"But why?"

"It was in him to do it, I guess. Just his way."

As the war drew nearer to Muldoon County, and it

52

became increasingly obvious that General Hood would never contain Sherman's forces, most of the gentile populace of the county fled to Atlanta. Surely the Yankees would never attack there, they all believed. Those who doubted remained in Muldoon County, placing themselves in the hands of fate, before the Yankee advance. Along with most of the plantation slaves, they watched in horror as their houses and plantations were destroyed. While the Confederacy retreated and the Union advanced.

Becky had remained behind in anticipation of word from her father. Days, then weeks, passed, but no word came. To pass the time Rebecca returned to her favorite pasture and painted. She captured landscapes and portraits of the field hands and the bivouacked soldiers. Despite the great stress placed upon her, Rebecca's artwork vastly improved, and the remaining townspeople marvelled at her work, finding it brought forth the last remaining beauty which existed in their county.

In the midst of the Union soldiers, the southern townsfolk came and went about their business. At first there was little friction between them. All Yankees were ordered to treat the populace with due courtesy. It remained so, despite the soldiers' restlessness and the fearsome stories the townfolk related among themselves. They told of the looting, pillaging and plunder. Frightened by all, the people of Muldoon County watched their history disintegrate before their eyes. Their present fell to shambles, and their lives were stained with uncertainty. But it was their inability to foretell the future that really drove them mad. All the while they maintained a facade of nonchalance before the gazes of the Union troops. It lasted until the Yankees began advancing upon their women.

"It's because we're trying to free the slaves," Shelby explained to Rebecca. She wasn't listening. Both knew that he was lying. "All right, so war is terrible. What else is new?"

"Nothing. The blacks are still black, and hated for it. And

the poor are still poor. And after this mess is over, not one thing will have changed. Except the names in government."

"But, but didn't you hear what Lincoln said?"

"Who's Lincoln anyway? Is he able to foretell the future, or relate the past to the present? Soon, when all the speeches are finished, and the last ounce of glory is squeezed from the dead, it will pass from his hands. Memories will fade with time, and time will show Lincoln was just another man, confined by his own limitations."

"You sure talk funny for a girl," mused Shelby.

"Nothing funny. This war has cost me plenty. It's brought ruin to my people, destroyed the fields where I once played. It stabs at my soul to think one day there'll be parades and banquets where so many have died. Souvenirs and pennants will be sold along with preachings of apology. My only fortune is that I won't live to see it."

After each of their meetings, Shelby would return to his tent and ponder what the lady had said. Her words bit into his flesh, tapped at his veins until her spirit became part of his. It was not her words, or even her explanations, but her manner that disturbed him. She appeared unlike anyone else he had ever seen. He began to see the world through Rebecca's eyes. He assumed a portion of her soul, of her posture. His voice acquired a new cadence, and his inflection softened his words. He knew he was in love, but it was his touching of her spirit and not so much of her body that had caused the romance. In a sense he had consumed her, so she fortified the bare spaces within his psyche. Yes, it was love. Surely. But more than love, he had discovered a greater level of consciousness, one in which two people can share. It was a strange awakening for Shelby Lopez, alias Billy Brick. For in his heart, and in his mind, Rebecca Maltesin would exist forever.

Chapter 5

Hours passed and the storm's intensity did not diminish. Barbed gusts of sand swirled across the land. Everything was in disarray. The world had gone beserk. No sign of unity was evident anywhere. Rock formations, brush and creatures were buried beneath the howling storm. The surface of the plains was constantly changing. Color had surrendered to a gritty yellow, obscuring the drifting plains with sullen translucence. All was tarnished and trembling with the reformation.

Shelby thought he could bear it no longer. Nothing in his life appeared like the sandstorm. All exposure to humanity's bizarre idiosyncracies had not prepared him for the undermining cruelty of nature. He shivered intensely, grimacing in the face of the howling fury. No longer was there life or death, but a constant bombardment of the same sensation. So naive to believe he could speculate as to what life held in store for him. How stupid to believe his imagination, in making allowances for his death by exposure or starvation, or murder by hostiles, would've dared acknowledge this heinous convulsion.

Looking to his left, Shelby caught sight of the large pile of sand atop Thunderbird's hat. For some odd reason the mound of sand had not blown away. It remained in crown and brim, forming an asymmetrical crown of old. Shelby laughed. It was the first thing funny he had seen all day. And Hawkins. He appeared like a variegated clump of rags deposited on a wayward horse. Together horse and rider swayed back and forth, onward toward the far edge of the southern mountain range. Rainbow-striped, Thunderbird flashed like a daydream on a boring day. Shelby's heart went out to the Indian. It was Thunderbird who was giving him comfort. With it came the realization that Lopez wasn't going to die that day. No, there was little need to fear the sandstorm. The panic of death began to fade from Shelby's system.

Hawkins was leading them toward a cluster of boulders, looming before the piss-colored sky like mounts of the gods. The horse plodded through knee-deep sand. Finally, when the beasts could carry them no longer, the companions dismounted and waded through the sand drifts. Each step was more painful than the last. Legs and hearts pounded. But breathing was the worst of it. Each breath was another emergency, drawing with it spoonfuls of sand with each gasp of air. At last they arrived at their destination. Ducking between the boulders, they unsaddled their horses.

Shelby feared they'd be taken by the storm. Buried beneath the drifting sand, they'd be left forever, the mounts of the gods marking their tomb. Before such fear could overcome him, Lopez was once again reminded of Hawkins, and once more his panic subsided. With Spartan relish he took his seat on the ground and awaited the storm's onslaught. Beside him sat Hawkins, curled among the ribbon of colors. Only a tiny spot on his forehead was visible. Shelby scrunched his hat down over his ears and pulled up his collar. Cross-legged, he wrapped his bedroll around him and prepared for the worst. Comforted beneath the covers, he found they offered childish protections. Satisfied with his new arrangement, Shelby put his finger to his nose and blew the sand from his nostrils.

In the darkness of his blankets, Lopez closed his eyes and found Rebecca Maltesin waiting beneath his lids. So petite and gentle was she, wearing a cream-lace dress beneath her coiled black hair. In a flash she disappeared. Corporal Kip Kearney replaced her. Following Kearney were his three cronies: Hutt Jameson, Roy Barlow and Walker Straughan, the giggling fat man of Company C. Shelby's nerves wiggled and his guts were attacked by thrusts of nausea. He was reminded of Kearney's wicked smile, Jameson's crazed eyes and the obese Straughan's lecherous slobber. A howl in the distance interrupted his thoughts. Lopez cringed and felt terror far greater than the sandstorm advancing against him. Before his eyes, Kip Kearney, Jameson, Barlow and Straughan lay dead or dying. The howling erupted again, this time from a new location. But Thunderbird Hawkins seemed to hear nothing.

"What the fuck's going on out there?" Shelby cursed under his breath.

"You're chickenshit, Brick," he heard inside him. "Jus' a crusted turd hangin' from a rooster's ass."

It was Kip Kearney speaking. Walker Straughan was standing beside him. "You're a spineless worm," guffawed the fat man. His fist twisted into his other palm.

Behind Lopez, up the hill a bit, in the old chickenshack, Rebecca Maltesin lay like a doll fallen from a shelf. Her slim legs were spread and protruding from the doorway. Her dress was ripped and torn away from her body, revealing bare white thighs and shadows between them. Though her face could not be seen, Shelby already knew the answer to his fearful question. Rebecca Maltesin was dead. She'd been raped and murdered by Kip Kearney and his three playmates. As the vomit surged from his throat, Shelby ran up the hill to take one last look at her body. He reached the doorway, looked in, horrified. He placed his hands on his head and wondered what to do.

Lopez had first met Kip Kearney in Tennessee. A few weeks later they'd fight side by side in the Battle of Chickamauga. Unlike Kearney, Shelby was a replacement, a raw recruit who could barely manage to clean his rifle. Under the name of Billy Brick he had enlisted in the Union Army just a short month before. After a couple of weeks of training, he was shipped to Tennessee to bolster the flagging units.

Kip Kearney had been in the Army for close to three years. He was a seasoned veteran of many a major battle. He had fought at Antietam, where he first met Walker Straughan. Later he participated in the Battle of Chancellorsville. There he met Jameson and Barlow. His three cronies were compulsively drawn to their leader. Without question they would do his bidding, accompanying him on his series of forays throughout the countryside.

"We don't meet many like you, Kip." Walker Straughan had expressed the feelings of all.

"Not most who get t' feast their eyes on th' Savior of the Union," Kip answered. "Ain't easy, teachin' those Rebs a lesson."

"Where ya from?" Kip had asked Billy Brick, when Brick settled into their tent. He had replaced another trooper, who had lived among the foursome for nearly a year before his death occasioned a vacancy. Oddly enough, it occurred during a dice game. Kearney swore it was self-defense.

"Up North," answered Billy Brick.

"How far North?" Hutt Jameson wanted to know.

"Boston," Brick answered after a few moments hesitation. He didn't think it wise for anyone to know too much about him.

58

"When d'ya get in?"

"A month ago. Hey, what is this, anyway?"

"Jus' makin' sure you ain't no spy, boy. Tha's all. This man 'ere is the Savior of the Union. No sense in us takin' any chances."

Brick frowned and pondered his new tentmates. Of all the tents . . . he began to think. "Where you from?" he asked the Savior of the Union.

Kearney seemed surprised. One by one he regarded his cronies before answering. "Maryland."

"Where in Maryland?"

"Maryland," Kearney repeated. "Lissn, Brick, we have our work to do. You kin come wit' us or you kin stay. Sure, it's hard, bein' the Savior an' all, and it's purty demandin'. But in between we do manage a little funnin'. Some might say we have a purty good time."

On cue all the cronies laughed. Billy Brick wondered why. Later he was to learn that the funnin' Kearney referred to was their forays about the countryside. In methods honed well from practice they terrorized the native residents, focusing most of their attentions on the blacks and the poor white trash. Women were raped and men were beaten. Livestock was taken and eaten. What couldn't be used was left to rot in the fields.

Kip and the boys were notorious looters. It was no secret among the ranks that many Yankee soldiers took what they wanted, chalking it off to the spoils of war. But the more grisly elements of theft remained in the domain of Kip Kearney and his fellow soldiers. Even wooden crosses were removed from historic churches, to be dragged off and used as firewood.

"I just love to see th' damn things burnin'," Kip had commented on more than one occasion. "Almost as much as seein' these farmers cry whenever we take hold o' their women. What gall they have anyways. Should be out doin' a man's work. Gittin' killed in th' war. No honor."

At first, Shelby, who was embroiled in despair and very

bitter, thought Kearney and company amusing. On a few occasions he went out with the boys, storming about the countryside. Little destruction was caused. A few chickens were stolen and slaughtered, a general store was burned down. A few barns were reduced to ashes. But not much else. Oh, now and then a handful of white trash did try to intervene, but the corporal and his men were quick to put an end to that. Easily the settlers were subdued and strung up by their wrists.

"We could skin them alive," proposed Hutt Jameson. "I jus' love th' sight of fresh, raw meat."

The others laughed. The thought wasn't far from becoming an action.

"It'd teach 'em a lesson, it would," noted Roy Barlow. " 'Bout time these bastards paid th' price for livin'. Whatta ya think, Corporal?"

Kip Kearney folded his arms and eyed Billy Brick. "I don't know. Let's leave it up t' Billy, here. Whatta ya say, Brick? Ever skin a man?"

The mortified Billy Brick shook his ragged curls. "No, I can't say I have," he answered, trying to be casual.

"Ya begin down th' chest," Kip instructed, his knife pressed against a hanging farmer's rib cage. "An then ya work your way down, hack off his balls, 'n' work up through his ass and up his spine."

Upon hearing what was to be done with him the poor farmer squealed in terror. He wiggled madly, kicking his feet against the sky. Kearney and his fellows roared with laughter. All except Billy Brick. He stared down at the ground.

"Too much for ya?" quizzed Walker Straughan. "Jus' as I thought. This one can't take it. Ain't man enough for real action. How d'ja think we'd win this war, anyways?"

Billy didn't answer. His head felt too heavy to lift in Straughan's direction. For Brick the joyrides had ended. No more excursions with the Corporal.

It was Jameson who wished to press the issue. "Well, boy, ain't cha gonna answer Walker?"

Brick shrugged and refused to lift his head from the ground. He couldn't bear to view the faces of the hanging farmers. Four of them there were, wriggling like fish on the line. ›

"Hey, boy, you're bein' spoken to."

At last Brick managed a look at Straughan. He hated the fat man, despised his hog face and constant slobber. "It's no way ..." he started to say.

"No way for what?" It was Kearney this time, pressing Brick for an answer.

"No way to fight a war."

"Then you tell me what is."

Brick didn't have an answer. "Just ain't right, that's all."

Kearney eyed the hanging farmers, studying each one in turn. "How else they gonna know their betters?"

"That's right," Jameson was quick to agree. "Cuz ya know damn well the Corporal's the Savior of the Union. He's said it himself, a hunneret times at least. No one would dare claim so, if they didn't know for sure."

Brick laughed at the ludicrous position in which he found himself placed. How he wished he was back among his own, the merchant-husband of Sherri Seltzer. Even capture was hardly worse than this. He should've listened to his Uncle Shmuel and never joined the Army.

"I think I've had enough of this," he said after much hesitation. "You do what you want, but I'm going back to the camp."

The four others regarded each other, shaking heads as they passed around the most treacherous of expressions.

"Now ain't that something," spoke Walker Straughan. "He's leavin' us."

"Do what you want, says he. But leave me out of it."

Squealing among themselves, the foursome had a good time mimicking Billy Brick. The dangling farmers didn't enjoy it any better than Billy. Their eyes wide with horror, they stared down at the heads of Kip, Jameson, Barlow and Straughan. Their hands throbbed from the constriction of the ropes around their wrists, and their feet were consumed with pins and needles. Sweat covered their undershirts.

Billy hadn't noticed that Straughan and Barlow had moved closer to him. By the time he did conceive of their conspiracy the fat man was already on top of him, thrashing madly with his beefy arms. Roy Barlow did the kicking, methodically working over Brick's shins and stomach. Kearney and Jameson stood back, watching, laughing.

Straughan had him pinned to the ground and was about to cut his throat with a hunting knife when Kearney called a halt to the exercise. "That's enough. It's no good to finish him all in one blow. We have all the time in the world."

"Let's rip off his peter, for now," suggested Roy Barlow. His knife was at the ready to do the cutting.

Kearney feigned concentration before rejecting the proposition. "Later, when he thinks it's all over with. One day, in the camp, when all's quiet."

"The nerve of him, to ruin our reputations. Who's he think he is, messin' with the Savior of the Union?"

"I didn't mean any hard feelings," Brick apologized, after Straughan had let him up. "I just don't have the stomach for it, that's all."

"No hard feelings?" mocked Kearney. "You're tryin' to walk out on me. Anyone who does a fool thing like 'at should expect some hard feelings. Now you get out of here and we'll tend to you later."

Billy regarded Kip's dark, stringy hair and the sparse mustache adorning his upper lip. He noted the missing teeth and the cruel lines around the man's mouth. One day he'd kill Kip Kearney. Of that he was certain. But this wasn't the day. Sucking in a great breath, Billy sprang for the nearby woods. He ran madly, in a zigzag pattern. Behind him shots were being fired. Where they were aiming, Billy wasn't sure. He assumed they were being thrown over his head, just to scare him. Whatever, they were successful. Brick ran even harder, feeling his heart pounding beneath the uniform he had begun to despise. At last he reached the woods and turned to look over his shoulder. From behind a tree he peered toward Kip, Barlow, Jameson and Straughan. Their shots had not been wasted. The four farmers had been murdered. Their bodies now dangled lifelessly, while the blood dripped to the ground beneath them. Nearby, Kearney and his men were still laughing. Occasionally they'd gesture in Brick's direction. Whether they had seen him or not, he wasn't certain. Billy allowed the scene to make its final impression, before he turned toward camp. Once there he cleaned his belongings from the tent and searched for another place to sleep. At last he found one, among four Yanks who did little else but trade stories about their women, or play cards. It was a pleasant relief, when compared to Kip Kearney and his men.

During the coming months, Billy Brick learned awareness. His senses stretched to new regions. He was able to spot danger long before it happened. On many occasions his keen abilities enabled him to avoid Kip Kearney, Barlow, Jameson and Straughan. Despite his ability to elude them, Brick believed there would indeed be another meeting. Probably not of his liking or of his choosing. The mere thought of it made Billy Brick feel lonelier than ever. No one could help him. All those who had once been part of his life had little to offer. His father, his mother, Aunt Belle, Shmuel and even Sherri Seltzer, his obligatory girl friend, were of no use in this crisis. As for Rebecca Maltesin, she was best left out of it.

As the days passed Billy was overcome with an odd sense of relief. In the face of doom he had found his salvation. He was no longer afraid of being scared. He found the war, the storming of fortifications, to be ridiculous and nothing more. No more fear, or worry of dying. He had seen the worst of it and had endured.

Oddly enough, the worst had occurred when he was least

prepared. There he stood, in the midst of the battlefield, the enemy all around him. And his fucking rifle wouldn't fire. Struggle as he might, he just couldn't get the thing to do its duty. Bullets whizzed by and the air was filled with shouts and war cries. And he was helpless. He prayed they wouldn't spot him. But one did. A Rebel infantryman, about twice his age, thrust his bayonet at Billy's chest and came charging from across the field. Brick looked on, more amused than frightened. Paralyzed by his own curiosity, he made no move to defend himself. He would bear witness to his own demise.

As the Reb drew nearer, a pistol shot rang out from behind Billy Brick. The Rebel soldier fell forward, his bayonet grazing Shelby's thigh as he swept past. Brick, with morbid interest, stared down at the fallen soldier. The man was dead. Looking about him, Shelby sought the one who had saved his life. The god who had interrupted a certain course of destiny. From the corner of his eye, Billy caught a rider loping off, down toward the other end of the battlefield. There was nothing Billy could learn of the man's features, for his back was turned and he was bent low over his horse. Shelby waved at his fleeting vision and hoped one day they'd meet again. When they did so, Shelby would thank him properly.

The battlefield incident and his relationship with Rebecca Maltesin compelled Shelby to change his ways. Rapidly, he was becoming a new man. He sensed it in the very depths of his soul. He was proud he could change in a time of crisis. His enthusiasm caused him to overlook the oath of vengeance Kearney and his men had taken against him.

Life was too good for that. The war had faded into the distance, and his days were occupied with his beloved Becky Maltesin. They took long walks, and talked between themselves for hours on end.

"I love you," he swore repeatedly.

Rebecca only shrugged it off. "Perhaps. But love, Billy, is

not our concern. The substance of life itself is what exists between us. It is a strange brew, the mixture of you and I. So drink now, for our time spent together will soon be over."

Becky's eyes had turned toward the ground. Billy grew worried. He stared on uncertainly. "What's wrong?" he managed after several moments had lapsed in silence.

"Nothing is wrong. Everything is as it's supposed to be."

"Then . . . then why are you saying . . . ?"

"It's what I know."

"But I don't understand."

"If you were meant to, then it wouldn't bewilder you so. Sometime in the future, what has taken place will be reviewed with no surprise."

"Oh, Becky. To say these things . . . only scares me."

"You said you were no longer frightened. The incident in the battlefield, you claimed it took fear from your heart."

"Only a certain kind of fear. Other things still frighten me."

Becky only shook her head. "My father's a prisoner," she claimed, trying to change the subject. "I found out from Mrs. Sedgewick. Somehow she received word from her husband, Clayton. They're both held in a Yankee camp somewhere in the West."

"I'm sorry," offered Billy with his head bowed. "I hope he survives."

"So do I," said Rebecca, her eyes focused somewhere else, another world perhaps.

"You will," he assured her, a weak smile on his face.

Becky said nothing. Believing she wished to be alone, Brick kissed her on the lips and bade her farewell. What he didn't know was it would be the last time he'd ever see Becky alive. For Kip Kearney and his men, who had been watching in the bushes, were only waiting for Shelby to depart. When he did so they burst from their hiding place and quickly captured Rebecca Maltesin. As punishment to Billy Brick, they tortured Becky for several hours before they

65

actually killed her. The frightened townfolk and black field hands, who heard the commotion, made little effort to stop it. For they too had experienced the fierce Kip Kearney and his pals.

"That's what he gits for messin' wit' the Reb girls," laughed Kearney after they had done their worst. The mangled body of Rebecca Maltesin lay beneath him. She was badly bruised and her skin was covered with burns from cigar tips. Her death was simply horrid.

When Shelby returned to the chickenshack, he could barely gain control over himself. While the chickens cackled and strode about, Becky lay before him, her arms and legs spread toward the four corners of the world. Kip Kearney, Barlow, Jameson and Straughan stood nearby, still laughing at their horrid prank.

"We did some rearrangin'," Straughan jested.

The foursome broke into fits of hysterics. Pointing at her corpse, the boys pounded each other on the back and shouted further insults for Shelby's benefit.

"Well, Brick, after this 'sperience I dare say she won't be talkin' to the likes a' you."

Billy started to cry. He could contain himself no longer. The harder he cried the louder Kearney and his pals guffawed. To them the spectacle was the funniest thing they had ever seen.

"Why?" wailed Billy Brick. "How could you do such a thing?"

"Determination, Brick. Can't be done without determination."

With that as their explanation, the foursome backed out of the chickenshack. Brick watched through tearful eyes as, arm-in-arm, the men strode back down the hill. Tentatively his hand reached for his pistol. He found the revolver in his hand, quavering between his fingers. Using both hands, he aimed the pistol at the backs of the four men and fired his first shot. Barlow dropped instantly Jameson followed, a

66

slug tearing through his heart. Brick's third shot missed, allowing time for Kearney to get hold of his gun. Meanwhile, Straughan was rushing Billy, his arms outstretched as if he was a bear. While Shelby prepared for Walker Straughan, Kearney fired his pistol. His shot grazed Billy's arm. Brick returned the fire, hitting Kearney squarely in the chest.

"I'll kill you, Brick!" Straughan was bleating from less than ten feet away.

Shelby fired again, hitting Straughan in his inflated belly. It seemed to do no good, for the fat man of Company C kept right on coming. Again Billy fired, this time ripping off the top of Walker's head.

Believing he had killed them all, Shelby dashed up the hill. He took one final look at Rebecca, bidding her a silent goodbye. Behind him, plantation residents and assorted troopers had arrived on the scene. They were pointing at Shelby, and quickly he realized his own version of the story would never be believed. Not by Major Claymore Rayburn.

"I don't give a fiddler's fuck for what they do with the women as long as they kill plenty of Rebs," Major Claymore Rayburn had declared in confidence on many occasions. And the good major would hardly overlook the shooting of four Yankees to avenge the murder of one southern girl. "Don't make sense, boy," the major would declare.

With the vision of a firing squad standing before him, their rifles aimed at his breast, Shelby took off across the fields. He ran and ran, until he could run no more. At last he came upon an abandoned farmhouse, and he took refuge for several days. When the pursuit appeared to have slackened off, he fled Muldoon County, making his way through both Union and Confederate defense lines. At last he was able to reach Philadelphia, nine weeks before Lee surrendered at Appomattox.

Shelby Lopez had enlisted in the Army under the name of Billy Brick. As Billy Brick he fought in a series of decisive battles, beginning at Chattanooga and ending in an encampment in Muldoon County, Georgia. He had fought well and had killed his share of men. He had joined the military to escape the coercion at home, and he fled as a deserter. In between he had suffered from his own ignorance, but had also been imbued with a new sensibility, a greater depth of emotion. He had come to know love, and had experienced fear at its most precarious levels. He had attempted to understand the confusion about him. Upon killing many good men, all of whom he hadn't known, he was applauded. Upon killing the vilest of all possible creatures, he was pursued. Isolated, he had no longer a place to call his home.

As he sat tucked inside his bedroll, with Thunderbird Hawkins beside him, he recalled once again the pretty image of Rebecca Maltesin. Then, quite suddenly, she was reduced to a battered corpse. His heart pounded as he recalled it all—remembered casting off the name of Billy Brick, resuming life under the name of Shelby Lopez. For, despite all he had been through, and what he had endured, Billy Brick would live no more.

When he was still a boy, Shelby often visited the Liberty Bell and the adjacent plaza. Free at last, or at least temporarily, from his obligations at the family store, he'd take his own sweet time walking north along Delaware Avenue. His feet scuffed across the cobblestones, and his lungs filled with the breeze coming off the adjacent river. Beside the piers and numerous warehouses, laborers and sailors mingled, trading stories as they polished off their bottles of wine and beer. Railroad cars crept along the myriad tracks imbedded in the cobblestones, pausing before the old brick warehouses to load and unload freight. With the assistance of tugboats, ships travelled about the port, settling at last at their proper docking spaces.

Upon reaching Market Street, Shelby turned west, listening as he walked to the voices of the pushcart vendors as they hawked their wares in as many languages as there were countries of the world. The pushcarts eventually yielded to the permanent stalls, where slaughtered pigs, cattle, chickens and rabbits hung by their feet. Clothing for sale was piled on tables, as were work tools and hardware. Fruits and vegetables were arranged in baskets. Merchants and customers talked their business, gesticulating wildly, as if their waving arms were signals to distant ships awaiting entrance to the harbor. Gossip was traded, mingling with the aromas of baked goods, fresh meat, human body odor and the industrial smells coming off the river. It was all very pleasant to Shelby Lopez. He wished the river would roll on forever, its banks adorned with the strange beauty of urban behavior.

But soon enough the markets ended, and he was once again confronted with Independence Hall. Inside, the chairs and tables, quill pens, inkwells and documents of historical significance adorned the different chambers. Time and again Shelby toured through the rooms, at last arriving in the center hall, where the Liberty Bell hung from its resting place. He always studied its contour, exploring its famous crack for further signs of wear. When the guards weren't looking he touched its surface, making sure its formation was less abstract than all it symbolized. After walking around the bell, Lopez smiled to himself. So odd, he thought, for a single bell to exert its powers over so many millions, while it hardly relieved the bondage he experienced from just a few blocks away.

It wasn't that Shelby didn't love his father or respect his merchant's qualities. It was, perhaps, that he didn't fully believe in him, or in his theory that his business was worth maintaining at all possible costs. For Leonard had often

69

acknowledged the store he owned was more than a business now. It had become an institution, a tradition of itself. And it was in the name of tradition that Leonard insisted his son take over when he passed it on. Not just a store was Shelby inheriting, but something solid. A responsibility.

"You'll have to look no further for what you should do," Leonard insisted. "It's here, before you. Sensible."

"But I don't think I want to be a merchant," Shelby responded, wishing some of the Liberty Bell's magic would release him from his bondage.

Leonard looked at his son as if he were crazy. "You must be insane," he ranted. "My father and I worked for years to build this. Our lives were devoted to its very maintenance. And now you want to turn your back. Just walk away, as if it never existed."

Shelby looked to his mother for her understanding. Automatically, her eyes were cast downward. Wrinkles formed at the corners of her mouth, like she was working overtime to keep silent. "I just don't think it's for me," said Lopez. "It lacks the adventure."

Leonard frowned, smashing his hand on the counter by the register. "Whatta ya mean, it's not for you? Adventure? What's with the big ideas about adventure? You get into something solid, and you build from there. Who needs adventure. Business is enough adventure on its own."

"No. It isn't."

"You're ungrateful, is what you are. Isn't he, Sarah? God knows it isn't easy building from the bottom up. But when you're finished, it's something. A monument to yourself. What my father began, I completed. And you shall be here to carry it on."

"You don't leave me with much of a choice."

"Choice? I'll hear nothing of choices. I'm telling you. Get the shit out of your ears and listen."

Shelby refused to listen, and Leonard shouted to make himself clear. Often they'd battle for hours. Back and forth they'd hurl their exchanges, each wishing the other would change his attitude, or disappear from sight and mind. By means of threats, insults and withholdings, Leonard persisted. Shelby's leisure was determined by the hours the store was open. He was assigned to the stock room and later to the upstairs, where he was supposed to wait on customers. He was a poor salesman and was again relegated to the stockroom, shipping and receiving. And then, at last, Leonard discovered a better use for his son. A compromise, said Leonard. Shelby would have more leisure, as long as he spent it in the company of Sherri Seltzer, daughter of Morton Seltzer, a local manufacturer. Willing to do anything to escape the horrid store, Shelby agreed. He would become the future fiancé. He would learn to love Sherri Seltzer.

"See how nice they look together," was Leonard Lopez' favorite claim. "In a few years they'll be ready to cinch the knot."

Morton Seltzer raised his glass and beamed with pride. "It'll be a wedding," he promised, "like none other this town has ever seen."

Though their parents thought their names sounded cute together, Sherri and Shelby were hardly compatible. Sherri detested young Lopez' coarse manners, much of which he had especially affected just to be released of his bride-to-be.

"I prefer gentlemen to young boys," she often claimed. Shelby was quick to agree.

As the months passed it became increasingly clear to Shelby that the only knot he was ready to cinch was the one on a rope around his neck, provided his family still insisted he marry Sherri.

"I can't do it," he'd complain on a regular basis.

No one listened. Not even Sherri. It wasn't that she desired Shelby any more than he did her. In fact, besides hatred, she felt little emotions at all toward the young man. But Sherri, as her parents claimed, was a "traditional girl," and traditional girls do not allow ruinous feelings to stand in the way of a proper marriage. That is, until she fell in love with a real gentleman, one who was only slightly younger than her father.

"I'm in love," she confessed to Shelby during one of their walks through the park.

He stared at his future fiancée with all due incredulity. "C'mon," he begged her. "Don't make it worse than it is."

"You don't understand," she intoned, disgusted by his lack of belief. "I've found another man."

Immediately Shelby's heart climbed to levels of unknown pleasure. "Who? Where?"

Sherri smirked her thin, red lips and widened her eyes. "He's a man," she insisted. "Not just a little boy with big ideas."

"Marry him. Believe me, I'll understand."

"How can I marry him," she smiled, "when I don't even have the chance to see him? Most of my time is taken up by you. My father forbids me to see other men."

Lopez didn't know what to say. Somewhere there must be a way out. If only . . .

"I have an idea!" screeched Sherri. Shelby could've guessed she had it planned all along. "Suppose we only pretend to see each other. You pick me up, walk with me a few blocks, and then I'll go my way and you'll go yours. We'll meet back in the park, say in a few hours. No one will be the wiser."

No one was ever the wiser. Despite Sherri's constant tardiness, for she was never in the park on time, Shelby was ecstatic to be relieved of his horrid task. The wedding ceremony and all its encumbrances were already receding from conjecture. Every night he prayed Sherri would remain in love with her newest suitor. He appealed to all the forces of the universe that the older man shouldn't die before young Lopez could be relieved of his responsibilities.

In his newfound leisure Shelby visited the various museums or wandered up to the university where he took his place among the students. On warm days he sat beneath his favorite shade tree and watched college life pass him by. On cold days he hung about the union building, sipping countless cups of coffee in his isolation. He wished he could really be a part of the university. He'd have given anything to become a student. But Leonard had forbidden it.

"The store will be your education," swore the elder Lopez. "There you'll learn everything. And that should certainly be enough for you."

Leonard's rejections caused Shelby to wish he'd been sired by someone else. By Shmuel, maybe. Or Seymour, Leonard's older brother. He had been educated.

"He's dead!" was the response when Seymour's name was spoken. His father wanted no part of his older brother. "Dead! So don't bring up his name again. Let the dead lie still."

"What's with Seymour, anyway?" Shelby finally asked of his Aunt Belle in desperation.

"Seymour was your Grandpa Lopez' favorite, honey," Belle answered with her usual candor. "Your father was forced to ˈstay home and mind that store, while Seymour went off to school. It was your grandfather's wish that Seymour become a doctor."

"So? What happened?" pressed Shelby.

Belle shrugged and flicked the long ash from her cigarette. "He became an artist. A painter, I think he was. And later he became a radical. Moved in with a shiksa and took up with the union causes. Your Grandpa disowned Seymour and gave the store to Leonard."

"But why? Why'd he disown Seymour?"

"For one thing, Seymour was dead. I guess in your Grandpa's mind, that made it easier. God knows what he would've done if Seymour had remained alive. You see your Grandpa Lopez wasn't any fonder of Leonard than I am. Like so many others, he thought Leonard a schmuck. If you'll excuse the expression."

"That's all right. What about Seymour?"

73

Aunt Belle sighed and took another drag on her cigarette. "Like I said, Seymour was the favorite. Don't you dare repeat a word of this to anyone, or dare tell your father I told you so, or he'll forbid me to come to the house. But Seymour was the favorite! Believe me, your Grandpa Lopez would've gladly died in his place ... or sent Leonard to heaven instead. A real bright, sensitive kid, Seymour was. A few years younger than Leonard. Barely see his face. Always was polite, even to me.

"He was sent away to school, a fine university somewhere in New York. He was gone about two years when he suddenly takes up with this girl. Faye was her name. Faye Gestalt, I think. It's been so long. Anyway, even though she was a bright, sweet girl, she didn't strike the mark with your Grandpa Lopez. So he put his foot down. Either Seymour gives up this shiksa, or he gets no more support for college."

"Then what happened?" Shelby asked, his interest steadily growing.

Belle stared at her nephew and smiled. A glance at his face caused her to fear what he might be denied in life by his father. "You know, your father can be a terrible schmuck," she admitted. "He really can annoy me."

Shelby ignored it, and bade his aunt continue with her story.

"Oh! Like I said, Seymour was young and impetuous. Not much older than you. He told his father, if you'll excuse the expression, to go fuck himself. He'd had enough of school anyway. Besides, his ladyfriend was strong-minded and was willing to back him up. She was a firebrand, that one. I only met her once, when she was down for the holidays. Leonard had just fallen for Sarah, and he invited us all over for dinner. Even Shmuel. Anyway, she encouraged Seymour, and he became more involved with the union causes. He painted a good many of their posters. And then one day he was no more."

Shelby regarded Belle's mournful expression before he asked what happened.

"He was killed in a riot. A demonstration became violent and they found him dead, after. Police said he was trampled by a horse. No one knew what to believe. Your Grandpa Lopez was out of his mind with grief. He couldn't bear the death of his favorite son, so he disowned him for all previous disagreements. He allowed the authorities to bury the body somewhere in New York, and never again did he mention Seymour's name. A little screwy, your Grandpa was. And boy, did he ever take it out on Leonard. Poor Leonard! He forced him to work some sixteen, seventeen hours a day in that rotten store of his. No wonder Leonard later had so much trouble with ... with...."

"With what? Aunt Belle."

"You shouldn't be told at your age. Later, maybe ... in a few more years."

"About what?"

"Never you mind, about what. Anyway ... where was I? ... Oh yes, a month or so before Seymour was killed Grandpa Lopez had gone up to where his son was living. He figured a personal appeal would stir some sense into Seymour. He failed, and returned to this city more disgruntled than ever. It was the last he ever saw of Seymour.

"You'd be surprised how similar you look ... you and Seymour. I have an old photo around here somewhere. One day I'll show you the picture. It's frightening. Small wonder you have so much trouble with your father. Every time he looks at you he sees his dead brother."

"What about the girl? This Faye Gestalt?"

Belle shrugged and flicked another ash. "Who knows? No one ever heard from her. She shipped back everything Seymour owned and disappeared. Had rich connections in Chicago. Her father was a brewer. Besides his letters, she only kept one thing that belonged to Seymour. A book, she said. It was important to him, she claimed, so it would always be important to her. Always!"

Shelby was deeply moved by the story. At last he felt like he had known his dead uncle. The man's behavior had

75

excited him. Especially if he was as similar to Seymour in appearance as Belle had claimed. One day, vowed Shelby, he'd visit the grave of his Uncle Seymour.

Not long after Belle Gluntz had related the story of Seymour Lopez, the conflict between Shelby and Leonard erupted into open warfare. Each was hard pressed to stifle his disdain for the other. Sarah remained on the sidelines, her head hung low, tears in her eyes. Occasionally she ranted about peace for the sake of family unity. But her appeals were never strong enough.

"I don't like him," Leonard always retorted. "It's as simple as that. Wherever he goes, whatever he does, he brings trouble to me."

"If you weren't so concerned with my affairs, you wouldn't assume my troubles."

"Contention! Nothing but contention. Why couldn't you be like the others?"

"What others?"

Leonard spat on the floor. Thinking better of it, he wiped it up with the sole of his shoe. "Never mind what others. All you've done is bring grief to me."

"What kind of grief? All I want. . . ."

"Is to give me aggravation. If you ever agreed with what I said, the sun would rise in the west."

"And then you'd have to rearrange your display windows to keep the sun from bleaching the merchandise."

Leonard was furious. "And you wouldn't be there to help me. Gone. Never once are you around when I need you."

"I have other things on my mind besides this lousy store."

"Don't curse at me! What could be more important than your family?"

"Myself."

"Yourself? You're selfish. Selfish to the bone. To the marrow. For years I obeyed my father. I worked for him, downstairs, sorting stock from morning until night. In season I barely saw the light of day. And you say you can't even work for me. What kind of son are you?"

76

"The wrong kind, I guess."

Leonard grew hysterical. "Get out! Get out! I can't stand the sight of you. Never again will an ingrate like you have anything to do with me."

"Fuck you," Shelby muttered, peeling off his apron.

"What?" Leonard demanded.

"Nothing."

"What?"

As Shelby made for the door he noticed his father reaching for the nightstick he kept hidden behind the counter, in case of a holdup. What he'd ever do with the stick, Shelby had no idea. At last it found its purpose. With little fanfare Leonard hurled the stick at Shelby. It bounced off the young man's shoulder and then struck a nearby showcase. The glass fell out of the panels and shattered on the floor. Shelby laughed and stepped over the wreckage. His shoulder ached, but young Lopez refused to reveal any sign of pain. For a few moments he stared hard at his father. The older man's eyes had softened.

"I guess it would've been different if you were Seymour," sighed the younger man, sorry he mentioned it as the words parted from his lips.

"Don't you ever mention his name again," warned Leonard, the door slamming shut on the last of his words.

After he completed a tour of the streets, Shelby went to visit his Uncle Shmuel, at his plush office in City Hall. Years before, the burglarizing uncle had been taken under the wing of Giles Havelock, the behemoth mayor of the city. At the time Havelock was only a councilman, but he entertained high aspirations. Even the mayoralty was only a stepping stone toward grander horizons. When his second term of office ended, Giles hoped to pocket the state. Certainly there was room enough in his size 48 trousers. As for Shmuel, he would continue to enjoy Havelock's protection in return for services rendered. It was no secret that Shmuel Gluntz was considered the mayor's noblest counselor. It was Shmuel whom Havelock sought whenever trouble reared its ugly head in his fair city. And Shmuel always had a solution. Legal or otherwise, Shmuel always had a solution.

"Come live with me," Shmuel offered his nephew, once Shelby had settled in his office.

Lopez stared at his uncle from across the huge walnut desk. He studied the gray, wiry hair, the piercing eyes, and the cold cigar which rested between his uncle's fingers. He recalled all the gifts Shmuel had given him. His uncle's advice was always good, the words conveying authority blended with experience. Shelby believed in him, though he often disobeyed his uncle's suggestions.

When Shelby didn't respond, Shmuel felt obligated to go on with his explanation. "It's not that your father's necessarily a bad man. Just that he's so self-righteous. In his store the moral standards of the world are tenaciously upheld. He may cheat a little here and there, swing things one way or another, but he calls it his business. He may go out on your mother, but he calls it a man's right. But when it's me . . . then I'm the crook of his family. He's so wrong. So damned self-righteous. What he doesn't realize is we're all crooks, stealing our lives away under assumed names. No one's any different. Any better or any worse. Except for your father. He believes the world's nose should be stuck up his ass. But they'll fuck him. With broken glass, if he's not careful."

"So . . . what should I do?"

Uncle Shmuel paused to brush his sleeve across his nose. For some time he stared down at his desk, refusing to lift his eyes. He played with his paperweight, and stirred the pencils in his cup. "Come live with me," he said finally. "I could really use a bright kid like you. We know each other. We like each other. It's not often, in this business, I meet people who I like. You know, you'll always have the best of everything when you're around me."

"Thanks, Uncle. I promise to think it over. What about the Army? I thought I'd join, just to get away from it all."

Shmuel bit down angrily on the tip of his cigar. "Schmuck!" he cried. "You'll get away from nothing. A war's going on, and it's no place for a smart kid to be. Any dummy can get his ass shot off. It takes one with brains to stay the hell away. You want to be some fuckin' putz, get up at five in the morning because some fuckin' redneck is barking in your ear? You want that? No breakfast, no comforts of modern living. Just a fuckin' battle on a hill no one ever heard of before. Only a putz would do such a thing."

Shelby enlisted anyway. It wasn't that he disagreed with Shmuel, or that he particularly wanted to join the Army. No. It was for neither of these reasons. Something more basic had arisen in Shelby's life. Sherri Seltzer had been knocked up. She could have had eight kids for all he cared. A full litter of them pouring from the womb. However, the only problem was that dear Sherri had placed the blame on her future fiancé. Very creative she was in including Shelby in her story. Bravely, she stood before both sets of parents and described in sordid detail how Shelby, overcome with frustration, his dick in his hand, attacked her one sunny afternoon. She had no choice in the matter. All Shelby's doing. And, quite naturally, Morton and Leonard believed it. Shelby would be forced to pay his dues.

"I never touched her," swore young Lopez. "Not even on the arm."

"What was it then? An act of God?"

Shelby paused to imagine God, white haired, white bearded, standing before Sherri in his floral patterned underwear. His dick was long and menacing. It parted the fly in his boxer shorts. Sherri lay curled on the bed of clouds. Tears were in her eyes as her legs were forced apart by His majestic lever.

"I didn't do it," repeated Shelby. Before either his father or Morton Seltzer could object, he laid out the entire story of Sherri's affair with an older man. He claimed he only dropped her off at the park and then met her there later in the day. "She was always late," he added to his explanation.

When he was finished, young Lopez sat back with his arms folded and watched the two older men deliberate. Panic appeared in both sets of eyes. It was not that they necessarily disbelieved Shelby, although they never admitted it, it was just that Sherri had left them in a bind. An unmarried daughter with unborn child was simply more than they could handle. What could they do, sit like two fools while the girl swelled through the months, the object of every gossip in the neighborhood? Send her away? Who would have her?

"What should we do?" whispered the nonplussed Morton Seltzer.

Out of duty to his creditor, combined with the desire to see Shelby married and settled at last, Leonard turned back to his son. "What kind of bullshit are you trying to give us?" he demanded.

"Yeah," took up Morton. "You mean you left my daughter unescorted while you went off somewhere on your own."

"It was her idea to go our separate ways," insisted young Lopez.

"I don't care whose idea it was. You're responsible. One way or another. You should have more sense than to leave her alone like that."

"She wasn't pregnant when I left her. Only when she returned. I swear, it wasn't me."

Morton and Leonard would have none of it. "I hope you enjoy your lives together," they said, each pausing to toast the future couple.

Several days later, Shelby enlisted into the Union Army. He demanded to be accepted right away. They took him, under his assumed name of Billy Brick. With other enlistees he was shipped to basic training and later sent to join Yankee forces in Tennessee. Soon after he became one of thousands committed to the Battle of Chickamauga.

I didn't want to do this, Shelby told himself, just as the battle was under way. I should've listened to my Uncle Shmuel. But such deliberations were soon to pass into history, as Shelby spent the coming days charging up and down the dreaded hillsides. As weeks passed into months, his prior life had all but vanished. The war had absorbed him. When he entered Muldoon County with his contingency of Union forces, it was quite clear who was going to win the war. This fact made the fighting seem all the more absurd. Why didn't the Rebs just give it up? he often wondered. Retain what's left of their slaughtered populace and their has-been antebellum culture? They must have been as tired of the killing as he was. More so, since everywhere they searched, defeat was there to oppress them. They were dressed in rags, these Rebels, covered with blood. Part of an arm, a leg and even heads had been severed. Yet the war still continued.

In Muldoon County, Shelby found time to reflect upon himself. He wondered what he'd do when the war was finally over. He thought of his home and his family. Certainly he could never return to the store. He pondered his being saved at the Battle of Chickamauga. Time and again, he relived his experience on that battlefield. The nameless Rebel soldier came charging forward. Suddenly he was no longer in command of his actions. A bullet had ruined it all. He staggered several feet before collapsing just behind Shelby. His bayonet nicked Lopez as he passed by. And somewhere behind him, Lopez' savior galloped off, his image fading amidst the gunsmoke and war cries.

When he could no longer ponder what fate held in store, Shelby grew restless and began to wander about the plantation on which his troop had bivouacked. The Hackett Plantation it was called in better times. Now it was a shell-pocked, withered image of a bygone era. Everything lay in ruin. Everything, that is, but Rebecca Maltesin. She had smiled apprehensively at her first sight of Shelby. Immediately he had fallen in love.

From inside the Indian blanket he had secured like a miniature teepee, Thunderbird Hawkins reviewed his father's arrival in the desert. On many occasions, in dreams and in reality, he'd seen Burning Bush. Hawkins had sought his guidance and communed with his spirit. Much like he did while living, Burning Bush was usually reluctant to discuss himself in great detail. Perhaps he remembered little, or the events leading up to his death were so inconceivable he still failed to acknowledge their occurrence.

Thunderbird, when envisioning his father, usually contented himself with his mere image. He never imposed upon the presence of the spirit by asking too many questions. Of course there were times when the spirit of Burning Bush voluntarily discussed his life, so, bit by bit, Hawkins was able to accumulate the details of his father's existence. And as the pieces fused together, Thunderbird discovered a greater awareness of his father, not as he had lived in the past, but in the framework of Hawkins' own life. In trancelike states, while wandering about the Massive Desert, Thunderbird had witnessed key events relating to his father's life. While travelling about the country, Hawkins often sensed he'd come upon an area his father had visited many years before. The sense was little more than a spark of emotion, igniting a portion of his consciousness. It was enough. It was fulfilling.

Thunderbird had learned in his meetings with his father's spirit, and while in his trancelike state, that Burning Bush had roamed the world for many years after he was banished from his tribe. With only his blanket, essential weapons and

82

the Great Necklace in his possession, he had set forth from Sour Broth's camp in the Swamp Land. For the first time in his life Burning Bush was confronted by his own solitude. He was awkward at first, alone, left to his own devices. He missed the quips and the ancient stories often passed among his fellow tribal warriors. True, he had borne much of the brunt of their jokes, but he'd also returned them in kind. Though he was disliked, he was also feared and even envied. Always he was the focus of much attention.

"The Great Necklace will be yours," Sour Broth had ordered. "But you will leave this tribe, never to return."

Some of the elders had disagreed. "The Necklace?" they questioned. "How will we ever survive without the Necklace?"

"We will survive," Sour Broth had confirmed. "It was Sacred Heart's final wish that Burning Bush be given the Great Necklace. My only concern, as should be yours, is respect for his wishes, not the questioning of motives."

"But it's only natural to wonder why," the elders complained.

Exhausted by the preceding sequence of tragedies, Sour Broth cast a weary glance to the spot they were burying his Gopher Tracks. Even before his son's duel with Burning Bush, Sour Broth had known who would emerge the victor. He had sensed destiny and could ill afford to stand in its way. His awareness of destiny had allowed him to yield to Sacred Heart's last wishes. Sour Broth did not know why the old medicine man had wanted Burning Bush to have the Necklace. Perhaps it was due to nostalgia. For it was no secret among the tribal elders that, long ago, Sacred Heart and Fair Rainbow, Burning Bush's mother, had had an affair. A brief encounter, no doubt, yet shortly afterward, the middle-aged and previously barren woman gave birth to her only child. In the depths of Sour Broth's memory, he recalled the tribal gossips counting the months. He remembered there had been some confusion. Burning Bush was born a month too early. Even so, the rumors and gossip were quickly stifled, out of deference to Green Lizard, Fair Rainbow's aging husband. Once a great and noble warrior, Green Lizard had grown senile through the years. Rarely was he coherent. And when he was, the occasion was frosted by his lament for his inability to produce an heir.

Even while the duel raged between Gopher Tracks and Burning Bush, Sour Broth had considered all of this. It pained him deeply to relinquish the coveted Great Necklace to the arrogant Burning Bush. Had the request not come from Sacred Heart himself, had it not been heard with his own ears, Sour Broth would've ignored the plea. However, to ignore the wisdom of his medicine man was to reject the forces existing beyond the limits of his own understanding. This he could never do.

With all this in his consideration, Sour Broth turned and faced the tribal elders. "The last time we questioned the motives of Sacred Heart it nearly led to disaster. Although I am at times a foolish man, I'll not repeat the mistakes of my ancestors. Burning Bush will possess the Necklace. He will take it from the tribe. Forever."

Again the tribal elders implored Sour Broth to relent his decision, but he stood firm.

"What Sacred Heart has done was with the benefit of the entire tribe in mind. He was a wise medicine man, a great leader who was always available for consultation, be it day or night. I won't dare profane his wishes."

The tribal elders turned to talk among themselves. Some discussion of rebellion arose among the least contented members of the council, but their suggestions were overwhelmingly rejected. Others at last began to understand Sour Broth's own point of view. Collecting his thoughts with theirs, they espoused the wisdom of Sacred Heart, conjecturing that the same inspiration which had caused the medicine man to send Fair Rainbow alone to retrieve the Great Necklace had also caused him to bequeath the Necklace to

Burning Bush. The merits of Sacred Heart's past decision were recounted. It was pointed out that Fair Rainbow had been a heroic figure, had later become a wise and efficient counselor, never once taking advantage of her powers. As the first female ever to serve on the tribal council, she heard arguments from all standpoints, receiving the praise of many. When she passed away, the entire tribe paid tribute at her grave.

It was said that the Great Necklace had been in possession of the tribe for many hundreds of years before its removal. It was traded away by Movement Reformers who acquired blankets, furs, trinkets and assorted steel weapons in exchange for the treasure. The Movement Reformers believed the Great Necklace was no longer necessary. It was a hindrance, disrupting the progressive elements of the tribe. For years these Movement Reformers had attempted to undermine the power of the Necklace, to abolish the rituals in which the Necklace was involved. Constantly they failed, although they argued, pleaded and even threatened the more conservative tribal members. But under the council of patient face, Sacred Heart's father and previous medicine man, the Movement Reformers had failed to gain ground. At last, caught in the hold of grievous frustration, these Reformers decided reform wasn't enough. Something drastic must be done. Something radical.

When Patient Face died and Sacred Heart assumed his title as medicine man, the Movement Reformers at last seized their chance. They argued that Sacred Heart was too young for the role of medicine man, that an alternative tribal philosophy must be established. Strange Steed was named its director, and the Reformation Movement relocated in a teepee at the far side of the campsite.

While still grieving for the death of his father, Sacred Heart assumed his title. He had never dreamed of such a conflict existing among his people. Certainly life before was never like this. Chaos was everywhere. His tribal members were desperate for a new leader, and there was little hope one could be found. After much deliberation, Sacred Heart met with the tribal elders.

"I will first go to the mountain and look down from its peak. I'll meditate and learn the secrets of my ancestors and the powers of my spirit. As they were passed down to my father, if my task is noble, they will be passed down to me. When I return from the mountain I'll contain a new sense of direction which can be invoked upon our tribe."

"It's a helluva time to be going away," several tribal elders admonished. "With our tribe in a state of crisis, you're going to disappear. We can't see the wisdom at all."

Ignoring all other threats and pleas that he remain with his tribe during its hour of need, Sacred Heart packed a few belongings and headed for the mountains. He travelled slowly, with great care and deliberation, believing too hasty a step would cause him to miss the insights he'd receive while climbing the mountain. At different vistas he paused for hours, overlooking the territory his tribe called its own. The splendor of the land renewed his determination, provided him with strength. He was overwhelmed by the beauty and consumed by understanding. He had risen above the Swamp Land and gazed down into a fragrant milieu of smoke-water green. Sunlight shimmered from the Swamp Land. Leaves and fronds glistened with moisture. Enchantment was all around him. So little was defined, yet all was essential, fitting together like lone sprouts upon a field of crops. He recalled the many times he had gone with his mother and the other women and children of the tribe to plant crops in the few open spaces. He remembered the prayers, the ceremonies and the good feeling toward the beginnings of a fresh season.

"We plant in good faith, with the understanding we may not be present to share the harvest," the elders chanted from a circular position. "But it is in our interest that we ever perpetuate the powers of the earth."

The planting ceremonies reminded Sacred Heart of the

winter solstice, in which the powers of the Great Necklace were again invoked. He remembered the year he joined the other youngsters who were first initiated into the Rites of the Great Necklace. It was among the fondest of his memories. He saw the smoke rising from the center of the giant teepee, the pipes and herbs being passed among his tribe. Proud birdfeathers adorned the entrance to the teepee as the tribal members huddled together to guard against the cold. For hours they prayed, chanting, each pursuing the elements of his own particular fascination. Visions, stories of the past, became intensely recognizable, reinforced until their very images were projected onto the teepee walls, or materialized within the haze of fire.

As the pipes were passed and the herbs digested, the elders recounted the origins of the Great Necklace. One by one they expounded upon the episode by which the Great Necklace was acquired. They told of the Conquistidores' dispersement of the tribe driving them deeper and deeper into the Swamp Land. All who floundered were destroyed by the invaders.

Under the leadership of Twisted Branch the tribe retreated deeper into the Swamps with the foolish Conquistadores boldly in pursuit. When he was able, Twisted Branch turned and fought his enemy. Valiant were his stands. Guerrilla tactics were employed, enabling the warriors to isolate small pockets of Conquistadores who were soon put to death. It seemed the war would never end.

In their haste for treasure the Conquistadores had spread themselves too thin and were now unable to support their occupied territory.

"I think they may have exhausted themselves," Twisted Branch announced to his warriors. "They have chased us until they've become bogged down in the Swamps. Their superior weapons have become useless in the marshes. No longer are we the prey, but the predators. We have endured, and now we will emerge victorious."

With renewed vigor the Indians rallied round their chief,

launching a series of counteroffensives. With each success, confidence was bolstered, until a false belief in Indian superiority was instilled among the warriors. The years of retreat, of brutality, of suffering, were forgotten. Old memories were replaced by torture and sexual acts bordering on the sadomasochistic. As each new group of Conquistadore prisoners were marched into camp, new tortures were originated. Blood sizzled as it seeped into fires which had been stoked for the branding of prisoners.

The Indians were consumed by their desire for vengeance. In its seeking, old customs were abandoned in favor of the lurid and the brutal. Tribal elders pleaded with the more influential warriors to cease their actions, lest the tribe fall into total ruin. They begged they return to the ancient rituals and customs, abandoning all acts of vengeance.

"Let the remaining Conquistadores return to their people," they insisted.

Plead as they might, the new order of influence refused to heed the elder's warnings. "This war has forced us to witness our own doom, and now we must behave according to our experience. We were once a peaceful tribe, but such days are finished. What lies beyond us is cruelty. We must be protected against its intrusion. For there can be no values, no judgments established in a world without rules. For us it is over. Our fate has been aborted, for we've been denied all claims to our territories. Killing the invaders is inconsequential, for as we move toward our own oblivion we rediscover only the desires of the flesh, which for so long have been largely concealed by the desires of the spirit."

"No, you are wrong," argued the elders. "You will destroy us as you've destroyed the Conquistadores. Corruption has run amok. The will to transcend base pleasures has all but disappeared from the hearts and minds of our youngsters. Few care, and even worse, fewer maintain the capacity to care. Our relationships have regressed to our crudest principles. Life is tentative, consumed by an emotion which is too easily exhausted."

A stalemate was established, dividing the tribe. Time passed and not much changed. The delirium that had once been aroused during acts of vengeance and torture had been depleted. Even brutality had been undermined by the inescapable formation of a new pattern, a routine which soon grew as boring as the rest. By now the traditional had been forgotten, left to rot beyond restoration. Only conceptual fragments of the past could be proffered, and they did little to sustain much interest. Once-abundant mythology relinquished its influence to little more than vacuous ideologies. The tribe believed its end was soon.

It was quite by accident, during one of their many battles with the Conquistadores, that the tribe acquired the Great Necklace. Weary and unenthusiastic, the warriors marched their prisoners into the camp to prepare them for the now dull ritual of slaughter. Matter-of-factly the Conquistadores were lined up and slain with arrows and spears until only three men were left. One, a wounded young soldier, was wearing the Great Necklace.

"Take this," he offered to Twisted Branch in exchange for his life. "It has come from far across the sea, from the oldest of civilizations. Those who possess it are said to have reached a greater understanding. To unlock its mysteries means possession of the wisdom of the world, the destiny of man."

Twisted Branch scornfully examined the Necklace and then passed it among his counselors. "This is nothing," he claimed. "We, in the past, have created necklaces that are far more beautiful than this mere trinket."

Before the young soldier could reply, Twisted Branch called for his own collection of necklaces. He presented these in confirmation of his tribe's ancient craftsmanship.

Pained by the wound he received in battle, the young Conquistadore managed a weak smile. He pushed the necklaces away. "No. You don't understand. With this Necklace and the Great Book, the key to its mysteries, one can know the destiny of man. Many have pursued this answer, as they have chased across continents for the Great Book and the Great Necklace. But never have the two been brought together."

"And the destiny of man?"

"It remains unsolved. Only when one has possession of the Great Book and the Necklace will he ever know. And even then, mere possession is not enough, for it is said among the ancients from across the sea that one must be able to decipher the code scripted within its pages."

Twisted Branch fingered his chin. "How'd you come by this Great Necklace?"

"A favor from a lady. An heirloom. Her family were once explorers from far away."

"The Necklace. What good will it do without the Book?"

"It is considered an honor to seek the Book. The search alone has been proven vital to many."

Skeptically, Long Claws, the witch doctor, moved the Necklace through a number of positions. Quite as he had expected, nothing happened. He snorted, before casting the Necklace down in disgust. He started to walk away, his followers behind him. Suddenly, a snake appeared in his pathway and, before anyone could react, it bit Long Claws on the calf, killing him instantly. The snake slithered away, successfully dodging all attempts to stop him.

"That is an omen!" sniffed Twisted Branch.

"A great opportunity," espoused the young soldier. "One day your tribe could learn the destiny of man."

Twisted Branch stooped down and retrieved the Necklace. He carefully examined it again, noting its symbols, its metals and general texture. He bit down on one of its medallions. At second glance it seemed much more exotic. The coloring seemed brighter. He pulled at its ends, before returning to his captive. His eyeballs burning, he stared deep into the young soldier. He searched for his insincerity but found nary a trace.

"All right," he said wearily. "I will keep this Necklace.

You shall have your freedom. Take your companions and leave this camp."

When the Conquistadores had fled his captivity, Twisted Branch displayed the treasure for all to see. Though he still may have doubted the Necklace's powers, he saw it as an instrument by which his tribe could escape its quandary. New myths could be created. New forces could be set to work. At last, at long last, there was something to believe in.

"From this day on," commanded Twisted Branch, "we will remove all evidence of our reign of vengeance, which for too long has debased our better nature. All acts of torture and barbarism are condemned. We possess the Great Necklace, and we shall seek the Great Book. Heroic warriors will search the earth for its location. Once it is retrieved, we shall unlock its mysteries. Then, and only then, can one dare venture an answer regarding the destiny of this tribe."

Old ritual was gradually resumed and incorporated within the new. Practices invoked in their former territories were now being employed by even the younger members of the tribe. Belief in tribal salvation and redemption before the greater forces of nature was restored. The war with the Conquistadores passed into history. Though it was recalled in song and ritual, never again was its violence relished.

"We have entered a new epoch," announced Twisted Branch, just a few days before he died. "I have borne witness to much suffering and to much brutality. I have seen the collapse of our tribal character and then observed the resurgence of our better spirit. This is certainly enough for one man to see. Happily, and in much contentment that I have performed my duties, I can take leave of this world."

Each year at the winter solstice, the Rites of the Great Necklace were performed. This ancient story was disclosed as were tales told of valiant efforts to retrieve the Great Book. Tribal elders related their own adventures, and hoped that the younger warriors would profit by their experiences. As the spiritual fervor increased, and as the herbs and the pipes worked their magic, the Great Book once again rose from within the fire. Its pages opened, turning, the Great Book revealed a mere glimpse of its secrets. A myriad of shapes and forms and ancient languages were seen by all whose state of consciousness had risen to the occasion. Then, without warning, the Great Book vanished, inviting only the bravest to seek its whereabouts.

The day before his ill-fated duel with Gopher Tracks, Burning Bush had had a vision of the Great Book. It loomed above him, uncomfortably translucent and foreboding. Burning Bush concealed his face before its image. But the mysterious code drew nearer, implanting its image on the palms of his hands. Nonplussed, Burning Bush shrieked and fled his teepee. Oddly enough, when he trekked across the Massive Desert, his vision of the Great Book became his sole source of comfort. It was desperate consolation for one who had been cast upon the plains, sentenced to the life of the constant traveller.

Chapter 6

Burning Bush often resented the quality of his life. His exile made it even more distasteful. Gladly he would've suggested Sour Broth shove it up his dead son's ass had not the other warriors seemed as prepared to back their chieftain. One by one, Burning Bush trained on their faces. When he reached the end of the line, he spit in the dirt and wiped his ass, a tribal symbol meaning "you can eat shit for all I care." Although several warriors stepped from the line, and murmurings persisted throughout the ranks, Burning Bush was allowed to gather his few belongings and leave the camp.

"You will walk from here," he was told by Sour Broth. "Each step will remind you of this day. May your feet tread on jagged stones and broken bits of pottery. For you have shamed us all."

His journey wasn't easy. He had braved many dangers on his way west. He had defied alligators, quicksand and the incursions of hostile travellers. He had encompassed many miles, from the Swamp Land to the Massive Desert. He had experienced many changes in terrain and climate, many hours of loneliness, reducing gradually to a listless solitude. And as he walked he thought many thoughts and reached many conclusions. These were soon erased, substituted for new answers to his questions a little further up the trail. Again and again, he phrased silent questions and answered them within. A cycle, a given rhythm, was established as he traversed the earth. Soon a system was developed, by which he could calibrate the distance travelled by the number of the questions asked and answered. Burning Bush discovered he received approximately four sets of questions and answers for every seven miles travelled. Over dangerous terrain his ratio varied.

His duel with Gopher Tracks and his confrontation with the remaining warriors had exalted Burning Bush to a new level of arrogance. He was instilled with a deep sense of pride and a dash of hatred for all. Except for his mother, who, long ago, had inspired him with courage. He often considered her as he walked, imagining the path by which she had travelled in her quest to recover the Great Necklace.

"Fair Rainbow will seek the Necklace," Sacred Heart had announced to his people. He had just returned from his second meditation trip upon the mountain. He was tanned and looking splendid in his first set of medicine man robes. "She is the one who holds the power."

"Fair Rainbow? A woman? C'mon now. At least shouldn't a warrior accompany her?"

Sacred Heart said no. "She must go alone," he explained. "Only then will she be able to find the Great Necklace. Sending two would be like sending no one."

The Necklace had been traded to a one-eyed travelling peddler, who carried a walking stick adorned with a ram's head, and who spoke in a bare whisper. That was all Fair Rainbow had to go on when she left the camp. Her departure marked her first venture away from camp, outside the Swamps of her people. Her journey would take her well beyond its boundaries. She would explore the white man's world, a territory of which she was ignorant. She headed for the Mississippi River and New Orleans where the peddler was said to winter.

Her emotions were mixed when she left the camp. At once she was fearful, yet exhilarated. Free from all other obligations, she believed she'd miss her own home, her living with Green Lizard. Not that the once-noted warrior was any great catch. At nights he snored loudly, the saliva dribbling from the side of his mouth. A bit senile, hard of hearing, and a sloppy eater, Green Lizard usually dwelled in a world all his own. It was a small world, consisting of himself, his invisible friend and a wide variety of stand-ins. Only on rare occasions did he emerge from his state of confusion.

Alone in the white man's world, Fair Rainbow missed Green Lizard. She longed for his youthful smile, his wide-eyed innocence and lack of inhibitions. The gray-haired old man had brought her more laughter than she had ever realized. His spirit had touched her, made her more than his servant girl.

"Take care of him," she advised her cousin, Leaf Beneath the Rocks. "Feed him and keep him clean. Walk him occasionally. Otherwise, he should be no trouble. Goodbye, Green Lizard."

"Don't talk to me like that or I'll close down shop," he replied with a wave of his hand.

Fair Rainbow passed through the Swamp Land without incident. Except for its natural dangers, the Swamps displayed no outward signs of hostility to the Indian woman. Her steps were firm, crossing the lands with which she was most familiar. Occasionally a small tribe of Indians or a lone hermit living in his thatched hut was sighted. It was not until she reached the other side of the Swamp Land that Fair Rainbow first set eyes upon white men. A small community lay before her, its people hustling about their morning routines. Wagons creaked through dusty streets and the morning breeze hissed through the palms and the jungle brush. Indians were a common sight to these settlers whose community stood at the end of the Swamp Land, and Fair Rainbow was able to pass through their town without incident.

The apparent futility of her quest developed melancholy within Fair Rainbow. Isolated, far away from home, she had found no one to turn to. Assistance, if it was given at all, was given grudgingly. Days passed, and she ached for the sound of her tribal tongue. In desperation she turned her attentions elsewhere. Ignoring the warnings of her tribal elders, she drifted closer to the white folk. She became interested in their habits and began to study them as one would any society of animals. From behind rocks, trees, and in the far corners of their senses, she hid herself from the white folk, secretly observing their habits. She learned of his eating habits, how he courted, how he made love in the bushes by the running streams. She peered out from her hiding places to see the white man at prayer meetings, his hands raised in praise of his God. Little by little she came to know his language. Certain words were familiar. With hand gestures and her small vocabulary Fair Rainbow discovered she could approach the white man, asking of the peddler whom she was seeking.

"Ain't no one-eyed peddler been through here," the more courteous whites answered. Others demonstrated what louts they could be on short notice.

"Hahaha, what'd he do, knock ya up?" they quizzed.

"Ya askin' for a piddler or a peddler, hahaha?"

Fair Rainbow had little understanding of the white man's humor. Until she had been sent to recover the Great Necklace, she had only met a few. And they were well-rounded people, those who were bold enough to make their way into the Swamp Land to trade with the Indians. But these, these townfolk, they were something else. Their humor seemed intricate, complex, if they found much humor in the travels of a one-eyed peddler. Uncertain, Fair Rainbow posed a smile on her face. The smile, she was assured, would keep her from harm's reach. Appearing before the whites with a smile on her face demonstrated her ability to blend with the people, to gain admission to the different communities in the path of her journey. How wrong she was.

Upon seeing her smile, a gross fur trapper strode forward and demanded he make her his. Mammoth, drunken, the fur trapper wore a scraggly red beard and bushy mustache, the likes of which Fair Rainbow had never seen before. His cheeks puffed out and his eyes were beady. He investigated her with the swipe of his ornery paw.

"I jes' love these heah red squaws," he roared to the men who were standing behind him. He puffed and snorted, and waved his arms over the Mississippi, shining in the distance. Like a man sent to judge a good horse, he approached Fair Rainbow and circled her with a trader's caution. He pinched her flanks and tapped at her breasts, slobbering down his deerskin jacket.

Fair Rainbow stood still. Mortified, she found she was unable to move. The trapper leered into her face. The men behind him roared their approval.

"Well I'll be," he declared. "What have we here? Think she'll do, boys?"

"Yeah, she's fine, Lloyd."

Lloyd the trapper turned back to Fair Rainbow. For her benefit he spoke again. "It's a rough winter without a meaty woman to sidel close to. All tha' 'ere trappin' 'n' peltin' 'n' huntin'. Makes a man hunger for some relief. Knotholes and goat pussy jus' won't do for a man like me."

With no further ceremony, he grabbed Fair Rainbow. He enslaved her, using her body for his sex releases. She became his servant, waiting on his slightest wishes. If she failed to anticipate what he desired, she was beaten with a leather strap. Lloyd the fur trapper grabbed her at will. The weight

97

of his corpulent figure, it seemed, was constantly pressed against her. She could barely move or breath when he neared her. He bit her cheeks and pinched her breasts so she yelped in terror. He drove his dick inside her as if he wanted to kill her. At no time was he ever a pleasurable lover.

At first Fair Rainbow attempted to resist his efforts. But he was much too strong for her. Lloyd was too big, immovable, capable of hurling her across the room with a mere shrug of his arm.

"Why do you treat me like this?" she pleaded. "I'm a free woman."

He roared back at her. "No you're not! You belong to me. You're sent by the heavens to keep me company durin' mah trappin' season."

"And when it's over?"

"We'll git ready for the next year."

To further humiliate her, the gruesome Lloyd often tied Fair Rainbow to his wrist with a six-foot length of rawhide. Whenever it pleased him he'd suddenly yank the cord, knocking his slave from her feet. Dazed, Fair Rainbow struggled to regain herself while the fur trapper kicked her, a reminder of his great prowess and her vulnerability.

Most nights Fair Rainbow cried herself to sleep. She prayed the spirits would relieve her suffering. Nothing happened. Days passed into weeks, weeks into months, and still there was no escape. Just when she believed she had neared her end, Fair Rainbow discovered the ice was breaking on the streams feeding into the Mississippi. The sky was clearing, shining blue from just beyond the recessive winter clouds. Fresh green appeared on the empty branches, peeked through the melting snow. Spring was here. Soon the fur trapper would be breaking camp, heading for wherever he sold his pelts.

"It's time to be gone, woman," Lloyd announced one day. With no further explanation he then secured Fair Rainbow to his wrist, loaded his mule and set out toward the river. They walked for days, in silence mostly. On the few occasions Lloyd saw fit to speak with Fair Rainbow, she answered quickly before turning her head away from the man she hated so.

At Jast they came to the river. For several days they walked southward on its eastern bank, until they at last encountered a group of strangers, travellers like themselves, who'd had their boats overturned by a sudden shift in the river's current. Their despair had since come and gone, and now they killed time by playing cards. Occasionally one or the other would lament his misfortunes, recounting for the umpteenth time the quantities of freight and livestock he'd lost with his flatboat. The businessmen, who had only lost their luggage and who had ruined their dark wool suits, cared little for the boatmen's miseries.

"Deal," was all they said, their eyes shifting from the several boatmen to a wizened stick of black licorice, a slightly built and aging gambler known as Moses Moriarity. Those who'd known him throughout the years preferred to call him Mo.

He was a wisp of a man, with overgrown, talonous hands and a thin, hooked nose he had broken in a fistfight many years ago. His head was nearly bald, save for the gray brush on the fringes of his skull. His skin was leathered and wrinkled with age. His eyes were dark, shifting, searching the thoughts of his opponents. He displayed no signs of noticing Fair Rainbow when she and her beefy master first approached the group. Only slightly did his eyes shift in her direction. He liked what he saw, but his attention was soon drawn to the mammoth trapper who had claimed his right to join in the card game. Soon he was losing his wealth, all the pelts he had trapped in season.

"I got a dollah, three pelts 'n' mah huntin' knife," proclaimed Lloyd when it had reached that point. His

99

fingers trembled when he fanned his cards for one more peek. " 'N' I want to see your han'," he told Mo Moriarity after some deliberation.

Normally Mo would've told any man to kiss his ass for trying to match high stakes with a dollar bill, a hunting knife and a few smelly coon furs. The pot had long since passed the trapper's limit, and Lloyd's meager offering should've appeased no one. However, a glance into the man's eyes informed Mo that he'd better go along with the trapper. So many times the aging black man had seen it before. Frustrated, angered, there was no telling what a man like Lloyd would do if he were cleaned out. Soon enough, they'd know, thought Moriarity, reviewing his full house for the final time.

"All right," he said rather tentatively. "Y' can call me with your pelts an' dollar bill."

"What've you got?" demanded the trapper. His eyes betrayed his intentions. Obviously he was threatening the smaller man, hoping he would back down, throw in his cards, rather than face the menacing hunter.

"A full house," Mo declared, as poised and as calm as he always seemed. "Threes over jacks."

"You sure?" warned Lloyd.

"Read 'm for yourself," he said, laying the cards before him.

Lloyd stared at the winning cards and wiped snot from his nose. Without anyone asking, he launched into a lengthy explanation regarding the purpose of the pelts. "They were supposed to stake me to another try on the plains," he noted. "Jus' give me a grubstake t' get me some furs," he said, as frightened as he was angry.

No one said a word. The big man turned from one to another. His brow knitted, his eyes flashed. He was becoming more menacing with each moment that lapsed in silence. "Y' hear what I said?" he challenged the gamblers.

They had all heard too well. Especially Mo, who had

quietly slipped his derringer from his vest pocket. He counted breaths awaiting the hunter's imminent aggression. It came soon enough, with Lloyd giving out with an animal's cry as he lunged from across the makeshift table. His ass left the log as his hands reached forward for Moses' throat. His sudden movement proved so shocking to two of the businessmen that they fell backward, clasping their chests. But Mo Moriarity wasn't shocked. He'd seen it all too many times before. He greeted Lloyd the trapper with the sting of his derringer. A hole appeared in the big man's forehead as he fell across the wiry gambler. In an instant Moses rolled the hunter off him and climbed to his feet. He stared down at the gasping man.

"Oh God! I'm daid, I'm daid," cried the trapper. Blood seeped from the spaces between his fingers.

"Die hard, you rotten bastard," Fair Rainbow suddenly howled, her first full sentence in the English language. Cursing and crying, she kicked at the hunter, who rolled about the ground as the life slipped from him. "Agguaaha," he cried, his body trembling with pain. Even the businessmen were amused.

Exasperated, Mo Moriarity stared at Fair Rainbow. "I thought he was your husband!"

"He enslaved me. I hated him. He can't die fast enough to suit my needs."

Mo glanced at the hunter again. He was dead. Slipping his derringer back into his pocket, he regarded Fair Rainbow a little more closely. "He's dead now," he told her. "Where do you expect to go from here?"

In desperation Fair Rainbow explained to Moses all that had come upon her. She told him of the Necklace and of her intentions to retrieve it for her tribe. She described the miles of her journey, the places she'd seen, the things she had done. He listened intently, posing kindness in his flashing black eyes. They talked well into the night.

"You can come with me," he volunteered. "I'm only

waiting for the next flatboat. It should be comin' down soon."

When the next vessel arrived, they boarded, along with the others who had survived the accident along the river. Their presence overloaded the small flatboat. Its deck was crammed beyond its capacity, and the boat rode low in the water. Sweating travellers, the stench of the livestock and added aromas made passage on the flatboat nearly unbearable. Still, it was better than waiting alone by the river. It was only a matter of time before stragglers were discovered and slain by hostile Indians or the ferocious pirates who roamed the river according to their whim and fancy. The very thought of the river pirates aroused a lump in the pit of a boatman's belly.

"You were quick to kill him," Fair Rainbow suggested to Moriarity.

"He was a big man. No sense in tangling with the likes of him."

"But it happened so fast. And yet, you were ready."

Mo smiled and toyed with the grip of his derringer. "I've seen them before, the likes of him. They like to maul, beatin' people who are smaller. Saw one once who ripped a woman's arm right from her shoulder. Just for a laugh, claimed he. Yeah, I've been up 'n' down this river for so damn long. Too damn long, I think, sometimes. Seen belts made from human hair. Pouches outta breasts. Even seen hollowed dongs used as snack sacks. Yeah, I've seen it all. Disgusting. Yet I've endured all the perils of this river. I've survived. Like back there. I knew I'd have to kill him sooner or later. I hoped I wouldn't but, from the moment I laid eyes on him, something told me I'd have to see him dead. Just as soon get it over with, says I. Keep him from markin' me."

Fair Rainbow reached out and stroked the black man's forehead. Gently she rubbed the fringe of hair, toyed with the curls of his ears, and then brought her hand down along the outline of his chin. "You seem compassionate. Not a killer. Perhaps not yet is your mystery unveiled."

Mo laughed his laugh and regarded the Indian lady with kindness. "I'm a nearsighted visionary. Ain't got nothin' but dreams. 'N' a few old suits. Someday I'm gonna quit this river. Someday."

"Where will you go?"

"Don't know. A little nook or cranny where no one will bother. Have enough food, a roof over my head, not much else. Just sit down and think. Do some reading, believing in more than the turn of another card. Never was meant to be a gambler. Not the way I lose."

When the flatboat had been secured for the evening, Fair Rainbow led Mo Moriarity away from the camp. In a soft nest of brush he made love to her. She did not really enjoy it, nor did she expect to. It wasn't unpleasant either. Just uneventful. She had expressed her gratitude and mixed it with her pity. She had sensed this was what he wanted, and allowed his dry, taloned hands to roam over her body. She smiled at his caution, his immeasurable sense of order. He fondled and stirred according to his sense of proportion. He refused to mount her until he believed Fair Rainbow had been aroused. To keep it from continuing all night she feigned desire and at last he climbed inside her. Fair Rainbow saw herself as a granny, lying back with a child on her lap. Mo rocked back and forth in the gentlest of fashions. At last he came, rolling off with his final spasm.

"Thank you," he nodded. "It's not often that I get the chance."

"Never think of me as a lover, but as a friend."

He flashed his teeth. "I never had a lover," he lamented. "An occasional girl friend, whores, the palm of my hand. But never a lover."

"One day it may come to pass."

"It's passed already. Passed me right by, is what it did. What about you? What's . . ."

Fair Rainbow cut him off. "My husband is older than you. A good man, but a little crazy. I was offered to him as a favor, one he's never failed to appreciate. In his own peculiar way."

His curiosity aroused, Moses Moriarity searched his mind for added questions. They reached the tip of his tongue before they were interrupted by the boatman's warnings. "We're approachin' Massacre Bend," he shouted. "Everybody keep a sharp lookout for them pirates."

A collective chill ran throughout the flatboat. Overloaded and extremely vulnerable as it was, the tiny vessel was sure prey if the pirates spotted them.

"See anything?" Mo heard one man ask the next.

"Not yet."

Hands rested on pistol grips, hammers were cocked on rifles. Boat poles slipped in and out of the water, knocking ominously against the sides of the vessel.

"We're almost clear."

"No. It's a good mile before we're out of danger."

"Damn those pirates. Why can't they find work like everybody else?"

"They say there's good money in bein' a pirate. My own kid threatened to run away and join them, he did. Got as far as the freightyards, before he came home beaten and yelping. Some teamster had kicked his ass."

While the men laughed at the boy's misfortunes the first of the pirates' canoes slipped from the foliated blinds. A war whoop rose from the shoreline as the lightweight vessels streaked through the water. Obscenities were shouted as the pirates advanced, the canoe leaders firing as the others paddled. They were nearing the flatboat.

From behind their luggage and stacked cargo the passengers opened fire. A few pirates fell out of their canoes and plunged into the water. A stray bullet caught one passenger in the face. He howled before falling backward, his arms dangling from the flatboat's edge. Gunpowder smells mixed

104

with sheepshit and the farts of terrified human beings. It was clear to all that they would be overtaken.

Mo Moriarity picked up a discarded rifle. He discovered it wasn't loaded. After deliberating on its usefulness he flung it into the water. A fellow passenger turned to demand an explanation but he was struck by a rifle shot before he could protest.

Mo sighed and rubbed Fair Rainbow's rounded buttocks. "We'll never get out of this one. They'll soon board us."

"What will they do?"

"Me they'll probably kill. You ..." he decided best to leave it go at that.

By the time the pirates prepared for boarding, most of the passengers had been killed or wounded in battle. No one dared resist them when the pirates advanced on deck, kicking the dead and wounded over the side and into the river. The rest were stood in line and bound by their hands. The cargo and other booty were taken aboard the canoes. When the vessel was emptied it was set afire and allowed to drift down river as a warning to all those who might spot its charred remains.

At the pirate headquarters, Moses Moriarity and Fair Rainbow found a slew of pirates awaiting their arrival. They laughed among themselves, jabbing each other with the points of their elbows. Behind them a myriad network of caverns revealed an almost fortress-like protection. Believing the worst was about to befall them, it came as a surprise to Moses and Fair Rainbow when they were separated from the surviving prisoners. Still bound, they were led to a cavern located around the other side of the hill. They were escorted inside, to where an older Elijah Hawkins was seated at his table. With hands folded he regarded the two prisoners. He said nothing.

Moriarity wondered where he'd seen the face before. Probably in New Orleans, at the mouth of the river. It was not uncommon for pirates to venture into that city. Loaded

105

with booty, they spent many a day partying inside the brothels and casinos that lined the riverbanks. They could celebrate for weeks on end, Mo had once heard. Such a reminder, at a time like this, made him smile.

Upon seeing the gambler's smile, Hawkins recognized the wizened Moriarity. "I've seen you, travelling up and down this river," he gestured. "You've been a losing gambler for a good many years now."

"That's right," laughed Moriarity, who was always eager to share his gambler's woes. "Ain't been worth a single dime since hair left the top a my head. Except for the few dollars and fur skins you took. . . ." He allowed his voice to trail off.

Hawkins nodded. "Food is waiting. After you eat something we'll talk some more."

While the two ate their meal, Hawkins sat across the room, his hands propping his chin. He listened to teeth gnashing food, frowned at the few comments exchanged between Fair Rainbow and Mo Moriarity. The silverware tinkled against the dishes. Overhead an exotic chandelier, which once burned in a banker's palace, extended candlelight against the surrounding darkness.

"What will become of us?" asked Fair Rainbow, once she finished eating.

"He'll be placed in a rear chamber. You'll stay with me."

"How cruel. To confine a man in darkness."

Hawkins smiled and wiped his mouth. "It's done every day," he noted. "Besides," he paused, "the other prisoners are already dead."

Haughtily, Fair Rainbow drew herself to her full height and raised her voice. "That's not always the worst choice."

"You think so?" With no further comment, Hawkins suddenly rushed forth, a knife in his hand. When it seemed he was prepared to plunge it deep inside Fair Rainbow's chest, the Indian lady threw her hands up to guard herself. She never said a word. Hawkins backed off, smiling.

"You think you're something," she challenged him.

"And you thought you could die so easily."

"What do I know, with all this loathing and terror rising up inside me."

"Life will be better. You'll see."

For the next few days Fair Rainbow was forced to sleep with Elijah Hawkins. She hated the man, despised the very ground he walked on. Or so she thought. But as the time passed she came to know more of him. She allowed him time to fondle her, to rub against her body, slipping his fingers inside her vagina. When he kissed her, she kissed back, opening her mouth so his tongue could slide inside. With each passing day her breasts hardened all the more. She found she desired the once-terrible pirate, no longer spreading her legs in mute acceptance of her fate, but arching herself so she was more receptive to his offering. In time Fair Rainbow found she missed Hawkins when he wasn't there beside her. When he was off on the river, plundering flatboats.

"You're not like other pirates," she told him. "Why do you live this life? Live with these scum and do what you do?"

Hawkins paused to consider her question. "I've had little choice in the matter," he explained. "Once I was a believer, a hero fighting alongside the notorious Yonkel the Privateer. He was a great commander, a man of revolution. But ... when he was no longer needed, he was made a villain. Yonkel and all of his crew were taken. They were tried by fools and executed by scoundrels. All but one, who found refuge in Yonkel's home."

Fair Rainbow could not avert her eyes. A power inside Hawkins was drawing her closer, more intently than she would ever have imagined. Beneath his haggard posture a greater mystery lay waiting for the searcher. She reached out her hand, stroking his beard. She noted the rutted channels, the lines of his face, in which all the worries and impressions of his time had travelled. Perhaps his life had been harsh,

107

even cruel, yet if it had left him bitter, he was also tempered by forces few ever realize. The exhaustion, the raggedness and perhaps even the viciousness were only postures, camouflaging depths of personality of which Hawkins was not yet aware.

Hawkins kissed Fair Rainbow's hand before lifting his bottle of wine. He pulled long on the neck of the bottle, swallowing in great gulps. "For years we terrorized British ships," he went on. "We laid the finest ships of the line to total waste. Or took them as prizes, which were later divided with Congress. Yes, with all their guns, their mighty frigates, our rum runner and a few cannon ... Oh, but that was so long ago. And for you, an Indian, a woman of the Swamp Land, it probably never existed at all."

"And now? What meaning has this for you?"

"Revenge," he said plainly. "Even so, even now I'm growing tired of the river. Of piracy. It's not been a bad life, but the edge is dulling more rapidly than I can rally my senses around my old desires. There was a time when the rush of enthusiasm sparked my very day. When all I had to do was spot a craft in the water and I was elated by the thought of plundering ship and crew alike. But all that's tiring anymore. I want to be left alone, yet wherever I go, to seek my solitude, trouble is waiting to face me."

"And now I must share your misery. Moriarity as well."

Hawkins scoffed at Fair Rainbow. "You should be thankful I took you in. Even so, it was their capture of several new boatloads of cargo, with women and crews, that prevented their demanding your heads. River pirates don't enjoy captives hanging around for too long. They fear they'll become attached to their victims."

"That wouldn't be so terrible. Besides, you're a leader. You must have some say in matters concerning who dies and who lives."

"I have a sense of duty. Of pirate honor."

Fair Rainbow drew the wine to her lips. She had grown to like the taste. After a long pull on the neck of the bottle she returned her eyes to Hawkins. "Piss on pirate honor," she exclaimed as the wine dribbled from between her lips, staining her deerskin shirt.

Hawkins stared incredulously at his captive. "Why did you journey down the river, anyway? You're so far from home."

Before she answered Fair Rainbow thought back to her tribe. It seemed like such a long time ago. Even her husband, Green Lizard, was barely a memory. Her heart grew heavy, speculating on her return to her tribe. Or if she'd ever be able to return at all. "All the adjustments I'll have to make," she thought aloud.

"What?" asked Hawkins.

"Just thinking."

When Hawkins seemed content to listen, Fair Rainbow launched into her story. She told of her search for the Great Necklace, described its value to her tribe. She related her stay with the fur trapper, her rescue by Moriarity. In detail she described her impressions of the white folk she had encountered. It all poured forth, a stream freed of the mud, rocks and woodpiles blocking its flow.

When she'd finished with her story, Hawkins said nothing for several moments, at least. He stared down at the table, the candlelight reflecting in the pupils of his eyes. He seemed lost in a trance of his own inducement. Fair Rainbow was startled when he suddenly snapped up his head. "And now you believe yourself a failure for not retrieving the Necklace."

"My tribe prides itself on its possession. Without the Necklace there'd be little reason for most of our tales. Our stories would have no meaning. The end of our task would seem a myth without legend. Empty and searching our lives would be."

109

"Hahah," laughed Hawkins. "Such anxiety over another necklace, a simple piece of jewelry. You need just one and I have so many. Would you care to see my collection?"

"No." Fair Rainbow didn't want to see. The spectacle of the assortment of necklaces would only deepen her sense of failure. But Hawkins insisted, and she was led by the hand through a natural corridor, to an alcove whose entrance was blocked by a huge wooden door. Iron locks held it safely in position.

"I have the key," explained Hawkins, removing a ring of keys from his belt. It didn't take him long to find the right one. Soon they were inside the storage chamber, their eyes unfolding on a room stuffed with booty. Treasure was everywhere. Jewels, coins, valuable art objects were mixed with bolts of silk, velvet and ladies' gowns.

As one does in an old cellar, Hawkins shoved objects and materials aside as he waded through his pirate booty. At last, after much crashing and banging, he came to a small safe he had long ago imbedded in the shadow of the rocks. He flipped its dial in several directions and then pulled open its door. Before him was exposed one of the most magnificent collections of jewelry in the world. Rings, necklaces, chains and tiaras abounded. Its collective glitter was assaulting to the eyes.

"Some of it's fake, of course," laughed Hawkins. "Piracy on the river never pays as well as piracy on the high seas. And of course there are other forms of piracy that pay better than all. But that becomes another matter. Here, is this what you're looking for?"

Fair Rainbow was disbelieving. For several long and anguishing moments she stared speechless, her eyes never once averted from the necklace laid in Hawkins' hand. The Great Necklace!

"My God, all this way," laughed Hawkins as if he were reading her thoughts. "And now here it is, nearly lost among a pirate's aimless rummage."

"I had come so far. Given up all hope. Never did I believe I'd ever find it."

"Well here it is. You can even take it back to your people. Provided that's the direction in which you wish to travel."

Fair Rainbow was truly amazed. "You mean ... and Moriarity? What about the gambler?"

"He'll go too."

"And you? What will you do?"

"I've been tired of this pirate business for a long, long time. The killing and looting's been a bother for years. Bad for the nerves. I need a rest somewhere, a chance to start anew, to seek what it is that stirs inside me."

"You could come with me, back to my people."

"No. I'm afraid not. Dreadfully so. For I know I'll miss you."

"Then where will you go?" Fair Rainbow made no attempt to conceal her sorrow over losing her pirate lover.

"The Massive Desert. It's a sight I'd like to see. Perhaps I'll find the solace I've been looking for. Certainly better than this river dampness, the noise erupting from the cavorting, boasting pirates next door."

"I'll miss you so," declared Fair Rainbow. "Never again will I ever know a man like you."

"We'll meet again. In some way. By another fashion."

Under cover of night the two captives, led by Elijah Hawkins, set forth from the pirate caverns. Crouched and dressed in dark clothing, with only sacks slung over their backs, they darted in and out between the drunken pirates who were in the midst of a boisterous celebration. Another boat had been plundered, one containing several more female passengers as well as a few rich gentlemen they hoped to ransom.

It was Hawkins' hope that his absence wouldn't be noticed until long after daybreak. By the time the pirates extricated their minds from the past evening's confusion and discovered the escape, the cagey pirate hoped to be long gone, lost in the Swamps branching from the river. In the murky marshes, and through the high grasses, few pirates ever dared tread. Besides, Hawkins had only departed with but a small portion of his treasure. Taking only a few things, those which he knew were valuable, mostly coins and such, he left the thick wooden doors to his storehouse opened to the greed he was sure would be aroused among the pirates. Certainly they would spend the remainder of the day fighting over his booty rather than pursuing the escapees.

"It's not like pirates to pass up blood for treasure," Hawkins had informed Mo and Fair Rainbow. "But with them being hung over, and the good lead we have, there's a fair chance we'll be successful."

What Hawkins had not allowed for, and was pleasantly surprised by, was Fair Rainbow's talent for walking among the marshes. Her homeland had provided her with all the expertise of the best of the Mississippi trappers. She walked easily, seeming to float upon the deep murky waters. He was warmed by her delicacy, her agility in stepping over vines, passing through the marshes, the brush and the dangerous waters. So ironic her movements seemed, especially when contrasted with those of Moriarity. The poor gambler was a tired third, sweating and panting, the flaps of his jackets pulled by current so they stretched out from his body like two feeble water wings.

"Hey, wait a minute," Mo would plead every mile or so.

"It would be easier to carry him," suggested Fair Rainbow.

"He'll make it on his own," replied Hawkins. "We'll give him all the time that's needed."

After much struggle they reached safety in the small river town of Pourlebesse. After a bath, a good meal and a few drinks among them, Hawkins removed the treasure from his pouch and divided it into three equal sections. He gave them each a share and bid them all the luck in the world.

112

Before much sentiment could be raised to meet the solemnity of the occasion, Hawkins was up and gone, leaving behind a quick handshake for Moriarity and a kiss for Fair Rainbow. He headed west, toward the Massive Desert, while Fair Rainbow departed for the land of her people. With the money Hawkins had given her, she was able to go first class, taking coaches all the way. It would have been easier for her, perhaps, to have taken a small boat to New Orleans and then caught a ship bound for the eastern ports. But before she left, she had sworn to Hawkins that she wouldn't dare travel down the river. Moriarity, with his share of the treasure tucked away, headed north for Chicago. He was certain it was there he'd find his home.

When she at last arrived in the camp of her people, Fair Rainbow was barely remembered. After much discussion, the tribal members gradually warmed up to this myth come back to life. In a hero's procession she was led to Sacred Heart, who proclaimed her the first true heroine of the tribe. He appointed her to the tribal council and demanded her word be regarded with those of the wise. He claimed Fair Rainbow had seen new things and had learned many different ways, all of which could be beneficial to the tribe.

For several days the tribe celebrated the return of the Great Necklace. All tribal members were overwhelmed with joy. Even those of the Reform Movement had to admit the Great Necklace was part of the magic.

During the time of celebration Fair Rainbow and Sacred Heart formed a brief liaison. Sacred Heart was later to claim he always had a fondness for elder women. The affair lasted for but a few weeks and the two parted as friends forever. It had been easy for each to admit the affair was one of gratitude, one consummating the blend of heroics and face-saving they both had achieved in their lifetimes.

Many nights would pass thereafter when Fair Rainbow lay awake staring at the stars above. She recalled her

113

adventures, relived her life among the white folk. With intense hatred, which had not diminished with time, she remembered the fur trapper who she had fucked out of fear. She thought of Moriarity, who she had fucked out of pity, and Elijah Hawkins, the dashing pirate, with whom she had fallen in love. There were times, fleeting instances while doing the wash, or with arms folded among the tribal counselors, when she envisioned Hawkins alone on the Massive Desert, seated in a cave which was hidden in the mountains. She smiled at the warmth of his body, his tenderness and concern for her welfare. She felt his lips pressed against hers, the tongue stabbing at the insides of her ear, and the palms of his hands cupping her breasts. Sometimes, despite her being in the midst of a council meeting, of their own volition these thoughts occurred. At such times Fair Rainbow laughed inside herself upon finding her nipples hardened with bygone lust. It was one aspect of her personality they would never eulogize when she passed away.

As for Mo Moriarity, he too sometimes appeared in her vision. He was travelling up the mighty river to Chicago, where he fell prey to his usual streak of bad luck. All the jewels were lost in a six-handed poker game. Relieved by his sense of failure, Mo vowed never to gamble again. He took a job on an estate, as caretaker to the grounds and the people who lived there. He maintained the gardens and cleared the land. He listened to problems and heard stories of the past. There was much time which he spent with himself, enclosed in the modest cabin Doug Culvane had built for him. In the afternoons, when school was over, Lana Culvane, the little girl, would come for a visit, sitting on her favorite lap. Or in the chair Moses Moriarity had especially made for her. With her hands folded, her feet swaying from side to side, she listened to the old man's stories. Time and again he repeated for her fancy the tales along the Mississippi River, and his account of the river pirates. Just by the way he told

114

his stories, Mo filled Lana with an everlasting lust for adventure. And by the way he described him, the tall, dashing figure whose face revealed so many trials and tribulations, Lana Culvane was imbued with love for Elijah Hawkins.

Chapter 7

After months spent wandering about the desert, Burning
Bush knew he'd reached his end. Simple as it was, his body
refused to carry him further. His legs ached, his bones
creaked, and his muscles slackened beneath the heat of the
raging sun. He looked upward and found the sky was
laughing at him. Its blue light dismissed all suggestion of
redemption. The mountaintops appeared like monstrous
teeth rooted in the gaping mouth of the Devil. After all the
miles he had travelled, all the dangers he had defied, what
hazards he had borne in life, yet he was still faced with his
heinous, spectre of ignorance. Why had it not disappeared,
left him alone to be what he was, without ever suggesting he
attempt to change his ways? He would've eagerly ignored
the burden of living, had not death seemed such a futile
attempt to escape his gradual decline. Yes, all those miles,
his ridiculous duel was Gopher Tracks, his travels. Every
step of the way he had been tested. Chiefs, disguised as
generous hosts, had fed him, provided him with shelter, all

116

so he could provide entertainment by dueling with the strongest and toughest of the defending tribe. Playful combat they had named it, and yet it never ended in the same spirit as it began. Temper and wounded pride had been the end to many a well-intentioned exhibition. Mere demonstrations of ability were rapidly transformed into mortal duels.

In all, during his trek to the desert, Burning Bush had fought more than three hundred and sixteen duels with champions of hosting tribes. Much to the displeasure of their chieftains, Burning Bush had defeated every opponent. Fortunately, not all exhibitions escalated beyond his control, but enough warriors lay bleeding on the ground after the contest had ended. Burning Bush himself had been wounded on many occasions. He had been exhausted, his will to battle had been overcome with inexorable fatigue. No longer did he wish to fight. Even his famous temper, the idiosyncracies which formed the very source of his anger, had lapsed into despair. To be left alone was his only desire.

Seated on a bit of jagged rock, lost among his lugubrious considerations, Buring Bush didn't hear the approaching footsteps. It was not until his back muscles sensed someone near him that he pushed himself from the rock ledge and crouched in the direction of the noise. From out of the shadows stepped a lone Indian girl, a wisp of innocence converting her obvious fright into a more amenable posture. She smiled shyly, extended the blanket and sack of food she had clutched in her hands. Burning Bush regarded her with mute intensity.

"I thought you might be hungry," she said. "And the desert chills at night," she continued, raising the blanket.

The girl must be an apparition, capable of disappearing on a whim. Burning Bush was struck by this thought, and he stepped closer to the girl to best examine her texture. Tentatively, more frightened than she, he extended his hand and touched her. She smiled, reached into her basket and offered him a slice of bread she had prepared from corn.

Eagerly he snatched the bread slice and gulped it ravenously. Each mouthful seemed to further deplete his self-pity.

"I am Cactus Flower," said the girl, offering Burning Bush another bread slice. "My tribe lives just beyond these hills. Had you climbed to the top you would've seen our dwellings."

"Why did you bring these to me?"

"A voice told me to do so."

"What voice? Where?"

"A voice," she repeated, gesturing about her. "On the desert there are many voices. Which does the speaking is of small importance. What matters is to which you choose to listen."

His eyes consumed the barren plains as Burning Bush glanced around him. For the first time he took special note of the different plant and animal life which surrounded him. Their configurations were remarkable, so revealing of their interminable struggle to survive. Such contrast his environment held to the vision of loveliness which stood before him. So frail and helpless she had first appeared. It was not until later that he first became aware of her inner strength.

"It comes from my people," she explained to him, after he remarked how easily she climbed the steep mountain faces. "My tribe is a desert people. We are capable of existing where others fear to tread. We know what we know and have little use for different explanations."

"Funny. All this time I thought I was walking alone out here."

"You were alone. And still would be, had not the voices been so urgent."

When they reached the mountain's summit, they were able to gaze down at the tribal dwellings. Made from adobe, the houses were formed in pueblo fashion, differing only by the boldly colored symbols and various paintings which covered the fronts of the houses. The assorted hues of green, red, yellow and blue glazed when reflected by the sun. Burning Bush promised himself a closer look, despite his dread for the imminent contest between himself and their tribal hero. A pang of anxiety breached his stomach when he considered it was time for him to lose a duel. How ironic, after coming all this way, to end his life face up in the desert sands, his last ambitions mocked by the laughing blindness.

Cactus Flower was compelled to explain her tribe's existence. "It's not in spite of the desert that we live, but because of its tidings," she said as they descended from the mountain. "Few ever challenge us, for they know they can never replace our lives with their own. So there would be no purpose for their invasion."

"There are many who care little for purpose," Burning Bush answered.

Cactus Flower did not reply. For the remainder of their walk she led Burning Bush along her well-chosen path. The number of times she had travelled this path, there was no telling. Yet ever so lightly, with unprecedented grace, she danced across the precarious terrain, never stumbling or taking her eyes from the village she called her home.

Once inside the village, Burning Bush was introduced to the woman's father, Crater Lake, a jolly man whose deep-rooted intelligence was hidden beneath his pretense that little concerned him. He laughed, snorted and slapped Burning Bush on the shoulder. Soon the two men were seated around a fire, smoking pipes and passing stories of the world outside. Crater Lake claimed he had once ventured away from the pueblos. Disgruntled, he later returned to his people, to never again leave his village.

"For many years, since returning to the pueblos, I have felt secure, protected from the outside. But now more and more whites are coming to the desert. In huge wagons or on horseback they come, feeling noble with intent and purpose. Signs of their invasion are everywhere. Old containers, wrappers, broken wagons and discarded food are strewn across the plains. And then, of course, there are the ranchers, who believe this desert is nothing more than a toilet for their cattle. Our presence here, these ranchers believe, will disrupt their ʹcattle's bodily functions. No longer will they bring a high price at the market."

"And what have you done about it?" Burning Bush asked solemnly.

Crater Lake erupted with laughter. He pulled on his pipe for a good many seconds, inhaled, exhaled and grunted before answering Burning Bush. "We're a tribe who does little of anything. We live . . . like the coyote, the snake, and even the cactus . . . struggling, but always in the celebration of life itself. And like the coyote, the snake and the cactus, we see no direction but the satisfaction of our own basic needs. There is no absolute meaning or purpose to our time spent on earth."

"I came from a tribe who believes it couldn't survive without purpose, mythology."

"We are among the few," acknowledged Crater Lake. "It's grievous at times, when sense of purpose is extended into another man's solitude. For the desperate power of the will sets it all into motion. The ranchers, they are willful people. They have expanded the plains so it may serve in ways different from those my people know. Much variety is created but from a single effort. Yet when that force of will is corrupted, we all become enslaved by its dread powers. Soon, I'm afraid, it will be upon us. Hopefully not before this season's crop of smoke has been harvested."

For some time Burning Bush studied the man before him. He searched his eyes for his sincerity, hung onto his eyes, until the man was forced to avert them. It became obvious Burning Bush's distrust annoyed him. "I was seeing if you were serious," he apologized to Crater Lake.

Crater Lake knocked his pipe against his leg and watched intently while the ashes poured from the bowl. "You don't look to me for sincerity," he muttered, his eyes raised to

120

meet Burning Bush's. "I've only spoken, a very simple thing to do. But it is you who does the listening."

Reluctantly, Burning Bush nodded his head and looked away from Crater Lake. His eyes caught hold of Cactus Flower, who had just emerged from the pueblo. She was carrying a tray laden with food. Stooping over so her breasts nudged the inside of her multicolored blouse, she placed that tray between the two men. Smiling at Burning Bush, she took her leave, returning to her house.

"You have a beautiful daughter," commented Burning Bush.

Crater Lake showed his delight. "You've noticed," he said with mockery in his voice. "Yes, she is very pretty . . . and in need of a husband."

"Once again I've caught you selling our daughter," scolded Woman of the Shadows, Cactus Flower's mother. She had just emerged from her house. "Time and again I've found you bartering for her attachment, to a man of all things. If I've told you once before, I've told you a thousand times, Cactus Flower will find her own."

"I'm not even sure I want one," defended the lovely daughter. "That is, until I'm sure one truly wants me."

Crater Lake scoffed at them both. "Woman, dammit, I'm not selling. Only suggesting. It wouldn't do us harm to see a grandchild come into this world. What pride to have a grandson named after me."

"And if it's a granddaughter, then what do we do, you fool, kill it?"

"Woman! Don't talk that way. By now you should know me better that that."

"Yes. I do. That's why I can't stand it when you talk such foolishness."

Burning Bush and Cactus Flower pretended to ignore the argument. Each found solace in the other's embarrassment. "It's always like this," explained Cactus Flower. "It means nothing. There has always been much love between them."

121

Crater Lake had signalled to Woman of the Shadows that it was quite enough. His attentions were now turned to Burning Bush. "We'd like for you to remain with us," he explained, "unless your journey ends in a different location. Then, you are free to go, with our blessings and the supplies you can carry."

By shutting his eyes Burning Bush grew aware of a strange exhilaration burning inside him. The passing of the smoke pipes had lightened his burden. His legs numbed, his heart overshadowed by gloom, he had arrived at what he had once deemed nowhere and found involvement mixing with love and pleasure.

"I've killed many men in battles," he found himself confessing. "I am tired of fighting, weary of the anger I've carried inside me. Since my youngest days I've been torn between despair and animosity. Throughout the years the demands placed against me by these two forces have left me homeless and with a broken heart. So, if it pleases you, then it pleases me. I will stay. Gladly."

The smile of a man about to lose himself in celebration burst across Crater Lake's face. "I am very pleased," he confirmed. "Woman of the Shadows, it is time for celebration. Bring out the best of our smoke and summon our friends and neighbors. We will engage in merriment, until the last glint of moon disappears behind the mountains. Then the sun will shine and we'll all face a new day, complete with another member of our tribe. Certainly this is an evening in which to rejoice."

All night long the Indians partied. Dancing and general raucousness permeated the campgrounds. The pueblos were alive with people doing their best to sustain the momentum of their joyousness. Never before had Burning Bush seen anything like it. With complete abandonment bodies were flung every which way. Naked squaws and braves danced about the fires before going off in flocks to fuck among the pueblos or down by the stream which trickled by the campsite.

Yet when morning came, the party was over. Tired men and women lay where they had fallen, their children being especially careful when treading among them. No one dared make a sound. Inside the pueblo, Burning Bush lay with Cactus Flower. Long before daybreak they had gone off by themselves, and with the assistance of the smoke and the general merriment, they had fallen in love. Occasionally they were interrupted, but Burning Bush didn't mind. Intrusions hardly aroused reminiscences of his tragic encounter with Swan Lake, so stoned and overjoyed was he. Not in ages had he felt so good. Even his winning the coveted black feather hadn't filled him with the pleasures of his one night spent with the desert tribe. The intensity of his anger had diminished. He vowed he would fight no more.

Just as his head was clearing, Crater Lake approached Burning Bush through a rear entrance. He hovered above the naked couple, appearing like a wise old owl. He smiled his smile, making light of the previous evening. He reminisced briefly over parties he had held in the past. This was the best of all, he told Burning Bush.

"I'm glad to see you two are getting along," he giggled, before starting for the doorway.

"I'm in love with your daughter," Burning Bush announced through undertones of apology.

Crater Lake smiled at the young brave. "I'm sure you are. She's a very fine woman. Been raised with great care."

"I'd like her to be mine."

It was some time before Crater Lake answered. He shook his head and closed his eyes before he attempted speaking. Upon opening his eyes, words appeared in his mouth. "She'll never belong to anyone. But you may share life together in love and harmony. If that's your true desire."

"It is," answered Burning Bush.

123

"Then it shall be."

With negligible ceremony Burning Bush and Cactus Flower were married. While Gray Bear, the medicine man, stood in as best man, Crater Lake nodded his consent, as did the Woman of the Shadows, and the wedding ceremony was finished. Joined by the other members of the tribe, the newlyweds then constructed their own section within the pueblo's foundation. Useful household items were offered as gifts, along with valuable animal furs and a horse presented by Crater Lake. No one ever asked to examine their wedding sheets or ever inquired of Burning Bush if he was satisfied with the purity of his wife. With little ritual, they were simply included among the tribe. For years they lived happily, their only uneasiness arising from the increasing encroachments of the white folk, the ranchers in particular. Stories prevailed concerning the horrid practices the ranchers imposed against stray Indians. Occasionally the corpse of a beaten Indian was found or a ravaged woman managed to drag herself back into camp. It was a grim reminder of the world outside, rapidly approaching their interior.

Not long after their marriage, Cactus Flower gave birth to a son. He was called Thunderbird and was raised in accordance to the customs of his tribe. He was taught to hunt, as he was taught to cook and make pottery. The craft of weaving became his, though he learned the use of weapons. Little emphasis was placed on warfare, for the tribe had not been to battle in several decades. Life for Thunderbird was pleasant and uneventful. He grew into manhood along with the other children of his tribe. Despite youthful impatience, he rather liked childhood and the leisure it afforded. Such spare moments were enjoyed with his playmates or spent by himself in spots he liked to call his own.

Change came suddenly, shocking, as the cataclysm unfolded on what had appeared to be a normal day. He had awakened with an uneasiness implanted in his senses, an intangible despair that rendered him groggy until late in the day. His ignorance of what affected him caused Thunderbird to pass it off as indigestion. Fond of eating, he was known to stuff himself during the evening meal and wake up the following morning with a hardening ball in the center of his belly. Too listless to play, he sat outside his family's pueblo waiting for his mother to return from her errands. While looking out toward the horizon, he noticed an odd occurrence. Four Thorns, their neighbor and his mother's best friend, was returning without Cactus Flower. She appeared in shock, as if the total horrors of the universe had been inscribed on her cheekbones. Her eyes were glazed, her mouth open, allowing feverish gasps to come forth, alarming young Thunderbird.

"Is your father here?" demanded Four Thorns, barely in control of herself.

"Around back, helping build new ovens," gestured Thunderbird.

When Four Thorns dashed off in search of his father, Thunderbird felt compelled to join her. He trailed behind, his short little legs unable to match Four Thorns' galloping stride. Out of breath, he reached his father just as Four Thorns related her news. Cactus Flower had been murdered, raped and brutalized by several ranch hands. In charge of the assault was Hal Pardee, Junior, the spoiled son of the biggest rancher in the territory.

"It meant nothing to them," complained Four Thorns, the tears pouring from her eyes. "Just a way of passing time. Me, I'm weak and gave into them. One by one they mounted me, and I let them have their way. But Cactus Flower, she fought against it. She enraged them. While they beat her I was able to run off. There was nothing else I could do."

Her explanation finished, Four Thorns broke into hysterics and fell to her knees. On and on she ranted at no one in particular. She sobbed, muttering non sequiturs about

125

helplessness and her frustration in leaving Cactus Flower at the hands of such men. It was all Burning Bush could do to pry the location from her. Once he acquired a general idea of where the incident took place, he dashed off, taking with him his weapons and several days' supply of food.

"Don't go," begged Crater Lake, sensing it was revenge Burning Bush was after, not the retrieval of his wife's corpse.

With a fanatic's harshness Burning Bush turned on his father-in-law. Cruelly he laughed in the man's face, until grief overwhelmed the younger warrior. Barely able to maintain his composure, he clasped Crater Lake's shoulder and tried to explain his feelings. There was little he could say. Shaking his head, he mounted his horse and rode off. Through tear-blurred vision, Crater Lake watched him fade into the background. He was sure it would be the last time he'd see Burning Bush alive.

Burning Bush arrived in town just after nightfall. Luck was with him, for he was hardly noticed. Just another Indian, passing between the shadows. He walked with his head bowed, so no roving eyeball would detect the oddity of an Indian openly flaunting his anger. At last he reached the saloon often frequented by Hal Pardee, Junior, and the other ranch hands. The place was crowded, filled to the brim with cowboys and townspeople bent on getting loaded. Unnoticed, Burning Bush crept through the mob until he reached the edge of the bar. There he found young Pardee, his back turned to the Indian. He was laughing, retelling his adventure to an attentive buddy. At the appropriate moments his pal snorted and pounded the bar with the palm of his hand. Satisfied, young Pardee poured his buddy another drink from the bottle he had ordered.

"Pardee?" whispered Burning Bush when he had snuck behind the young rancher. Junior turned around to find the business end of Burning Bush's blade pressed against his throat. With no further explanation Burning Bush slashed the man from ear to ear and backed quickly out the side

126

exit while Pardee's companion searched his drunken mind for familiar cries of alarm. By the time the ranch hands had recovered, Burning Bush was riding out of town, armed with a rifle and pistol he had taken from a horse's back.

Word spread throughout the territory. A price was placed on Burning Bush's head. it was a handsome reward, exceptionally high for the death of an Indian. Nevertheless, Hal Pardee, Senior, was adamant Burning Bush pay for his crime. No price was too high to capture the slayer of his son.

"And if he isn't found," Pardee insisted, "hell will be to pay for those Indians. For too damn long they've been living on my land. Been nice to them so far, and this is how they thank me for my efforts."

Knowing his return to his tribe would only instigate dreaded reprisals, Burning Bush headed away from the pueblos. He climbed the mountains, growing increasingly savage with each passing day. They would kill him for sure, he knew that. So while he lived he would do his best to avenge the sufferings of his people. Hardened beyond any concept of mercy, he raided wagons and small communities, swiftly riding through the settlements, his rifle blazing. Alone he was responsible for keeping half the territory panicked. Never did they know where he'd strike next. Posses were mounted, but all in vain. No one was able to capture Burning Bush.

Months passed, and the reward was increased accordingly. For every white he killed, for every wagon he robbed, ample funds were contributed by the more respected members of the community. Funds were accumulated through bankers, ranchers and stage offices in every settlement. Trackers, lawmen, ruthless killers were hired to hunt the man down. To the last man, they failed.

Believing he was hiding out among the Indians, Hal Pardee, with the aid of local marshalls, launched a terror campaign against the pueblos. For every white person Burning Bush attacked, for every wagon, stage or bank he robbed, several Indians were willfully slaughtered. Still, even those who knew his whereabouts would not give in to the white men.

As the ranchers' acts of reprisal grew more forceful, Crater Lake thought it wise for young Thunderbird to flee, before his true identity was discovered. As a hostage, he was sure to lure Burning Bush out of his hiding. Even then, his son's life would never be assured, especially when in the hands of Hal Pardee.

After packing enough provisions for his grandson, Crater Lake escorted the young man to the fringes of his community. "The spirits will watch over you," said Crater Lake. "Of that I am sure. For enough harm has already come to this family. You ... you will wander, and you will grow weary of your loneliness. There will be many hardships that you will encounter. But you will survive."

Unable to speak, Thunderbird nodded solemnly and kissed his grandfather goodbye. He then rode off, hoping to find shelter inside the desert. Deep inside him he kept alive his greatest desire, to discover his father, living high among the mountains. But even as he rode off by himself, Hal Pardee, with his newest employee, Lorenzo Stokes, was closing in on Burning Bush. Through torture and other methods of brutality Pardee had learned of the Indian's whereabouts. The hunt was narrowed to a small area on the northern face of the mountain range. Slowly, deliberately, Pardee and his men formed a constrictive ring around Burning Bush's hideout. So many men there were, a small army by anyone's estimation—this time it would be impossible for the great warrior to escape.

From the mountain summit, Burning Bush stared down at the approaching army. Hundreds of men, stalking him as if he were a rabid dog. He laughed bitterly, considered the irony life held in store for him. Gently he pressed his fingers to his lips and blew out a series of kisses, one for each

128

member of his family. Tears came to his eyes when he thought of Cactus Flower, so lovely had she been. And Thunderbird, how anxiously Burning Bush had desired to watch him grow. But all that was over now. Only a torrent of gunfire, of days of starvation, lay in his future. The warrior closed his eyes, for the first time in ages, dreaming of his Swamp Land home.

"I think he's up 'ere," gestured Lorenzo Stokes. "Pretty soon it'll all be over."

"Could never be soon enough," hissed Pardee. "We'll use him as an example, a warning to all those who attempt to interfere with law and order. Jus' like the old days, we'll hang his body high, for all to see."

"Might make 'm a martyr," noted Clarence Thizzel, respected marshall of the territory. "Already made him a hero, among Indians and some o' the white folk as well. If we'd left him alone he might've gone away, drifted below the border, out of our hair."

Pardee took special exception to Thizzel's reaction. "Odd talk for you, a marshall, to be pouring in my ear. Any white man th' sees him a hero has gotta be part savage himself."

"Even so," answered Clarence Thizzel, pausing to spit out a wad of tobacco, "ain't everybody that sees it like you do, Pardee. Some claim it's all been a big waste o' time."

"I could have your badge for that," warned the rancher.

"You could," the marshall admitted, as the first shots rang out from above.

Obsessed with killing Burning Bush himself, Pardee ended the dispute and bounded up the mountain slopes. By now the entire army had opened fire, shooting at anything that moved.

From inside his cavern hideout Burning Bush watched the advance of the posse. He bided his time by stacking the boxes of shells he had accumulated for such an emergency. When they fell into rifle range he would be waiting,

129

prepared to end it all in the grandest of exhibitions. His final defense would be an exploit discussed by Indians and whites alike for many years to come.

Carefully, Burning Bush took his rifle up to his shoulder, laying the barrel across the rocks. He squeezed the trigger and a man fell several hundred yards below him. Before they could find adequate shelter, he dropped several more. Indeed, it would be a good day to die, laughed Burning Bush. Moments passed quickly as the tension built up all around him. Burning Bush waited for his order to surrender. He wasn't surprised when the invitation wasn't extended. Pardee's doing, he assured himself. Just once, for a single moment, he'd like to have the rancher in his sights. The thought of dropping the rancher so far from his castle thrilled Burning Bush. He squinted, searching for Hal Pardee.

More shots rang out. Bullets ricocheted from distant rocks. The posse still wasn't sure of Burning Bush's true location. The warrior laughed again, reloaded his rifle and gunned down two more men who attempted to outflank him. It would be a long afternoon. Perhaps even days would pass before they were able to kill him. And then, if luck was with him, Burning Bush could disappear into the darkness, once again eluding his captors. It was a hope, not lasting very long, for the posse was once again advancing against his position.

Volley after volley was poured into the cavern. They had discovered his hideout. Bullets ricocheted wildly, whining, tearing sections of earth and pieces of rock as they whirled by. Soon it would be over. At long last. Grave relief overcame the Indian. It wouldn't be long before he could relax, find the tranquility in death that had been so elusive during his lifespan.

"Fuckers!" he hollered over the gunfire. No one seemed to hear him. He fired madly, catching one or two before his gun was emptied. He reloaded, taking special note of his remaining ammunition. Not much was left. He smiled, estimating the men he had dropped on the mountain slopes.

"It's getting toward nightfall," Hal Pardee warned from down below. "Might lose him in the darkness."

Lorenzo Stokes regarded the worriment on the rancher's face. "Not much we can do about it. He's holed up 'ere pretty damn good."

"Charge him then. Get it the hell over with, already."

Marshall Clarence Thizzel was the only one to protest. "We'll be slaughtered if we go charging up that hill. It's tragic enough, what we've lost to that Indian."

Hal Pardee regarded Thizzel with a drastic sneer. "You yellow baby bugger," he shouted, much to the marshall's embarrassment. "I swear I'll have your badge for this."

"It's all yours," retorted the marshall, his ire truly aroused. "Provided you're the first one to go charging up that hill."

Awkward silence lapsed among the three men. Stokes turned away, feigning disinterest. Only a paid servant, he told himself. He wasn't there to interfere with the town's personal business. In a few days he'd be off wenchin', gamblin' and drinkin' himself silly in the cities up North. He didn't need this extra shit. No siree.

"Advance!" demanded Pardee, ignoring the marshall's suggestion. "I'll tend to you later," was all he had to say on the subject.

With one great battle cry the entire posse came charging up the hill. Burning Bush had a field day. His rife overheated with its constant operation. Possemen fell like saplings before a woodsman's axe. Still they came, urged on by Pardee, who time and again repeated the figure he'd established as a reward.

From his hideout Burning Bush glanced at the sun, which was just fading beyond the horizon. He noted with sadness that it was the last time he'd ever see the awesome spectacle of a completed day. With no ammunition left for his rifle,

Burning Bush raised his pistol, taking careful aim. Two more men fell before him. Before he was able to get off another round, a bullet struck him in the chest. Another hit him in the arm, a third penetrated his abdomen. Life faded from him. Just the image of Hal Pardee was all he wished for. To see him coming over the rise, falling into Burning Bush's sights, was his final desire. But no Pardee. More bullets struck him. Quickly, Burning Bush fired off his remaining rounds of ammunition. He then lay down, playing dead. An overly eager soul came bounding into the cavern. With his last remaining breath, Burning Bush knifed him in the belly.

Moments later Hal Pardee arrived with Marshall Thizzel and Lorenzo Stokes. Before anyone could object, Stokes plucked the Great Necklace from Burning Bush's body. The marshall viewed Stokes with contempt.

"A trophy," the killer greedily replied.

When they returned to town, Marshall Clarence Thizzel was relieved of his duty. At Pardee's insistence, of course. He left the town, never to be heard from again. Stokes was sworn in as marshall, and he remained in office for several years. But after falling out of favor with Hal Pardee, Lorenzo Stokes was caught red-handed, fumbling with the drawers of the mayor's eleven-year-old daughter. He was dismissed from duty and banished from the town. Penniless, dishonored, he drifted west, at last finding employment with an English midget known as Big Ben. Ben had come west and established a small empire consisting of whorehouses, saloons, casinos and a fair piece of the town itself. As a favor to the impoverished Stokes he also purchased the Great Necklace, which he placed on display, along with his other genuine artifacts, in the Lost Hope Saloon. The showcase had often attracted tourists who passed through the fledgling town of Star City.

At the time of his father's killing, Thunderbird was miles away. Yet he was overcome with stabbing pains throughout his body and was forced from his horse. Exhausted, he lay there for several moments, trembling with inexplicable grief. When he lifted his head he discovered a man standing over him. More myth than man was he—the hermit discussed in much of the Indian legends. He was believed to be in command of special powers and was left to himself to dwell among the mountain peaks. Even the whites spoke of him, passing him off as a stray from society, another fool ensnared by his more primitive instincts.

With much apprehension the young Indian allowed the mythical figure to approach him. He inspected the hermit's soft eyes, and folds of white, unkempt hair. Gentleness and understanding abounded in his mannerisms. He smiled at the boy, reaching down to place his hand atop his head. Anticipating the worst, Thunderbird closed his eyes, only to discover the hand had instilled him with comfort and not the fright he had expected. He glanced upward, tears in his eyes. For the first time since he had learned of the death of his mother, he wept openly, wiping his tears in the crook of his arm. The white-haired man looked on sympathetically.

"Come with me," whispered the lanky figure. "You'll always find safety with Hawkins the Hermit."

The storm abated as abruptly as it began. Torrential winds were reduced to gentle breezes. To the west the setting sun cast shadows upon the land. Only a few bare threads of purple light were able to penetrate the hollowed rock formation in which Shelby and Thunderbird sat like two cigar butts stubbed out in nature's ashtray. A mere portion of their rainbow-colored blankets was distinguishable from any distance. All the rest was buried in the sand.

Grateful for the storm's termination, the companions dug themselves out of their shelter and stood for the first time in many hours. With great care they surveyed the landscape, taking note of its changes, the debris and rock formations exposed by the storm. They noted what had been swept beneath the gusting sand, and thanked the spirits they had not been buried alive. In a glance they pondered the less fortunate creatures whose rotting carcasses protruded from the heaps of sand. Upon viewing the dead, the companions grew aware of the living, the countless pairs of eyeballs peering from shelters, gazing apprehensively at their new surroundings. Nearby, in a narrow crevice between two towering boulders, stood their horses, battered, frightened, but generally in good condition.

"We've survived. We've survived. I can't believe we've survived."

Hawkins laughed at Shelby's exhaltations. His young companion was prancing about, a bit of an Irish jig, his hands clapping above his head. "It's part of the magic," said Hawkins, giving no further explanation.

Intrigued, Shelby stopped his dancing. "What magic?"

Thunderbird paid him little attention. With one hand cinching his saddle's girth, he gestured obliquely with his other. His arm spun freely over his head, making circles.

"What are you saying? I still don't understand."

"Part of the magic," repeated Hawkins.

"Oh." Before he had much chance to continue with his inquiry, Lopez noticed Thunderbird had saddled his horse and was preparing to make off without him.

"Where are you going?" he asked. "The sun will be down soon."

Thunderbird nodded. "Yes. It will."

"Then why bother packing for just a few miles of travel? We could camp here and start fresh in the morning ... I'll gather the wood and you can. ..."

"No good. We must leave here. Now."

"But ... but I don't understand."

A faint smirk appeared on Hawkins' lips. Refusing to

134

answer, he slung his leather sack over his horse and prepared to ride off. Thinking better of it, he offered Lopez one final explanation. "The storm has made this spot dangerous. The evil spirit lurks here now, waiting to carry the listless to their doom. We must travel. Quickly!"

Shelby wiped his mouth, attempting to suppress a laugh. A vague utterance slipped through his lips, annoying Thunderbird. "There's no spirit. What are you talking about?"

"Part of the magic," the Indian repeated. "Trouble lurks here."

"But ... that's ridiculous." He paused, aware of the hurt exposed on Hawkins' face.

It was difficult for Hawkins to keep his temper. He attempted to conceal his anger with his last appeal. "Is it? Then you stay."

With no further words of explanation Thunderbird rode off, leaving Shelby standing with his arms at his sides, his mouth wide open.

"Hey, wait a minute," he called after the Indian. Hawkins refused to stop. Never even did he bother to look back. "Hey, hold on a minute, will ya? I'll be right there."

Haphazardly, Shelby scrambled for his belongings. In a few moments he was mounted on a loosely girthed saddle, which swayed precariously back and forth as he chased after Thunderbird. He galloped frantically, calling Hawkins as he rode. Only when he drew alongside him did Thunderbird acknowledge Lopez.

"I believe ya. All right? I believe ya."

A brush of his nose, a sniff of the wind, was Hawkins' sole response.

"I'm sorry. Honest, I am."

"It's to your advantage. Unless you'd rather die."

"No. I don't wanna die. I should listen to you. I mean, what do I know about the desert?"

"A fool is a fool wherever he travels. One with wisdom obeys the commands of his nature, not of foolish reasoning."

135

"I wasn't thinking."

"Yes, you were. Without feelings. Just thoughts."

"I have feelings. I do."

"I know." He handed Shelby a pipeful of burning smoke. "I never doubted your feelings, just the wisdom by which they are governed."

Shelby drew on the pipe and scowled at his mannerisms. "I'm sorry," he repeated. "Only . . . since my Army days it's like one big toilet reversed its flush on me. Shit everywhere I look. Everything I touch is covered by it. Everything . . . just everything."

"And now you're bitter."

"Naw. I'm through feeling bitter. Just disgusted. If only one thing had turned out the way it should, I would've claimed there was hope."

"It did turn out the way it should," Thunderbird insisted.

Lopez frowned at his own considerations. "Maybe so," he admitted through a sigh. "Strange, one minute I'm over-joyed I survived the sandstorm. And the next I'm feelin' so low."

Hawkins barely heard him. Affected by the smoke, he delved into his own memories, recalling the man he had once known in the desert. Again the white-haired, lanky figure appeared vividly before him. His arms hung down to his sides, his huge hands were spread against his thighs. Hawkins remembered those hands. How tranquilizing their affect when they were laid upon him. Soothing, making life seem less dangerous.

The hermit never asked many questions. In time, and with patience, he knew the answers to all that was plaguing Thunderbird. Hidden among the mountains, he allowed weeks to elapse, never pressing the young Indian boy for a single comment. All the while, Thunderbird sat across from the hermit, anxiously waiting for the man to attack him. Reminiscences of stories dealing with hermits crossed his mind, reminded him of their feats of magic, their rituals and

136

their predilection for solitude. Certainly this hermit only wished to fatten up the young Indian so he could later have him for a ceremonial dinner. How awful was this consideration, especially when compounded by the endless remorse he suffered still concerning the death of his mother and father. Time and again he visualized their departures from this world, the terrible rape-murder and the final hunting of Burning Bush. He would avenge his father, vowed Thunderbird. Sooner or later he'd slay the men who killed him.

Months passed, but still Thunderbird cried openly when he remembered his mother, joyous when she sang by the well. Her voice, transforming into a wail of agony, often roused the boy from his sleep. He awakened in a sweat, his fear subdued at last by the hermit, who lulled him back to fitful slumber.

"You should eat something," the hermit insisted, his huge hands offering a bowl of broth. "What's been done can never be repaired through your starvation."

Still believing Hawkins the Hermit planned to fatten him up for his ceremonial dinner, Thunderbird usually refused the food. He went to bed, listening to the growling of his empty stomach. He resolved he'd be a miserable dinner for the white-haired old man. Gradually, however, he warmed up to Hawkins, thinking, with the passing of days, the hermit was less threatening than he first appeared. His trust increased, and he soon accompanied the older man to the hot springs where he bathed every morning. The water soothed him, its pacifying temperature relaxing the tensions of the past. He began to eat more regularly, and even accepted the hermit's invitations to walk with him along the different trails. In their passing, Hawkins often pointed out many things, sights often unnoticed by the different members of his tribe. Alone, unhampered by interruptions, Hawkins the Hermit had borne witness to more events of nature than any other man. Thunderbird was most impressed by his dexterity, his agility in climbing up and down cliff faces and mountain trails. A metamorphosis had taken place. Part of the nature of mountain animals had taken hold of the hermit's senses. There was little wonder no one could ever catch him, or even spot him for any great length of time.

"How did you come here?" asked Thunderbird one day, after curiosity overcame his reluctance to speak.

Hawkins repressed his delight in the young man's questions. "I was a pirate. It grew tiresome. Meaningless. So one night, I walked away."

"Just like that?"

The hermit laughed, high-pitched and nasal. "No. There was a woman who helped me escape. An Indian woman. A fine lady. Brave and capable."

"Whatever became of her?"

"My, you do ask your questions once you set your mind to it," the hermit mocked. "Where is she? I have no idea, although I'd give the mountains and the hot springs to see her one more time. But that was so long ago. And you're so young."

Thunderbird was compelled to protest. "I'm not so young," he said angrily. "I've already seen tragedy. Not once, but twice."

"Unfortunately, you'll probably see even more before your days escape you. And from the horror your life will gain direction. Purpose will be established, a path you must pursue."

"You seem sure of it."

"A feeling. Nothing more. Whatever I can pass on to you will be of service. With the desert so huge, it wasn't coincidence that caused us to meet each other."

Thunderbird rubbed his cheeks and stared out toward the mouth of the cave. "One day I must return to my tribe. I must recover my father's necklace."

Abruptly Hawkins turned to the boy. "What necklace?" he demanded.

138

"My father's necklace. Its possession holds part of the key to the wisdom of the world."

Excitement surged through the aging hermit. "Whoever told you that?"

"My father's tribe believed it. In the Swamp Land they called it the Great Necklace. It was taken from the Conquistadores hundreds of years ago. My father told me ... not long before he died. As if he sensed his doom, realizing his necklace was all he had to offer."

The hermit's hands trembled so badly that he spilled water when he attempted to lift the cup to his mouth. A mixture of love and long, lost regrets fell upon him, a forgotten structure come tumbling down. He thought of Fair Rainbow, relished the nights they had spent together. Her departure, his pangs of regret, the tears trailing behind her retreating footsteps. He remembered the Necklace as well. Not a very pretty thing, though he could easily recognize it in a chest of treasures. It had the power, that's for sure, to capture the attentions of the roving eyeball. Never did he actually believe it contained part of the secret to the wisdom of the world. An Indian legend, that was all he ever considered.

"You must have the Great Book before the Necklace becomes of much use," Fair Rainbow had explained so many years before.

Of all the jewelry he had locked in his vault, this was all she had treasured. Priceless rings and diamond broaches were mere trinkets in her eyes when compared to her possession of the Necklace. He had laughed at her, good-naturedly, but with little regard for the customs of her tribe.

"You've come all this way for a mere trinket. I'll never see the point. What could ever be so important as to risk life and limb? Yet my admiration extends beyond the nature of your search, to your journey and all you have endured."

Sad-eyed and exhausted, Fair Rainbow took a seat beside her lover, concealing the melancholy she felt inside. "Unless

I find the Great Book, I'll never even learn the secret of the Necklace."

"But no one has ever seen this Book. How would you even know what it looks like?"

Fair Rainbow closed her eyes. "It's covered with thick, brown leather, free of all inscription. On the inside, its pages are made of thick parchment, and mysterious scrawls and etchings cover both sides of each page."

"How can you be sure?"

"During the Ceremony of the Great Necklace, we've seen the Book. Like a ghost it rises from the fires of our worship, pages turning for all to see. Yet we can note nothing but odd markings and alien pictures. I'm sure there's no other like it."

"It would certainly ruin your tribe if it became known that an entire series of Great Books were being published."

Fair Rainbow received the Pirate's jokes with solemnity. "That is not the case. Of that I'm sure we're both aware."

Years passed before Hawkins the Hermit was again reminded of the Great Book and the Great Necklace. They appeared suddenly, a majestic swirl of colors suddenly unleashed upon his cavern wall. In the center of the tinted storm the Great Book and the Necklace materialized from a mass of vibrant hues before dispersing back into the ellipse. Shrouded in its shadows, Hawkins the Hermit looked on in horror, searching his soul for the exhilaration he knew was there. Before his emotions reached their peak, the Book and the Necklace were gone from view, leaving Hawkins with little more than a trace of their images. So impressed was he that he considered all the other images that may have appeared before them. Gradually he prepared his life for new discoveries, searched the secrets of his mind for the means of summoning other visions. Gradually he increased his expertise, able to summon apparitions at his command. Among them, initially, appeared Yonkel the Privateer. His image presented Hawkins with his greatest pleasure in years.

140

Joyously the man and the apparition reminisced over old times. The hermit sipped spring water while Yonkel swirled above him. Much to his relief, the wise Yonkel congratulated Hawkins on his relation with the pirate's mistress, Culavara Ulmstead.

"I would've done the same thing," insisted the noble pirate, traces of his old smile evident on his translucent mouth. "In times of great tragedy, it is often necessary to seek relief in the arms of a lover. You did what I would've done," winked the old commander. "I dare say you may've done it better."

By summoning visions, Hawkins the Hermit was able to receive bold premonitions. No longer did he feel as alien to the world beyond the desert mountains. He learned of advancements in technology, of forthcoming wars abroad and the subsequent onrush of civilization, which threatened the Massive Desert and its surrounding territories. In time he learned how to control such visions, brightening their focus for a better impression. Through such impressions he grew alarmed by the passage of time on earth. Once again he felt unsatisfied, incapable of dispelling his fears of the coming world. Increasingly desperate with each passing day, he searched his mind for a solution to his restiveness. The Sea, came the answer. Before all was lost he must journey to its coastline, die listening to its waves surge against the ragged cliffs. From where it began it all must end, travelling like the sun, his dissolution in western water.

"Who was your grandmother?" asked the excited Hawkins the Hermit, his attention returned to young Thunderbird.

Before answering, Thunderbird launched into a lengthy explanation about his father's famed trek to the desert. In detail, as if he had been there himself, the young Indian described the Swamp Land and the passage westward. "As for his family, my father never much discussed them. They seemed to bring him more pain than he cared for. His

141

mother was called Fair Rainbow. Supposedly she was the tribal heroine, who crossed the country in order to recover the Great Necklace. His father, Green Lizard, was a constant source of astonishment to Burning Bush. He never understood how such a senile old man could've ever produced a son as strong as himself."

Hawkins the Hermit grew delighted by the prospect that young Thunderbird might be his grandson. "Your father told you that?" he further quizzed.

"Yes, what of it?"

"Nothing," said the hermit, who wasn't about to let slip a secret kept hidden for so many years. "Just an old man's curiosity, is all. Where is this Necklace now?"

"Taken by the man who killed my father. Lorenzo Stokes is his name. One day I shall find him and cut him down."

"I'm sure you will," smiled Hawkins the Hermit, ever aware of his task. "But first I must teach you to take care of yourself. A fool seeks vengeance. You must accept the justice at hand."

"I don't know what you mean," protested the young Indian. "And why do you care if I ever find this man? What does he mean to you?"

His secret refused to get the best of the hermit's wisdom. Once again he didn't let on that he might be partially responsible for the youngster's lineage. "More than you may ever know," was all he said. "That is all I can ever tell you."

The years did much to change the features of Thunderbird Hawkins. His voice thickened to a muffled growl, his muscles hardened and his chest bowed to the proportions of a thick, iron kettle. Despite his short limbs, Thunderbird still maintained a handsome face, his dark eyes ignited with the zest and fury passed on by his ancestors. As a man,

142

Thunderbird became sure of himself, reinforced by the white-haired hermit. The old man had taught Thunderbird many useful concepts, so adeptly did he blend customs of mind and body to form a unique perception. Never again did Thunderbird experience life as he had through the eyes of his mentor, Hawkins the Hermit. How invigorating the white-haired old man remained. So eager he was to tread boldly where few men dared wander. Fearless were his footsteps, stalking precarious mountain trails or sections of the mind worn hollow by the shifting tides of his restless soul. He devoured all that he learned, so increased knowledge and advanced wisdom stirred the very impulse by which he survived. Yet the old hermit never seemed satisfied. With the end of each day he grew increasingly restless. Often Thunderbird discovered the hermit singing sea shanties or expounding naval jargon to invisible sailors.

Although the old pirate never declared his intentions, Thunderbird sensed that his life would soon be changing. For the worst, imagined the young Indian. He feared being left alone, yet shunned the thought of returning to his people. They weren't his people anymore. In some ways it was as simple as that. Besides, what really drew his attentions was the wide world lying beyond the Massive Desert. So open for his exploration it was, yet he dared not take the first step in any one direction. He feared he'd be incorrect. When he asked the hermit for his assistance, Hawkins only laughed.

"You'll know soon enough," was the best he could get from Hawkins the Hermit.

"I could seek my father's Necklace," Thunderbird proposed now and then.

"The wisdom of the world, the destiny of man. It would surely be a worthwhile item to pursue."

"I can recover what they took from my father. What they stole from his corpse."

Hawkins only smiled. His eyes were filled with sadness.

"No, you'll never recover what they stole from your father. Anymore than the ranchers can destroy the legend they've created. Try as they might, they can never prevent the tale of Burning Bush from being passed from one generation into the next. Time and again, they'll pay for their foolishness. Constantly they'll be reminded of cruelty's futility. Somewhere the spirit of your father lurks. He is laughing. Laughing hard at the ranchers, fools that they can be."

"Why hasn't my father come, whenever we've summoned him?"

"It's his business. Maybe one day you'll learn the answer."

Thunderbird closed his eyes, allowing his father's memory to overcome him. Bitterness forced the young Indian to clench his teeth. "What is there for me to do?" he asked of Hawkins the Hermit.

The hermit stroked his beard and studied the blazing planets. His eyes blinked, his ears quivered as he listened for the sound of their movement through space. His thoughts were punctuated by the howl of a lone coyote. "You should live your life. That's all. Acquire experience of that which belongs to the world of humans. It is time for you to be going, as it is also time for me to return to the sea. I'm getting old, tired. It's time to travel just one more time. To the ocean. It's where I'd like to die."

Thunderbird tried to control the tears that had formed in his eyes. One by one they escaped his blinking and slid down his high, puffed cheeks. He had dreaded this announcement with all his heart and soul. All prior speculation had proved correct, try as he might to discourage such projections by thinking happier thoughts. Emotions prevailed, although his sense of logic could never accept the hermit leaving the desert.

"Not really. You just couldn't leave the desert."

Hawkins' eyes retained their focus on the tearful Indian, the child become a man. They had been companions for such a long, long time. "It has to be," said the hermit, before sentiments could overtake him. "Something is calling me, and I must go. I began my life in the east and must end in the west, along the route of the daily sun."

"Then I'll come with you."

"No. It's time for you to go on your own. Our life, thus far, has been rich and complete. But now we are threatened by outside forces, as well as our own stagnation. It's time for both to travel on."

"But we could continue to share our experiences. I've always liked the ocean. Of what I've heard you tell, anyway."

"I'm sorry. Our efforts would remain incomplete."

"B-but you've always told me that nothing is ever completed."

The hermit nodded amiably, but he refused to capitulate. "There are times when we must all contradict ourselves."

"Then much of what you've said in the past is a lie?"

"At the time I believed whatever I told you. That's all you can ever expect of anyone. No matter. We'll never be separate. For too long we've exchanged much of our spirits. We've shared much of our personalities. Thoughts, gestures, expressions will remain long after we've departed. This is the greatest treasure of all . . . to retain part of another's soul."

Several days later, Thunderbird watched the hermit pack his few possessions and exit the cave for the last time. Every few paces he glanced over his shoulder to the cave's yawning mouth. Inside stood Thunderbird, also packed and ready to leave. He would travel in another direction, north toward the cities and towns that had developed since his departure from his tribe. Within the new towns and cities lived settlers, who created and maintained new methods of living. From new inventions, differences were spawned. Opposing opinions ignited controversy, alienating one from the next. From heated tempers and verbal differences, a war would erupt, scarring the country from one end to the other. Lonesome Thunderbird would be snared by its bitterness, confronted

145

with its ruination. The terrible machinery of war would sweep him, bale him and store him, to later dump him as additional refuse into the terrible conflagration.

In the coming years he'd become a scout, proclaimed a hero and displayed to all as a symbol of equality as expressed by the military. The war would carry him to many places, allowing him a chance to participate in different experiences. He'd travel to eastern cities, learning the ways of their people. He'd pose as a performer in a Wild West show, as a gypsy, a laborer and a man out of luck.

Still, despite all his travelling, the new experiences and what he was forced to endure, whenever he closed his eyes and wished for peace, the serenity of emptiness, the beauty of naked space, Thunderbird Hawkins always knew the desert was eternally his home.

Chapter 8

Riders were approaching. A half dozen of them, at least, were coming from the west. Thunderbird had sensed them long before he had seen the dust clouds rising in the distance. His hand over his eyes, his tongue running across his lips, Hawkins considered what should be done. Although he had no logical explanation, he was certain the riders were hostile. Hawkins frowned at Shelby Lopez, then turned his eyes to the ground and considered their best move. He discounted a run for it, since he doubted Shelby could outlast the more experienced riders. Plus any sudden moves on their part would only draw the riders to them. Hawkins, after a few moments of deliberation, decided to remain where he was, hoping the trouble would pass.

"Whatta ya think?" asked Shelby Lopez.

"Doesn't look so good to me. I draw trouble from their dust cloud."

"Yeah?" pondered the nervous Shelby. "How can you tell?"

"By the color of their dust," answered Hawkins with a straight face.

Shelby refused to question it further. "Looks like we're fucked," was all he said, as the riders appeared to be turning in their direction.

Desperately Hawkins searched the plains for reasonable shelter. Through squinted eyes and shaded brow he at last spotted a ruined adobe house set atop a rocky hill. The house afforded a perfect view in all directions. Crumpled, roofless, it appeared from the distance like a primitive crown worn atop the rocky face of a weary king. Thunderbird smiled at the appearance of the house on the hill. He knew they would be safe there. He and Lopez would recover from what dangers they were about to face.

"We should make for that abandoned adobe," pointed Thunderbird.

Despite all attempts, Shelby was unable to notice the distant hilltop. "I don't see nothin'."

"A house is there, or what's left of one. It'll give us cover."

Shelby looked over his shoulder. Even he was certain now that the riders were coming toward them. From the present size of their dust cloud there appeared to be more than a half dozen riders. "We're fucked," Shelby whispered under his breath.

"Let's ride!" commanded Hawkins.

At a full gallop the companions sped off toward the adobe shack. The tension mounted inside them as they neared their destination. Any minute now the riders would be upon them, firing their weapons as they pursued their intended victims. A brief glimpse of failure, of being knocked from his horse before he could reach the adobe shack, travelled through Shelby's mind. Quickly he dispelled it.

When they reached the adobe shack, the travellers dismounted, stripping their horses of saddleguns and extra ammunition. They left their horses saddled, in case they had to make a desperate break.

148

"Stash them inside that clump of rocks," urged Thunderbird.

Shelby obeyed, just as the riders approached the bottom of the hill. He scowled, noting there were fourteen of them, all well armed and very angry. They were attempting to arrange formation.

"Hey, get that horse next to Buck's," one shouted amidst the confusion. He seemed to be the leader, a tall man who wore a handlebar mustache and a black derby. "C'mon, get'm closer together. Tighter, goddammit! C'mon, get'm tighter!"

Horses whinnied, some reared, and several riders were tossed from their mounts. Abundant curses came from the riders. Shelby and Thunderbird were forced to laugh. These were no experienced, hardened riders. They were townfolk, a posse formed for a single purpose. Few had been on long trips in ages, it seemed, judging from the way they kicked, cursed and floundered among their ponies.

Their leader, the sheriff, was shouting again. "C'mon, what is this? Johnson, dammit, get your fuckin' horse pointed in the right direction. Shit!"

Shelby and Hawkins turned to each other, amazed by the performance of the posse. They howled with laughter, more determined now than ever to keep this motley bunch of warriors from taking them in.

"Damn you, doncha know how t' ride a horse?"

"Whoa, big Spike. Whoa!"

"Lookit the assholes," suggested Lopez.

"That they are," Hawkins was forced to acknowledge.

Lopez sighed and wondered what it was all about. If life was simply as crazy as this, as being hunted by the wrong men for crimes you never committed. It is crazy, he decided, reminding himself of his father, who, time and again, swore warrants against the sanity of his only son. His general fear of his own insanity reminded Shelby of his Aunt Belle, whom they had deposited in Poor Yussel's Home for the

149

Insane Aged. But she had escaped, hadn't she? Gone off, taking her pirate spirit with her. No, Belle wasn't that old, or that crazy. He laughed, thinking of her, remembering her dark hair, now streaked with gray and bits of platinum. Curly, it was. Her eyelids were green with shadow, her lips the color of the setting sun. Big-busted, stout, loudmouthed and crazy. Yeah, she was crazy, after all.

Shelby laughed aloud. He was reminded of Ida Gluntz, no less crazy than her daughter Belle or her son Shmuel. It was Shelby's mother, Sarah, who had been the oddball in that family. So meek and tormented she always appeared. So desperate she was for the security she was never given by her abandoning father. Mad Gerson Gluntz he was called. No one spared the accent on the mad, either. Ida's husband. From whence he came or to where he departed no one ever knew for sure. Rumors were spread, and squashed years later when all tracks led to futile attempts to make contact. Shelby recalled the sole photograph of his grandfather. Dressed in a wide-brimmed slouch hat, an oversized black overcoat, a scarf flapping in the winter breeze, he'd hawk his papers up and down the streets, offering his inspirations to anyone who'd listen.

"My own work, my own thoughts," he shouted through the neighborhoods, waving his paper creation above his head. "Taken from cosmic inspiration, how the world began and how it will end. Read all about it. Two bits, only two bits to know the future of the world. C'mon now, don't be bashful, learn the truth. The truth ... for only a quarter."

One day Mad Gerson Gluntz left forever, leaving behind his moldering stock of handmade newspapers, his wife and three children. Oh, he was a crazy man, complete with straggly beard, zealot's eyes and a balding head. Despite all he had done, leaving his family impoverished and struggling, Belle always spoke fondly of him. Even Shmuel was imbued with understanding for his missing father. Still, it

150

was Belle who loved him so. Her thickset lips would flare into a smile whenever she mentioned his name.

"A crazy bird, he was. You know what he'd write in those papers of his? He gave his own interpretation of life on Earth. He believed we were fugitives from another galaxy, refugees who somehow escaped to Earth. Somewhere, there lurked the rulers of the distant galaxy, who believed us incapable of colonizing other planets. They believed they were compelled to destroy us, to keep our inherent sickness from spreading throughout the universe. So, according to my father, they searched everywhere, but could never discover the whereabouts of the refugees, those who escaped the great war of the distant galaxy. But they keep on searching. Every day they check new planets, ask questions, chart maps. And one day they'll find our hiding place. And all this will be over."

"It's possible," Shelby said, attempting to placate his aunt.

"Don't kid me, buster, the old man was madder than a bedbug. But I loved him, even if he did run off."

"And you never heard from him again?"

Belle shook her head. "No. Never. Some say he opened a bookshop, specializing in volumes of alien literature. Others say he went off to die. I doubt that. Not with his spirit."

"Why'd your mother ever marry him?"

Belle settled back in her favorite chair. She flicked the ashes from the tip of her cigarette, watched impassively as they missed the tray and cascaded upon the carpet. "He was an actor, and she loved the theater. To her it was the greatest treasure of the past. It was Ida who urged me to pursue the stage. And to sing. But I never had much of a voice, and my mind rambled too much for me to concentrate on my characters. But I did find a nook for me, I did. The floozie. You should've seen it, fluttering my eyes, acting lewd, vicious beneath my sweet surface."

151

"And Shmuel?"

Belle laughed, taking another drag on her cigarette. She hefted a bottle of cognac and took a healthy swig straight from the bottle. "Shmuel? He was born to be a thief. He could crawl between bricks, if money was on the other side. He was good at it. I'm tellin' you. Oy, am I tellin' you! Mother would kill me if she ever heard me talk like this. But it's the truth!"

What truth was there? wondered Shelby as the first shot recovered his present senses. "Ah, shit," he moaned as the posse began its charge. They had formed a ragged line and were now advancing up the hill. Shelby rested his weapon on the flat of an adobe brick and aimed just above the horse's head. Carefully he squeezed the trigger. A rider dropped from his saddle. He looked to Hawkins. The Indian was smiling.

Shots were ringing everywhere. Gunpowder assaulted the nostrils, as the ricocheting bullets reverberated through vacant space. Bullets whizzed past Shelby's head. Again he leveled his rifle, fired, this time missing his target. He fired again, catching the horse so it fell, crushing the legs of its rider.

Beside him Thunderbird Hawkins fired at will. He had already dropped several members of the posse. The butcher, the roofer, a liveryman and the leading merchant's son were out on their ass. Gradually the posse retreated.

"Where do you think they're from?" asked Shelby during the interlude. "What do they want?"

"Beats me."

"Maybe they think we're someone else. Maybe we should call out and ask them."

"No. We'd better not."

"Why?"

"They might be right."

Before he could respond, Shelby's hat was knocked off by a lone shot. His red curls waved in the breeze, a banner

152

unfurled, a thousand snakes let loose to register the defenders' determination. Thunderbird regarded the free-flowing curls as a good sign. With renewed vigor he pumped five shots at the posse in rapid succession before discovering he was running low on ammunition.

"How many bullets left?" he asked his companion.

"Here," said Lopez, passing his ammo pouch to Hawkins.

Hawkins opened the pouch and frowned at the meager supply of ammunition. "Assholes," he muttered as a bullet ricocheted past him.

"I thought for sure we'd be dead by now."

Thunderbird nodded. "They'll come again. More slowly this time."

While he awaited the posse's advance, Shelby was drawn by memories of Belle Gluntz. He wondered where she had gone and what she was doing. He reminisced about the better days, when his aunt had him propped on her copious lap, relating adventures of her family. Time and again, she'd describe to her nephew the stories of Yonkel the Pirate. When the facts were depleted, she manufactured stories, often giving the battles Yiddish names.

Interspersed with images of his aunt came pictures of Uncle Shmuel, the infamous cigar inevitably placed between his fingers. He chewed his tongue and pondered the world around him. He scratched the bald spot at the back of his head, in preparation for one of his stories. "When I was a thief . . ." he would begin. A good man, despite all the negative propaganda dished out by Leonard Lopez and the opposition press. Not everyone enjoyed Shmuel's politics.

Where was Shmuel now? He, like his sister, had disappeared. Last they heard, he had travelled south. His intentions were to become a carpetbagger. Trouble in the city had forced him to leave. The demise of Shmuel's superior, one Giles Havelock, aspiring candidate for governor, had created the ruin of the party machine. How badly Shelby had needed his uncle's services after he had deserted the

Army. How disappointed he was to discover the man had left the city. Alone, despondent, with no soul to talk to, Shelby turned back to his father, hoping the older man would provide assistance, if not some means of understanding. It had been years since he had spoken to Leonard, even written him a letter. Time and absence would heal the wounds between father and son. Desperately Shelby believed it.

"So where the hell have you been?" asked Leonard when he looked up to discover his only son before him.

Shelby related his story. He described his tour of duty, the great battles in which he had participated, and his love affair with Rebecca Maltesin. Drawing a deeper breath, he related his misfortunes, his encounter with Kip Kearney, and his despair and frustration upon finding Rebecca had been mauled and murdered by Kearney and his friends. "So I killed them," he sighed, looking up to meet his father's eye.

Leonard's black eyes darted back and forth. Excited as he was, he couldn't stifle the twitch that had appeared in his face muscles during the past few years. He twitched uncontrollably now, regarding his boy for agonizing moments. At last he spoke.

"For a stranger you brought this trouble on yourself. All this aggravation for a lousy tramp."

He caught Shelby speechless. Despite all anticipation, Shelby never dreamed his father would react this way. He hadn't expected sympathy but had failed to conceive of such unabashed callousness.

"Don't you understand?" implored Shelby. "Don't you see it at all?"

The older man had not comprehended a thing. "For a stranger you did this? All this trouble for someone you hardly knew? What's the matter with you? Are you crazy? Haven't you learned a thing? Not even in the Army?"

His father's chin protruded. The eyes were bloodshot and his face was ignited with fury that had lain dormant for all

154

these years. **How** stupid young Lopez had been. He should've known his father was waiting, holding at the bit, so it could all gush out in one terrible explosion. The hostility he had been forced to suppress due to the absence of his son now surged ahead of what sensitivity remained inside him. Instantly he had become **a** monster, bellowing over treasures, not chivalry, that had been lost through the ages. After three years of fighting, Shelby had returned to this? A repeat of the same moment he had left the house, only with substitutions for different characters over whom they could feud.

"You're scum is what you are," shouted Leonard. "You're even worse than your uncle, a thousand times worse if you ask me. Like that lousy aunt of yours, you were never meant for anything decent. No pride, no sense of responsibility. Get away. Leave this house and forget about ever running my store. Bah, I'm finished with you."

Lost in the mists of his tearful despair, Shelby made for the door. Every nerve ending made its presence known. His chest throbbed violently, a machine suddenly overloaded. He searched for words, found nothing, and returned to his father a flip of his finger. Why did he ever allow the man to even tie his shoes? he wondered as the door crashed shut behind him. All the shelves he dusted, material folded, stacked neatly in place, inside that wretched fucking store. What ever became of the insights, the confidence a father instills in his son? A vacuum, that was all he had ever created between Shelby and Leonard. A vacant space filled with the ideas, the perceptions of others. Fortunately there were others, who could at least attempt to fill in the answers to the questions the young man held inside his mind. His father's word was gone now. Dead and buried beneath a heap of store receipts.

On the other side of town Shelby Lopez sat inside a barroom, a beer in his hand while he contemplated his future. After searching his mind for possibilities, he at last

155

considered Shmuel's old profession. It was the most immediate, needed little education, and he could easily be accepted among the fraternity of thieves. Shmuel's word, passed on to the older burglars, would be enough to admit him. That was it. He'd become a thief. A much better idea than a job as an office clerk or a trainee. Never would Shelby dare dream of his own business. The very concept hung over him like cancer. Any enterprise would destroy him. Be self-employed, he told himself. But own little. A few more drinks flushed down his blues, and he found himself leafing through the paper, searching the name and address of his first intended victim. Luck was with him. Sherri Seltzer had been married that very day. Fortunately, as Shelby had learned through the grapevine, she had miscarried the one embryo who had set his life into new directions. As was the past, the coming child was over and done with. It was only Sherri Seltzer, a few years older, prettier perhaps, and contented. She had married Nathan Hamstrunk, a young intern from a wealthy family living on the other side of town. The announcement in the society page described the new house, a small affair, barely furnished but laden with gifts presented for their wedding. Yes, the couple would reside there, remaining in town for several days before embarking on their honeymoon to Niagara Falls. Nathan had an examination coming up which he couldn't afford to miss.

Young Lopez chuckled and slapped the paper across the bar. "Another drink," he demanded. At long last, he had something worthy of celebration.

Late in the night Shelby appeared beneath the window of the Hamstrunk residence, his heart pounding. He carried a leather satchel, a doctor's bag he had acquired in a late-night pawnshop. Dressed in black, wearing rubber soled shoes, he had slipped in through the rear entrance, having climbed the garden wall. With a small screwdriver he jimmied the latch on the window and raised himself, taking care not to kick over anything loud and breakable. Success.

He stood inside the Hamstrunk house, surveying the multitude of gifts, some of which were still wrapped in packages. Why hadn't his father mentioned anything about Sherri's wedding? he wondered as he crept about the house, examining all the items. Hungry, he paused to remove a smoked herring he had brought with him. He took a bite from its belly and decided against the rest. Shelby stuffed the herring back into his pocket and searched the house for money. After rifling through several drawers he decided it must be with the newlyweds, somewhere inside their bedroom. Taking the greatest care not to wake them, he nudged open the door and stepped inside the master bedroom. It contained only a bed and several bureaus. A large mirror rested on the floor, waiting to be mounted. Surreptitiously, Shelby advanced on the couple, stared down at their faces. A hard day and an eventful evening, he assured himself. They would be out for the night. His confidence renewed, he searched the drawers, at last coming upon a large packet. Inside an assortment of bills, checks and money orders just waited for the taking. Some were still contained inside the special gift cards. "Best of luck, Harry and Jean. May you lovebirds perch on a growing tree, Hortense and Julius." Lopez snickered and stuffed the envelopes inside his leather satchel. He loaded his pockets with the jewelry lying atop the bureau, discovering in the process that he still had the herring. As an afterthought he tossed it lightly on the bed, so it landed between the newlyweds. He laughed, picturing their reaction in the morning.

Working his way downstairs, he found several more valuables and also stuffed them inside his satchel. Satisfied, he left the house, laughing as he closed the front gate behind him. His first attempt at burglary had been a grand success. He pictured Nathan Hamstrunk so unnerved that he failed his critical examination. "I'm sorry. I didn't mean to kill the bastard. My hand slipped. That's all." Poor Nathan. Well, fuck him, on second thought. Condemned to a lifetime of

157

manufacturing partnership with Morton Seltzer. Shelby smiled. The downslide of life had at last reversed itself, curling upward to new levels of consciousness, where murky layers of the past separated, exposing daring new concepts of truth and freedom.

Spaced yards apart from each other, the posse members sipped from their canteens and contemplated their next action. They had the abandoned adobe shack surrounded, but their forces were hardly capable of overtaking its defenders. A brief debate had erupted between those who wished to send for reinforcements and those who didn't. Those against reinforcements finally had won out after Sheriff Tad Buchanan had the last say. His concern over the town's reaction to his asking for new volunteers had kept him from sending a man back. Already he'd have a hard enough time explaining the deaths of four of his men. Three others were injured or wounded. It didn't look good at all. Look worse, come election day.

"Let's smoke," offered Thunderbird while they waited for the posse to make its move.

Shelby accepted the pipe with his regular gratitude. "Whatta ya think they'll do?"

Thunderbird was nonchalant. "Charge us. From all directions at once."

"Doesn't sound so good. Think we can pick them off as they come rushing up the hill?"

"Let's hope they're slow runners."

The sheriff was advancing toward them, a white flag waving in the air. Hawkins and Lopez regarded each other with mutual surprise. "Whatta ya suppose he wants?"

"Hey! You men. I want to talk with you."

158

"Talk!" ordered Shelby, giving his impression of a Rebel's drawl.

"We'know it's you, Curly Bill. Though we ain't sure who your friend is. If you come out peaceably it'd make a lot more sense than fightin' in all this damned heat."

"Which one's supposed to be Curly Bill?" wondered Shelby.

Thunderbird smirked. "You sure it's not you?"

"Never heard of Curly Bill. Curly Bill who? Hey, this idiot has the wrong idea. ... No one here named Curly Bill," Lopez called down the hill.

It was the sheriff's turn to snicker. "Hear that boys? We got the wrong man. Don't bullshit with us, Curly. We can spot that head of yours a mile away."

"What about it?" Hawkins asked again.

"Ain't me, Thunderbird."

Hawkins grunted. "And I thought their shooting off your hat was a good omen."

"Just a few more minutes, Curly. Then we're comin' on up."

"If he hadn't tried the flag of truce after we killed his men, there might be a chance they'd listen to reason. But not now. They'll hang us for sure. That is, if they can find a tree."

"This is some load o' shit," Thunderbird acknowledged.

The posse waited the allotted time for Curly Bill's answer. Before making preparations for their final charge, they called up the hill once again. There was no reply. High and feeling good, Shelby and Thunderbird were too busy laughing to answer foolish questions. Of course they weren't going to surrender. It would be a desecration to the notorious Curly Bill.

"Fuck you," giggled Lopez, while Thunderbird drifted off into his thoughts. He remembered taking leave of the hermit's cave, wandering aimlessly in search of his destiny.

159

He knew so little about the workings of the white man's world. Only armed with what Hawkins had told him, he walked about, confronted by his own sense of alienation. Since he had lived with a hermit, he had become a hermit himself, and was prone to strange behavior. His unconscious antics amused and antagonized the citizens of the towns he passed through. They were embarrassed whenever he relieved himself in public areas. He openly picked his nose, slept wherever he wished until he was chased by the local constable. He was hooted and hollered. Many laughed in his face. Children jeered in his direction, and women were swept from the streets in order to avoid his passing. Thunderbird was considered an ill omen. Wherever he travelled, he was believed to have left bad luck behind him. Sooner or later, as word spread, he was herded off before he could even reach the different towns.

In those days he looked strange. His hair was much longer, his face shrouded in the mystery of his inner self. No one dared search his eyes, even if they were able. To them, Thunderbird Hawkins was a leper with no colony to call his own. Like lepers locked inside ugly bodies, he found beauty within himself. Time and again his own sense of worth saved his life. He developed his own aesthetic perspective, a sense that could be evoked in others like himself. Occasionally he met mutual strangers, passed them by, or paused to camp beside them. Out of loneliness they told their stories over and over again. Each version seemed different than the last. It wasn't the substance but the simple tone of the human voice that made the retelling of each tale seem like a fresh variation.

Hawkins wandered for years, working odd jobs when and where he could. Gradually his dress and mannerisms conformed more to the standards of the community. From working odd jobs he advanced to become a ranch hand. His experience developed and proficiency at riding and roping became his own. He could ride herd with the best of them.

Hawkins often remained aloof from the cowboys. His preference of solitude estranged him from the group, arousing unspecified antagonisms among the bulk of ranch hands. It wasn't that he was disliked, really, just that he was marked as the obvious target for their practical jokes. Through the years he had borne the brunt of their childish humor. He preferred laughing with them to displaying his deeper feelings. Anger and hostility did not mix well with those who had him outnumbered. A big smile on his face, Hawkins allowed the cowboys to place cowpods in his bedroll, said nothing when he found his knife hidden in the wastes of last night's meal. Even when they chided him about his sexual prowess, declaring Indians always had the edge on white men because they were so primitive, Thunderbird laughed, shrugging it off as typical humor when they asked to see his dong.

"I'll bet you're something else with women," a cowhand started in one day. His compadres laughed expectantly.

Feeling vulnerable that day, Thunderbird confessed his innocence. "I wouldn't know. I never had one."

The cowboys regarded each other incredulously, each waiting for the Indian to break out with his shit-eating grin. He didn't. "Whatta ya mean you never had one?"

"What's it mean? To have."

"It means nookie, boy. A fella your age without no pussy ain't never gonna be a man."

"I guess we'd better show him how it's done."

"Damn. He'll give us cowboys a bad name if word spreads there's an unfucked Indian among us. Sheet."

Thunderbird laughed at their jesting. Underlying his pretense of humor, he could feel the rattler coiled inside him. More so than ever before, it was ready to strike, unleashing its venom at the first bare hand.

"Before he gets with a woman he better have some

practice first. Yo' know how embarrassin' it'd be to take him down t' Mabel's an have him lay on one a' her girls like a dead slab a' beef."

"Yeah. Let's show him a little practice."

At the group's insistence, Thunderbird was led from the corral to the barnyard. With great ceremony he was escorted inside the hog pen, where a prize hog was selected for his first sexual experience. The sow stared balefully at Hawkins, its eyes human with their expectations. Unthinking, Hawkins stroked the sow behind the ear.

"Yeah, that's it. She likes 'at."

"Get her worked up first. He's catching on pretty quick."

"Now mount her. That's it. Slip your tomahawk right in 'ere. In th' hole, boy. Yeah. that's it. That's right. Now, rock back and forth. That's it. Yeah, yeah, that's right. You got 'er now, boy. Just keep rockin'."

At first the sensation was pleasant. Having nothing to compare with the sow, Thunderbird was enraptured by the sensations. But gradually, as he was acclimated to the effect, he found himself disturbed by the cowboys' hysterical jeerings. Something was wrong. The hands were laughing harder than they ever had before. Slapping each other on the back, pointing at Thunderbird, making the sow quiver beneath his plunging cock. Yet the harder he rocked the better it felt. The better it seemed the more the cowboys laughed. Thunderbird was caught inside a terrible dilemma. Try as he might, he simply couldn't relinquish the sow's cunt.

Just as he came, Rancher Lee Kane broke through the ranks of cowboys. Kane wasn't laughing. Outrage was expressed all over his face. His fists clenched and unclenched, his teeth bit down hard on his lips.

"What the hell's the meaning of this?" he demanded. "That's my prize sow."

Thunderbird had no explanation. He was a cowhand, not a hogbreeder. One sow to him looked about the same as the

162

next. Before he could offer any explanation, Kane had slapped him from the hog, knocking him into the mud. Hawkins looked up at the rancher, dumbfounded.

"You ruined my prized sow with that damned Indian sperm o' yours," howled Kane. "What the hell gives with you?"

Thunderbird caught on that Lee Kane was working himself up into a terrible fury. Firing the Indian was simply not enough. While Hawkins attempted to brush the mud from his clothes, Kane studied the other cowboys. They were laughing harder than ever. Kane smiled cruelly, while the cowboys looked on expectantly. Hawkins regarded them all, noting the ring of teeth and eyeballs that surrounded him. None of them had ever been his friends. Few had barely exchanged decent words with him. Suddenly Thunderbird was angered. Before he could shout back at the rancher, Lee Kane caught him with an uppercut, knocking Hawkins back into the mud. The cowboys clutched at their stomachs, they were laughing so hard. His head clearing, Thunderbird looked up at the rancher. How wrong he had been to allow all this to happen to him. He had borne the brunt of one too many jokes. He had laughed his last laugh at his own expense.

With his head still clouded from the uppercut, Thunderbird realized Kane was pulling him out of the mud with intentions to strike him again. Catching his wind, Hawkins barely ducked under the rancher, who slid over the Indian's back, depositing his own self in the hog slime. The cowboys watched, astonished.

"I'll kill you for this," Kane threatened. Hogshit was all over his face. He charged for Hawkins, but the Indian deftly sidestepped his advance and knocked the rancher back into the mud. Kane slowly climbed to his feet. More sober he appeared now, knowing he was in a fight.

"You redskinned sonofabitch," he hissed, rushing forward a second time. Thunderbird met him head-on, driving his

163

shoulder into the rancher's solar plexus as they fell to the ground, each struggling to climb atop the other. Over and over they rolled, the spirit of Burning Bush showing its familiar prominence within his son. New power surged through Hawkins. With unbelievable strength he lifted the rancher over his shoulders and slammed him against the pen's fencing. Without breaking stride, Hawkins then kicked Lee Kane squarely in the face. Again and again, his foot found new sections of the rancher. The man's head slackened. He was unconscious.

The cowboys weren't laughing anymore. They stared mutely, their heads bowed toward the ground. Cold-eyed, Hawkins walked past them, gathered his few belongings and made for his horse. He rode off uncontested, although more than one ranch hand considered shooting him down. Had Lee Kane regained consciousness, it's probably what they would've done. However, as the hands later discovered, the rancher would never again come to.

Having been the first on the range, and after successfully defending his territory from hostile encroachments from sheepherders, squatters, Indians and outlaws, Lee Kane had acquired a fortune in cattle, land and horses. Hogs were only a sideline with him. He had become one of the most powerful men in the territory, his empire extending as far as the eye could see in any direction. Hundreds of men were employed by his ranch. His woman, a dark-haired Mexican beauty, made him the envy of the land. He kept her locked away in his palace. Yet, despite all his wealth, his power and his fame, Lee Kane lay dead, his face impressed in fetid slime.

The posse prepared for another charge against the adobe shack. With surprisingly little concern, Thunderbird watched them load their rifles. Shelby, meanwhile, ambled around the adobe shack, scuffing his boots against the wreckage. Accidentally he turned over something, a book, its title barely visible. He stooped down, taking the book in his hands. It was what was left of a family Bible. "Hawkins," he called, displaying the book to his companion.

"A Bible?"

"Yeah," answered Shelby, flipping through the pages. Much had been charred when the house had been burned. When he reached the end of the Bible, he turned what appeared to be a blank page. On its opposite side a record of the family's events was neatly inscribed. Birth dates, deaths, business matters and random notes were neatly listed. At the bottom of the column another note was written, this time in a different hand. Not as neat as the initial scribe, the penmenship depicted urgency in its wavering hand. Shelby brushed off the dust and charcoal and squinted at the inscriptions.

"Fuck God and Hal Pardee—Clarence Thizzel."

Lopez blinked his eyes and looked again. Nothing had changed. A laugh escaped him.

"What's a' matter?" asked Hawkins.

"This," Lopez pointed, handing the book over to the Indian. "It's a helluva place to plant a curse."

Hawkins' brows knitted at the inscription. He couldn't believe it. So this is what became of Sheriff Clarence Thizzel, after the town council had submitted to Pardee's demands and dismissed him from his duties.

"He was the sheriff in charge of tracking my father," Hawkins explained. "That was a long, long time ago."

"So there's no tellin' when this house was burnt. It could've been ages."

Thunderbird shrugged and touched a section of the wall. "Adobe is mud. Who can tell the age of mud?"

Mutely, Lopez agreed. He was about to add something when a cry rose up from the posse. They were charging the defenders. The companions took positions behind the adobe wall and waited for the riders to draw closer. When they

165

did, the travellers unleashed a terrible volley of rifle fire, sustaining it for as long as possible. Members of the posse fell from their horses, while others dismounted and struggled for cover. They were picked off before they could find safety behind the rocks. Only one man made it up the hill. He was the blacksmith, a large, burly man, who out of civic duty had accompanied Sheriff Tad Buchanan. The smithy got off one shot, killing Hawkins' deerhorn pipe. Angered, Thunderbird gutted the man with his hunting knife just as the blacksmith came over the wall. When the firing ceased, only Sheriff Tad Buchanan remained standing. He had retreated to the bottom of the hill. Shelby considered putting a bullet in the sheriff's back, but decided against it. He crouched down behind the wall, allowing Buchanan a chance to check his wounded. Thunderbird shifted alongside him.

"You know, my father sought revenge against the killing of his wife. They raped her, then beat her to death. My mother. He killed the leader and then moved off to the mountains, launching raids against the white man. Years passed before they found him. Nineteen men were sent to kill him. Sheriff Clarence Thizzel was one of them. Lorenzo Stokes another. Hal Pardee, a big-time rancher, was most insistent that my father not be taken alive, although I doubt that possibility because of my father's pride. Anyway, they surrounded his hideout, attempting to gun him down. In the process he killed eight of them and wounded several more. It was a slaughter, a valiant effort on the part of my father. In the end Clarence Thizzel was dismissed for cowardice, and Lorenzo Stokes was put in his place. Stokes had taken the Necklace my father always wore. The Great Necklace, his tribe had called it. It was supposed to contain many powers. Stokes was later found with the daughter of the mayor. She was only eleven at the time. He was dismissed and disappeared from sight. Hal Pardee died several years later, cheating my chance for revenge by dying of natural causes. My one consolation was that my father, Burning Bush, had killed his only son, and Pardee lacked a successor. His ranch fell into ruin and was later divided among the squatters, sheepherders and neighboring cattlemen he for so long had detested. Thizzel, as we see, died here, cursing the man who ruined his career. Only one is left. One that I know of. Lorenzo Stokes. He still may possess the Great Necklace. It's my duty to recover the Necklace, in the name of my father and a man known in the legends of the white man as Hawkins the Hermit."

When Thunderbird had finished, Shelby hung onto his eyes, unsure of what to say.

"This Bible has given me hope," added Hawkins, reading Shelby's thoughts. "I've been inspired."

Lopez glanced over the adobe wall, down to where Buchanan was still checking the wounded. His fellow townspeople moaned in agony, while their sheriff looked on, nearly out of his wits with grief. He had led the posse into catastrophe, despite the uncertainty they had been chasing the wrong man. Ashamed of himself, he removed his shirt and hung it across the barrel of his empty rifle. "You men. You men," he called. "I want to talk with you."

Neither Shelby or Thunderbird could bear to answer. While Hawkins gathered their things, Lopez looked on at the sheriff who, through different contortions, resembled Barney Muldoon, Shelby's favorite jewelry fence.

"You're really something, kid," Muldoon used to say. "Keep goin' at this pace and you'll find yourself a cozy lil' room in Eastern State. 'Specially wit' dat fuckin' herring gimmick. A dead fuckin' herrin' dropped in the middle o' the victim's bed. Jus' what th' fuck are ya' tryin' t' do?"

Shelby had little idea what he was trying to do. Maybe that was the fun of it. If so, the pleasure was beginning to run out. For Lopez was forced to agree with Barney Muldoon. It was only a matter of time before they nabbed him. Already they were closing in, moving about his hangouts, asking too many questions. With several years of burglaries under his belt he had pushed his luck well past its limits. A new election had brought into office another series of law-and-order candidates. The streets were hotter than ever.

"I've been thinking about leaving town," he admitted to Roxanne, his girlfriend, one fine day. A stiff breeze had recently swept the clouds from the sky. The weather was balmy, promising for a picnic. But what burglar had time for such frivolities? It depressed Shelby to be struck by such a thought. He had become a burglar in order to elude responsibilities, but he found after a while that he had much research to attend to in order to keep from getting caught. Every day he had his duties, visiting and checking out his intended target, even going as far as to pose as a serviceman in order to gain entry into the house. Once inside he could case the valuables, deciding what to steal and what to leave behind. And then, of course, he had to visit with his fence. Muldoon was always good company, but seeing him had become a chore, along with everything else.

Roxanne brushed her hair back and turned for a better view of herself in the mirror Shelby had recently stolen for her. A Victorian affair, embedded in silver casing, with a swordfish leaping across its top. "Where will you go?"

"I don't know. West. Maybe."

"West? What could I possibly do out West? What about my career?" she asked, calling attention to her aspirations as a model.

"I wasn't thinking of taking you," admitted Shelby.

"Oh. I'm sorry."

"About what?" he asked, admiring the thickness of her hair, the texture of her naked back. His penis quivered inside his pants.

"That we've lived together for so long, and yet there's nothing stronger between us."

"I know. It's sad. There was a time when I wished for more."

"Then what happened?" asked Roxanne, turning around to face her lover.

168

"I just realized . . . not this time around."

"Nothing to do with our differences in age, does it? I mean, I am a few years older. Maybe that annoys you."

"Has nothing to do with it. Chemistry. The wrong blending of elements."

"Except in bed," Roxanne corrected. "We've always been great in the sack together."

"Yeah, we sure have." The very thought of fucking Roxanne made Shelby's dick stiffen. "Want to go again?"

"Not now, Hon. I have an appointment in about an hour. I really must get ready. If he likes me, he'll use me in an ad for Sears' Catalogue."

"Sure. I can see it." On sheer impulse Shelby jumped from the bed and rummaged through his drawers. One by one he found and removed different objects, dividing them into different piles. When he had finished, he threw his clothes, a few jewels, some cash and his pistol into his suitcase, and closed down the lock. Satisfied, he returned to Roxanne, who was looking on over his shoulder. She expected an explanation. Without hesitation Shelby handed her several minor treasures and some cash. In all, she received seven gold watches, four rings, two of which were diamond, a pearl necklace, several gold bracelets and a pair of diamond earrings. "This should keep you in money for a while," he explained.

Roxanne nodded and accepted the offering. She stared silently into the palm of her hand. "That's nice," she acknowledged. "The last guy who I broke with left me with a black eye and a pair of swollen lips. You'll always be all right with me."

Lopez grabbed his suitcase and faced Roxanne. "If there's anything I can ever do. Ever . . ."

"Sure. I know. I'll just come an' look you up. Take care o' yourself, sweetheart. Someday you'll be good for someone. I hope she deserves what she's gettin'."

Guilt mingled with the silence. Shelby found a lump

swelling in his throat. His emotions surprised him. He never thought he'd dread this moment. Not the way he did. In a flash he recalled all the good times he'd shared with Roxanne. Never had there been trouble between them. Still . . .

"I feel awful," he confessed.

Roxanne tried to cheer him. "It's hot for ya' here. Think it'd be better for me to see ya sent up the river? Kill me, it would. A nice fella like you."

"We couldn't have that now, could we?"

Roxanne shook her head. "No. We damn well couldn't." She kissed him lightly on his lips and withdrew her face. Her eyes blinked, forcing back the tears. "You'll miss your train."

Shelby smiled, noting the jewels and money he left with his lover. "Sure it's enough?"

"Plenny. You'll need money for lunch. Take care, kid. Real good care. Y' hear. An if you're ever back in town . . . we'll celebrate. On me."

"Sure. Be good to yourself."

"I'll try it out. For a change. My love to the West."

Despondently, Shelby opened the door and pulled it closed behind him. He looked back once before descending the three flights of stairs to the street below. From now on, he'd call himself Clifford Dash.

"I thought justice was supposed to be meted out swiftly," he quipped to Hawkins, now that Sheriff Tad Buchanan was approaching, his flag of truce waving in his hands. "Not take all damn day."

"Life is slower on the desert," Thunderbird replied wearily. Silently he surveyed the carnage left from the battle. Horses and men covered the hillside.

"You men," repeated Sheriff Buchanan. "If you come back peacefully, I'll promise a fair trial. On my word."

"Where's he get off bargaining with us?" Shelby wondered.

170

"He's trying to save his face," was Hawkins' insouciant reply.

"If he wants to save his face, he'd better get his ass outta here. Otherwise I'll put bullets in both his ends."

"Leave him be," said Hawkins when Shelby raised his rifle. "There's enough he has to answer to."

The sheriff still advanced. Even from the distance the companions noted his glazed eyes, the vacuous expression. He was a man in shock, an animal carrying on long after his conscious senses had disappeared. Quite possibly, Tad Buchanan would go stark raving mad.

"Let's go. So we can make time while the sun still shines."

"Yeah," said Shelby, retrieving his bag. While stooped over he noticed Hawkins' deerhorn pipe. In the battle it had been shattered into a million pieces. The stray shot from the blacksmith had ended its days of pleasure-giving. Shelby was saddened by its loss.

Once mounted, Shelby took a final look at the ruined humans and horses. He was sickened by the sight, reminded of the grim aftermath on the battlefields where he once had served. Now, as he witnessed the torn bodies of men and animals alike, he found emotions welling up inside of him. He didn't know what to say, what final comment would somehow arrange it all inside his mind.

"Sorry about your pipe," he at last told Hawkins with morbid finality. "I hope you'll find another."

Chapter 9

One night, just after supper, Thunderbird poked his nose into the evening air currents and sniffed the ocean. He related his find to Shelby, who allowed himself the luxury of a triumphant smile.

"It's a few days off, at least," Hawkins cautioned his companion. "I can barely detect the change in the air."

Shelby heard none of it. "It's hard to believe. We made it. We finally made it."

"We've only changed places. Nothing more. Soon green will begin replacing sand, scrubs will become trees and rocks blades of grass. The change will be gratifying, at least for a while."

Heeding the conservatism implied in his friend's tone of voice, Shelby eased off his celebration. "I'll fix some coffee," he said abruptly, taking into his hand the pouch of coffee beans. Miraculously, their meager supply had lasted all this time. Lopez then filled the pot with some water, added the beans and waited. Occasionally his attention was drawn from the boiling water to the Southern Mountain Range, barely perceptible in the darkness. The ragged silhouette still appeared very distant, unreachable, no matter how much time was allotted for the journey. "We must still cross those," he gestured to Hawkins.

Despite the ardor contained in Shelby's gesture, Hawkins refused to turn around. He rolled his dark eyes around his head, sniffed again and waited patiently for Shelby to pour hot coffee into his cup. "It'll be nothing at all," he said easily, now that his throat was refreshed with coffee. "With the weather as it is, the season, there should be few obstacles."

"No more sheriffs with their posses," smiled Shelby. "You promise?"

"What good's my promise against the unknown?" came Hawkins' reply. "Besides, it's not the first time we've been hunted."

Thunderbird's intimation startled Shelby. Cautiously, he searched the Indian's eyes for his meaning. Nothing was revealed. "You ever done time?" he asked a little too easily.

"No."

"Neither have I."

"I know. It doesn't show in your character."

Lopez snickered bubbles into his coffee. "What does show?"

"That you've been hunted."

A slight nod of his head was Shelby's lone acknowledgement. He sipped his coffee, waiting for Hawkins to continue.

"I've been hunted. But they never found me. I lost myself in their Army. With the war on, it was quite an easy thing to do."

"Even for you? An Indian?"

Hawkins drew himself up to a boastful rectitude. He laughed, regarding Shelby's face as he explained. "I played the Indian Scout. A fine performance. So valiant I must've appeared, riding at the head of the troop. Big Stuff."

"And I'm sure you loved it."

173

"It beat th' hell outta sleeping with my pistols cocked by my side. Scared me. Thought I'd roll over one night and blow the hell out of my chest. There was a price on my head. Not a big price, but then again ... I wasn't Crazy Horse neither."

"What were you?" asked Lopez, his free arm draped casually across his lap.

"A murderer," replied Hawkins, startling his companion. "I killed a rancher. He tried to humiliate me. Beat me to death. I'd had enough of humiliation."

In the course of his drinking several cups of coffee, Hawkins explained his story. He recalled his years on the run, the endless search for work, a decent hiding place. As a wanted man, he learned never to linger too long in any one place. Odd jobs compounded, led to the acquisition of varied but superficial skills. Hawkins had worked everywhere, including a whorehouse, where he laundered the linens, whitened the ladies' undies. He also served in the kitchen, assisting the chef with banquets, as well as the seemingly interminable task of cleaning up. How many pots, pans and dishes he must've scrubbed in that kitchen escaped the more liberal estimates of his imagination. Still, it was a job, out of sight and out of mind. And it was a job in the whorehouse, where favors were returned via ways of the flesh. Often ladies would tap him for errands, asking Hawkins to relay messages to beaus or even families lying somewhere beyond the fantasies created within the posh bordello. A great place to work, it was. The windows were adorned with luxurious velvet drapes, the rooms with the finest in carved or upholstered furniture. An opulent bar surrounded by original oil paintings fronted the lounge, and a piano stood off in the corner. At the busiest hours it was played by one of the finest musicians ever to reach the territories. A passion for women and drink had caused his ruination along the more formal music circuits. But with the Grand Bordello he had found his home, satisfying all his urges at once. Lou Lavins was his name, and he and Hawkins became good friends. Many hours he had passed with Lou, playing cards, smoking, drinking or accumulating assorted favors with the ladies.

But whenever he could, Thunderbird snuck off to spend his time with Marlene Hobson, a sultry woman of mixed blood. She claimed the heritages of the Asiatic, the Indian, the Negro and the white. Her features verified all she said. Tall, dark-skinned, her eyes slanted, Marlene never walked, but floated across the surface, her hips swinging from side to side. Her expression was always sultry, concealing the laughter and wit she often liked to sneak into her conversations. That is, her conversations with those she admired. For her tricks, little more than a whore's smile and a quick piece of ass were ever offered.

She loved Thunderbird. Often they took walks together, shopping for sweet frillies about the town. Cod-faced women scorned and barflies snickered whenever the pair walked past. But few could hide their envy, the ladies wishing to be Marlene, the men comparing what they had to Thunderbird Hawkins. Proudly walked Thunderbird, his head barely reaching Marlene's squashed tits. He didn't mind. Not at all. For he knew when it counted, Hawkins could reach all that was necessary.

"We've been good for each other," Marlene declared one night, as the two companions stared into the approaching dawn. A bottle was passed between them, along with his pipe and tender compliments. "Maybe one day, we'll get off, be by ourselves."

Struck by the smoke, the booze and Marlene's kind words, Hawkins frowned with self-pity. He knew, as he had always known, they would never be together. Time and all its dreaded past events were rapidly catching up with him. Soon he'd be forced to move on, a stranger once again, visiting the barren faces and places he never wished to see. "I wish I could believe it," he smiled. "But our lives together have been too simple, too easy for us to continue like this. For you know that we were never meant to live with simple lives."

"I' know. But what does it matter? The uncertainty of each new day refreshes our love. It's the best we could ever expect. The best I could hope for."

"One day you'll meet someone, a person very much to your liking. You'll grow to love him, as you learned to love me. It seems impossible now, but sometime it will be simple."

"Sometime! I'm running out of sometime, Thunderbird. I'm a whore and each waking day I discover new wrinkles on my face. My ass bags like it never used to, and my breasts curve to the side. A few more years and . . . I'll begin my decline. What then? A series of brothels, each one more dreary than the last. I'd take my life before that."

Marlene's voice was weighted with despair when she speculated upon her destiny. Her eyes cast downward, her fingers stroking the waves in the sheets she and Hawkins had hewn with their passion, she recounted her early days as an urchin. Outside her room, two whores cackled in the hallway. Footsteps were heard thudding up and down the staircase. Hawkins diverted his attentions to the layout of her chamber. Nothing personal, despite the opulence, the lavishness of the draperies, the bureau, and the four-poster bed. With the exception of her clothes and toilet articles, everything belonged to the house. For nearly five years Marlene had resided there, and had little to show for it. Even the house itself no longer belonged to LuAnne Brady, its madam. Two years ago she had sold it to a corporate interest of physicians, attorneys, businessmen and the local sheriff, who received his share for exerting the proper pressures on LuAnne.

"She never would've sold, if it hadn't been for that creepy sheriff," claimed Eleanor Tracy, LuAnne's longtime lover.

"Go someplace else? I couldn't," LuAnne wailed, whenever her whiskey had gotten the best of her. She remained, as did her women, secure, stable and always open to receive the incursions of the corporate members. Usually they came late in the night, when they had less chance of being noticed.

Thunderbird studied Marlene's long, lean legs, her firm, round breasts and the shadows of her hollow eyes. He tried to assure her things would work out. Life would be okay, he insisted, his hands running down the curve of her back. Yet, despite his efforts, neither he nor she was at all reassured.

"I guess what will be, will be," Marlene brooded, her sadness evolving into tears. For the first time he could remember, she cried openly, filling Hawkins with the same sense of despair. He brought her close to him, allowed her to weep in his naked lap. Tenderly he stroked her back, his senses aroused by the mood of the moment. He patted her ass, running his fingers along its crack, slipping one, then another, into the hole. Marlene stirred beneath him. Her hand slid along his thigh until she found his cock. She stroked it firmly, working it up into a full erection. Her fingers ticked at his balls. Thunderbird grabbed her head, hoping to lift her from his lap so he could kiss her. Marlene refused to raise her head, preferring to secure her mouth around Hawkins' cock. She sucked him hard, pausing to flash her tongue over his swelled cockhead. In a few moments he came, and she pulled her head back, just as there was a knocking at her door.

"Marlene! Marlene," Eleanor Tracy was calling. "There are men here to see you. Ready, willin' an' rarin' t' go." Their laughter followed behind Eleanor's attempt at a joke. "Marlene, Marlene," the madam's lover called again.

"I've been off work for four hours," scowled Marlene.

"Too bad, honey," shouted Eleanor in her truer tone of voice. "Madam says you're drafted."

Marlene sighed, regarded Hawkins sadly. She embraced him, her long arms barely reaching around his midsection.

"I guess you'd better go," she whispered. She then turned toward the door. "Tell them to wait downstairs. Until I'm ready."

Reluctantly Thunderbird pulled on his clothes. When he finished dressing he checked the revolver he kept under his blanket, examining it for cartridges. He promised himself he'd clean his revolver someday soon. Kissing Marlene goodbye, he exited and started his descent of the staircase. The cowboys were climbing them, too drunk to see the Indian until he stood just above them. Only then did one cowboy open his eyes. He reared back, horrified, his mouth dropping open. "It's him," he shouted. "Goddammit all, it's him."

Through bleary eyes, the other two cowboys peered at the figure. It bounded backward, hopping away from them, its pistol drawn. Hawkins had recognized them as men from Lee Kane's ranch. Clumsy were the cowboys in bringing their guns to fire. Hawkins' first shot caught one hand in the face, another was struck in the chest. The third was shot twice, the second shot killing him before he tumbled to the bottom of the staircase.

His gun still smoking, Thunderbird raced for Marlene's room. He flung open the door, found her on the other side. She stared at his face, then turned to the pistol. Her eyes asked why.

"There's no time for that," he said, reading her thoughts. "Another time, perhaps."

"I'll come with you."

"No! I couldn't allow it. Not with the law one step behind me."

Three whores and two tricks had appeared in the hallway. All were naked, screaming, racing around, unsure of what they should do. Only after a while did the tricks allow their modesty to overtake their morbid curiosity. They scrambled back inside their rooms, slamming the doors behind them.

Madam LuAnne appeared at the foot of the stairs. "What's goin' on here?" she bellowed.

"¡Just a shooting," Marlene called back, trying to calm her down. It was then she noticed the sheriff, and signalled to Hawkins that he'd better leave. With one final kiss, he departed through the rear exit.

He rode hard, on a horse he had stolen from the bordello stable. The stallion belonged to one of the cowboys and fortunately came equipped with all Thunderbird needed for his escape into the desert. For several days he c‒‒‒‒nued riding at an arduous pace, pausing only in hamlets to restock his food supplies. And as he galloped toward freedom, he was again reminded of his father, Burning Bush, and those who had pursued him so many years ago. It occurred to Thunderbird that he too would be chased, tracked down until he was finally executed. Meanwhile, he'd do the best he could to stay alive.

In the tiny hamlet of La Pinza, Hawkins paused to refresh himself in the town's only cantina. In the deepest corner of the ancient adobe building he overheard two villagers speaking of the Army's attempts to recruit them for active duty. Thunderbird's interest was aroused. "Where are they accepting enlistments?" he asked the peasants.

The oldest of the two men raised his eyebrows at the stranger. With little difficulty Thunderbird found the man believed him a fool. Refusing to speak to the Indian, the older man only pointed, an obscure gesture with his finger. "Over there," his companion grumbled. "Tha's where you'll find the Army."

Still confused by the peasants' reaction, Hawkins ambled toward the compound where the recruiting station was situated. Sergeant Edgar Thrombattle was signing new recruits. So far, after several hours of arduous persuasion, promises of bounty and such, he had only signed four men, three of whom were too drunk at the time to know what

179

they were doing. Thrombattle was most surprised to see Hawkins approach him.

After a brief discussion, in which Thrombattle did his best to mislead the Indian, Hawkins finally signed the papers. What better chance for escape than to join the Army. Only then did he learn he was to be an Indian scout, not so much an Indian scouting Confederate positions, but actually participating in the surveillance of Indians. Apparently a series of uprisings had alarmed the Washington government, and a rigid band of hardline soldiers were sent to form an effective campaign against the renegade Indians. To support their efforts, Rebel prisoners, convicts and assorted vagabonds were cajoled into enlistment. Needless to say, discipline was strict, if not harsh and unbearable. For the most menial of infractions, soldiers were flogged, imprisoned or even hanged as an example to the remainder of the troop. Unwittingly Thunderbird Hawkins had become part of this force, the command headed by none other than the notorious Major Francis Solgenson, or "Bloody Frank" as he was called by the men who feared him.

"You'll be an Indian scout," Solgenson had commanded.

"That's fine with me," replied Hawkins, not caring on which side he fought, be it Confederate or Union. How surprised he was to learn he'd be fighting Indians, renegades who had enough balls to stand for their convictions. His heart was leadened by the burden he had taken upon himself. Despondent, he spent many a long night smoking, attempting to justify the act he had committed. He couldn't. No possible rationale ever appeared. Resigned to his plight, he went on scouting expeditions, content to allow his white counterparts to do the searching. When it was possible he did his best to throw his fellow scouts off the trail of Indian bands.

Frank Solgenson, or Bloody Frank, disliked his new duty. It had been delivered as punishment for his alleged brutality against Rebel prisoners as well as his own men. The Military Command, upon realizing Solgenson's underlying talents, believed the major could do best when in conflict against the heathen savages he'd encounter out West. So, from the front lines in Maryland, Bloody Frank was shipped out West, accompanied by his noble and faithful companion, Sergeant Edgar Thrombattle. What Solgenson commanded, Thrombattle effected, often adding his own peculiar brand of relish to the task. No flogging could be worse than when administered directly by Thrombattle himself. Of course his personal hand was always saved for the worst infringements or turned against those he personally disliked. This amounted to several dozen soldiers, and quite regularly they were stripped of their back hides.

"Under no circumstances are we to encounter Confederate soldiers," Solgenson had commanded, the undertones of bitterness evident in his manner. "It's our job to kill Indians, not Rebs, and we'll do just that."

"And if we spot a Rebel Patrol?" asked Hawkins at a tactless moment.

"Then avoid them. Tell me and I'll devise our evasion tactics. This, of course, will not be necessary, since no Rebel force of any size has been sighted in this area in at least six months."

If Thunderbird had not known better, he would've believed that Solgenson's own comments set off the chain of events that was to make Hawkins a military hero. For only a few days after the major proclaimed there were no Confederate forces in the area, Thunderbird quite accidentally came across a sizable division of fresh Confederate troops. Immediately he reported his discovery to Sergeant Thrombattle, who in turn related the message to Bloody Frank Solgenson. The major scoffed at the report. "Had it come from a white man, I might've given it more credence. But coming from my one Indian scout, I can only assert that he is attempting to avoid his duty by attempting to divert my strength away from the Indian concentration. Are you a spy, man? Is that what it is?"

Thunderbird shook his head. No, he wasn't a spy. "I saw what I saw."

"You saw nothing of the kind," demanded Sergeant Thrombattle, jumping on his major's side. "It's a deliberate evasion of duty. We should have you whipped for this."

Before Thunderbird could explain himself, Thrombattle had him shackled and led outside to the damned whipping post. With little ceremony, the sergeant unfurled his celebrated whip and administered a half dozen lashes. Hawkins' back was a bloody pulp. Through tear-blurred eyes he noted Solgenson himself, applauding in the distance. He swore he'd kill him, and Thrombattle right along with him. By the soul of Burning Bush, he'd see them die.

Several days later, the other scouts reported a buildup of Indians to the southwest of where the Army was stationed. Believing Hawkins would learn his lesson in battle with his blood brothers, Solgenson assigned him to the scouting party. He rode out alone, ignored by his comrades. No longer was he trusted. Little did he care. When the troop turned up nothing, Hawkins thought it best to veer off to the right, climbing the nearby mesas to gain an overall view of the surrounding terrain. The other scouts left him to his own devices, believing it would be best if he wandered off alone and was taken and tortured by his fellow Indians.

"A lesson you'll never forget," warned one scout, partially wishing this dastardly fate on Thunderbird.

When he reached the peak of the mesa, Hawkins took in the splendor beneath him. Adjusting to a better perspective of the world, he sat down on a rock, removed his Army rations, his pipe, smoke and the remaining possessions that added to his comfort. He ate slowly, happy to be on his own again. In the middle of biting down on his ration of cheese, he sighted movement at the far end of the valley. He dashed to his saddle, retrieving his binoculars. Peering into the distance he spotted a large troop of Confederate soldiers. They were heading in his direction. Following their projected trail, Thunderbird noted Solgenson's ragtag army was advancing toward the Confederates. Neither side had spotted the enemy yet, since the valley's breadth extended to more than fifteen miles, with assorted mesas and ridges impairing the view. It would be several hours before they discovered each other, in a head-on collision. For a brief moment Thunderbird considered warning Solgenson. As quickly as it came, the impulse passed right through him. "Fuck him," he muttered to no one in particular. "They can all go to hell."

His legs crossed, his pipe in his hand, Thunderbird sat contentedly at the edge of the mesa and watched the two armies collide. "We'll see who's nonexistent now," he snickered while the two armies prepared themselves for battle. As the time passed, Thunderbird was able to spot flashes of cannon fire, even hearing the dull murmur of reports, the cries of the wounded. For several hours the battle raged, each side slaughtering the other. When the armies were reduced to bare semblances of their former strengths, the reluctant commanders finally called a halt to the battle. Both sides retreated in opposite directions, easy prey for the hostile Indians, who lurked on the fringes of the battlefield, licking their lips at such a moment. Among those who failed to return from the battle was Sergeant Edgar Thrombattle. Major Solgenson did return, along with Thunderbird Hawkins, who drifted back into the regiment just before they reached their base.

"You were right all along," Solgenson acknowledged, still in a daze. He was so stunned by it all he could barely function. Upon learning that his sergeant, the loyal Thrombattle, had been slain in the fighting, the weight of his despair forced from the major a series of incoherent proclamations. Even the dullest of troopers could see that Bloody

Frank had gone buggers. A terrible, terrible day for the military tradition.

When word spread to his superiors, Major Frank Solgenson was relieved of his command, a degradation of his character from which he was never to recover. He spent the remainder of his days locked away in military institutions, babbling paranoiac intrigues to anyone who would listen. He died by his own hand ten years later, by strangling himself with his own beard. He had allowed it to grow to unfathomable lengths during his last sequence of intrigues, by which he believed himself to be the reincarnation of John the Baptist.

As for Thunderbird Hawkins, he was promoted, receiving several citations attributed to his keen eyes and general sense of awareness. In a token military gesture he was paraded about the East, lauded as a fine example of the equality found inside the Army. When the accolades died down he was discreetly shipped to the front lines in Tennessee, just prior to the Battle of Chickamauga.

Chapter 10

When the war finally ended, Thunderbird Hawkins headed north toward the major Union cities. His curiosity was aroused by the Eastern seacoast, the former stomping grounds of Hawkins the Hermit and Yonkel the Pirate. The journey north was crowded with others like himself who had been dismissed by the military and left to their own devices. Most attempted to get home the best they could, while others sat around makeshift living quarters deliberating on their future.

"I'm not gonna blow it this time," Hawkins overheard from the men talking around the evening fires. His horse's clopping punctuated their remarks. "The war has taught me a lesson."

"Me. I'm gonna get me a lil' ol' farm an' plow dem fields. I don' wanna know 'bout nuthin."

"Not me. I'm gonna speculate with th' money I saved from my pay. Make me a rich man, I damn well am."

"What about you?" one soldier would occasionally ask of

Hawkins whenever he joined in around the fires. "What will you do?"

"Don't have the vaguest idea."

Bewildered, the men stared at each other. The Indian's honesty surprised them, forced bitterness from their own sense of futility. Everything they had fought for, their ideals, fabricated or otherwise, had receded to mundane levels. Hopelessness, lack of change was what they already had begun to sense. A different perspective of life in general was perhaps all they had acquired. After relinquishing countless bodies, arms, legs, the fear impulse had nearly strangled their passions, and all they would receive for their efforts was a lukewarm welcome home.

"I betcha he's good at scalpin'," another soldier laughed bitterly. He managed to raise a brief laugh from his comrades. "How many Rebs y' scalp with yore license? Huh?"

"Only those with lice in their hair," replied Hawkins who was now tired of the same old jokes.

"Didja like it? All the legal killin' 'n' all? Didja?"

"Not much."

"Then tell us. How many Rebs ya kill? How many got caught in yore sights?"

"Only one."

"Only one?"

"I was a bad shot," snapped Hawkins, taking his leave of the soldiers. Fuck them, he thought, leading his horse away from their fire. Further up the highway he reflected on the one man he did shoot. A lone soldier who was advancing on a Union infantryman. He was never sure why he intervened. Playing God was never his foremost thrill. Had he allowed it to take its natural course, the Yank would've died and the Reb would've been praised by his superiors. But as it was, Thunderbird had stopped all that. Perhaps it was the mawkish look on the Yankee's face. He seemed more curious than afraid. And so simple it was for Hawkins to pull the

186

trigger. Out of necessity he had done so, the type of necessity of which he was never able to define.

His position in the war was something Thunderbird never grew accustomed to. When they shipped him East, he discovered the true irony of Army life. What good would a desert Indian scout possibly do the Yankees in its southern campaign? He knew so little of the verdancy of the East, the long-bladed grass surrounded by countless trees and bushes, dissected by rivers, interspersed with cities. A totally different terrain. Nothing he could ever be sure of.

Gradually, however, he did grow accustomed to his new surroundings. He didn't even do badly as a scout. Fond of the new forms of wildlife, the shaded green and sweet moisture, he loved to go on solitary patrols, ostensibly to seek out Rebel positions. But once he was free of the camp, he would find a quiet, hidden spot and laze about for hours. Ensconced in a thicket, he could lie unseen by all but the reflections of his own thinking. He soaked up the tranquility of his atmosphere, while a nearby stream moved southward, its crystal voice blanketing the surrounding threat of war. With his eyes closed, his pistol by his side, he dreamed great dreams, often thinking of Cactus Flower and Burning Bush. He thought of the women in his grandfather's tribe and speculated on which would've eventually become his wife had things not developed as they had. He laughed at his own projections and transferred his attentions to Hawkins the Hermit's trek to the Western Sea, recounting the journey with what he believed to be inexplicable accuracy. His vision of the hermit, his account of his every resting place, intrigue and encounter seemed all too vivid to be relegated as a mere impression. Trembling with the impact of what he saw, Thunderbird recounted Hawkins' long, white hair, the gentle gray eyes, the tanned and wrinkled skin. He searched the wiry frame, acknowledged its wisdom, the spirit with which it was imbued. He laughed, delighted that Hawkins still lived inside him, sharing his trek to the Western Sea.

187

And among his fondest memories came those of the desert. Too often life on the outside, away from his home, had led him to failure, disgusted him with its trite complexities. It forced him to wish for more than he had once ever expected, creating frustration when less was delivered. Not much of anything outside the desert appealed to even his minimum expectations. Upon this frequent realization Thunderbird found himself increasingly depressed. Certainly there was something available to relieve him of his spiritual decline. Limbo was made for the languid, not for the active such as he.

When he at last reached the northern cities, Thunderbird took his usual sequence of odd jobs, each one more demeaning than the last. Desperate for a change of pace, relief from the mundane conditions by which he found himself surrounded, he joined Ardmore St. James' Wild West Show. Naturally, Thunderbird portrayed one of the numerous blood-curdling Indians. The show toured through many cities, stopping in the smaller towns where public reaction always seemed greater than that in the larger cities. Even so, despite the arduous pace by which the show travelled, it wasn't able to meet its bills. St. James' socialite name couldn't sustain the creditors any longer, and the Wild West Show folded abruptly, stranding its participants in central New Jersey.

"What do we do now," sobbed Florine Divinci, a gypsy woman posing as an Indian princess in the Wild West Show. She also served as the assistant to Elmer Langer, the trick knife thrower. Hers was considered one of the most hazardous tasks, since Langer was a reputed alcoholic. "I never yet stuck my helper," he'd brag to anyone who'd listen. Few did.

"Nothing much we can do," muttered the forlorn Thunderbird Hawkins, his ass planted beside the railroad tracks. "Find a job somewhere, an' start over again."

Moved by his honesty, Florine sat down beside the former

blood-curdling Indian. In a few moments her gypsy ways enabled her to elicit easy responses from him. They talked for several hours, speculated on the misery of their futures, at last deciding to head off together, forming a fortune-telling partnership in a Jersey ocean resort.

"If we dress you right," proposed Florine, "we could pose you as a gypsy and open ourselves a business. Take tourists for whatever they're worth."

"I don't know. There's so little I know about gypsy life."

Florine smiled, resting her hand on Thunderbird's leg. She rubbed his thigh, attempting to arouse his senses. At last he turned to her. "Whatta ya think I knew," she laughed heartily. "I used to work in a bakery in Brooklyn."

"Where's Brooklyn?" wondered Hawkins.

"It doesn't matter. Only another state of mind."

His senses placated, and taking full note of Florine's heaving bosom, Thunderbird finally agreed to a trial partnership. Her dark eyes, thick thighs, big breasts and wide ass were simply too much to refuse. At once he would've traversed the world on a tightrope had she but offered him a mere taste of her womanly virtues. "What about the knife thrower?" he asked reluctantly.

"He drinks too much," scoffed Florine. "You'd better not drink too much, or I'll cut your throat."

"I don't drink much at all."

"Good. Cuz' drinkin' men are more affectionate wit' their whiskey than wit' d'ere women. Unnerstan'?"

"Sure. When do we get started?"

Florine smiled, arousing Hawkins' most protective instincts. "As soon as you steal us a horse."

Throughout the night Thunderbird prowled the town in search of a decent horse and buggy. Most were kept under lock and key, a most discouraging predicament. But at last he came upon an old swayback mare and an ancient buggy. More rusted than paint, the buggy squealed like a beaten demon when he attempted to wheel it from the farmer's

189

yard. The noise panicked Hawkins, making him wish Florine preferred hopping freight trains. But she had refused, claiming she'd rather travel in style. Some style, he muttered, believing the farmer would be relieved to discover the rig was missing.

Just as he justified his act, the first shot rang out over Hawkins' head. Fortunately the farmer had only a shotgun, and the range was too great for him to do any harm. Hawkins scrambled like a coolie, leading the horse away by the reins he held in his teeth. Further up the rode he paused to attach the horse to the buggy. He then raced to town over the torn and pot-holed road, hoping to pick up Florine before the farmer had aroused the countryside.

"We'd best get out of here," he yelled to Florine, who had been standing impatiently by the railroad stop.

"In that you want me to travel?" responded the indignant Florine Divinci. "Dat thing? You must be crazy!"

Hawkins had no time to argue. He jumped from the buggy and loaded Divinci's things. "Will you get in, woman, before it's too late?"

"Some thief. You steal a man's garbage. Dis is junk. Gypsies do not ride in junk."

Unable to tolerate her continued ravings, Hawkins lifted the kicking Florine and deposited her inside the buggy. He climbed upside and drove off, picking up too much speed for her to jump to freedom.

"I'll scratch your eyes out for dis," she howled. "One night, when you're sleeping, you'll wake up wit' no ice," she said, pronouncing eyes in her most severe of gypsy accents. Her taloned fingernails were offered as evidence.

By the time they reached the Jersey seacoast, Florine's anger had diminished considerably. She joined Thunderbird for a walk to the edge of a jetty. They sat down in silence, taking in midnight impressions of the sea. Foam-capped waves were just barely perceptible in the full moonlight. Waves rolled against the jetty, misting their faces.

190

"I like this," admitted Thunderbird.

"Not much like the desert. Eh, Indian?"

"Much like the desert."

"The desert is dry. This is wet, fool. I may be a gypsy, but I'm certainly no one's fool."

"The desert is massive. So is the sea. They both offer hope, a light beckoning from the distance."

"Paha, there is no hope in the desert. Only sand."

"In the ocean, too, there is also sand. Lying beneath the water."

"But on the desert there is no water."

"There is. Lying beneath the sand."

"Indian. You are crazy!"

"And you, gypsy. Tell us our fortune, before evening's pleasures fade away."

Florine turned upward, facing the full moon. She cupped its shape into the palm of her hands, expelling phrases as she moved her arms from side to side. She seemed entranced, her eyes glazed and blazing with the spirit of lunar tranquility.

"Gypsy, gypsy what do you see?"

"Faces and places, and the voice of a friend. He speaks of ships and sailors and battles for glory. He talks of plunder, a woman, a child and a song. In his words there is knowledge, in his eyes, wisdom."

"This man. What does he look like?"

"A smile in the shadows, passing forth like a sail without a ship. A traveller, hindered by conditions of space and time."

"His name? He must have a name."

"No name. But an expression. Hushed by the turbulence of the coming storm."

"What storm?"

"There!" shouted the gypsy as the first drops of rain fell upon her outstretched arm. A minute later a series of clouds burst upon them, drenching their skins. About the jetty the

191

ocean gurgled anxiously, attempting to climb from its mysterious bindings. The winds blew stronger, as lightning flashed from above.

"We best find a dry place," said Thunderbird.

"Yes, we should, shouldn't we?" smiled Florine, her magical arm draped across Hawkins' shoulder.

While the rain beat against the windows of their modest hotel room, Hawkins and Florine sat nude on the bed, drinking wine and smoking. They talked for many hours, pausing from conversation to make repeated love. On each occasion, Thunderbird entered Florine Divinci from a different position, often obeying what she demanded. They wrapped themselves tightly around each other, two spirits merging into one, breathing in unison while the fire in the fireplace chased the moisture from their skins.

Outside the ocean was churning, a vast agitation machine washing the stains from its own impeccable facade.

The Southern Mountain Range at last was behind them. The Western Sea lay ahead. In three days they had crossed the mountains at the junction where the peaks turned northward, separating the desert from the fertile plains. Around them the landscape was steadily transforming. Colors were darker, the increasing foliage assuming richer shades of green. The ground was moister, more earth than sand now, and clusters of wildflowers appeared on grassy knolls. Even the air was thicker, permeated with the fragrance of vegetation mixed with salt. Their trail led to Star City, along a rutted highway which carried them over sequences of hills, squirming through the different rock formations that stood in their path. Occasionally they sighted other travellers, who waved greetings or ignored them, preferring to keep their chins on their chests when they passed the two companions.

"I wish we'd get there already," moaned Shelby Lopez, his ass and feet aching from the journey. "I could sit in a bath for days. Just to lie in a bed again ..."

Thunderbird ignored him. He crumbled leaves into the wooden pipe he had kept in reserve and offered it to Lopez. "This will lift your spirits. For life has been good to us during this journey. We've covered much ground and shared many things, including friendship."

Shelby was touched by Hawkins. "I've never been this close with any man," he confessed. "Rebecca, Lana, they were the only ones I've ever cared about. And Rebecca's dead and Lana's been missing for years. So now there's only you."

Thunderbird's hand came down on Lopez's shoulder. He clasped him firmly and then let go, smiling as he retrieved his arm. "Our friendship has been tempered in the best of manners. We've learned to share instead of justifying our existence by stealing from that of another."

"It would be stupid. When there is so much to be achieved between us."

"It's not of our choosing, but that of the elements, the forces which surround us. The spirits, scattering souls to the corners of infinity, where they are swept together by the hands of God. All becomes everyone and everyone becomes all."

Shelby stared down at the pipe. He was bewildered. "And then what?"

"The spirits? They channel our destinies, filter our thoughts. They applaud our prowess, our awareness, and laugh at our foolishness. Spirits are always understanding, but rarely are they ever sympathetic."

"They must do a lot of laughing among themselves."

Thunderbird agreed. "At times you can hear them. In the

193

trickling of a brook, or within a pile of hay. When the leaves rustle they are sighing. When the skies roar they are angry. When the rain falls they are weeping."

Embarrassed, Shelby laughed at the rantings of his companion. "I think the smoke has gone to your head."

Hawkins knocked the ashes from the pipe and pulled his blanket around him. A buzz filled his ears, his lips were dry. He considered a swig of water, decided to let it go. He pressed his tongue to his dry, cracked lips for confirmation. His hand was stretched before him, his eyes exploring its shape. He was reminded of Florine Divinci, recalled all the hands he examined in the name of telling fortunes. Some of the predictions he had made appeared to him. Hawkins laughed, again recalling the series of scams in which he and the gypsy woman had engaged. The contour of Florine's swollen bust made him tingle down below. He would gladly pay a handsome ransom to have another go at her copious buttocks. The sound of her voice lingered within him.

"We do well together. No?"

The tips of his fingers traced the lines of her face. Eagerly he would've spent the rest of his life in bed with her, vowing never to leave her side until he was a corpse. But time was money then, during that one brief season when tourists flocked to their door, spending vacation money to hear their fortunes told. Later they would dip into their savings, relinquishing hard-earned money to rid themselves of the different curses Florine Divinci swore had been placed upon them.

"Evil will befall you and your family," she'd say in her most mysterious manner. "You must do as I say."

And most of them would do it. Nothing worse than a gypsy's curse. The profits mounted, enabling the couple to move to new and better locations. Each place was fancier, more luxurious than the last. Soon they were living in the best hotel, running their business from a shop located on the most prestigious street in town. Still, they could barely meet their expenses. Florine's lavish spending saw to that. It seemed they were always in debt, a bill owed here or there. A few more scams, a series of fortunes, and they were back on their feet, just making ends meet before the end of the month ran out.

"We should really put some aside," warned Thunderbird.

Florine would hear none of it. "Nonsense, Indian. Only a fool saves his money. He will put it away, to return to find it stolen. We must spend it, freely, without a care for the coming days."

"What about the future?"

Florine smiled wickedly. "The future, my friend, is no concern of mine."

Then one day the tourists came no more. Perhaps word had spread through town that the fortune-telling shop on the most prestigious street in town was nothing but a hoax. Perhaps the season was over. Then again, Hawkins often wondered, had not some stranger entered their establishment and placed a curse of his own upon their business? No answer ever seemed to include a solution to the many questions Hawkins held in mind. Some things, even barely perceptible issues, were left to speculation.

With each passing day, the partners lapsed into further stages of poverty. Their credit ran out, and they were forced from one hotel to the next. Their establishment was removed to a location on the edge of a commercial pier. A small shop it was, made of wood and tin. A potbellied stove was their only source of heat. Located on the very tip of the pier, the shop was always cold, and the dark draperies and a dim candlelight added a somber texture to the atmosphere. The tougher it became to survive, the darker was the one bare room they used for living space. Eventually even Hawkins couldn't free himself from the gripping moroseness. Futile was his attempt to escape from the sullen conditions created by their new mode of living. Florine and Thunderbird grew to hate each other, as they did the conditions of

195

their surroundings. To make matters worse, winter crept into the ocean town, covering the boardwalk, the beaches and the empty streets with a blanket of snow. The meager, wood-burning stove vainly attempted to throw back the cold, but its task was impossible.

"We should leave," said Hawkins. "And return with the season."

Florine lifted her head toward her partner, revealing the most lugubrious of expressions. "There is nothing to leave, nothing to gain," she chanted wearily. "We rot while we sit. If our lives together were meant to be different, we would've been south by now, a wad of money in our hands."

Thunderbird shivered, listened to the wind churning outside. Through the frosted windowpane he observed the rippling water. He was chilled by the mere suggestion of the ocean's presence. Time and again he wished he was back on the desert. Impressions of the midday desert sun offered him slight consolation.

"Maybe it's over between us," offered Florine Divinci, interrupting his thoughts. Her hands trembled when she tried to bring the cup of soup to her lips. "For some time I have thought such thoughts," she continued, pausing to touch the wrinkles in her face. "You are a traveller, but not a gypsy. We are almost too much the same, and yet we are so different."

"I'd hate to leave you," acknowledged Thunderbird, reminded of their efforts in bed.

"It would be like this," explained Florine, placing the palms of her hands together then pulling them apart. "No one leaving no one. Drifting away. A mutual separation. Believe me, Indian, there is much to be said for the harmony in separation."

"But where would you go?"

"I've said. To the south, where it's warm. But that's not for you to worry. For you must return to your home. Where you belong. The cities of the East are the dark spots in the palm of your hand. Little fortune waits in store for you. Not here. You belong beneath the heat of a midday sun, not trapped with a gypsy gripped by the winter's cold."

Thunderbird shuddered at the thought of being alone again. "I'll think it over," he promised hesitatingly.

"You do that!" cried Florine, her hand slamming down on the tabletop. Obviously she was annoyed. "I'm going for a walk."

"Shit!" cried Thunderbird after Florine had departed. He sat still in his chair, angrily observing the wood diminish inside the stove. He felt no desire to replace the logs, contenting himself to look at the room around him. He noted the seance table, the crystal ball resting on its top. He fondled the candelabra before turning back to the crystal ball, his attentions drawn to its center. Unwittingly he rubbed its surface, flicked it with his fingers and cursed what it had done to him. He was most surprised when a figure appeared before him, a slithering apparition, diaphanous before the winter sky. Hawkins the Hermit it was, floating above the table. Whisking about the room he conveyed the sounds of runners cutting through snow. Thunderbird was frightened, overcome by guilt.

"The Necklace," whispered Hawkins the Hermit. "Whatever became of the Necklace?"

Thunderbird lowered his eyes, trying to avoid the apparition. But the spirit quickly dove beneath his chair, appearing at his feet. The hermit demanded an answer.

"Gone," Thunderbird sadly admitted. "Gone forever. Lost among the confusions of my life."

The hermit shook his head sympathetically. "You've remembered so much, but practiced so little of what I once told you. You are not condemned to repeat the same mistakes of those who went before you, yet you follow suit. You've been whirled about, whipped into states of utter confusion. Off balance and befuddled, you've attempted to flee the horrors of the past. Blindly you've thrashed only . . ."

197

"Only what?"

"Only to find yourself in the wrong direction. Once again your course must be corrected by a hermit, an old pirate who only wishes to rest in peace. At long last, where the ocean converges against the shoreline."

"Where are you?" asked Thunderbird. "Where do you rest?"

"In the heart and soul of another. One who you must find."

"Where?"

The apparition, as if to demonstrate its dexterity, weaved in and out of the crystal ball, becoming concave and convex in accordance with the sphere's refractions. "From sea to shining sea," laughed the hermit, mimicking the patriotic.

"Florine! She put you up to this."

The hermit laughed his pirate's laugh, his hand resting on his translucent belly. "You knew so little about her. She too was an apparition, transfixed against the eyes of the forsaken."

Thunderbird argued. "She is a full, rich woman, complete in mind and body."

"Only a figment of the imagination, primed by the spirit of your own lack of decision."

"No. She is real and among us. I should know, for all the time we shared in bed."

"Among *us?*" laughed the hermit, heartier than before. "She was a fantasy. A sensation. A fleeting orgasm, dissolving as it happens. Passing through the system, spasmodically. And ... she will come no more. She's gone now, back to the source from which she first embarked."

Thunderbird stood out of his chair and traced a line through the frost on the windowpane. He stared out at the snow covering the beach before him. The ocean seemed rougher, more abusive then ever. He shuddered involuntarily, relieved finally by memories of his life first shared with Hawkins the Hermit. He remembered their cavern home, the crackling fires and the sounds of lizards rustling through the dried desert brush. There came the howl of the coyote, followed by the hissing of the snake. Cacti rose about him, as distant mountains were flushed with the violet of an aging day. When Thunderbird returned his attentions to the hermit's apparition, he felt relieved, less weary than he had been in ages.

"She will return," he insisted to the hermit.

Hawkins laughed his pirate's laugh again. "No. She served her purpose, only to bring you in sight of a better vision."

"I'll wait for her," Thunderbird insisted.

"While the Necklace waits for you. Do as you choose. You were always rather stubborn."

Thunderbird said nothing, but stood with his arms folded, watching Hawkins the Hermit propel himself about the shack like a whirling human comet. He observed the twists and bends of the apparition's supple movements, thinking it wouldn't be so bad to be a ghost. And then, as quickly as he appeared, the hermit was gone, his faded image sucked away as if by an invisible vacuum. Thunderbird removed himself to the cast-iron stove and awaited Florine Divinci's return. Hours passed, and she still hadn't made her appearance. Hawkins grew angry, glancing constantly at the table clock, their last valuable possession. Anger evolved into worry, and the ocean outside retreated into the blackness of nightfall.

Peering through the frosted window into the darkness meagerly punctuated by a few gaslit streetlamps, Hawkins imagined Florine returning. The fabricated clicking of her boots against the wooden pier floor aroused his sexuality, forced his dick to stiffen against his woolen pants. He longed for his ladyfriend, grew tired of his longing, and he began to justify her absence. "Dammit," he asked no one in particular, "where is she?"

By early morning Florine had still not returned. It was a

most unusual situation since, despite all she did on her own, Florine claimed preference for sleeping in her own bed at night. Thunderbird searched for another explanation, found none and fixed himself a fresh pot of coffee. His fingers trembled from the cold when he removed them from his blanket to set the pot on the stove. Beside him the clock ticked onward, its metronomic rhythm becoming more annoying with each passing second.

Returning to his chair, a cup of coffee in his hand, Thunderbird propped his feet on a nearby table and hummed to himself. He listened for the sound of footsteps but heard only the ocean rustling beneath the pier. When there was nothing else to do, Thunderbird recalled the better times, when business flourished. Tourists, students and their sweethearts had lined up before their parlor, listening intently, their eyes wide when they were rewarded for their wait by Florine's projections of coming times. Some became nervous, fearful of another breath, as if it might be their last. Others seemed satisfied, content to flirt with Florine Divinci, or, in some cases, give Thunderbird the eye. Others were set up for one of the partners' many scams.

The clock neared six, and dawn made its obligatory appearance. Hawkins was unnerved by its presence. In desperate search for consolation, Thunderbird was again struck by the words of the hermit's apparition. "While the Great Necklace waits for you," echoed in his mind. He was frightened, yet thankful the apparition had appeared before him.

"I'll always remember you," he whispered, unsure if his words were directed toward the hermit or to Florine Divinci. He then climbed from his chair and began his packing. Little was left that he cared to stuff into his leather bag. He looked around for additional belongings, just as the clock tolled seven. Hawkins was impressed by the comfort offered his mind by the seventh bong. He considered taking the clock along, but decided against it. He left it behind, its octagonal face looking out toward the ocean.

As gently as possible Thunderbird Hawkins closed the door behind him. He felt neither angry nor confused upon stepping out into the brisk morning chill. A sense of comfort embraced him, now that he had reached his decision. He would return to the desert. In all, the journey would last nearly two years. During that time Thunderbird would work odd jobs, again serving as the proverbial jack of all trades. Often, on his westward trek, he considered Florine Divinci and their fortune-telling parlor in the resort by the sea. He held neither remorse nor bitterness for the time they had shared together. It had been a joyous occasion to live with Florine Divinci. For she had been the last in a long line of efforts to seek relevant direction. Inadvertently, it was she who had shown him the way. And though her body was gone, dissipated, lost to the mystery of its source, her memory would always be lasting. So with mixed emotions Thunderbird Hawkins left the parlor, his retreating footsteps concealed by squealing freighters preparing to embark from the harbor.

Chapter 11

Belle Gluntz peeled back the draperies from the windows enclosing her third floor office suite and gazed out onto the street. She didn't like what she saw. Her eyes had traversed the sections of avenue until she found Big Ben standing before his Lost Hope Saloon, his hands clasped behind his back. His oily head shimmered beneath the sunlight, reflecting pointed, golden flashes against Belle's eyes. It pissed her off that even from a distance, unwittingly, the midget could annoy her.

"That greasy little fart," she cursed for Shmuel's benefit. Her brother was at his desk, seeing to his daily paperwork. "I could squat on his head, if the mood struck me. I'd love to ... shit down his collar and pat him on the back."

"Don't **aggravate** yourself," Shmuel warned in a typically brotherly **fashion**. "It's bad for your digestion."

"Little bastard," hissed Belle. "Only man I know who can bump his head against a horse's balls."

While Belle spoke, Crosly Finch appeared alongside his

midget boss. From the distance the two men seemed like matched twins, made from uneven amounts of raw materials. For both men were beetle-browed, wore their hair parted in the middle, dressed in three-piece suits, with golden watch chains attached from belt loop to pocket. Handlebar mustaches separated lips from noses, and their beady eyes darted about their faces. Finch, however, was much larger than Ben. Up closer, traces of his early life were revealed by the scars and lines in his face. He was pockmarked, dimpled and rutted, so his nasty puss resembled farmland after a lasting drought. A touch of red spotted one of his eyeballs, and a pie-wedged slice was carved from his left ear. His nose was twisted just above the nostrils, and a bald spot revealed where a splotch of hair had once been torn from the top of his head.

For many years Crosly Finch had been Big Ben's lieutenant, faithfully obeying the slightest wish and command of the midget boss. On drunken nights, when he strode about the Lost Hope Saloon, Finch lauded Ben's rescue of him from downtrodden days in the past when he served as a mere pug, performing his services for anyone with spare change. But all that had changed since he'd first been adopted by Ben. The midget dressed him, taught him at least the basics in manners and movements and then dubbed him with the title of vice president for Ben's multiplicity of enterprises.

"I love that lil' feller," Finch shouted for all in the Lost Hope to hear. "He pulled me from tough times, he did. Damn good to me. Made me a vice president an' everythin'. An' lookit dis. Just lookit it. A hand-tailored, custom-vested suit. Ju' for me."

"Very nice," acknowledged the barfly Finch had confronted. "Lovely."

Satisfied, Finch then stalked onward, rambling on about his blind loyalty to Ben, pausing between words to slap the dancehall girls across the rump. "I'd kill for the man." And many times he had done so, exercising a variety of methods. Crosly was feared by many and loved by none. Yet no one ever dared face him down and lived to discuss it. Years passed and Crosly Finch endured assassination attempts, free-for-alls and numerous power conflicts. He survived, his right arm raised triumphantly, used without thought or consideration for personal consequence as if it was attached to Big Ben himself.

"I met him in Abilene," Ben often bragged of his finding Crosly. "He was down on his luck, living in shantytown, in a house made from trash and castaway crates. I was passing through, returning from business in the East, when I found him. I fed him, cleaned him and generally restored his health. He owes his life to me. Otherwise, he'd be little more than another forgotten pug, washed away by whiskey and time."

No one ever refuted Ben's story. No one dared. All eyes were cast in Big Ben's direction, attentive to every word the midget ever had to say. His cockney accent, through years of living in the West, had assumed a slight western drawl. His voice was a strange mixture of the old and the new, the inherent and the adopted. His inflections were especially effective when he became angry and his voice heated to a steam-laden shriek. Hands went to ears, covering up the terrible sound. Even the toughest of gunmen, Lorenzo Stokes and Kip Kearney, yielded to Ben's angry admonitions.

Big Ben always carried a walking stick, his mark of status. A derringer was concealed in its handle, always ready for use. On numerous occasions Ben had been threatened with his end, until the famed derringer emerged from concealment, killing the foolish assailant. But such challenges to his person had diminished through the years. Big Ben was by now the undisputed baron of Star City. The respectable townsfolk, despite their rhetorical speeches for law and order and even a little sanity in their town, allowed Big Ben to continue with his ownership of a good portion of the town. Besides the notorious Lost Hope Saloon, Ben owned a series of restaurants, theaters, distilleries and a short-haul freight line. Money just poured into his stubby little hands. In the town of Star City, even the simplest of fools, the grandest of drunkards, fully understood that absolutely no one fucked around with Big Ben.

All that changed when Belle Gluntz arrived in town. The local political flaks, the respected business community and the clandestine vigilante brigades had good reason to rub their eyes in disbelief. For in a matter of days she had accomplished what all others had failed. Belle Gluntz had stood up to Big Ben.

Dressed in a brocaded cape, a velvet dress and wide-brimmed hat, Belle Gluntz stepped from the Alaskan Queen, her acting troupe in formation behind her. Twenty of them in all, comprising a versatile mixture of performers, including jugglers, acrobats, dramatic and comedic actors, dancers and singers, had taken leave of the frozen North country to resettle in Star City. The Sno' Fuck Follies, the troupe was called, a transposition of the expression "fuckin' snow" often used by the miners in the frozen wastes. Up the street the Follies marched, banging drums, tumbling, juggling, singing and parading for all of Star City. Eyes were upon them from everywhere as they paraded, deftly avoiding the spittle and horseshit that lay in the streets.

Big Ben was also watching the spectacle. Increasingly irritated, he demanded to know of his lieutenants why he wasn't apprised of the invasion. "You mean they can just walk up and down my streets as if they belong here?"

"No one knew nuthin' about it," Kip Kearney insisted.

Ben wasn't listening. The vision of such shapely ladies and refined gentlemen all combined into an extraordinarily talented troupe of performers had become too much for him. Especially when he compared the Sno' Fuckers to his own band of toilet jokers, tit wagglers and cunt croupiers, who lifted silver dollars from the tables with the lips of their snatches.

"What the hell's going on here?" he shrieked. "See who they are, where they came from. Find out what their price is. I'll buy them out, I will. And if they refuse, I'll gun them down."

Crosly Finch joined his boss by the window. "See that lady, the fat one? She runs the show. Came down from Alaska, for the change of climate. Big stuff up 'ere."

"She won't stay here. Not alive, anyway. Can't have no woman fuckin' up my act. Before they settle too comfortably, we'll pay 'm a visit."

A few days later Ben, accompanied by Crosly Finch, accosted Belle inside her new combination saloon and cabaret theater. It was part of a compound she had purchased from a real estate broker who failed to warn her of Ben's domination of all entertainment within the limits of Star City. For a mere couple of thousand dollars, Belle had purchased the saloon and the entire L-shaped compound, including the hotel and livery stable. The entire complex was surrounded by high stucco walls and would be used to house her Sno' Fuckers as well as serve as a showcase for their entertainment. Naturally, Belle Gluntz was thrilled to have purchased it for so little money.

"It's a damn good buy," she assured Lemon Lime, her assistant and the creative director of the Sno' Fuck Follies. "We'll call it the Alaskan Queen, for my precious Micha."

A day later the trademark sign was erected over the saloon. "The Alaskan Queen," the sign announced in silver script. Beneath the lettering stood a facsimile of a grizzled miner in drag. His bearded wrinkled face protruded from a tight, sequined dancehall dress. A beauty mark was penciled on his cheek and lipstick highlighted his mouth. He smiled suggestively, luring potential customers toward the entrance placed beneath his bowed and hairy legs. Big Ben and Crosly Finch were the first outsiders to walk beneath the sign.

"I want you out of here," Ben demanded, before Belle had even a chance to react. "This is my town, and it ain't big enough for both of us."

"Anything, pisher, is big enough for you. So mind your manners before I snub you out in my ashtray," warned Belle, indicating a nearby container of sand.

Ben was too surprised to speak. He stammered, befuddled, looking to Finch to gauge the big man's reaction. Finch's mouth hung slack with astonishment. Enraged now, Ben moved forward, ready to take a swing at Belle.

"Try it," hissed Belle, "and I'll scratch your fuckin' eyes out."

Exasperated, Ben stepped back and muttered inaudibly. "So what's this about you setting up a theater in my town?" he quizzed in a softer voice.

"That's just what it is, a theater. We're feeding people a taste o' class, instead of the garbage you've been serving over at your place."

Surreptitiously, Ben slid his hand toward his notorious derringer. He was halted abruptly by a cry from Jason, Belle Gluntz's longtime bartender. Jason had a shotgun pointed straight at the midget's belly. "Try it, man," warned Jason.

Belle laughed, gloating over the midget's reaction. "Jason used to work in the circus shooting cigarettes out of mouths. Ever see him miss?"

To back her up, Jason raised the gun higher, so it was pointed at Ben's greasy head. "There's one for you and one for your ugly friend."

Ben sucked air between his teeth, curling and uncurling his fingers. Finch remained beside him, bewildered by the sudden change in events. Even he was not about to tangle with a shotgun held point-blank at his head. His body trembling, Ben backed for the door, Crosly alongside him. He stood in the entrance for several moments, glancing about the saloon. "I'll be back," he warned ominously.

"It's two bucks in advance an' three at the door," laughed Jason.

"You'll be sorry for this."

"Listen, pisher," growled Belle. "It'll take more than you to force me down."

"I have more than me."

"Then you best keep it inside your pants before it gets away."

"Cow cunt!"

"Rat dick greaseball."

"I think we have some troubles," Belle admitted once Ben and Crosly had departed.

Jason agreed. "He's a-goin' to give us trouble. I kin jus' feel it in mah bones."

Belle nodded toward the aging black man and ruminated in silence over her projected course of action. She thanked Shmuel for being there, giving practical advice. She smiled at the thought of her twin brother, a man she hadn't seen in ages. Not since she had escaped from Poor Yussel's Home for the Insane Aged had Belle communicated with Shmuel. She missed him. They had always been close. Last she had heard, Shmuel was down South, starting afresh as a carpetbagger. Why he had fled from the city was only one of many secrets she had shared with him over the years. But as if God willed it, Shmuel appeared. He was always there when she needed him. Always. Especially in a town like Star City, one so laden with felony, vice and discord, Shmuel could hardly resist it. To Shmuel, life in Star City was a home away from home. A terrible standard of living.

"Where's Lemon?" Belle asked of Jason. The bartender shrugged his shoulders and resumed his stocking the bar. They would be opening the saloon in just a few days, and the whiskey had only arrived.

"When you see her, tell her I'd like to talk."

"Sure thing. D't crazy Lemon ain't gonna let no midget push her aroun'. Too much starch for dat nonsense. She'll cut his throat wit' dat big ol' knife a' hers."

"I hope so," replied Belle, retreating from the dust particles apparent in the sunbeam. Little could she predict the series of robberies, muggings and brutal beatings of her Sno' Fuck performers. Everywhere they went they were accosted by Ben's men. The women were raped, the men nearly killed. By the end of the month it was increasingly clear to Belle Gluntz that the situation was far out of hand. Little she could do in retaliation for Ben's vicious acts. She lacked the manpower. Even her own strength, the vitality of her pirate's spirit, had waned through the years. The roughness of Alaska, and now this. Having little recourse, Belle went to court, aided by George Maltesin, the one-armed lawyer. He was the only attorney in town with the balls to brush against Big Ben's power. But even his principles and legal expertise were applied in vain. The court was packed with Big Ben's paid employees.

"This is an outrage," shouted George Maltesin, his one arm waving at the judge. "This is no courtroom, but an alleyway, covered by the stench of graft and human garbage. And you, suh, are no judge, but a contemptible figure of corruption."

Impassively, the judge studied Maltesin's missing arm. "And you, lawyer, have no sense of enterprise. A man, an impoverished midget, comes to this town, penniless, a dream in his eye. Through hard work and years of experience he builds an empire, which you insist should be taken from his hands."

"You defile the very system you claim to enforce," retorted George Maltesin. "This is not free enterprise but travesty ruinous to the fabric of this country."

"It may even pull the wool over your eyes," roared the judge, amused by his pun. The courtroom laughed along with him. Once again Ben had packed the gallery with a mass of obnoxious slobs. "Nevertheless," continued His Honor, "I am the judge, and as the judge I rule deliberations between your represented party and that of Big Ben is not within my legal jurisdiction. All litigation will have to rest until the higher courts agree to a hearing."

"And when will that be?"

"A year. Perhaps."

"But people have been murdered, abused of their rights."

Laughter erupted behind Maltesin's final plea. "There will be more, I'm sure," replied the judge, once the noise had died down. "If I were you, I'd advise your client to leave this town for territory where she'll be free from adversity."

"And where would that be?"

"Mr. Maltesin. In case you haven't noticed, I am a judge, not a clairvoyant."

"I'm sorry we ever came here," Belle admitted to Jason, when the courtroom was adjourned.

"Can't beat it. Even if it belongs to a midget. I guess maybe we should move on."

"Maybe."

"It would break Maltesin's heart though. You know the way he loves defending lost causes."

"A mensch," Belle agreed. "Believe me, he'd be better off without this aggravation. Poor thing that he is. All those years in a prison camp, with no food, no medical attention, not even a crossword puzzle. Worked in the mills for nothing, his one arm bandaged above the elbow."

"Jus' like a slave," moaned Jason.

"We're all slaves. Held captive by our own dying animal."

"Huh?"

"A line from an old play. One of the few roles where I didn't play the floozie. A heart-rendering production with no commercial appeal. I should know, I was having an affair with its creator. Poor Simon. The production opened on a

Monday, folded on Tuesday. By Thursday Simon killed himself, leaving behind a long, heart-wrenching letter. Oy, I'm tellin' you, such sadness. Wouldn't you know, a third party finds the letter and sets it to music. It becomes the hit of the year. Made three actors famous. I had to settle for a bit role in the chorus. Nothing much. A bare living. The dead playwright ... I could never guess what his reaction could be. Anyway, the program gave him partial credit. From a story inspired by, it said. Poor Simon. We are all slaves, held captive by our own dying animal. He'd stand in the middle of cafeterias and spout off lines like this. Scare the hell outta the luncheon crowd."

Later, in the safety of her apartment above the old saloon, Belle Gluntz kicked off her shoes and thought of happier times. She remembered her fortunate escape from Poor Yussel's and her trek to Alaska. Why Alaska? everyone had asked her. Even now she didn't know the answer. Yet it was in Alaska where she met Micha Petrusky, a kindly old man who spoke of his grandchildren like they were idols of the ancient civilizations. Bearded, wrinkled and prone to over-sized clothing, which he stuffed with rags for added warmth, the old boy was immediately taken with Belle Gluntz, whom he followed about the muddy streets like a sex-starved adolescent. Belle enjoyed his attentions, grateful that a man still cared for her womanly charms. The pouch of gold he had hidden beneath his rags was only incidental to her.

Micha Petrusky had been a miner, a lucky one who had struck a modest vein of gold quite by accident. Before he met Belle, and her cameo face found room in his heart, he had squandered much of what he had at the many gaming tables and women of the streets. He was a lonely old man and was known to pay handsomely for companionship. Yet he always remained proud of his mining skills, swearing it was better than serving dead meat to annoying customers. Once he had been a butcher, until he renounced his vocation for the fortunes to the north.

211

"I'm closing up shop," he informed his customers after several hard weeks of deliberation. "I'm going off to seek gold in Alaska."

"Ridiculous. You'll never make it," was the most constant response from friends and acquaintances. Everyone felt compelled to reveal their opinions.

"You'll be back in a month. You know how cold it is up there? Prices are so expensive. Know what they charge for a loaf o' bread?"

Petrusky knew little about the secondary considerations involved with his journey. What he did know was that adventure and even riches lay in waiting. For an aging butcher, that was all that was necessary for him to sell his butcher's shop, purchase a heavy coat, supplies, pick, shovel and mining pan, and set out from Washington State on the Alaskan Queen. For years he dug alongside the multitudes, finding little more than a few nuggets. Barely enough to keep him alive. Time had exhausted his energies. He had aged well beyond his middle years and found his determination flagging. At last Micha Petrusky decided to give it up, find a job somewhere cutting meat again. Perhaps he could work in a delicatessen. It would be less responsibility than running his own shop. With tears in his eyes he slumped down into a mound of snow. No sense in going on, he told himself. Exhaustion, blisters and a leathery skin were all he had to show for his years of effort. His head clasped in his hands, he lay against the mound of snow, overwhelmed by his desolation. Then, quite suddenly, he found something hard hidden beneath the snow mound. He scratched at the surface, growing more excited as he threw the snow behind him. After digging for several feet he discovered the body of another miner, his shovel still clasped in his hands. Micha attempted to remove the man, but found he wouldn't budge.

"Dammit! Just me an' a dead man," he cried out to the

barren valley. He listened for his echo but it didn't return. Strange, thought Micha. Ever since he had first explored this empty valley, his echo had always returned to him. He had passed many days of his solitude arguing with the rebound of his very own voice.

"Christ," he attempted, but the words refused to form. His vocal cords were seized by some inexplicable paralytic force. His lips were frozen, locked in place by something other than cold. He placed the blame on the corpse of the miner, pounding through outrage its protruding rear end. It was not until he calmed down that Micha Petrusky noticed the glistening beneath the snow. He passed his nose over the ground, sniffing for explanation.

"Gold!" he shouted, surprised his voice was again operable. "Dammit to hell, it's gold!"

For over a year Micha Petrusky milked the claim for all it was worth. He worked night and day, storing his treasure in a hidden cave. Never once did he let on to other miners or the land claims office that he had struck it rich. When his time ended, and he had enough gold to last him in case he lived forever, Micha Petrusky called it a day. He would enjoy his riches before he died. Already he had sensed his heart had weakened from the strain of grueling work and solitude. It was time to return to town.

He spent the next few months gambling and whoring about town. Never did he admit he had struck it rich, claiming he had a modest find and could barely afford the vices he was fond of. It was in a small cabaret, a little joint on the edge of town, that he first met Belle Gluntz.

"You are my sunshine," he toasted her one winter's day. His glass was raised to her health.

"Then let me shed my light on thee," she smiled back. Micha was touched by her answer.

"Want to see pictures of my grandchildren?" he asked the waitress, his hand nervously scratching his ashen beard.

Belle accepted the wilted photos. The creases and stains made the images barely recognizable. A boy and two darling girls there were, all smiling at the camera.

"What are their names?" Belle asked, catching Micha off his guard.

"No one ever asked me their names before," he admitted. "No one. All they ever do is say 'that's nice' and ask how I'll keep them warm."

Belle was moved by the miner's honesty. He was no ordinary miner, this Micha Petrusky, for, despite his age, he was still much in touch with his deepest affections. She sat down beside him and began a conversation that was to last for many years. In time they became a couple, moved into a finely constructed home in the best sector of town. The house had gabled windows and a long runway for visitors to wipe mud from their boots. They lived in reclusive harmony, happy to relate to each other's stories of their pasts.

Micha was impressed with Belle's early career in the theater. Time and again she'd recite her stories, causing the miner to laugh into his soup.

"They'd become so enraged they'd throw shoes at me," smiled Belle, "Always one. Never a pair."

Petrusky laughed and rubbed against his ladyfriend. He still found her flesh to be soft and receptive. Occasionally, when weather and physical circumstances permitted, they made love in their giant feather bed. It was on such occasions Micha wished they had met earlier in life, exchanging fish-eyed glances over a tender leg of lamb.

"I have a confession," Micha announced one day. He trembled with apprehension.

"What is it?" asked Belle in her gentlest tone of voice.

"About my grandchildren."

"Are they sick?"

"No. They're not even mine. I made them up. With a picture I found in the wilderness. I took it at first as a keepsake. But after a while . . . a man must have something to leave behind."

Belle closed her eyes in sympathy. All too well she understood. Clucking her tongue with inspiration, she reached in her handbag and removed a photograph of Shelby Lopez. "He's my nephew," she told him for the first time. "You can share him with me."

"Is he a good boy?"

"A very good boy. Good-looking too. Must be handsomer now. Been so terribly long since I've seen him. But here, take this picture. Show him off as your own. To anyone you chance to meet."

Micha's eyes filled with delight. He imagined the ladies who lived in the saloons drooling over his new nephew. His sister's boy. Yes, he'd like that very much. Inspirational to have a beer.

"Maybe we should find him . . . send him some money?"

"One day he'll find us."

"For me there's not too many days left, I'm afraid. This," he claimed, patting his chest. "It's no good anymore. Soon it'll stop beating, and I'll be dead. My money goes to you."

"Micha, you're crazy."

"Death doesn't wait for crazy men either. It'll be right there on schedule. Just like the Alaskan Queen. Fine ship that she is. Brought me to riches and love, it did. When all I possessed was dead meat and freezers. I wish to die on the finest berth."

Belle attempted to laugh it off. "You and your Alaskan Queen. Maybe you should buy it and sail her in your bathtub."

"No. She belongs at sea, outshining the ice floes that wait in her path."

"Don't talk foolishly. You're not about to die."

Despite Belle's insistence, Micha refuted her claim. "We'll

215

see. By the next time the Alaskan Queen comes to port. We'll see."

True to his wishes, Micha Petrusky died in the finest berth aboard the Alaskan Queen. Belle had paid the captain in advance to postpone departure for three whole days. With Micha beside her, weakened and coughing, she boarded the ship.

"Where to, sir?" asked the captain, pretending nothing was wrong.

Micha regarded the man with his sad brown eyes. "Where I'm going can hardly be determined by the price of a ticket," he wearily responded.

Grief-stricken from Micha's demise, Belle turned to the theater to free her from her bereavement. She hoped the activity would rechannel her commitment to living. This time she shunned acting, preferring the organizational activities of the producer to actual performance on stage. She would hardly be convincing as an aging floozy, even if she cared to affect that pretension. In time she mustered the Sno' Fuck Follies, organizing the finest bunch of performers the north country had to offer. With the assistance of Lemon Lime, who had wandered into town from parts unknown, Belle established a local theater. Jugglers, dancers, singers, actors and acrobats performed on her stage. Soon the Follies received praise from every station. Even the Eastern papers lauded the originality of the performers. The Sno' Fuck Follies went on tour, filling houses all over the northwestern part of the country.

Yet, in the late night hours, after each performance, Belle Gluntz returned to her hotel alone. A bottle of scotch was set on the table, with one empty glass. With her aching feet propped on the plush settee, Belle remembered the times she had had in her life. Sadness and joy intermittently exchanged places in her mind. And as the evening wore on, faded into morning, she dreamed of Micha Petrusky, the ex-butcher who had struck it rich in the Alaskan gold fields.

Her heart fluttered with the rapture of his memory. She laughed, noting the irony of it all. She had known so many men in her life. Politicians, prophets and pricks. They flashed before her, their images like boxcars on a pounding freight train, encircling space like a garland of love, a memorial wreath of past opportunities, at last coming to rest on top of the grave of Micha Petrusky.

Chapter 12

Shmuel Gluntz regarded his sister with compounded respect and sympathy. The end of his pencil tapped aimlessly against the papers he had stacked on his desk. He was hardly aware of the constant sound, for Shmuel was studying his sister's profile, remembering the features as they once were, more elastic with better definition, unhindered by age and added flesh. The tissue had softened, hung from her face in places that had once been the highlights of her gorgeous profile. Her hair had been cut for practicality, no longer worn so the curling tresses fell upon her shoulders. Still, in certain moments, when Belle was lost in thoughts, her tongue curled and twisted around her mouth ever so delicately, elevating such innocent movements to new plateaus in sensuality. Shmuel laughed, considering if there had been some genetic transposition during his mother's period of gestation, he would've been Belle and she would've been born her younger brother.

Belle was older. By two minutes. As children it was a point Belle would use to her advantage. Two precious minutes became a standard of rank, a means of leverage to win her way during their frequent sibling arguments. Being two full minutes older, she was able to take command, have final say on any matters she deemed important, whether it be who received the new pair of shoes or the last piece of chocolate cake. Yet despite all his protests, Shmuel never minded his sister's advantage. For he alone knew he would've allowed her the choice even if she lacked the two minutes of birth time to hold over his head.

"Do you love me like a sister?" she used to tease him. "Or is there more than meets the eye?"

Shmuel flushed, his fingernails scratching at the cement of the sidewalk. He shook his head, concealing the widening of his eyes. "No," he'd lie to her. "You're just a sister to me."

"Oh come now. I must be more than a sister. With all the time you spend with me."

Usually he refused to answer. How could he possibly admit to his sister that her image was so strong in his mind that she'd become the standard to which all other women were compared? "No," he claimed, after an adequate lapse in their conversation had passed. "You're just a sister. A simple sister to me."

With the passing of years an extraordinary closeness had developed between the twins. Their interdependence was astounding. Shmuel appeared as Belle's most frequent escort, always presenting her with flowers and corsages. He traversed the city many times in order to view her performances.

"Boo, hiss," the audience shouted, much to Shmuel's dismay.

"Stupid bastards! What do they know of talent? Of theater?" Shmuel's face was purple, his mind surging with plots of vengeance. "She should be a star, not wasting her

219

time before these simple goons. The press, critics, elegant gentlemen should be calling on her every night. She should be a lady in waiting."

"Waiting for what?" Belle laughed at her brother's suggestions. "For the world to pass me by? Believe me, there're worse ways to make a living. I could've been scrubbing floors or taking in laundry."

"You'd never scrub floors. Not while I'm alive."

"Uh huh. Just be thankful Mother preferred the theater to three square meals a day. Otherwise . . ."

"What?"

"It all would've been different. Where are you going tonight, anyway?"

"Out."

"Oh. The natural thief is at it again. I thought we were going to slacken the pace this month. Getting more silver for Mother, I suppose. Already she has silverware for an army and tea sets galore. All with different initials. The other day she threatened to take them to the silversmith, so he could change the initials."

Shmuel was alarmed. "What did you tell her?"

"I said it was much too expensive. Besides, her good son Shmuel would gladly do it for her. Won't you?"

"Certainly."

"That's awfully nice of you . . . good son that you are."

"I take it you were over there."

"Yes. Last night. Mother had a cough. She wanted me to come have a listen."

"And . . . ?"

"I can hardly tell her what it is. Poor thing. She loses any more weight and we could bury her in a soap box. I feel so bad."

"And Sarah?"

"As usual. Sitting in the corner, won't say a word. Sucks her fingers and stares at you from the corner of her eye.

Strange girl. Mother asks and answers for her. So tell me. When are you moving from the basement?"

Shmuel allowed a brief laugh to pour from his mouth. So strange, Belle was. One minute she'd discuss her mother's tuberculosis, and the next she'd be chastising Shmuel for living in his basement flat. He had lived there for nearly five years now and had no intention of moving. Why could never be explained. Certainly there was little to behold from beneath the street, with the exception of the ladies' feet, scuffing about the sidewalk as they shopped for produce in the market next door. Since he had lived there, Shmuel had grown to know all his female neighbors by their shoe styles and the shapes of their legs. Hardly much to desire, since hard work and large families had added flab and varicose veins. Nevertheless, Shmuel remained in his basement dwelling, unrecognized by all but those who travel at night.

"So? Why don't you move from there?" Belle urged again.

"I'm safe there."

"From what?"

"My own depression. When I feel blue at least I know I can't leap from my window."

Belle refused to laugh, making Shmuel nervous. "You'd just better be careful. You'd look like hell with bars on your face. Bad for your complexion, which is bad enough as it is, considering the life you live."

His head nodding wearily, Shmuel removed a wad of bills from his pocket. "Here. Give this to Mother. Tell her to take Sarah and go out of town for awhile. Down to the beach. The sun would do her good."

After she had stashed the money in her bag, Belle regarded her brother with the deepest expression she could muster. "You're all right, you are," she said, bending to kiss him on the cheek. "You just be careful tonight. You hear?"

Choked by his unrequited passion, Shmuel didn't answer as he made for the door. An hour later he had entered the house of Giles Havelock, ambitious city politician. Already Havelock was on the city council and was bucking for the mayor's office. Even the opposition party claimed the portly Havelock stood a very good chance, considering his strong-arm tactics and voter manipulations. It was no secret that he had the entire south side of the city locked up and was advancing against the western edge. With those sectors in his control, conquest of the north and east became a very simple task. For surely the pols who had ignored him or opposed him up until then would lend their influence to such an adept bossman as Giles Havelock.

Minutes after he had entered the house, Shmuel had found the Havelock safe, hidden behind a copy of a Van Dyke painting. With professional ease, Shmuel turned back the replicated crucifixion, exposing the safe's dial. He pressed his ear to the digits and began to twirl. Somewhere in the house a grandfather clock ticked ominously, sending chills up Shmuel's spine. He reconsidered his objective, even thought of backing out. After listening for other sounds throughout the house, Shmuel went back to his safecracking.

"Good evening," came a voice from behind him. It was Giles Havelock, a revolver brandished in his meaty hand. Havelock lit a nearby table lamp and stepped closer for a better look.

"You were supposed to be giving a speech," Shmuel retorted, surprising himself with the accusational tone in his voice. Only one more number had been left to discover. To the right, once, perhaps twice around and bingo, Shmuel Gluntz would've been a very rich man.

"Just don't be foolish. I could drop you without even trying. You can lower your hands now. I don't like gazing at sweatstains this hour of the night."

Shmuel obeyed, cautiously taking a seat across from Giles Havelock. He wondered why the aspiring political figure didn't summon the police. The publicity would've certainly been worth his energy. For it was an election year, a law-

222

and-order construction of platforms and speeches. Havelock's apprehension of a crook in his own home would certainly go over big in the eastern sector of town.

"How long have you been a practicing burglar?" asked Havelock, eliciting a smile from Shmuel.

"A few months," lied Shmuel, inadequately concealing the smile on his face.

"I asked you a question," snapped Havelock. "And I expect a proper answer." He lowered the gun so it was pointed at Shmuel's chest.

Shmuel had no answer for the fat man. He hemmed and hawed, hoping Giles would shoot him already, call the police ... do whatever it was that he was going to.

"You're the same one who knocked over Winthrop Kahn's ... and Joe Simone's. I can tell by your style. Besides, no amateur would dare bust in here. What'd you come for, anyway?"

Unable to stifle his laughter, Shmuel replied. "Money! What else?"

"Being a man in my position, I am susceptible to many transgressions. The theft of money is only one of them."

"Negotiable securities would also go," answered Shmuel, aware of what Giles wanted to know.

"I see. And for money, and at no one's bidding, you dared enter my home?"

"The lock on your rear door. It's nothing. A kid ..."

"But we're not talking of kids," interrupted Havelock. "We're discussing criminals. The kind who, without adequate protection, can be sentenced to long years in prison. You do see my point, don't you?"

"Very clearly. But I'd say you have me cold."

"True. Very true, Mr. ..."

"Gluntz."

"Ah yes. Shmuel Gluntz. I've heard the name before. Well, Mr. Gluntz, you must realize, however, that first and foremost I'm a businessman. And as such, there's always

223

room to make a deal. Regardless of all else, no crime can be too great or too small that a deal can't be made. I take it you're getting the gist of what I'm saying?"

"I'm not stupid."

"I thought not. Otherwise I wouldn't be talking with you like this. I merely would've blown your brains out and declared myself the victor of a most ferocious battle. They'd love it over on the east side of town."

"I'm sure they would."

"Hmmm. Here's a drink, Mr. Gluntz. It's good for your nerves. Drink! It's a gesture of my hospitality."

In silence Shmuel observed Giles Havelock while he poured two drinks and handed one to the burglar. He couldn't avoid wincing when he thought how easily Giles could've shot him dead. Dying was definitely not one of Shmuel's best considerations. He sipped his liquor and reclined in the chair, awaiting Havelock's proposition.

"You see, Mr. Gluntz, despite our being at opposite ends of my revolver, there is one thing we share in common."

"We're both crooks," offered Shmuel between sips of his liquor.

Havelock's jowls wriggled when he nodded his giant head. "That's right, Mr. Gluntz. We're both crooks. But there is a major difference between you and me. You lack protection. You have no class, because you have no cover. You've become little more than a cheap burglar, vulnerable to the lowest elements of law enforcement. You are captured and you pay for it. Dearly. When I'm captured I pay off the judge. It's that simple. Really."

Shmuel snickered, nonplussed slightly by Havelock's honesty. "I doubt if you'll get caught breaking rules you've created for yourself."

"It's not easy. But, then again, there always is the possibility. I'm the type of man who prefers to alleviate all risks. Like you for example. It's quite conceivable that you one day may receive my protection. Provided, of course, you

224

protect me in turn. You see, Mr. Gluntz, I do have enemies. Malicious pissants who wish me dead. Yet their obtrusions against my person have caused me to witness their flaws in personality. As do we all, they too have something to hide. Even those who claim the best facade of nobility. We are all equal in our deviations from the path of righteousness. Just that we leave from different points. It would be your duty, Mr. Gluntz, to find out where my opponents deviate from their general facades. Is it women, gambling ... men? How can I nab them before they grab me? That, Mr. Gluntz, is the name of the game. And I daresay you can help me play it."

The politician set down his glass and poured himself another round. He then proffered the bottle in Shmuel's direction. After brief hesitation, Shmuel accepted the liquor into his glass.

"How do you know you can trust me?" he asked Havelock.

Giles sighed, denouncing the futility of such a question. "If you screw me up, Mr. Gluntz, you'll serve so much time behind bars you'll need three lives to complete your sentence."

"I see."

"Do you, Mr. Gluntz? Really? That's good. For there are so many who only pretend to see, and by covering their eyes, amounts of greed grow inside the lids. They no longer are trustworthy, but become treacherous to myself and my ambitions. Then, quite suddenly in fact, they are removed. Reduced to a mere name, a listing in the city annals.

"But for the others, those who remain with me, the rewards are numerous. A man like yourself, for example, can readily be elevated to respectable status. You will hobnob among the great city fathers ... while you pluck their safes for your own purpose as well as mine. So, tell me, Mr. Gluntz, how does it feel to be employed?"

"Much better than jail, I'd imagine."

Havelock paused to ream his finger around his mouth. His nail scraped at the space between two molars. He cursed silently, removing the finger, examining the drool which he wiped off on his lounging robe. "There's, ah, only one more thing then, Mr. Gluntz. A small matter. Concerning your sister. You see ... I've been an admirer of hers for quite some time. At my nearest convenience I'd like to have you ... ah ... introduce us. If you don't mind."

Caught by surprise by Havelock's final demand, Shmuel sat speechless, staring down at the nub resting between the legs of Giles' silken pajamas. Compared to his belly, it seemed the politician's cock was so small it would be incapable of spanning the distance between balls and paydirt. Three inches away from pussy it would spit out the results of its excitement, falling limp before the precious cunt it had so desired. Shmuel laughed just to think of it. He would've laughed harder, had it not been Belle whom they were discussing.

"What's so funny?" Giles demanded.

"How do you do it? On top or bottom?"

Havelock's lips stretched reflexively, revealing his annoyance with Shmuel. "Listen, you. I'm doing you a favor. A thousand punk burglars would be delighted to work for me. But I chose you. Remember that. And have your sister here. By Saturday the latest."

"Suppose she won't come with me."

"Then, Mr. Gluntz, I suggest you make her."

For the next couple of days Shmuel paced about in a quandary, endlessly ruminating his predicament. He weighed the pros against the cons, subtracted the flaws from the merits, and found he was no closer to reaching a solution. Gladly he would've presented Havelock with a dozen beautiful women, all built better, more lascivious than his sister. But not Belle. How could he ever relinquish her to such a sacrifice? Family honor was at stake. What little of it remained. No, Shmuel admitted, it wasn't family honor, but his own sense of pride, his own desire to keep his sister from being submitted to such degradation. And if he didn't . . .

"So that's all you want me to do?" laughed Belle after Shmuel had told her his story. "What's the problem? I arrive, he comes, and I depart, twenty minutes later if what I hear is true. That's it."

"Do you know what he looks like? Ever seen the size of him?"

"Not where it counts. I'm sure. What does he want from me? To act like an innocent? As if I was being offered up for sacrifice? What's his game, the trick that best turns his precious political dingle into an ounce of flaccid mush?"

"It's against your dignity. Your pride."

Belle rested a loving hand on her brother's shoulder. "Listen, honey . . . years ago, when we were poor, I used to sacrifice my dignity occasionally to the grocer, for nothing more than a loaf of bread and an old salami. Finkel, the landlord, let me pay the rent with my pants down, and Addison, the tailor, used to lick it between his alterations. Had him so cockeyed he used to make your pants so one leg was longer than the other. Remember?"

"I always thought he needed glasses."

"So what can't I do, what indignity is too much to suffer to keep my own twin brother out of jail? Besides . . . who knows . . maybe Giles and I will fall in love. See the two of us come waddling down the street? Our first child we'll name for you."

"I'll get him for this," Shmuel vowed before his sister. "One day, when he least expects it, I'll slip it to him. For good!"

Many years passed before Shmuel made good on his promise. In that time the former burglar advanced through the gears of Havelock's political machinery. As Giles himself rose from councilman to mayor, whose office he maintained for three consecutive terms, Shmuel won acclaim as an astute politician. For it was Mr. Gluntz, as Havelock still

227

affectionately called him, who made sure the mechanisms of political power were well oiled with funds and negotiable information. Gradually, Shmuel was able to gain his own power. His figure was recognized, wherever in the city he travelled.

The machine expanded, spread throughout the state, linking its powers with the smaller influences in the towns and cities surrounding the mayor's own province. Advances against the state's major political figures were being made with increasing frequency. Giles Havelock III was expected to run for governor and win hands down. Every poll, every political commentator predicted an easy victory. Shmuel himself was charged with management of Giles' campaign.

"If I win," snorted Giles, "you, Mr. Gluntz, will be my noble lieutenant. It's your reward for years of faithful service."

Quite tragically, if not dramatically, Giles Havelock III was removed from contention. No one ever discovered who it was who planted the bomb in his desk about a week before the primary election was scheduled. One inquiry flowed into the next, all encapsulated by molecules of liquid rhetoric, floating aimlessly toward the ugly surface of the political arena. For what it actually amounted to was no one cared how or why Giles Havelock III was assassinated. There was always someone else eager to take his place. But not Shmuel Gluntz. To the astonishment and concern of his followers, Giles Havelock's second in command stepped down from consideration, citing the danger of assassination as his main reason.

"My grief for Giles and my general concern for my own personal safety has deleted all my political ambitions," Shmuel announced at a press conference called by his party. "It's impossible for me to consider running for office at this time."

"What will you do?" asked a reporter.

228

"Nothing," said Shmuel, stepping from the platform. "It's all been done already."

With Havelock dead, and Shmuel Gluntz gone from the party, the machine slipped its gears, falling into the hands of inept political hacks. Although they were able to win the governor's race on sheer party reputation, it inadvertently became the final cause of their ruination. Scandal and manipulations were exposed everywhere. Resignations were demanded. City and state politicians were in disgrace, booed wherever they reared their ignominious profiles.

In the midst of the confusion, Shmuel Gluntz was able to disappear, unnoticed by all but his sister and a few familiar faces. He travelled south, intending to become a carpetbagger. A few bucks could be made, he thought, among the corrupted survivors and the chosen darkies who had gained favor with the powers that were. He would fade away from the furor he'd created up North, making hay while the gluttonous sun burned upon the ravaged heart of Dixie.

From her side-view window Belle observed the usual array of Saturday shoppers filling the streets. In wagons, on horseback and on foot they came, arriving from neighboring farms and ranches, mingling with the tourists and townspeople. By noontime Star City was jammed with people, the sun-bleached faces indistinguishable from one another from Belle's vantage point.

Rain from the night before had drenched the city, and the wagon wheels, horses' hooves and boot prints had churned the streets into a rutted, muddy mess. Fresh dresses, trousers, boots and faces were splattered by moistened clods, while families and loners attempted to pass through the mire. Despite the shining sun, the perfect sky, the promise of

229

a beautiful day, the slow plodding somewhat modified the carnival atmosphere permeating the streets. Yet the vendors hawked their homemade and manufactured wares, children squealed, running, slipping, sliding with laughter in their hearts and mud on their hands and faces. Family men bargained for farm supplies, weapons and tools, while the women purchased materials and foodstuffs. All in all, it seemed like a pleasant day.

Belle Gluntz closed her eyes and felt the sun's warmth resting upon her cheeks. A soothing elixir, it was, dissolving her troubles, making her wish she was standing outside. She weighed the dangers of exposing herself to Ben's evil guns, deciding to risk it before she had considered all the obstacles.

"Go take a rest. Get the sun. It's good for ya."

It was Shmuel calling from behind her. Once again he had read her thoughts. "I'd take Jason. Just in case. Damn that little pisher. That we have to live like this."

Shmuel climbed from behind his desk, advancing alongside his sister. He patted her shoulder, following her line of vision out the window. "His time will come. That I can assure you."

Belle smiled warily. "What will you do? Remodel his desk for him?"

"If need be. Anyhow, I know his type. They never last long."

"They last," sighed Belle. "Forever and a day, these bastards remain like stale odors in small kitchens. The question is ... will we?"

"Sure we will. And if not, there's plenty of other places to go."

"Not for me, there isn't. I'm tired, Shmuel. This runnin' around is getting to me. I'm old, my feet tire easily. It's no time for western showdowns."

Shaking his head, Shmuel clasped his sister's hand. He

squeezed firmly for a second before releasing his grip. Much gentler now, he led her toward the door.

"C'mon. I'll see you downstairs."

When his sister and Jason departed for the market, Shmuel remained behind, his hands clasped behind his back, staring from the entrance to the Alaskan Queen. He breathed in deeply and closed his eyes, enjoying the sunshine. Just as a wagon drove by, splashing mud over the last of his custom suits.

"Dammit," hollered Shmuel, his fist shaking at the unwitting driver. Disgruntled, Shmuel stared down at his muddy suit, reminded of how much he hated mud. Even city dirt was better than mud to Shmuel. Piled garbage, blackened snow and the grit flowing through the windstreams down eastern streets were things Shmuel remembered with some nostalgia. Suddenly feeling blue, the old politician tried to soothe his nerves by bidding hello to the sweet summer ladies who passed him by. They ignored him or glanced scornfully at his mud-sodden outfit. Even more depressed, Shmuel returned to the interior of the Alaskan Queen and ordered a drink for himself. He then sat down at a table near the window and observed the pedestrians. His feet propped on the table, the mud drying on his shirt, his head listed gently in the direction of the sunlight. His revolver remained closely by his side.

After imbibing more than half a bottle of pure whiskey, Shmuel grew to feeling sentimental. He mumbled the choruses of his favorite songs while removing his wallet from his jacket. He examined several pictures, all of Belle in her younger days. And then came a photograph of Shelby in uniform and finally the likeness of Louise Bodine. Tall, lanky, seeming the color of coffee and cream, Louise smiled back at Shmuel. He sighed, touching his finger to his lips before he placed its tip against the picture. With his eyes closed, Shmuel recalled their first encounter. She wasn't

231

smiling then, but angry. Angry as hell. He was attracted to her bitterness.

She had appeared to him in the morning. She and a group of organizers had invaded his office in Muldoon County, Georgia. They had come to protest the treatment of the poor, justifiably so, since much of the funds allocated for reconstruction were falling into the hands of Zeus Duffy and his cohorts. Shmuel, as well, had been rewarded with a scant piece of the sour pie.

"Carpetbaggin' ain't what it used t' be," Zeus had told him on the day he hired Shmuel. "Politicians all over the South, desperate for a job. Too much competition now. Can't siphon what we used t'."

"I'll take it," Shmuel had told his employer. He was much too weary to argue. For several months he had travelled about, in search of employment. Positions were filled, even to the extent that an old political hack like Shmuel couldn't find any work. Having relinquished his powers in the city, Shmuel no longer retained the connections necessary to see him through rough times. And times were indeed rough for the former burglar. In the salad days he had spent his money lavishly, believing a bad tomorrow would never arrive on his doorstep. How wrong he was. How easily his former cohorts maneuvered his holdings right out of his hands, only to dash them into worthlessness against the gathering tides of scandal. Corporations, tax shelters, partnerships which he had so lavishly constructed with the assistance of Giles Havelock's political machine had been just as easily unravelled. Securities were worthless, reduced drastically from their previous inflated values. Even Shmuel's private bank accounts had been invaded by the nefarious officers he had, as a matter of procedure, signed to the corporate charters. And now, after months of wandering about the South, Zeus Duffy had hinted at a job. Gladly he'd taken it. Even if he was to be the fourth man in a three-man operation. What did it matter? As long as he was eating. Surviving in this vicious world.

And then, in the small district of Muldoon County, Georgia, Louise Bodine had appeared before him, her long, bony fist curled in the air.

"We've come to demand our lives back," she wailed. "Along with all else you people've stolen, considered of greater value."

Shmuel directed his eyes to hers, waited for a blink, a modest gesture of hesitation. None came. Her eyes wide, Louise glared at the shorter person, clenching and unclenching the hands which now hung at her sides. "Long enough you've made us pay penalties for the privilege of being born. There's too many poor folk who need food, jobs, medical attention ... while you're out spendin' on what you damn well please."

By the manner in which she spoke, Shmuel would've half expected to see an army standing outside his door, instead of a handful of paupers, their hat brims twisting in their fingers, their heads bowed self-consciously. He pitied them. He honestly did. Yet in all his years, Shmuel had never allowed such obscure sentiments as pity to interfere with his making a living.

"We're here to help you get on your feet. To start a new life, now that you're free."

"No we aren't free. Not nearly free enough. Not free until we're free from you. You and that Mr. Zeus Duffy. What's he pay you for this, anyway? How much you gettin', just to answer questions?"

"These aren't questions," Shmuel corrected, "but demands."

"Damn right they're demands. How much they paying you to listen?"

Just then a door creaked open from behind him. Shmuel didn't need to turn around to know it was Lem Halstrom,

233

Zeus' chief lackey, who was peering out from his office to see if a mob was coming for him. Recently, rumors had been spreading that with increased frequency carpetbaggers, bogus politicians and such were being subjected to all sorts of indignities. Some were merely tarred and feathered, while some were whipped and others hanged. Halstrom was obsessed with his fear of hanging, often complaining there was no justice found among a mob.

"Gluntz," Halstrom shrieked. "What in tarnation ar' ya doin' with 'em people? Throw 'em out an' be done wit' it."

Thyrone Norton was the next man to make his presence known. Black Thyrone had squirmed his way into power during the first occupation by Yankee forces. He had maintained, wisely yielding first command to Zeus Duffy when the old attorney announced before the county hall that "he personally was going to see that things got straightened out." Nearly a decade had passed since then. When Zeus had taken over, Thyrone had assumed second rank as county commissioner and Lem Halstrom ran a close third. As promised, the triumverate initiated a series of government-sponsored programs, all, on paper at least, nobly designed to lift the masses from their threadbare buttocks. And it might have been so, had it not been for Duffy and company's frequent dipping into the funds. Yet every election year, Duffy proudly mounted the podium, his cohorts beside him. He ranted and raved for an hour or more, giving out fried chicken to those who could bear his speeches.

"You wanted government programs. We gottem for ya'. An' still are people ain't eatin', ain't tastin' the waters that pour from the land of milk 'n' honey. Yet we go on. For we are a great people, proud of our heritage, fond of our past."

At such moments those who were still aware of what was happening, not fooled by fried chicken every four years, gazed up toward the steeple of the county hall. It had been split in half by cannon fire several years before. All about them, buildings had been shattered. Charred wood and blackened brick fireplaces stood in mute testimony to the holocaust that had once swept through the county. Everywhere they looked, troopers and private guards stood ready, willing and able to do Zeus' bidding. Armpits prickling with anxiety, stomachs bloated with fear and hunger, there was nothing for the paupers of Muldoon County to do but to listen to what Zeus Duffy had to say. As usual, he said nothing.

After each speech, the townfolk gathered around each other, cursing Duffy, wishing that he and life would soon be parted. They talked of the restiveness in other counties. Heard rumors of skirmishes, rebellions, the tar and feathering, even the lynching of carpetbaggers and scalawags. Each year's desperation was driving them further along, making them wish that for once they could witness Zeus Duffy being hanged by the intestines of his two lackeys. How they wished it, willed it to their gods and their superstitions.

And then one day Louise Bodine returned from her teaching job up North. People were fond of Louise, pointed her out as the first woman, black woman, that is, in the county who ever amounted to something more than a washerwoman or field hand. She was admired wherever she ventured.

"You're some fine woman, Louise Bodine," people would call after her. "Wish my Joni could be like you."

In due time Louise had things organized. She formed a school, teaching old and young alike the basic methods of the English language. She bought land with her meager savings from her teaching position and allowed the farmers to grow some food there. As poor as the crop yield was, it stood for more than a mere food supply. It was a symbol of defiance, a contradiction of Zeus Duffy, Halstrom and Thyrone Norton. Her flock gathering around her, Louise Bodine advanced further, pushing for demonstrations. She was blocked by Duffy's private army, ex-soldiers, now mer-

235

cenaries, who were designed to keep the paupers in line. But Louise Bodine was too determined a woman to be stifled so easily. With her closest disciples organized behind her she marched onward, headed straight for county hall and Shmuel Gluntz's office. He was the first in her path.

Shmuel had heard of Louise Bodine before he had met her. Somehow in his mind, Shmuel had pictured a fat, black nanny, too enraged to care about her own personal welfare. He saw her as being inarticulate, basically obsequious from too many years of wear and unable to find loopholes in the apologetics spewing from his mouth. He was wrong. Her hands on her hips, Louise now glanced defiantly at him. "Well? How much they payin' ya to listen?"

"Not nearly enough," Shmuel attempted. "Care to sit down?"

"I ain't sittin' anywhere you put your butt."

Challenges such as these were most distressing to Shmuel. With his bosses standing behind him, forcing him to stiff resistance, he'd better do something or else lose his job. Inwardly he laughed at the irony of it all. To have once been one of the most influential men in a major metropolis and to have become a shiftless little fart in charge of defending boorish ignoramuses was simply too much for Shmuel Gluntz to take seriously.

"You know how long, how far I had to travel, just to find this fuckin' job?" he asked Louise, hoping she'd see the humor. She didn't. Her eyes flashed the whiteness around her pupils.

"Your bosses," she retorted. "Y' ever see what they do to the poor folk? Ever see the way they torture these poor creatures of God? The murders, the beatings. For nothing. But money and power. Power. Damn them and their power. A change is coming this way, Mr. Gluntz. Jus' make sure you're not the last to know about it."

Shmuel clasped his hands behind his back and paced to his window. Outside of the county hall stood an odd

236

monument to an unknown Yankee soldier. Apparently, according to the legend that had evolved over the years, he had taken revenge against some fellow Yanks for slaying one of the native daughters. Multicolored, for the statue had been cast from assorted metals acquired through donations, the sculpture's appearance was almost comical. It portrayed a young man running, his head jerked back over his shoulder. His pistol was grasped in his hand, and steel wire, emulating smoke, curled from the barrel. At first glance Shmuel believed the statue to be in honor of Rebel courage, setting the Yanks on the run and such. It was not until later that its true meaning was explained to him, along with the legend that the Yank soldier lived on in Muldoon County, and on the eve of the full moon, he and his lover, Rebecca Maltesin, could be seen scampering across the distant pastures.

"Well," Louise demanded, interrupting Shmuel's thoughts. "What are you going to do about our demands, Mr. Gluntz?"

"Nothing," Shmuel answered, surprised by his sudden change in attitude. He reached for his hat and coat before extracting a battered suitcase from his tiny closet. He opened the suitcase for Louise's personal inspection. "See? Only a few shirts, socks, some underwear and mouthwash. No gold, no money, not even a few heirlooms I stole from someone's dying granny."

"Whut in tarnation ar' ya doin', Gluntz?" It was Zeus Duffy speaking this time. Halstrom and Norton had taken their rightful positions beside him.

"I'm leaving," Shmuel replied, pleased to see Louise Bodine was taken totally off her guard. "This carpetbaggin' shit has been enough for me."

Zeus would have none of it. He waved at Shmuel as if to abolish his stated intentions.

"You leave now, Gluntz, an' you'll lose th' respect o' all your peers. Is that clear, bub?"

237

Shmuel always hated when Duffy called him "bub." "If I lose their respect, then maybe I'll lose their habits."

"Whatta ya' crazy?" asked Thyrone Norton, jumping forward to confront Shmuel. "Ya kin't go do dat, leavin' heah jes' like 'at."

"Watch him, asshole!" Louise Bodine erupted with the giggles. She eyed Shmuel as if she were seeing her own dream come true.

"Ya bastud," squealed Lem Halstrom.

"You're finished, boy. You're through here."

"I should hope so."

"Bastud," repeated Halstrom.

"This is how ya' bite the hand that feeds ya?" roared Zeus Duffy.

"Feed them, motherfucker. Not me."

"Bastud," Halstrom repeated.

This time Shmuel refused to ignore it. "Lem, come here a minute," he softly beckoned. Obediently, the lackey stepped forward, promptly receiving Shmuel's gooey spittle right smack in his face. "Fuck you," said Gluntz, before making for the door. In a moment he was outside, sniffing the air, detecting an aroma he had not known for years. He walked on, headed for the railway station, when he heard a voice calling him from behind. He turned around slowly, half-expecting to see Halstrom facing him with a gun in his hand. Shmuel was pleasantly surprised to discover it was Louise Bodine, smiling as she shortened the distance between them.

"That was quite a performance," she smiled, after she had caught him. "Perfect timing. A bit rehearsed."

"A hundred times before. Mood was never as strong as it was then. I don't know. Maybe I wanted to do something heroic for once in my life. Take after my sister. She was an actress. Worked the stages for years before she retired."

"I was going to be an actress."

"What happened?"

"Figured I'd be more useful as a teacher. That is, before I discovered that it's here I do belong. Maybe it's the same for you."

"You mean, become a teacher?" laughed Shmuel, fascinated by the woman who stood before him. A quick sweep of his eyes accounted for her svelte figure, extending into long arms and legs. A little too lanky to be svelte, really, but in a town the size of Muldoon's county seat, Louise Bodine would do very nicely. For what, Shmuel wasn't yet certain. To gain time, he asked her for a drink. He was surprised when she accepted.

Later that night, by the light of a solitary lantern, they made love. One night, immersed in passion, accented by the crackling cornhusks beneath their naked skins. Around them the cabins and shanties darkened with the aging day. No longer could they hear family arguments, children shouting. Only lonely wolf barks and owl hoots punctuated their sentiments.

Throughout the night Shmuel held Louise against him, barely able to sustain his determination to leave in the morning. Another day, perhaps? A week? A month? For the first time he had found love, and yet he had to leave it. Depart an enlightened warrior fleeing from the contest. How satisfying could that be when compared to the carnal treasures he clutched in his hands? A lone tear fell from his eye as he speculated on his loneliness. Well, fuck it. Leave the crusades for the lions and the martyrs. He would no longer be among them.

"You know, I could really get to love you," sighed Louise, interrupting Shmuel's thoughts.

Moved by her sentiments, Shmuel pressed her buttocks, his tongue flicking in and out of the cleavage between her narrow breasts. His forehead against her chest, her thighs wrapped around his ribs, he searched again for an entrance, wishing it an exit, a sudden return to the void where all was forgotten. He wished Louise could feel him, not as a man, a mere prick inside her, but as an ideal, a revelation rising in her system. He wished to burn her from the inside out, branding her consciousness with his eternal memory, so that in all her future memories Shmuel Gluntz would never be forgotten.

Chapter 13

Lemon Lime tugged her leather jacket down over her narrow waist and settled on the wooden step. From her vantage point she could witness the marketing taking place on the waterfront just a few yards away. Her arms draped over her knees, her head tilted upward, she relaxed beneath the midday sun. Through the slits of her eyes she was able to maintain surveillance of any possible danger. Big Ben's men lurked everywhere, waiting to pounce on one's unsuspecting body.

As usual, Lemon felt very much apart from those in the marketplace. Deep down she longed to be among them, concerned with little more than the chores of another day. However, she understood she could never be contented with routine living. For a lady who once longed to be the first female President of the United States, a mundane existence was out of the question. Yet the camaraderie shared among the housewives, the merchants and even the dogs and cats scampering about in search of crumbs always attracted her.

So simple their lives always appeared. So easy. Lemon smiled. She knew better than to think anyone's life was easy. Having come from one of the richest families in Chicago, she was too well aware of the pitfalls awaiting clumsy feet. Even those who entered their journey with their eyes wide open were in for a few surprises. Such was life. Exaggerated, such was the life of Lemon Lime.

Her golden locket suddenly heavy around her neck, Lemon pulled it up to her eyes for a better examination. Carefully she opened its face, a ritual she had performed for many years now. Inside rested a picture of her mother, Faye Gestalt. Funny, thought Lemon, how her mother always seemed to be here and somewhere else at the same moment. Like she was only serving time with Lemon's father, Doug Culvane, while the essence of her vitality was devoted elsewhere. Of course Faye was often inaccessible to Lemon. There was seldom time for excursions, talks in the parlors, the sharing of table and card games. That is, until Moses Moriarity appeared in their doorway one fine day. Everything seemed to change with Mo's unannounced arrival. No sooner had her father hired the wizened old black man as the estate's caretaker than Lemon found herself drawn constantly to his side. She followed the old gambler about his rounds, talking her gibberish, while Mo smiled patiently, waiting for her to finish a sentence. Lemon had been young then, barely out of diapers. What an impression this man had made. As black as he was, so close. It was most uncommon then.

Turning over the locket, Lemon read the inscription out loud. "To my beloved Faye—from Sy," it read. Who was Sy? Lemon always wanted to know but had been afraid to ask. Did Doug Culvane know this ancient lover of Lemon's mother? Where did he come from, this Sy? More importantly, where did he go? How nice it would be, now that her mother had passed away, for Lemon to visit this man, to learn of this experience he had shared with Faye Gestalt.

This man, he must've been something to have been the first to put the gleam into Faye's bright, shining eyes. He who had led her to the waters and extracted a taste from its currents. She had not sipped but guzzled, apparently, for it was no secret that Faye Gestalt was never the same upon her return from the university.

"What are we going to do with you?" her father, George Gestalt, noted brewer, had asked of his only daughter.

"I don't know. Marry me off, I suppose."

As if it had been her deepest wish, George Gestalt set to the task of finding his beloved daughter a suitable beau. He appeared soon enough, in the form of Doug Culvane, middle-aged, but of good breeding, and wealthy in his own right. "No paupers, gigolos, for my only daughter," Gestalt had always vowed.

Shortly thereafter, Faye Gestalt and Doug Culvane were married. A few months later, Lana was born, prematurely, or so they said. Certainly Doug Culvane was an honorable man and could've never committed such a terrible misdeed as to screw the sole, beloved daughter of George Gestalt out of wedlock. Premature. Indeed!

Not long after Lana was born, Faye moved into her own bedroom, a suite actually, and lived there, more or less, for the rest of her life. On special occasions, business meetings, banquets, etc., she joined her husband, walking proudly by his side, her arm enwrapped by his. Otherwise, she strode about the huge estate, absorbed by its appointments as if she were just another piece of furniture.

"Your poor mama," old Moriarity often lamented. "Never yet seen the instant when she's been a happy woman."

Lana Culvane studied the caretaker, awaiting his further explanation. He seldom ventured more, instead preferring to return to his gardening or the mending of fences.

"What about the book?" asked Lana, aware of the volume her mother guarded so closely. Faye had returned from the university many years before, the book hidden inside her suitcase. A bizarre copy it was, inscribed with alien figures, indecipherable notations, all imbedded on pages reminiscent of a parchment texture. Yet the fabric was more supple, better-wearing than its parchment likeness.

"The book," frowned Mo. "Oh yes, the book. I keep meaning to ask your mama about that book. I'd like to examine it, as soon as I finish my other readings."

"Mama never reads it. She only turns the pages. She mumbles to herself. Reminds me of a child's teddy bear, the way she totes that book around."

Moses' curiosity was aroused by Lana's explanation. He too had noted Faye's strange behavior whenever she was away from the volume for too long a time. Her eyes glazed, her fingers trembling, she was distracted easily, couldn't concentrate on a damn thing, not even the simplest explanation of the garden's arrangement. She fidgeted constantly, her eyes darted back and forth, like an alcoholic in need of a drink. "What's the matter?" Mo asked on such occasions.

"Oh, nothing. Just a restless night, that's all." Faye would attempt to laugh it off. Mo always knew better. Any rational explanation could never deter the tragic expectations that crept through his body. Something bad was coming down. That he was sure of.

"What are ya' doing with that book in your hands?" Doug Culvane asked whenever he had time for his wife. A busy man, with a multitude of livestock and several processing plants to worry over, he was often gruff and unreasonable. "I would think by now you'd finish it. Bein' a woman with some college and all. Ed Clawson's wife, she reads three books a week, so he says. And she never attended anything other than finishing school. Like I've always said, the university is a bad place for a woman. Brings out the strangest of their actions."

Faye Culvane usually ignored her husband or regarded him with a condescending smirk. Such an expression always irritated Culvane, forcing him to challenge his wife's intentions. "You're tryin' to get at me. Aren't you? Always trying to get at me with those crazy looks of yours. What's the matter, woman? Something wrong with your eyeballs?"

Faye never did respond. "Pah," was the best she could muster before disappearing to the rear sector of the mansion, where she maintained her quarters.

It was Mo Moriarity who first broached the subject of the book in any serious fashion. Faye was astonished that the old gambler was interested in the volume. Although she was aware of the man's attempt to educate himself and had seen the numerous volumes he had piled in his cabin at the rear of the estate, Faye Culvane had not retained any such impression, preferring the image of Moses escorting her daughter Lana around the property. This vision was much more acceptable to Faye's imagination. Perhaps it was the suddenness of his request that caused her to hand the book over to Moriarity. "Who knows?" she smiled, "maybe you can tell me what it means."

"Where did you ever find this, anyway?" he asked after leafing through several pages.

Faye's head rolled back atop her shoulders as if she had been clipped by an invisible hammer. Her eyes widened, her head turned, and she confronted Moriarity as if the real Faye Gestalt, who had hung back in the waiting wings for such a long period of time, had suddenly rushed forward to make her presence known. Moriarity was frightened by the sudden change in personality. He stepped backward, just as Mrs. Culvane released an earsplitting wail, which caused the servants to rush out to the patio to see just what the matter was.

"Nothing," Moriarity assured them. "Go back inside." He then took hold of Faye Culvane and led her to her quarters. She trembled so that she would have fallen had not Moses been there to support her. At last they arrived in her chamber, and here Faye seemed to regain control of herself. By means of a slow process, a handling of all key sections of her anatomy, Faye Culvane at last brought about her normal composure. Mo waited patiently, noting she was about to speak.

"That book is one of the few secrets remaining in this world of mine," she admitted to the caretaker. "It's been in my possession since the time my life had meaning for me."

Mo diverted his attentions to the pages of the volume. He thumbed through, more slowly this time, becoming increasingly aware of the strange and magnificent powers of the book he rested in his lap. Never before had Mo witnessed such an exotic book as this. Certainly it was the type of volume that belonged to legends, stories of old, the mystical . . . and then he remembered, long ago, the pirate, the Indian lady, her indelible tale of the Necklace.

"Where did you say you found this book?" he asked again, a bit more cautiously this time, for fear he might instigate another round of histrionics.

"Are you able to read its language?"

"No. But there lies something in the symbols, an enchantment that befuddles the reaches of my imagination. I am almost afraid to declare myself, for fear that my speculations are justified. If so, then it means my duties in life aren't over yet. I'll be at it again, travelling, in search of an aging man, a man much like myself, yet so different. I am bewildered. Amazed really, by this strange occurrence. Never in my life did I . . . not here anyway. And you've so adamantly retained this book, yet you're unaware of its mystery, the secret it may reveal."

"The secret lies within me, and the soul of one who I lost such a long, long time ago."

"Who?"

"A good man. Lana's actual father. He's gone now. Killed shortly after I discovered Lana was encased inside my womb. I carried her around, at first like some unwanted fruit I'd be forced to bear in the springtime. Until I realized she'd be all that was left, all that remained between him and me. Except for the memories, the endless sequence of

246

memories which still invade my soul. Terrible, to spend all these years living for a dead man."

"So your father, the brewer, arranged for the wedding with Doug Culvane."

Faye's eyes widened with her memories. "No, I mean, yes. But my father never knew, nor did Culvane, that I carried a child inside me. How could I reveal myself to people of my father's station? Surely they'd force me to relinquish the child. So I pretended, I did everything I could to have someone marry me. Anything, anyone would do. Just as long as they did so before my secret was known. So proud Doug was to learn he would soon have a child. With his virility confirmed for all to bear witness, he stalked proudly about his empire, never once bothering to ask any further questions."

"And the other man? Who was he?"

"Seymour. He was the ideal, the values in which I truly believed. Until they became sentiments, bittersweet memories impossible to conceive of in the world in which I live. Seymour was a sensation, realized once, but never regained. How awful to possess something so dear, only to have it fade beyond restoration."

"So you settled for Doug Culvane. You became one of them."

Faye lifted her head so Mo could explore her bloodshot and tearful eyeballs. "I was always one of them. I couldn't help it. I was born that way. Seymour was my lone excursion toward another means of existence. Our lives together were so insecure, so abundant with fervor, I couldn't possibly withstand the tensions for too much longer. How I loved him. How I really did love the man. So tender and caring he was. So concerned with my slightest involvements. He could just stare at me and I'd fall to pieces. Seymour, that sonofabitch, why did he have to die?"

The tears falling again, Faye paused to rub her eyes and brood over her confession. She would've thought it odd if anyone had informed her that it would be Moses Moriarity

247

to whom she would have finally admitted the tragic affairs of her life. Old black Mo. She had passed him off as the caretaker, her daughter's aged playmate. Even Lana's idolization of the old gambler had been passed off as childish infatuation. Little did Mrs. Culvane realize the magnet to which she had been attracted, compelled to reveal her deepest affections.

Faye smiled unwittingly, her thoughts lost among the hours by which she had watched her daughter playing on the grounds with Moses Moriarity. She recalled all the stories her daughter claimed Mo had told her. Lana effused lavish tales of pirates, of gambling along the river. It was mythology to Faye, something dreamed up by the caretaker in order to entertain Lana, tighten his position with members of the family. The Indian, the pirate and the Great Necklace, what a tale it was, even in the bits and pieces Lana related to her mother. Her favorite story. A fable extending beyond the limits of reality, unbelievable for anyone with half a mind, yet nothing else, either real or tangible, could ever compare in arousing her spoiled daughter's interest. Gladly, Lana would've relinquished her dreams of becoming the first lady president in order to spend eternity listening to the embellishments of Moriarity's fable.

"Why do you remain aloof from your daughter then?" asked Moriarity, interrupting the lady's thoughts.

"She frightens me. Her father emanates from every act of her behavior. Dammit, she has captured his very mannerism. She'll be just like him ... as stubborn, as arrogant, as distasteful of anything conventional. And then where will she be? Seated on her hidden desires, wishing for her white knight to come along? How terrible to find she was only wasting her time."

"You never believed you were wasting your time," Mo defended.

"Not for a moment. Still. I don't know which is worse. To

248

reconcile oneself to a life lived with little affection, or one where the instant is so impassioned yet so fleeting, it forces all other moments to pale by comparison. Dammit! And here I am. A mental case. I despise my husband, recoil from his touch. Yet somehow, somewhere deep inside me, I can't help but believe I did my very best. That it was meant to be this way, if it was to be anything at all. At least I have that much . . . some odd belief in my one accomplishment."

Mo unfolded his hands and drew in a deep breath. "Soon I must be going, travelling once again. Just tell me. Where did you find this book?"

"I said already. Seymour."

"Yes. But where did he get it?"

An odd smile expanded across Faye's mouth. A finger came up to brush her lips, rub her eyes, as if she were recalling another buried memory. "By the university campus, an old man owned a stuffed and musty bookshop. I forget his name now. It's been so long. Something Gluntz, I believe it was. He loved Seymour, shared an indescribable affinity for my lover. They spoke to each other in coded utterances. What a strange little creature. His eyes were always filled with fire. Always talking nonsense about our being refugees who escaped from a distant galaxy. Can you imagine? Would go on and on about our impending doom. Just as soon as we were discovered by their armed forces. Crazy, he was. Wore an old slouch hat and a long, dark overcoat.

"But he did like Seymour. Always had a kind word and a funny story. He liked me too, but not the way he did Seymour. Yes, it was Gluntz who gave Seymour the book. One of the many from his 'alien collection,' as he called it. Told him to keep it. Always."

"And now it must be taken to its final destination. So the hearts and minds of others can finally have their rest."

"I'm sorry. I truly am. But I'd rather die first than relinquish the book."

249

"If you don't give it up, you'll die soon after. For no mere mortal can interrupt its rightful path."

"We'll soon see about that," cried Faye Culvane, growing angrier by the second.

"Don't say I didn't warn you," said Moriarity, in a solemn fashion usually reserved for funerals.

"Thank you. Now please return to your cottage. Where you belong."

Ironically, three days later, Faye Culvane was to make her first visit to one of her husband's several processing plants. All these years she had deliberately avoided any direct contact with the means by which Doug Culvane had made his living. A vestige of her old radical days, Faye Culvane preferred not to be reminded of the angst and suffering among the hardbitten who slaughtered, hauled and otherwise processed the carcasses of cattle and hogs. Upon sight of the hunchbacks, the infected and mistreated victims of the brutal plant conditions, with all their aches, complaints and festering sores, Mrs. Culvane collapsed on the spot, never again to regain consciousness. For three weeks she lingered between life and death, never transcending the coma. Despite all of her husband's urgings, his summoning of the best specialists in the country, Faye Culvane would not survive. When the end was near, Lana Culvane was notified of her mother's worsening condition. She left the university, arriving at the deathbed just as Faye was prepared to breath her last. One more episode transpired between mother and daughter before Faye Culvane (nee Gestalt) went off to sleep.

Soon after her funeral, Doug Culvane promptly called a meeting at the processing plant. He blamed the workers for his wife's death, for not looking their very best during her visit to the plant. He then fired the majority of laborers, without pension, of course, and hired a new unit. With that done, he turned his attentions to his daughter.

"You won't be going back to the university," he informed

her. "You know I've always been opposed to formal education for women, ever since I witnessed what it had done to your mother. During the past few months I've been making arrangements with Lloyd DePugh, of the Kansas City DePughs, for your betrothal to him. He's a fine man, from an upstanding family, which happens to possess a virtual gold mine in livestock. An alliance between his family and ours would enable us to dominate both the hog and cattle markets."

Before Lana could give her reply, Doug Culvane summoned Clifford Dash by tinkling the bell he kept atop his executive's desk. "I'm entrusting you to Clifford Dash, a promising talent for Culvane Enterprises. Dash will see that you safely reach Kansas City. Railway tickets will be waiting with my secretary."

"But . . . but . . ." Lana attempted to protest.

Culvane looked up from his paperwork. "But what?"

It was futile. Her father had never reacted favorably to any of Lana's proposals. Now would be no different than all other occasions. "Nothing," she said, her lips twisted with contempt for her father.

The train ride to Kansas City at first promised to be an uneventful vacation for Clifford Dash. He had longed to escape the confines of the meat processing industry for some time now. Eagerly he accepted Doug Culvane's proposition. "See that she gets there safely," was all Dash's employer had to say.

But as the days passed, Lana and Clifford had reached familiar terms. By the time they reached Kansas City they had fallen in love.

It was most distressing for Lloyd DePugh to discover his fiancée in the arms of one Clifford Dash. Immediately, DePugh sent word to Lana's father, calling off the engagement. Somehow the word was leaked, and stock for Culvane Enterprises, which had been rising in value with incredible speed, suddenly came to a halt, beginning its long, slow descent, creating the loss of millions. It was all Doug Culvane could do to recover from his losses. He worked many long hours to restore his firm's formerly solid reputation. He had only Clifford Dash to blame for the crisis, and true to form, Culvane vowed he would kill him. As did Lloyd DePugh, who never quite recovered from the lewd spectacle laid before his eyes. But by the time the two men had recovered from their different crises, both Lana and Clifford had disappeared, both absorbed by the territories like rain when it strikes the ocean.

Three of Big Ben's men were sidling across the street, approaching Lemon's horse. Her guts tightening as the three thugs approached the mare, Lemon prepared herself for the inevitable. She lifted her jacket so it cleared the hunting knife she had attached to her thigh. Her long, smooth fingers slipped inside her jacket, patting the .32 revolver she had concealed there.

Kip Kearney and his two cohorts hadn't noticed Lemon. Kip's brain was still raging, fuming over the altercation he had had with Shay Daniels back inside the Lost Hope Saloon. Kip had never liked the grizzly old-timer and never wasted an opportunity to tell him so. Despite the animosity between them, Kearney remained hesitant to push a show-down with Daniels. Somewhere, Kip maintained that, even though he was faster than the old-timer, Shay Daniels would easily kill him.

Ironically, the argument erupted over Lemon Lime. The gunmen had been discussing her womanly virtues, speculating on five minutes of fun with the director of the Sno' Fuck Follies. Lemon's legs, ass, tits and face were assessed as the conversation travelled counterclockwise around the table. Even Crosly Finch was present, swearing his amorous intentions.

252

"I'd like to get my hands on her," said Finch. "She'd learn soon enough what a real man's about."

Everyone laughed but Lorenzo Stokes. Foolish Stokes had to add his personal iconoclasm to Finch's fantasies. "That's what Jess Tulin said, before Lemon dug a hole outta his face wit' that knife o' hers." He then snickered at Crosly, proud of his chance to get in a dig.

Crosly had no time or tolerance for Stokes' humor. With a sweep of his apelike limb, he backhanded Lorenzo from his chair. Laughter ensued, as Stokes slowly climbed back onto his feet, wiping the blood from his damaged lips.

"I'm more than ten Jess Tulins," swore Crosly, to be sure Lorenzo understood. "An' I'm certainly more 'n a match for tha' witch of a bitch."

"They say it's true," threw in Shay Daniels. "They say she has the mark of a witch, right here on her shoulder."

"I'd love to have a peek," said another.

"Some say she's been raised by a she-wolf. A's why she's so mean."

"She-wolf, my ass," Kip had grumbled. "She'll stop scratchin' soon enough, when she takes a gander a' my big honcho. Measured nine inches, as of two weeks ago las' Friday."

"Hahaha," laughed Daniels, beginning the altercation. "Never knew a man who wasn't a damn fool for measurin' the size of his pistol. 'Sides, you go wavin' it at Lemon Lime an' she'll bend it in half for you. Be pissin' on your gunbelt everytime you went to take a leak. Hahaha."

Reflexively, Kearney backed off a few paces, his eyes narrowing at Daniels. He considered right then and there going for his gun, killing Shay before the old-timer had a chance to clear the table. "Don't be so funny, old man. Or I'll twist your beard like taffy."

As worldly as he was, Shay Daniels knew quick enough that Kearney was egging him on, trying to make him rush it. Wisely, Shay eased his own tension, while his eyes never left Kearney's gun hand. "It'll be the last thing you ever touch, farmboy," warned Daniels, hoping he was ambivalent enough so Kip didn't know whether Shay meant his beard or the gun near Kearney's hand.

Abruptly, the gun hand ceased its downward motion. A damn good idea. "I ain't got no time for fightin' with an' ol' ass like you."

"I didn't think you did," came Daniel's insouciant reply.

Suddenly Kip felt awkward. His hand suspended in midair, his brain searched for further insults. All eyes were upon him. His awkwardness changed to confusion, finally arriving at Kearney's personal sense of embarrassment. Even Lorenzo Stokes, his lips swelling, turning blue, was watching, waiting, hoping Kearney would make his move. Wisely Kip decided against it. "C'mon," he said to his underlings. "It stinks in here. Let's go get us some air."

Obediently the two cohorts, Patcheye Thorndike and Farley Ames, stood out of their seats and followed Kearney outside the Lost Hope Saloon. Once on the street the trio headed for the marketplace along the coastline. They walked with their usual swagger, their heads turning in search of trouble. With each footstep one or another would comment on the women they passed.

"She's too fat."

"Lookit that one. Ever see an' ass like 'at?"

"Well I'll be, take someone like me to keep her happy."

By the time they reached the marketplace the trio was laughing and clowning around once again. They jabbed and punched and poked at each other, guffawing for all they were worth. They returned contemptful glances at those who questioned their behavior. "Fuck you!" they challenged to those who had unwittingly turned their heads in Kip's direction. "What kinda town is this anyway? That can't see a man laughin' wit'out makin' a fuss?"

After the successful theft attempt of three apples, six oranges and a pear from the various stalls aligning the marketplace, the trio ambled on toward the edge of the water. Their boots squished against the mud. Their hat brims shadowed their faces.

"Hey, lookit 'at horse there. Know who she belongs t', don't cha?"

"Lemon Lime."

"Yeah, that's her horse all right. No one else in this damn town owns a paint like 'at one."

Patcheye Thorndike furtively glanced about with his one good eye. "See her aroun' anywheres?" he asked the leader of the pack.

Kip scoffed and kicked at the mud, almost slipping when he raised his foot. "Damn bitch! I'll kick her teeth down her throat if'n she gives me any trouble."

"She's a mean one, they say."

"They say! They say. Who says? I've handled more 'n one she bitch in my time. This one ain't no exception."

Before his buddies could protest, Kip moved toward Lemon's horse. He stroked its mane, fingered its saddle. He even undid the reins from the hitching post and was prepared to mount her, when he saw Lemon come charging from across the street.

"Hey, motherfuckers! Whatta you doin' with that horse? Get the hell away from that mare," swore Lemon when she neared the trio.

Kip stepped back a pace or two and smiled leeringly at Thorndike and Ames. "I thought this heah was my horse," snorted Kearney. "Foun' me one just like it. Jus' the other day. Ain't it right, boys?"

"Yeah. That's right."

"You motherfucker," spelled out Lemon Lime. "Move away from that horse before I kick your dick back out your ass."

"Well, now," snorted Kearney. "The lady talks dirty. In mixed company, no doubt. Should be taught a few manners. Doncha t'ink?"

Before anyone could answer Kip whirled around with a

255

wild left hook he had aimed for Lemon's head. She ducked under it and returned her own punch to Kearney's midsection. While he was doubled up she lifted her boot out from the mud and kicked him one, smack in his face. Thorndike and Ames grabbed for her, but Lemon was able to escape them by whirling and turning until she was free of their hands. She found solid ground, braced herself and kicked the onrushing Patcheye square in the balls. He dropped knees first into the mud.

Farley Ames landed a roundhouse right, which knocked Lemon from her feet. She rolled away from his ensuing barrage of kicks to her body and regained her footing. Meanwhile a crowd had gathered, most of whom were rooting for Lemon Lime. "C'mon, Lemon, whip his ass," they urged from the sidelines. No one dared come to her aid.

Recovered from their initial failure, Kip and his cohorts spread themselves out and rushed Lemon all at once. She leapt to her right, at Thorndike, hacking at his neck when she flashed by. Several blows landed on her head and shoulders but she was able to escape without much damage. She faced them again, her knife drawn in her hand. "C'mon, motherfuckers," she challenged them.

Patcheye Thorndike was the first to come for her. For his efforts he received a gash across his chest. Blood dripped between the ragged edges of his freshly torn shirt. He looked down, more surprised than dismayed. "What is it with her?" Patcheye asked of Kearney. "Is she crazy?"

Kip didn't answer. He advanced, his own knife drawn now. Farley Ames attempted to circle in from behind Lemon. She slashed again, cutting Farley's arm.

"Dammit, we gotta git organized," howled Kip, just as Lemon charged at him, hacking off a fair sized chunk of his nose for her effort. Kip yowled and put his hand to his face, leaving his middle unguarded. Lemon stabbed, catching the gunman's belly, but not severely enough to kill him.

"You'll die for this," howled Kip Kearney.

256

With Thorndike now somewhat recovered, the three men again attacked simultaneously. The weary Lemon Lime, this time, could not withstand their three-to-one advantage. After much struggle and a series of cuttings, kickings and oaths, the trio had her on the ground. With their knees pressed on her chest, Patcheye Thorndike and Farley Ames held Lemon's arms, while Kip Kearney hovered above his intended victim, gloating for all he was worth. "Now I'm a gonna kill ya," he declared, brushing his knife's cutting edge with the tip of his thumb.

In the midst of her struggle Lemon had noticed something strange. A familiar face stood out among the spectators. A face of old. It had been placed beside an extraordinary Indian, one who looked like he was peering from behind a leather kettle. An odd thought, she realized, perhaps her last, as Kip Kearney approached her with his knife. "Now I'm gonna show you jus' what you're made from," he hissed, revealing his intentions to slit her down the middle. He was suddenly interrupted.

"Kip," whispered a vaguely familiar voice. Kearney aboutfaced, the knife still in his hand. He was annoyed by the sudden interruption and was about to say so. What a surprise to discover Billy Brick before him, a .45 pressed in his hand. The barrel was pointed at the tip of Kearney's missing nose, its hammer cocked and threatening from just three feet away. Shelby wasted no time in pulling the trigger. Without another word he blew Kearney's head clean from his shoulders. It hung by a single tendon as Kearney collapsed to the street. Howls and cries rose up all around them. People crowded, pushed and shoved in order to cast their eyes on the grotesque spectacle before them. Except Thorndike and Ames, who by now had released Lemon Lime and were backing away from Shelby.

"Whatcha gonna do, mister?" pleaded Patcheye, his face covered with blood.

Lopez refused to reply. His revolver did the talking. In

rapid succession his next two shots killed Thorndike and Ames, the bullets' impact spattering blood on several onlookers, who fainted dead away. Thunderbird stepped forward and helped the battered Lemon Lime climb to her feet. Shelby turned his attention to the bystanders.

"I thought I killed him once before," he explained. "I guess now that this makes up for it." He holstered his pistol and assisted Thunderbird with Lemon.

"Clifford," cried the director of the Sno' Fuck Follies. "It is you, isn't it?"

"Yeah," answered Shelby, delighted to be standing by his lady once again.

After the town doctor had patched her up, Lemon and Shelby sat around his office discussing old times, bringing each other up to date on what had transpired since then. Lemon, slouched over, sat barechested, a gauze bandage wrapped around her shoulder where Kearney's knife had drawn blood. Except for the ugly gash, which required stitches to repair, and a few added bruises to her fine-boned face and torso, Lemon Lime seemed none the worse for her adventures.

"It's nice to see you," she laughed, adding special warmth to her statement. "Funny how you seem to show up at the right time."

"Whatever became of Lloyd DePugh?" asked Shelby, delighted she hadn't married the breeder.

"He's still in Kansas City, I'm sure. What was it you said out there? About you shooting Kearney before?"

His voice grown sullen with the memory of Rebecca Maltesin, Shelby related the story of Kearney, Walker, Barlow and Straughan. His guts quivered when he rediscovered his impression of Becky, her legs protruding from the rickety chickenshack. "All those years. I thought he was dead. Well, I guess it's finally the end of him."

Lemon's voice turned bitter when she recounted for Shelby ,the additional members of Big Ben's private army. "There's plenty more where Kearney came from. Dozens, at least. They're determined to hold on, retain power despite all the pressures against them. But their time is coming. I can smell it. Feel it."

A waning smile formed on Shelby's face. "Maybe," he said wearily. "And then again, maybe not. Either way, it ain't for me to decide. I'm too small a part of it to be fuckin' around with it all. Besides, I've other things to do. Me an' Thunderbird, we have business to take care of. Urgent business."

"The Indian?" quizzed Lemon. "Where'd you meet him?"

"In the desert. I was lost and he found me. We've been together ever since."

Musing briefly over Hawkins' comical appearance, Lemon attempted to be diplomatic. "He seems like no ordinary Indian to me."

"He's no ordinary anything," defended Shelby. "He's Thunderbird Hawkins."

Lemon wished to change the subject. "Y'know, many nights I laid awake, worrying if my father or DePugh had ever tracked you down. I would cry, thinking there was no chance I'd ever see you again. Whatever hope I had was lost long ago. I wandered about, dejected, just wishing we'd meet somewhere. God only knows the places I've been, the things I've seen and done. But no one ever took your place. All because we spent a few spare days together. Can you believe that? Just a few days, the only time we shared. Years ago. Yet, with all the days and weeks that have come between us, I keep returning to our train ride, our hotel room in Kansas City. Funny. I was just about to say I love you when DePugh broke down the door."

His jaw slack with astonishment, Lopez stared into the

259

face of Lana Culvane. An awkward silence passed between them, one encompassed by too many affections for words to express. A lump coiled in Shelby's belly. He blinked his eyes, uncertain if Lana's mud-stained face was merely another illusion. Tentatively, he reached out his hand and touched it. She turned her head in order to kiss his hand. Shelby bent over and lightly kissed her on her hairline. His prick stiffened down below. Another gesture of his affection. He ran his hand along her jawline, delicately twinking the corners of her mouth.

"I can't believe this. Nothing could be more surprising."

His discovery of Lana Culvane was to be only the first in a series of pleasant surprises. Shortly after he escorted Lemon from the doctor's office, he found himself sitting inside the Alaskan Queen Saloon. A half a glass of beer raised in his hand, he casually glanced toward the staircase, discovered his Aunt Belle Gluntz descending the steps. They stared silently at each other for ages, each too frightened the vision would disappear. Eyes blinked, hands trembled. Slowly, ever so slowly, Shelby climbed out of his chair and stalked toward the bottom of the staircase. Belle Gluntz remained on the third step, her eyes wide with surprise. "Shelby?" she asked softly, a voice that almost seemed one other than her own. "Is it you?"

Lopez nodded and lifted his arms. Belle stepped down and embraced him, allowing Shelby to pull her tightly to his chest. She pulled back her head, blinked her eyes and then plunged forward, her thick red lips leaving lipstick stains all over Shelby's cheeks and forehead.

"My God, my God, I don't believe it," she cried loud enough for all the world to hear. "It's a blessing, a pure blessing, straight from heaven."

Upon hearing the commotion downstairs, Shmuel Gluntz rushed to the staircase to see what was going on. "Who is it?" he quizzed from the top of the stairs.

"Shelby," replied Belle, between kisses. "He's here. Just

260

look at the size of him. My God. A regular cowboy, with spurs, a gun, boots and all. So big he is."

Demonstrating vitality he had long kept inside him, Shmuel raced down the stairs in a few leaps and bounds and joined the reunion. "I don't believe it. It's really Shelby." With that Shmuel managed to squeeze his arm between Belle and Shelby and take his nephew's hand. He pumped it vigorously, clapping Lopez on the back. When Belle stepped back, Shmuel embraced his nephew, pressing his cheek close to his. "Of all the fuckin' things . . ." he went on.

When the greetings had ended, Shelby introduced Thunderbird Hawkins, who had been patiently standing by. "We're friends," explained Shelby. "We met on the desert and have been together ever since."

Belle smiled at Thunderbird. In a flash her eyes ran up and down his portly frame, taking note of his blanket, the moccasins, the battered old top hat and the thick, dark hair that hung to his shoulders. It was difficult for Belle to determine if Hawkins was smiling back at her. "So what type of work do you do?"

Thunderbird shrugged, swallowed a shot of whiskey. "I perform the services required of Thunderbird Hawkins."

"That's nice. If you need work, we can always fit you into the Follies."

Shmuel had returned from the bar with bottles of whiskey clasped in each hand. Shot glasses, like transparent thimbles, were attached to each of his fingers. Upon setting the bottles down, Shmuel poured everyone a round. "May we all have years to share together," he toasted before downing the whiskey in one gulp.

"I should hope so," Belle intoned. "But who knows, with that little pisher across the street. . . . So what happened to you?" she asked of Lemon, noting for the first time the assorted cuts and bruises emblazoned on her face.

"I got into it with Kip Kearney. They were ready to kill me when Shelby stepped in."

261

Belle's head swung back in Shelby's direction. She awaited his further explanation.

"I shot him dead," he said simply.

Shmuel nodded and raised his glass again. "Mazel tov," he cheered, before downing another shot.

The reunited family drank until the wee hours of the morning. Stories were told, updating all that had transpired since they last had been together. One tale seemed to surpass the last in adventurous content. Names of places, people and things revolved around the table as if they had lives of their own. New realities, spawned from past experiences, appeared on the lips of the different speakers. The most harrowing, the more challenging of experiences were saluted with another shot of whiskey. By three in the morning, Belle and Shmuel were barely able to escort themselves upstairs. Lopez followed Lemon up to her room, while Thunderbird Hawkins prepared his bedroll in a vacant stockroom. Unable to sleep just yet, he took out his pipe and filled its bowl. He then sat back, drunk and contented beneath the amber light of the stockroom.

Inside Lemon's bedroom, the couple regarded each other in silence. Occasionally one's hand reached out to stroke the other, an eye winked and lips parted. Lopez wished for nothing more than to be locked in Lana's sweet embrace, aroused in the morning by sunshine conveying the aroma of bacon and eggs. Lana wished the same, but on second thought, she decided against it, remembering the injuries she had sustained during her fight with Kearney and his men.

"It's best that you leave tonight," she said reluctantly. "I'm in pain, and besides, it'd be best if I was alone to work it all out in my mind. You do understand, don't you?"

"Sure," replied Lopez, managing a weak smile for his lover. "Anything you say." With that he turned to go. Lemon stopped him, spun him around and kissed him on his mouth. "Go now," she whispered. "But don't go too far."

"If you need anything ... I'll be downstairs with Thunderbird."

Shelby found Thunderbird lost in his thoughts. In a trancelike state the Indian turned to him, his mouth parted slightly. "The Necklace is here. I can sense its presence."

Lopez knew better by now than to contest his companion's awareness of such matters. "The Great Necklace? Where?"

"Somewhere. Here."

"Then ... this may be the end of your journey."

"No. Journeys are like the turning of the Earth. Both continue in order to justify the original creation."

"Which was ... ?"

"For me, the seeking of the Great Necklace," came Hawkins' simple reply. "I've vowed to myself to retrieve it on behalf of all those who have gone before me."

"And the Great Book? What about that?"

"Yes, the Great Book," whispered Hawkins. "The two combined would reveal the wisdom of the world, the destiny of man. Once you learn their secret."

"You intend to find it?"

"I only intend to continue looking."

Shelby crossed his legs and took another hit off the pipe. "Then I intend to help you."

Hawkins smiled at his companion. "You already have. We've both been necessary for the benefit of each other. Tomorrow we shall begin our search."

"To tomorrow," laughed Shelby, the pipe raised in salute to the coming day.

"Tomorrow," repeated Thunderbird. "Without it, there'd be no sense in going on."

263

Chapter 14

As the dawn skulked behind a billowing curtain of leaves, Lemon Lime sat back and listened to the early morning wagon teams clopping in the streets below. The ocean breeze, with all its dampness, blew through the window, rippling the surface of the drink Lemon clutched in her hand. She shivered, pausing from her thoughts to rub at her breastbone for better circulation. In the mirror across the room a little girl pranced about on the pony her father had recently bought for her. Leading the mare was Moses Moriarity, his smile filling her day with childish optimism. Anything was possible when he was around, the little man with the balding head, his temples fringed with wiry ash. His old black gambler's suits seemed a might too tight for him, due to easy living on the Culvane estate.

Lemon's raising her drink to her mouth and then resettling the glass in her hand served as a metaphysical switch, changing the impressions she projected onto the looking glass. She was no longer a little girl, but much older, as was

Moses Moriarity. His hair was white now, his skin even more wrinkled than before. His suits were battered, shining in places. An old leather satchel hung from his hand. Moses was leaving. For good. Tears fell from Lemon's eyes as she watched him abandon her. He was waving goodbye, the broad smile still on his face. She cried bitterly, before her father yet, a man to whom she kept her emotions secret. He watched her, puzzled and dismayed. Culvane glanced up the road, viewing Moses Moriarity for one final time. And then back to his daughter.

"He'll be back," he mistakenly assured her. "People like him have no place to go."

"It's childish of me, I suppose, but never again do I feel I can expect anything to last."

One final sigh and Lana had regained her composure. She walked back toward the house, recalling her last visit with her mother. How frail and helpless the woman looked. As if this scrawny figure of a woman, this pathetic creature, was in fact all the time hiding just behind her matron's pretense. So large her eyes had seemed when set inside her head. Saucers looking up at her, staring straight ahead, yet saying nothing.

"Why doesn't she talk?" Lemon pleaded. But no one answered. A grim-faced doctor who was standing beside her father mournfully shook his head. As if it were a cue, he and Culvane departed, leaving Lana Culvane alone with her mother. "Mother?" called the daughter. "Come back. Please."

It appeared for an instant that Faye Culvane's eyes had actually fluttered. Her slackened jaw had regained a firmer posture. Her head turned, just slightly. "Mother?" called Lana.

Again the eyes fluttered. The head began to lift, raised slightly from the pillow. A little bit of clearance, a portion of space between head and mattress which revealed the difference between life and death. Lana looked on in astonishment. Faye's eyes were flashing, not fluttering now. Her

265

mouth had taken shape. Slowly it all turned from side to side, a dying woman's last request.

"No?" Lana whispered just loud enough for her mother to hear. "No what, Mama?"

But that was all. With a last gasp, the head fell back against the pillow, the jaw slackened and the eyes closed. Forever.

When Lana returned to her home Moses Moriarity was still there, packing his things. Upon her approach old Mo averted his eyes, afraid to reveal himself. "I'm sorry, little girl," he consoled. "Otherwise, there's nothing else to say."

"I know. Thank you." Her hand touched his shoulder. Mo looked up, his eyes a bit blurry.

"I'll be leavin' soon," he said, answering the question she expressed in her face. "Just me 'n' my little ol' bag." He didn't tell her about the book.

She sensed his awkwardness and wondered why. With little consideration, Lana passed it off as grief and sorrow for both her mother and his imminent departure.

"My mother's book," she asked of him. "Have you seen it?"

Mo's eyes widened. Again he turned his head away. "No. I can't say I have. I'm sure it'll turn up someplace. In the hands of those who'd know its power."

"Yes. But I wanted you to have it."

"Me? Why me?"

"Because. . . . now that my mother's gone, I feel it belongs to you."

His head nodding in capitulation, Mo bent down into his satchel and retrieved the book. "I lied to you, little girl. I have it here."

"But. . . . why?"

His leathery head swept from side to side. "Cause, this here book has an importance all its own. You an' me, we may never know what lies among its secrets, but there ain't no doubt that this book is something special. And I must take it away from here, to someone else."

266

"Who?"

"An old man. Like myself. Gettin' older by the minute. I know how he'd feel if he could see it but once. Call it a favor, if you will, a way to pay him back for what he done for me. But I'll be leavin' soon, jus' me and the book and my old leather satchel. Everything else I own is yours."

"But Mo. Can't you tell me more?"

"There is no more. Not that I will ever know. Lord, you know how I wish I did. All these years, studying, learning, trying to become an educated man. And all I ever kept finding out was how little I still knew. Except. ... except I knew about the Book. An' maybe that's all I ever needed to know in the first place. Cause it seems that was all that ever mattered. But you, little girl. ... a big girl now. You best take good care of yourself, an' live a good life for ol' Moses Moriarity. You keep him proud o' you. You keep him in love with the ground you walk on. Cause there's no one better than the likes a' you. My first Lady President."

With that Mo took hold and embraced her. They remained clutched in each other's arms for a long, long time, until they were interrupted by Doug Culvane's personal secretary. "Your pay is waiting for you on my desk. Mr. Culvane saw fit to leave you a little something extra," he said almost grudgingly.

Moses and Lana smiled at each other. "My father's such a generous man," she laughed sardonically. "A heart as large as the day is long."

The old man and the young woman followed the secretary across the grounds to the Culvane mansion. Mo received his money from the rickety hand and bowed deeply. "I thank ya, Mr. Silks."

The frozen Silks stared down his pince-nez at Moriarity. "Don't thank me. Thank Mr. Culvane."

"He wouldn't have the time to accept it," Lana interjected.

A few minutes later she was standing by the entrance gate to the Culvane estate. Her father was driving up in his carriage. He stepped out to say goodbye to Moriarity. The two men pumped hands for several moments before Moses departed. His back turned to father and daughter, Moriarity strode up the winding road, soon disappearing behind a clump of trees. Lana Culvane closed her eyes, clamped up her face in order to subdue the hysterics rising up inside her.

"Don't worry," her father repeated. "People like him have no place to go."

Chapter 15

Shelby Lopez watched the new day rise across the water. He breathed in deeply, his head still filled with smoke, his soul still tingling from the events of yesterday. Occasionally wagon teams, homeless drunkards and returning hookers passed him by. Above him the sky was clouded, threatening rain. With one giant step Lopez moved away from the street and entered the beach which led to the water. By now he was used to the uneven sand terrain and walked easily despite his present condition. What a relief it was for him to look up from his feet and be able to spot the wide span of ocean, just yards away. At last he selected his spot and sat down, a few feet from the water. For a while he thought of little more than the waves, their crunching power as they fell upon the rocks. He closed his eyes, suddenly struck with the belief that he was waiting for something, something to happen. What it was, he didn't know.

At last a numbness welled from within him. No longer could he feel, not even the soreness of his back, the stiffness of his legs. His head carried no weight, his eyes were swollen, sealed by an invisible pressure. He would've felt uncomfortable, helpless, had he been able to feel at all. Yes, indeed, something odd was happening. Something fantastic. A slight thrill cut through the numbness before subsiding.

It was then a man appeared. Who he was, Shelby had no idea. An old man, with long white hair, bearded and frail. His soft gray eyes were staring out to sea. Like Shelby he was watching the waves rise out of the water. This old man, he was sitting on a rickety old porch, a section of board protruding from an ancient wooden shack. A vacant chair stood nearby the one occupied by the old man. A small garden fronted the porch, leading into clusters of rushes, shrubs and elephant grass before terminating in a ragged precipice which fell some hundred feet or so before reaching the ocean. Neither the house, the grounds or the man had been tended to in years. Except for the garden.

So limpid were his impressions that Lopez soon began to feel that he was the man. An old man, white hair and all, just sitting in tranquility, staring out at the ocean. But wait, there was another man. A black man, as old as the occupant of the rundown shack. Dressed in an old black suit, the man approached from a narrow pathway, nearly recovered from the years untended. How the black man had found it, Shelby couldn't imagine. But he had come a long way. From his viewpoint atop the porch he noted the fellow's heavy steps no more than ten feet away. One boot had mounted the first step to the porch. He hesitated, awaited permission to continue his march. "You don't know me, do ya?" the old man smiled. His remaining teeth virtually gleamed from inside his wrinkled black face. "Look what I brought with me," he continued with pride. He extracted an old leather-bound book and handed it over. "Look, this is for you."

Shelby stared down at the book, unsure of his intentions. He didn't know whether to accept it or ignore it. Reluctantly he extended his hand, his limb feeling older and wearier as it stretched further into space. He had nearly touched the edges of the leather when he was suddenly interrupted. Someone was standing beside him. Shelby's eyes popped open as he prepared to defend himself from one of the vagrants who prowl the beaches late at night. He was relieved to discover it was Thunderbird Hawkins who was standing beside him.

"What's happening?" asked Thunderbird in a manner that betrayed his awareness.

"It must've been a dream. I felt like an old man sitting on a porch. When another old man, an old black fellow, came up to me and offered a book. I mean. . . . I didn't even know the man. He just appeared from nowhere, in the middle of nowhere. Somewhere along the coast, I guess."

"This old man. The one who you thought you were. What did he look like?"

"A tall, bony creature. With long, gnarled hands, a wrinkled face. Pure white hair hanging down to his shoulders. A beard. I don't know. I just don't know. I felt just like him. I felt I was him, only I knew I couldn't be. Cause I am someone else."

"That's true," Hawkins admitted. "But there's always more than one truth to fit an answer. This place you saw, would you remember it again?"

"It would be harder to forget than remember. It's not every day I have dreams like this. When I was a little kid I had a dream one time about a witch chasin' me. I couldn't yell, I couldn't call out. I was naked, with a gun in my hand. A little kid, armed with a pistol. But no bullets . . ."

"Yeah, yeah," Thunderbird interrupted, not at all concerned with Shelby's earlier dream. "But what about this house? Have you ever seen it before?"

Lopez shook his head no. "Why?"

"For I believe in your vision, or your dream as you call it, lies the secret of the Great Book. I believe you've discovered its location."

"C'mon," scoffed Shelby. "Why would the Great Book be

271

comin' after me? I mean, I'm no great seeker. I only promised to look for the Necklace because. . . ."

"Because what?"

"Because of what it means to you. Me, ah ... I mean, what would I do with the wisdom of the world anyway? With me it would probably only go to waste. I'd have some smoke, lie back and forget whatever wisdom that came to mind."

Hawkins laughed at his companion's perplexities. He patted Lopez's shoulder and assured him all would be just fine. "We must find this shack, and the Great Book. Together. For now I do believe I know why you and I were chosen to travel together."

Shelby was still reluctant to believe his dream held any credence. "You don't suppose it was something I ate, do you? Salami used to give me nightmares all the time."

"You explain too much," said Hawkins. "Your true feelings are hidden by a mask of poor excuses. This dream you spoke of will return. Until you seek the location of the Great Book, the same vision will come back, a reminder of a consciousness that dwells beneath all logic. Whatever comes next will never harm you. You have nothing to fear but your own confusion. Otherwise, all will be well."

"How do you know all this?"

"Because. ... Hawkins the Hermit is given to tender ways."

Her wounds and bruises stiff with pain, Lemon Lime awakened to discover she was still coiled inside her old, gray easy chair. Tentatively she straightened out her arms and legs, expected further aching when she attempted to get on her feet. Standing now, she glanced about her, noting it was late in the morning. While in the midst of a yawn, Lemon

272

stepped toward her bureau mirror, where she paused to inspect her lips and teeth. A delight it was to discover everything was still intact. Indeed she had paid a small price for the riddance of the deranged Kip Kearney.

Cautiously Lemon proceeded to wash and dress herself. When her face and body were cleaned to satisfaction, she searched her room for something fresh to wear. It was then that Lemon was struck by the fact that nothing she owned had belonged to her when she first met Shelby Lopez. Everything was different, less refined, not as frilly and pure. Even her more personal possessions had been acquired sometime after Clifford Dash had leapt from the window in order to escape from Lloyd DePugh. Her comb and brush, made from walrus tusks, had come from Alaska, her hand mirror had been stolen from the house of one of Lemon's many wealthy suitors. The dandy hunting knife had been a present from a knife thrower, a performer attached to Regis Perth's Actor's Troupe. Her shin-high leather boots, her jeans, her leather jacket, the silver concho belt, she wouldn't have dared wear such things when she was simply Lana Culvane. Well, she wasn't Lana Culvane any more. Time and experience had seen to that. Time, passing by in captivating ribbons, blending emotional polarities with new and strange sensations. Time, combined with distance, culminating in a novel expression of her human being. Lost in its confusion was Lemon Lime, unable to make the distinctions between the deliberate and the coincidental. It had simply happened to her as if, after leaving on the train from Chicago bound for Kansas City, an unsung switchman had switched the tracks, channeling her destiny toward the unexpected. What a nightmare it had been at first. Penniless, isolated, unprotected, she had been left to her own devices. There was no going home, that was for certain. Forward was the only direction. But where was that? How did you eat? What did you do?

Townfolk had been suspicious of her. The further West

she travelled, the rougher her life became. So much greater were the dangers found in the wild country compared to those encountered back home. Nothing compared to the constant threat against her life and limb as she journeyed West and then South, looking, hoping searching for a means to stay alive. When she could, Lemon worked odd jobs, most often as a waitress in a town's only hash house. In time her frilly dresses and luxurious accessories were exchanged for the durable jean and boot attire. Her hair was no longer dressed and teased, but absent of the coiffure's touch. Her golden tresses now hung loosely about her shoulders or were bound by a single ribbon or pigtails tied back by two leather thongs.

"Well, I never ..." bantered the respectable ladies who lived in the towns through which Lemon had travelled. Their fingers pointed to her ass, which was so well defined by her softening blue jeans, the ladies of the town would gossip among themselves, speculating on the scandals this strange woman would create.

"Hey, here comes Calamity Jane," bantered the barflies.

"Hi there, my name is Mike. Could I show you to my room?"

One town passed into the next. One job became another, and still a third, all continuing along an even plane, never rising to greater challenges, never transcending the confines of her awkward position. It was not until Lana had discovered Rue Halpern that she finally had a chance to settle down. If but just for a moment.

Rue Halpern had once been one of the territory's most notorious gunfighters. But he was old now, and all but forgotten, save for dime-novel legends and the barflies of Morganville who still called him friend.

"I'm tired," admitted Lana, after Rue Halpern had bought her a drink. "I can't go on like this anymore."

"Then set for a spell, my lil' lady. My cabin ain't much,

but it's as good a place as any to call your home. If even for a bit. Jus' a tiny bit."

She moved in, allowed the dubious freedom of Rue Halpern's two-room adobe shack, located just outside of Morganville's city limits. With Halpern being much older than Lana, he expected little from the willowy creature he loved to admire. Occasionally, on special holidays and during the times when Rue was able, they did get it on. Otherwise, Lemon was left to her own devices. As Halpern's companion she found credence and could stride about the town unchallenged and unmolested. Her confidence grew. Her mind expanded. Bit by bit she learned the ways of the West, the town and the surrounding desert.

"I'm gonna teach ya the pistol," Rue offered on many occasions. Before Lana could protest she was led out behind the house where Rue maintained a firing range, consisting of little more than a backdrop and whiskey bottles he had sucked dry.

"I'm really afraid of guns," said Lana, the weapon appearing so cumbersome when grasped in her hands.

"A lady on her own should learn how t' take care of herself. There's no tellin' what kinda trouble's brewin' out yonder. One day, what you learn from me might come in handy."

Between shooting instructions and long talks about the West, Lana and Rue shared many a bottle of whiskey along with their share of good times. Often they took rides up into the mountain country, where they explored the terrain. When the winter months set in they sat together by the adobe fireplace. Fortunately for Lemon, Rue Halpern never ran out of stories to tell. For the better part of his life he had been a desperado on the run from the law. He had robbed banks, trains, had served as a spy in the war and had been pardoned for his contribution to the Yankee cause.

"I've lived a damn good life," he declared when drunk.

275

"I'm not sorry for a bit o' it. No. Never been sorry at all."

"But how did you end up here?" Lana asked between exchanges of whiskey.

"Here's the same as anywhere. A bare bit of space for a tired ol' ass like mine. Now, if I had been younger, I would've done it differently."

"How?"

"If I wuz young like yourself, I would've gone off to Alaska. Gone lookin' for gold."

"But I thought you said you didn't need any more money than what you had?"

Rue blinked through his one good eye. He scratched at the patch which covered his other, the left one. He jerked his head, sweeping his graying hair across his shoulders. A finger came up to press down his mustache.

"It ain't for th' gold," he muttered. "Not for the gold a-tall. But for the adventure," he was quick to put in, in order to answer Lana's next question. "A man needs adventure in his life. Not just the gold. Tha's why I became an outlaw in the first place. Hell, my father was a doctor, a damn good one at that. Worked in the city, he did, and made plenty o' money too. Led a damn good life, but he had no adventure. Not the thrills 'n' challenges that I was cravin' for, anyways. I can see him now. Bald as a berry, he was. His thick finger always pointin' at me. Right here, he did. Right at my chest, like his finger was a pistol. 'Son,' he'd tell me. 'You ain't gonna amount t' shit.' 'N' with 'at, he barred me from his house. Told me he was gonna do the sensible thing. He'd take a vacation on the money he had saved for my education. Anyhow, they were raw days. No law for miles. 'N' no goin' aroun' pretendin' there was such a thing. Everyone for himself. No bullshit about it."

"Sounds like a bit of a struggle to me."

"It still is," scoffed Rue Halpern. "Only nowadays we make believe it's different. Well, it ain't different. It only looks different. That is, it looks different when you're at the

276

top. But when you're down here in the middle of it, like you 'n' me, then nothin's changed a-tall. Only fact is, I'm older 'n' slower 'n' more confused by the new ways o' killin'. Somehow it all climbed behind me. Jus' lurkin' there, waiting for me to make my one false move. And then it's over for Rue Halpern. Lived by the gun, died in confusion. Ain't no other eulogy that can closely fit mah life."

Winter passed into spring, and Lana felt restless. Still, she believed she owed much to her companion and remained with the former gunfighter, helping him with the garden he had cultivated alongside his adobe shack.

"Sometimes I feel I'm just growin' sand," Rue scowled at his little patch of cultivated earth. "Ain't no sense in tryin' to raise crops around here. Th' birds 'n' the dogs pick over the harvest anyway. Last season all I picked was but one tomato an' a few scoops o' beans. Not much t' live from."

"Then why go on with your garden?"

"Keeps me busy, I guess," laughed Rue, his laughter ceasing abruptly when he glanced back over his shoulder. His eyes narrowed in gradual recognition. Bart Kovacs was standing over him, his hand draped over his gun.

"Well, now," snorted Halpern. "If it ain't Bart Kovacs. Haven't seen you since the winter o' sixty-nine."

Kovacs said nothing. He turned his attention to Lana Culvane, immediately believing she was Halpern's daughter. As old as Kovacs was, just about as aged as Halpern, his eyes still twinkled at the sight of Lana Culvane. His pasty tongue slipped between the spaces of his decaying teeth, dabbing his lips with a fresh coating of moisture. His eyes surveyed the implicit delicacy of Lana's slender body.

"What can I do for you?" asked Halpern, interrupting Kovacs' lecherous glances.

Bart Kovacs was annoyed by the interruption. His head twisted back toward Halpern, his irritation carved in his features. "We got us a score t' settle," claimed Kovacs in his gruffest tone.

"What kinda score is that?" asked Rue, climbing slowly to his feet.

"An old score," added Bart Kovacs.

"Is that a fact?"

His eyes narrowed, Bart Kovacs watched apprehensively while Rue slipped his hand into his pocket and extracted a half-filled bottle of whiskey. He offered the flask to Kovacs, who cautiously accepted.

"Good for a dry throat, ain't it?" Halpern asked of Bart Kovacs.

"Sure is."

Rue took a long pull on the bottle and handed the remainder of its contents to Lana. She refused, at which point Rue polished off the rest. "Now," he said. "What about this score you've been keepin' for all these years?"

"An old score," Kovacs repeated.

To display his disgust for Kovacs' motivations Rue belched his whiskey in Bart's face. "Old scores belong t' old games," he contested. "If you'd just look aroun' you, you'd see that times are different. Everything's changed, including you an' me."

Kovacs heard little of Halpern's argument. "I've been huntin' ya ever since I found ya knocked up my Bessie. That it weren't my chile but yours that was makin' a bubble in her belly."

"So that's it," confirmed Rue Halpern, pausing to scratch his neck. "So you wasted all this time jus' to come see me about some woman you never loved in the first place."

"Love ain't got nothin' t' do with it. It's mah honor that counts. Man's got his self respect t' think of. Ain't a pretty thing to watch someone's chile born from your ol' lady's pussy."

"It could've been yours."

"Yeah. Sure. It could've been mine. But it wasn't. It was yours. Bessie tol' me so herself."

Halpern scoffed at Kovacs. "You never paid heed to one

278

damn thing your woman ever had to say. E'ceptin' that. Where's she now? What about the child?"

Bart Kovacs laughed bitterly. For a moment or two he seemed lost in the past, reflecting on his vengeance. "I took care o' em, in my own particular way."

"What is this?" Lana suddenly protested, startling the two old gunhands. "You two must be out of your minds. That was over, long ago. Hell, it's a rare day now when either of you can have it stand in the right position."

"She's right," Rue acknowledged. "It's too old to fight about."

"You fucked my Bessie!" Kovacs insisted.

"So I did. But just for a little while. Ain't much between us. Just a stiff dick for twenty minutes or so. I was tired an' lonely. ... An' I was on the run. Every sheriff in the territory was lookin' for us. A bullet in mah shoulder, sores on mah ass from all that ridin'. It was amazin' I lived through it all ... Would never have happened if you hadn't led us into that trap. Every citizen in the world was waitin' for us with a gun in his hand. Damn you!"

Lana could see that Rue was getting angry. She watched him touch the wound he had sustained many years before. Its scar still registered just below his shoulder. Up until now she had never known how he had come by his wound. "Runnin' from a posse," was Halpern's total explanation.

"C'mon now, let's settle down," Lana commanded. But the two men refused to listen. "Hey! What is this?" she cried when they backed from each other, their heads filled with memories, glories from the past. "Hey, come on now. Cut this out."

Rue wasn't listening. Neither was Bart Kovacs. They were a good fifteen feet apart from each other, their hands stretching, testing the reflexes.

"You're both too old to be fighting like this. Over a woman neither of you ever loved. Crazy! You must be crazy!"

"I'm a-callin' ya out, Rue Halpern," came Bart Kovacs' challenge. "It's high time ya paid for what you done to me."

"I did nothin' but fill in where you didn't belong in the first place. Damn fool! Couldn't plan a bank job right if your life depended on it."

"Hey c'mon," pleaded Lana, just as the guns cleared their respective holsters. "Bang, bang," two shots fired in rapid succession. Rue Halpern fell to the ground. Bart Kovacs clutched a nearby wall, gasping for breath. Blood dribbled from between his fingers. He had been shot in the gut.

Lana rushed to Halpern's side. He shrieked in pain when she attempted to turn him over on his back. "Rue! Rue?" she called, hoping it had all been a trick, a fantastic practical joke which had been designed by two near-senile old fools. It wasn't. The last bit of life was escaping Rue Halpern. "Rue? Rue?"

"Under the bed, there's a loose floorboard," Rue gasped. "A lil' money, left over from a job in '71. Take it 'n' go to Alaska. Your future waits in the cold."

Tears welled in Lana's eyes as, for the first time in her life, she watched a man die a violent death. Nearly a year had been spent beside Rue Halpern, and she had grown to love him in that time. Sure, being an old gunfighter and a confirmed bachelor at that, he had acquired slovenly habits and was prone to be drunk more than he was ever sober. But he had been kind and capable of meeting the challenges offered by Lana's inquisitive imagination. She had learned much from the man, and he had provided her with sanctuary, a place to exchange the patterns of her life for those she deemed more useful. And now he was dying, a gunfighter's death, but a foolish demise nevertheless.

By this time Bart Kovacs had managed to stagger forward, his hat doffed in deference to Rue Halpern. Tears filled Kovacs' eyes, those of sorrow indistinguishable from the tears of pain. It was increasingly evident that Bart

280

Kovacs would also die for his efforts. A gutshot was too difficult for a man of his age to survive.

"I'll have two graves to dig in the morning," Lana admonished the suffering Kovacs.

Kovacs blinked back the tears. "Side by side, the way it used t' be."

"You damn fool! Why did you ever do it?"

"I had nothin' else. Nowhere to be. It all slipped by me, before I ever had a chance to take o' hold."

"You could've stayed with us, sat about the fire, drinkin' whiskey, talking old times. Anything . . . anything would've been better than this."

"I'm afraid you didn't know Rue Halpern. I gave him what he always hoped for . . . a gunfighter's death."

"So you did."

Before more could be added, Bart Kovacs suddenly fell to his knees. His head lifted up toward the heavens as he mumbled his prayer, the last he'd ever recite on earth. When he had finished he collapsed at the feet of his old buddy, Rue Halpern.

By now a crowd had gathered around the scene of the recent gunfight. The town's sheriff, an old man himself, the barflies, stray dogs and children all gathered to see what was going on. Their collective eyes requested some explanation from Lana Culvane. "You tell me," she said before going off to retrieve her shovel.

The next morning, just before dawn, Lana Culvane saddled Rue Halpern's old horse and rode out of town. Her saddlebags contained a meager supply of foodstuffs, some clothing, Rue's old handgun, and the few pieces of gold he had left over from his last robbery. Before departing from Morganville, Lana returned to the grave of Rue Halpern. He had been planted in his own backyard, beside the body of his old companion, Bart Kovacs. Lana raised her arms skyward, above the graves of the two old and desperate men.

What a shame it was that Kovacs had been able to overcome all interference, the obstacles that stood in his way. A pity his journey hadn't changed him, hadn't enabled the gunfighter to see more than his object of vengeance. For what had taken place in Halpern's yard had not been the climax to their rich and colorful lives. Only an ending.

Like other instances in her ill-fated life, her embarkation for Alaska did not go as Lana had intended. While seated by her campfire in the open plains, two saddlebums attacked her, raping and robbing before leaving her for dead.

"You bastards," she had cried after her assailants, only causing them to laugh all the more. "Motherfuckers! One day I'll catch up with you for this."

"Ain't she purty there, Albert, all nekkid an' smooth 'n' jus' waitin' for some buzzard's love."

Naked, stretched before the two bums, Lana now wished she had paid more attention to Rue Halpern whenever he instructed her in matters of the gun. Like she had done with the piano, she had learned the mechanics of the instrument and then had failed to practice. Her failure ashamed her, for now she had been victimized by two motley saddlebums. "Bastards," she hissed again, the blood sticking to her chin.

"I got jus' th' thing to shut her mouth, Lamont," giggled the badman. Pressing his knife to Lana's throat, he knelt before her, his cock forced against her mouth. After resisting his first attempts, Lana finally parted her lips. Albert shoved his cock inside her. Unwittingly, Lana bit down on his sour penis. When he shrieked in agony her teeth clamped down even harder, forcing him backward, his hands clutched between his legs. "Aieie, yowww," moaned the saddletramp. "She bit my dick near in half."

Before she could gloat over her modest victory, the second

saddletramp leaped from her blind side, proceeding to kick her all about the campsite. Blinded by his rage, he kicked and pounded, promising he'd ruin her forever.

"You bit his dick, you dirty bitch," howled Lamont, while Albert continued to roll about in agony. "I'll kill you for this," he bellowed, bringing his pistol from out of its holster. The barrel was pointed against her temple before Albert intervened on her behalf.

"No," he roared. "Leave her to die by the buzzards."

"Yeah," Lamont was obliged to snicker. "She'll die much harder that way."

Her ribs broken, her face bloodied, Lana remained with her arms outstretched for the remainder of the night. Barely perceptible was the bandits' departure, as they took everything of value with them. Her horse, her gun, even her clothes were gone now. Only her naked torso flashing pale in the moonlight testified to the horrible assault. And in the morning this slight amount of evidence would quickly be gobbled by the vultures who lurked overhead. Before she lapsed into unconsciousness, Lana swore once again that she'd find Lamont and Albert.

Her promise would've been useless, and she would've died right there in the desert, had not a wandering theater troupe discovered her the following morning. Numbering five men and nine women, the four-wagon caravan was on its way to a nearby village when it discovered the half-dead Lana. They were prepared to bury her and had even dug a shallow grave when they discovered she was still alive.

"Do you hear breathing?" whispered Regis Perth to Pamela Terrace, his longtime leading lady.

"My God! She's alive," exclaimed Pamela, dropping her grip on Lana's arm.

"She won't be if you handle her like that," Perth admonished. "Dugan? Where's Dugan?"

"On the other side of the wagon, praying for the dead."

"Damn him. Get me some water."

Upon discovering that Lana was still alive, the remainder of the actor's troupe gathered around her body. Even Dugan Pompquist, Regis' youthful lover, was on hand to observe the reincarnation. They cheered urgently when Lana appeared to accept the water. "Do you think she'll live?" asked Dugan.

"How should I know? I'm not God, but his actor."

"She had quite a build on her," winked Pamela Terrace, running her hands across Lana's body.

"Keep those paws to yourself, you old hag. Whom you happen to be touching is Regis Perth's bright new starlet. Actors, meet the starlet. Starlet . . . meet the actors." Unfortunately Lana was too near death to respond.

For nearly two weeks Lana Culvane lay inside Perth's wagon, recuperating from her wounds. Gradually her feeling was restored to her arms and legs, and her anger aided in her ability to withstand any lingering diseases. In due time she was up and around, behaving as if nothing had happened. Nothing at all.

To help her regain her strength, Elmer Lanser, a former knife thrower in the St. James Wild West Show back East, offered to instruct Lana in the use of the knife. "Throw so there is only one turn of the blade between yourself and the target," he informed her during countless sessions. With the throats of the two motley saddletramps before her eyes, Lana was quick to adapt the knife as her weapon. In short order she was able to throw two daggers simultaneously, with each striking different targets.

"Bravo!" applauded Regis Perth, with Dugan and Pamela looking on from his side. "Bravo! Bravo! Bravo! But unfortunately a knife throwing act just won't sell tickets. What you need to do, my dear, is to become an actress. As part of this great troupe of ours, your ideals will reach fruition, your desires will multiply. You will shower enchantment, glory and fable . . . upon the coarsest group of roughnecks you've ever laid your eyes on. But they pay, and pay well too, for a

284

glance of ass, a peep at the thigh. And the businessmen, the fine citizens of the community, there is nothing that they wouldn't do for a creature as fine as yourself. As all the ladies of the troupe can proudly declare, there is no one more vulnerable than a bare-assed banker or a lawyer with his tongue hanging out from exhaustion. So you will render them, my dear, as we gad about from town to town, living from our nefarious earnings, money acquired both on and off the stage."

"What Regis is trying to tell you," piped in Pamela Terrace, "is that we get it wherever we can. There are no heights to which a gross bunch like ourselves cannot extend our talons and no depths to which we fail to stoop."

"Only if the price is right, my dear. And Lana Culvane, from now on we shall call you Lemon Lime. You'll make a fine dramatic actor, you will, and the desire of every stiff penis on this side of the Mississippi. For it is here, among this ragged band of creative crusaders, that you have found a home."

In the course of her touring with Regis Perth and his actor's troupe, Lemon encountered numerous exotic situations. She was wined and dined by the best of the territory's leading businessmen. Bankers, local politicians begged to do her favors. Ladies' clubs threathened to have her run out of town. Nevertheless, Lemon Lime was always able to return good bounty to the struggling actor's troupe. And when times were good and she and the other ladies were swamped in luxury, there was much occasion for celebration. During their wild festivities the actor's troupe became most intimate with one another. In time Lemon found herself experiencing all sorts of carnal delights in the respective wagons of Regis, Pamela and the remainder of the actor's troupe. Men slept with men, women lay beside other women. And the caravan wandered northward, out of one territory and into the next.

"You know, I've come to love you all," said Lemon one night over dinner.

Regis seemed most amused. "That's because we're actors. As such we portray what we please, what will bring joy, what will annoy and what will depress. There are so many out there who are incapable of performing the basic functions of changing moods, in the matter by which God had intended. For people to feel, to emote and to portray the very best of what they find inside themselves. So we are hired, a dime a dance, to spin around swiftly and then discard ourselves ... like ruined ideals. 'Tis a pity. A shameful pity. But without pity, tragedy and the likes, there would be no drama. And, my dear, without drama, Regis Perth could never survive."

Lemon struggled to lift the wine bottle to her mouth. "But all we do is exaggerate reality."

"Exaggerate!" exclaimed Perth, taking another nip from his glass. "Exaggeration makes things bigger ... all the better for the myopic to see."

"No. No. We only help them relish a brief instant of their lives. A small matter by which they can identify. A mundane occurrence that appears sensational when projected from the stage. We're just a particle of meaning, that's all, encountered somewhere between life and death."

"Oh, Lana," Perth admonished. "You really must do something about your attitude. Perhaps you should be the director. As the director you'd be able to gain an overall view of the total performance. You will be respected, revered even, if not challenged. Really. You must give it some thought. Before time slips away. Before you lose sight of your better nature and are stuck with the worst of the bargain."

So Lemon became a director. Her dramatic productions did enhance the credibility of the actor's troupe, and soon the more sophisticated of local papers began carrying pictures of the performers. The added publicity increased the actors' incomes, and Perth and his bunch even began to acquire their own brand of respectability. That is, until they reached Santa Placebo.

What had previously been a quiet, tiny village was now dubbed the "Anaconda of the South." Silver was everywhere, or so the legends said. Brochures, leaflets and souvenir maps abounded with inspiration, promises of riches. "If you're looking for wealth, fame and glamour, then you should be looking in beautiful Santa Placebo," the literature dutifully recited. It was all a hoax, of course, evolving from the rumor spread by the local idiot who came running from the public drinking fountain with a silver filling clutched between his fingers.

"I'm rich, I'm rich," he shouted for all to hear, rushing to the land office to stake his claim upon the drinking fountain.

Despite the outcry from certain sectors of the community, the shrewder businessmen refused to protest. The local idiot was allowed to stake his claim to the water fountain, while the prominent citizens set about the task of creating a stir. "Silver was everywhere," they swore to anyone who'd listen. "Come, come visit Santa Placebo."

Soon thousands had taken them up on their offer. What hotel accommodations had been built for the occasion were nowhere near adequate to assuage the gathering throngs. An outcry rose up, and the prospective miners were soon quartered in abandoned mineshafts and tent cities. Outrageous prices were charged for the luxury of a bed, and food was so dear only the wealthiest of individuals could afford to eat. Still they came. The additional fruitless mineshafts were soon converted into quarters in order to house the multitudes. Soon miners were everywhere, gathered in clusters, trading stories in the meager lamplight.

Though few claimed to have struck it rich, stories abounded in regards to friends who had met with fortune in Santa Placebo. Such stories travelled madly, expanded to new dimensions, split and expanded again, until the entire

287

town was virtually covered with rumors of fabulous successes.

Naturally, crime ran rampant in Santa Placebo. The local women were warned to keep off the streets at all times, and those who remained were considered whores and adventuresses, fair game to all concerned. With growing frequency, rapes and murders appeared in the pages of Santa Placebo's lone newspaper. But it was a small price to pay for the killing made by the local townsfolk. The grocer, the saloon keepers, the general merchants all made a fortune, which they barely maintained when the larger companies, the professionals, moved in on Santa Placebo. In short order, the once-innocuous village was divided up into different domains. All those who protested the invasion by the outside interests were quickly dispensed with. From this new base of conflict, new friction developed. Chaos was rampant. Free-for-alls, mass murders erupted extemporaneously. Men fought and men died, vying for the affections of the few women who offered their favors. In turn they were replaced by others who were ignorant of the strife which had befallen Santa Placebo.

It was in the midst of this chaos that Regis Perth brought his caravan to Santa Placebo. Even he, the worldly Perth, was astonished by what he saw. "By the looks of this," he said, "all towns must be remarkably pure, now that the scum of the earth have collected here." Upon the crowded, raging street he then stepped, alighting from the wagon with a deep bow to no one in particular, drawing his hat in a broad, sweeping motion.

"He'll get us killed if he behaves like this," sighed Pamela Terrace. She moaned bitterly as the crowd gathered by the wagons, pawing and whistling at the different actors.

"Now, now, my mortal mutants," scolded Perth. "In just a few hours this marvelous troupe will deliver the first in its series of fine performances. For it is our aim to raise the standard of culture in your delightful hamlet. To serve you as we've served the gentry of the land. Please bear in mind, tickets for this evening's performance may be purchased in advance, or at the door."

With that out of his way Regis Perth proceeded to bargain with the Chamber of Commerce for adequate theater facilities. After much haranguing, mainly in conflict over their share in the profits, the chamber finally suggested the Old Sloe Gin, a burnt-out saloon that stood at the far end of town. Angry miners had destroyed the interior as well as the roof during a recent outburst.

"I've never seen such a captive audience," proclaimed the overjoyed Perth, now that the arrangements had been made. "After months of lusting after phantom silver, these Neanderthals are about ready for anything."

"Even us," scowled Pamela Terrace.

"Remember," added Regis, speaking slowly for effect. "At intermission, when the lights go out for several brief but profitable moments, it will be our time to stake our claim. Dip into those ragged pockets for all your worth. Show them your boobs, your smile, your puckered behinds. But don't show them what you really came for."

"I think you're playing with fire," intoned Pamela Terrace. It was clear she didn't like Perth's plan one iota. "These are desperate people caught in a desperate situation."

"And what's more desperate than the plight of culture? Besides. What's wrong with fire? Is it not the gift of God?"

"I'll try and remember, when they boil you in tar."

"Come now, Pamela, my dear. What a terrible fate to be abandoned, left to the vices of a thousand slobbering miners."

"You wouldn't dare, Regis. Even you would be unable to recover."

"Enough of that," interrupted Lemon Lime. "We should

rehearse our performance, not rehash familiar arguments."

"They're one and the same to me," muttered Pamela before shuffling off to prepare herself.

Regis Perth clucked after Pamela Terrace. "One day she should wander into a pickax."

"You'd never know what to do without her."

"True," sighed Regis. "But I'd be brave. Oh hell, let's practice our Parisian Revue. Make it all the more risque so we can numb the bastards before we make off with their wallets."

"I'll see what I can do."

As expected, the crowd overflowed well beyond the capacity of the Sloe Gin Saloon. Fights erupted when extra bodies tried to push their way into the angry, crushing mob. A few innovative souls climbed the building walls, assuming precarious positions in the crumbling upper stories. Others shouted, raved, fired their pistols and jacked off in the middle of the scene. The excitement of witnessing live ladies half naked on stage was simply too much for the horny brood. Anticipation was high, the atmosphere frightening, when the lights dimmed inside the Sloe Gin Saloon.

The show began with its routine dance numbers and several comedy skits laced with double entendres. But as time elapsed, more skin and sass were gradually revealed, and frenzy encompassed the miners. Lecherously they licked their lips, soused their gills with rotgut whiskey and humped at the back of the fellows before them. More fights erupted, amidst the turbulent aura projected by catcalls, jeers and raucous hooting.

"A smash! A wonderful success," declared Regis Perth from the waiting wings. He then recited every cliché that was common among theatrical reviews while beaming from ear to ear. In the midst of his glory, Perth was eager to ignore the turmoil which had increased substantially as the miners attempted to drag the performers from the stage.

Pamela Terrace had just managed to escape and was back in the waiting wings exhorting Regis to halt the performance. As evidence she directed his eyes to study the sordid array of bruises and pinch marks she had incurred while before the miners. Perth ignored her.

"Nonsense. Nonsense. It's been so long since you've last performed before an appreciative audience that it's thrown your mind into a tizzy. You must have more appreciation for their accolades. You should smile, not scowl, when they receive you."

"Regis, I do believe we're stoking the very fires which may well consume us."

"So eloquent. She speaks with such flair, such drama. If one had not known her sordid secrets, he'd think she belonged to the finest stages of Europe."

"Regis ... please!" cried Pamela as intermission neared. But Perth would hear none of it. As prearranged, he cut the lights, hoping the performers would return from intermission with their pockets bulging with contraband.

"You've returned from your foraging. How nice," he said, when the different actors appeared in the backstage area.

"Regis," Lemon interrupted. "Maybe we should take these off," she said, pointing to her skimpy costume. "We're just asking for trouble."

"What? You have no desire to restore the light to the eyes of those weary souls who work the earth in our behalf? Where is your conscience? Your duty?"

"We may be killed."

"Nonsense. Performers never die. Only mortals die. Actors are as immortal as the roles they play. Now get out there and give them what they're looking for."

No sooner had the ladies hit the stage for the second act than the miners exploded. Frenzied, frothing at the mouth, they clamored, heaving and whipping as they dashed for the actors. Skulls crunched, bodies crumpled, while blood doused the floor of the Sloe Gin Saloon. Fires were ignited, the flames extending to nearby structures which were soon ablaze.

Doris Rengue was the first of the ladies to be grabbed, pulled from the stage, pinched and squeezed and ripped apart by the hysterical mob. Some pounced on her trampled corpse, still eager to make love. They were immediately bashed across the head by anxious replacements.

Regis and his troupe dashed for the wagons. All except for Lemon Lime, who made for the opposite direction. Finding a discarded woolen overcoat, she threw it over her shoulders, then donned a battered workman's cap before exiting the burning saloon. She soon found her escape afforded her little salvation, for the frenzy had spread throughout the town. Buildings were burning everywhere. Brawls and impromptu skirmishes permeated the streets. Bodies were strewn about. There was much screaming, unendurable confusion. Lemon raced for the stables in hopes of finding a horse still breathing. Shadows of men danced madly about her, darting in and out of the fires. The town was finished, a goner for sure. Purged from the earth by one round of frustration. But Lemon had no time for such insights and considerations. Clutching the knife she had found in the debris, she scurried across the open spaces, hoping she'd find cover before she was discovered by some raving band of lunatics. After much maneuvering she drew near the stables, discovering it still unmolested by the surrounding destruction. Her knife brandished, she made for its entrance. She had just reached the stable when two threatening characters popped out of hiding.

"Hi, there," said one of the men. "Well, looky here," snorted the other.

Even in the relative darkness Lemon recognized the voices and postures of Lamont and Albert. But before they neared her she managed to scurry inside the stable, climbing up to the loft while they struggled to find her. Desperate for a

292

moment, she searched the loft until her eyes met with a pitchfork, resting against the barn's siding. She smiled, relieved. With the pitchfork in her hands, she prowled over the side of the loft, discovering Lamont standing directly beneath her. She thrust the weapon down upon his back, catching him between his neck and spine. He cried out once, before falling face forward.

"Lamont? What's a matter?" asked Albert, stepping from the shadows.

"A shame there isn't more time," muttered Lemon before hurling her knife against Albert's chest. Her form was true, in accordance with that demonstrated by Elmer Lanser, the old knife thrower. Albert fell backwards, clutching the blade that had pierced his heart.

In an instant, Lemon was down on the stable floor, searching the corpses for any remains of her personal effects. Magically, she came upon the locket containing the picture of her mother. She tucked it into her costume before stripping Lamont and Albert of what possessions they carried. When she was finished, she saddled a horse. Before she mounted the frightened stallion, she bid a touching farewell to Pamela ˙ Terrace, Dugan Pomquist and the remaining actors. Even Regis Perth was included among her sentiments. For after all, Lemon was never one to bear a grudge.

Chapter 16

Sunday was almost startling with its weekend appearance. The contrast to Saturday, market day, was incredible. For the streets no longer banged, squealed and lurched with the endless procession of commercial vehicles. Except for the family wagons and buggies passing by, the streets were clear of traffic. Along the sidewalks ladies and gents in their finest attire promenaded toward the different churches which had been erected in the community. All about town the church-bells clamored, their syncopated timbre penetrating the waning fog, casting volumes of religious melody toward the balded mountains which in the distance loomed like a herd of elephants trailing toward the sea.

Above it all, Big Ben listened. He stared mutely at the wagons, buggies and assorted clusters of pedestrians who passed him by. He was surprised by the sight of all the familiar faces. So many of the Sunday gentlemen were frequent patrons of his various enterprises. Whether it be the Lost Hope Saloon, his gambling casinos or his cathouses they adopted for their hangouts, it was plain to Ben that even the most respectable of citizens in the community paid the midget more homage than they did any church in town. He smiled at the thought of the professionals and the businessmen joining with the hooligans, the farmers and the factory laborers in a bit of pleasant debauchery. Of course Big Ben had seen fit that the wealthier residents and tourists were directed toward the posher, more luxurious establishments, while the laborers, farmers and such were compelled to accept the hand-me-downs from the better houses. The older prostitutes, the poorer brands of whiskey and the less expensive gambling habits were all relegated to the sleazier joints in town. It was a good plan. For all Ben had accumulated during his long reign as head of his enterprises went not to waste, but was recycled so that every bit of utility was extracted from his property. And when the men, women and machines would function no more, they were then shipped off to other towns, where they were purchased as surplus. Or ripped apart right there in Star City and sold for scrap. Whatever. There were always other means to reap additional profits from seemingly wasteful material. One such plan that Ben had harbored in his mind, but had still failed to put into practice, was the mail-order bride business. His old hookers, barmaids and such would be shipped from the coast to the middle of the country where they'd be purchased by men in terrible need of companionship. Shipping and freight charges were to be included in the purchase price. Ben couldn't lose. Having set his accountants and attorneys to the task, Ben now awaited the results of their study.

"Here's your breakfast, sir," announced the cook, a silver tray resting on the palm of his hand. "More hot chocolate, sir?" he asked before returning to the kitchen.

Ben sipped his hot chocolate while examining what lay beneath the silver tray. He lifted the lid to discover his favorite, raw ground beef crowned with raw egg. Assorted rolls enveloped the platter. Taking his fork in hand, Ben stabbed at the naked egg yolk until it burst its yellow down the sides of the bloody ground meat. Ben then sopped up the mixture with half a heated roll. He chewed slowly, savoring the taste. He paused from his eating to have another sip of hot chocolate, smiling to himself when he remembered the old days, when he was just a poor, abandoned urchin left to the streets of London.

The butler appeared in the doorway. Ben nodded for him to enter. "Sir," announced the butler. "Crosly Finch and Mr. Lorenzo Stokes will soon be arriving for conference. Should I have the cook set places at the table?"

"No. I'll see them in the study."

When the butler had retreated, Ben found he was hungry no more. The business at hand, his meeting with Finch and Stokes, had ruined his appetite. For it would be Belle Gluntz and her Sno' Fuck Follies they'd discuss. In lurid detail, probing the strengths and weaknesses of their strongest competition.

Belle wouldn't run. That was clear enough. Despite all their attempts to frighten the head of the Sno' Fuck Follies, she hung in, across the street, diverting Ben's trade away from his establishments. It wasn't that she siphoned a terrible amount of business from his massive bulk. No. It wasn't that at all. What she attracted to the Sno' Fuck Follies, to the Alaskan Queen, the midget could live with. But if one tries it, then another will try it. And then a third. Before long, Big Ben would be forced to witness everything he had worked for laid to waste. Star City would be virtually swamped with enterprises maneuvering for power, vying for the trade. Confusion. Nothing but confusion. And Ben, for one, despised any lack of order.

"The Alaskan Queen's been enough of an embarrassment already," he had informed Crosly Finch.

"We could burn it down," proposed the big man.

"We could. But it wouldn't look so good in the eyes of the

citizens. We have to work more subtle ways. Give Belle Gluntz a chance to hang herself."

"How?" interrupted Lorenzo Stokes. "What could we do to make her look bad?"

While Ben and his men considered the question, Kip Kearney had performed a very stupid act. For his efforts, he had had his head blown off, causing Ben a terrible loss of face. So embarrassed was he by Kearney's sudden demise that Ben failed to step downstairs into the Lost Hope Saloon for the entire evening. He simply couldn't bear the stares, the questions written across his patrons' faces. It would have been too much for the midget. His credibility had suffered enough already. An inch he had given the Alaskan Queen had already expanded to a foot. Soon Belle Gluntz would have her mile. No. Not if Ben could help it.

"I can't sit back and watch my domain whittled away by the weak and the puny. Something must be done to reinforce our position here. Before the dam breaks and every group in town, including the vigilantes, come pouring down our throats."

"The vigilantes," scoffed Crosly. "I alone could handle the vigilantes."

"Not if they all come at once. And you should know by now, that's the only way they would have it."

"They're scairt o' ya," put in Stokes. "Plumb crazy scairt."

"And jealous. They want what I have. They believe it's been taken from them. That they are the rightful owners. Just because they play in my arena doesn't mean they own the grounds."

"Well, one thing's for sure. They don't like Belle Gluntz anymore than we do."

"That's it, then. Perhaps we could bribe them, pay them enough to burn down the Alaskan Queen."

"No, no. They'd rather sit back and watch you two go at it. And then, like vultures, scoop up whatever's left."

The men turned to face Bowsley Colgate, Ben's chief attorney, who had entered unannounced. As usual, he carried a packet of documents under his arm. All for Ben to sign. "If you ask me, it's still best to go through the courts. After all, they are locked up in your pocket. By a long, slow process, you could wear away any resistance that stands before you."

"Takes too long," Ben answered. "Besides, if I rely solely upon the courts, it would be too easy for my enemies to call attention to the preferential treatment I receive in the halls of justice."

"A showdown," offered Lorenzo Stokes. "Looks like it's the only thing."

Colgate turned derisively toward the former cowboy. "Is that all you can think of?" he chastised. "Just go out and shoot 'm up. Our best move is the retention of order, not the creation of havoc. Get it through your head that your methods don't work. Unless they're done quietly."

Ben was annoyed that the conference had turned into a debate. Time and unity were the main losers during such a confrontation. He hadn't clawed his way up from life's ragged underbelly for nothing. He hadn't lived among the worst rabble imaginable, sleeping in doorways, abandoned buildings and park benches, and remained naive. He well understood the brute facts of life. Belle Gluntz, the Alaskan Queen, and all other potential opposition must be finished once and for all.

"Lorenzo may be right," he put in, much to Colgate's astonishment. "A showdown may be necessary. Do it now, while we have the forces, the strength to take over easily. We can clobber our enemy and maintain order all at the same time. If we work quickly, decisively."

"Your best move is to wait and see," countered Bowsley Colgate.

"Wait and see?" mimicked Ben. "Wait for what? Another incident like Kip Kearney. Many more of those and we can all pack it in. Our credibility as the sole power of this town will be lost forever. Believe me, lawyer, it's past the hour for dirty legal tactics. Our situation is much more urgent than that. And though you may recoil from the heathen strategies expressed by either Finch or Stokes, there is some accuracy in what they say."

Colgate drew himself to his full stature. With professional rectitude he admonished Ben for not believing in the less direct methods involved with vanquishing one's foe. "You've not learned all that I thought you had. Unfortunately, the underworld still lurks inside you. Ben, you still wish to pick their pockets and get away with it."

"I did get away with it. For many long years. I made my living from the pants of others. I roamed all over London, advancing my practice until it included burglary and even murder. Yes, Lawyer Colgate, even murder. Cold, ruthless assassination. For a price, of course. What other course was open to me? A midget, mocked for my shortness. But even the biggest and the bravest, men as tall as Crosly Finch, soon discovered it wasn't my height that I should be measured by, but my ruthlessness. For with a dagger in my hand, a pistol, I could dispatch them as easily as I could flick my wrist or pull a trigger."

"He was even dubbed the 'Little Killer,'" put in Crosly in support of Ben's denunciation of the lawyer's attitude.

Ben smiled, appearing cherubic and lethal. "Yes, they called me the 'Little Killer.' All the better to fade in and out of crowds. No longer was I a mere scamp, a dirty face lost in the muck and rubble. I was someone, rising above the condemned and the squalid, transcending the levels of my comrades who preferred to languish about in threadbare garments. Not for me, it wasn't. For I was someone special. I was the Little Killer."

His hands running nervously across the documents he carried under his arm, Bowsley Colgate stared down at the floor, much to the delight of Finch, Stokes and even Ben

299

himself. For the chief mouthpiece had been treated to his own brand of poison. No argument he carried inside him could match the experience Ben had claimed for himself. The attorney could only nod his head. Obsequious was the fashion in which he presented the documents for Ben to sign. Finch and Stokes looked on, gloating over their vicarious victory.

"I still believe you're making a mistake," mumbled Colgate, after Ben had finished the signing of papers. "To show full power now would only reinforce the claims of your enemies. And you have many enemies. It's time to exercise more discretion. Keep to yourself. Let the Alaskan Queen continue its operation. In time, when the controversy dies down, who knows, by then we may have developed more effective tactics."

"By then we could be ruined," interjected Crosly Finch.

Colgate's head nodded slowly. He surveyed the room with magnified deliberation. "I'm sorry for the intrusion," he solemnly declared, before making his way to the door.

"It's time we got to it then," sighed Lorenzo Stokes, clapping his hands together. "I'll round up Junior Arroyo and let him help me git t'ings organized."

"Go with him, Crosly," Ben urged. "Make sure we have plenty of men. Round up every thug and hooligan who's able to stand. Give them guns, if they lack them. Pay them. Some advance. Some later. If they're still breathing. Let it be known that a showdown is soon to come. Have the cowards scramble for cover. I've listened to reason for the last time. Reason only affects the mind, not the surrounding conditions. Tear down the Alaskan Queen. Let its empty space remain in tribute to our power."

When he was left to himself again, Big Ben settled back in his custom-made easy chair to enjoy a few belts of whiskey. At last he had reached a decision, set his machinery into action. It was time for celebration, since indecisiveness was intolerable and, at last, it had been conquered. Feeling lazy,

300

almost passive, Ben closed his eyes and began to doze. Once again he listened to the traffic in the London streets. He remembered the various sights and sounds of his boyhood. He thought of the old crone of a tavern keeper who had raised him briefly, after she had discovered his infant self abandoned in the alleyway. It all came back, a winding spiral of imagery coiling inside him, refusing to dissolve, tinted slightly by the glasses of whiskey Ben had slugged down behind it. Beads of perspiration appeared on his forehead. His shirt was stained at the armpits, as was his suit jacket. He trembled slightly, managing to pour himself another round. His eyes closed again. Opened. It didn't matter. Additional images unfurled their grisly strips of Ben's personal history. Once again he was the midget, crawling about the refuse of the dingiest of London streets. He was the slave of the tavern keeper, saved from death if only to bear her constant errands. He was the pickpocket, prowling the busy sectors for an easy mark. He was the thief, the arsonist. And finally, he was the murderer.

Ben had always hated that expression. For he was no mere murderer. He was an assassin, paid well for his services. No family feuds, no insignificant bits of revenge would snare him. A planner to the last, he had built himself quite a reputation as the man who would see the job done. Perhaps it was his notoriety, his widespread reputation that forced him into early retirement. That caused him to flee England, in search of new opportunity.

With the hangman's noose carved on his fleeting heels, Ben arrived in the New World. He had seen the last of London, had slain his last Englishman. A Lord, no less. Lord Munson Turner was his name. A charter member of the ruling class, Turner's family lineage retreated beyond the deepest fathoms of history. His ancestors had been involved with the Norman Conquest, it was recognized. But when Ben was through, none would ever continue the lineage in Munson's name.

Chapter 17

Lemon was not surprised to hear a knocking at her door. She had expected Shelby hours before and had become alarmed when he didn't show. She smiled, pausing to brush back her hair before letting him in.

"Hi," he said, handing her a fresh bouquet of flowers. For several awkward moments Lemon examined the bouquet, along with the varying stem lengths and the assorted weeds. Having no vase in which to set them, she settled for her wash basin. There was some pleasure to be gained by watching the different flowers twist and float in the iron-stone bowl.

"I've been waiting for you," she admitted to Shelby, noting his ragged jeans, battered hat and the six-gun attached to his thigh. His linen shirt was clean but tattered, its basic pattern consisting of holes. The sun had wrinkled the skin around Shelby's eyes, and his lips were dry and cracked. The bath he had taken had done him some good, as did his shaving his face. He was handsome once again, appealing, if not as pretty as some of the fancy dancers from the Sno' Fuck Follies.

"Daddy should only see you now," giggled Lemon. "He'd never guess you were once Clifford Dash."

"I would, though. How do you feel?" asked Lopez, eager to change the subject.

"Much better. A night's worth of sleep has quelled at least some of the pain."

"Really?" tested Lopez, suspicious of something.

Lemon pretended to discover attractions outside her window. Her eyes turned in its direction. She hoped Shelby wouldn't press her about her rest. For it had been a long time since she'd had a decent night's sleep. Insomnia they called it. A mere word to round out the difficulties she had experienced for several years now. At first there were nightmares, and finally she couldn't sleep at all. Oh, a few restless moments when she lapsed into fitful slumber. But that was about it.

"So?" asked Shelby. "What do we do now?"

"You sound so urgent. After all this time you can certainly allow us a few moments to feel things out a little. My life has been different since I last saw you."

"I'm not Clifford Dash anymore, either. You said so yourself."

"I did. I know. Maybe that's what scares me. Maybe we're so much different that we'd hardly blend together. Perhaps the myth is far greater than the reality."

"It could be."

Lemon's head snapped in Shelby's direction. "What do you mean by that?"

Lopez smiled, brushed his mouth with his thumb. "I was just going along with you. To see where it would take us."

"Not very far, I'm afraid. Oh, Shelby, it's just that I'm so frightened. Until now, I've had no time for fear. But now, when there's something I risk losing, I begin to tremble. You'd think I should know better. I should. But I don't."

"Funny. I keep watching from the corner of my eye for the great blade to come smashing down, severing any remaining attachments. I'd hate to keep on drifting. Not after meeting you again. Not after finding Belle, Shmuel. I'm young, but I'm weary. So damn tired of it all. I've gone around and around, and around again. And I'm back in the midst of a struggle. Dammit."

He looked up from his brooding to discover Lemon was smiling. "What's so funny?"

"I'm just trying to picture you as Clifford Dash. You were so handsome then. With your curly red pompadour and your flannel suits. Your hair had the softest waves, the most irresistible coils of any man I've ever met. Oh, you were something then. Pens in your pockets, a tie tack in the center of your chest. You smelled of lavender soap and cornflakes. A small pocketknife you carried, just to keep your nails clean."

Shelby was forced to grin. He had never liked himself as Clifford Dash, but Lemon had painted such a funny picture. "And you," he replied. "In dainty dresses of ice cream colors. Your hair hung down in rows of ironed curls. Your lipstick was always a shade too bright. Remember, you once told me if it wasn't for your marriage to Lloyd DePugh, you'd probably become the first lady President. You believed it too."

"Nahh."

"Yeah. You did. You had speeches prepared and everything. Covering every crisis, every political situation. It was all solved, according to you, before it even happened."

"That was me, all right. Until I got to know better. Here, help me change my bandages."

Before he could respond, Lemon had removed her Mexican blouse, allowing Shelby opportunity to explore the contours of her back. She turned around slowly, revealing her small but well shaped breasts. They perched firmly against her chest. Lopez discovered pleasant sensations arising from his crotch. He moved toward Lemon Lime, his hand extended toward her shoulder.

"Ouch," she cried when he brought his hand down on her wound. "It hurts me."

"Sorry," he retreated. "Maybe I should. . . ."

"No. You do it."

Lopez smiled, accepted the package of gauze she offered. "That's a nasty gash," he said when Lemon removed the dirty bandage.

"It could've been worse," she answered, recalling what Kip Kearney had borne in mind. "It would've been a lot worse to have been slit from neck to navel."

"I'm sure. There. The bandage is on now. It should hold for a while."

"Let me hold you for a while," cooed Lemon, stepping into Shelby's embrace. She kissed him, passionately enough so hot pokers burned at his asshole. "Fuck me," she whispered, pulling him toward the bed.

Shelby was never one to argue. In a flash he had removed his shirt and pants. Naked before her, he assisted Lemon with her undressing. After she had removed her boots, he rolled her jeans and panties from her thighs and buttocks. She kicked them from her ankles, laughing all the while. "We're so perfect together," she laughed. "Like two rag dolls intertwined upon the hope chest."

Lopez fell beside Lemon, careful not to brush against her wound. In the flush sunlight that poured through her window he noted the puffiness around her eyes. She had been injured worse than she cared to admit. "Are you sure it's all right? With you being hurt an' all."

"I know of no better cure," she answered, driving her tongue deep inside his mouth. In another moment she had straddled his legs and was working his hands along her crotch and chest. She bit at his lip, twisted her tongue inside his ear. He returned her kisses while passionately stroking her teardrop buttocks. He kissed her everywhere, beginning

305

at her mouth, working his way downward, pausing self-consciously at her knees. She sighed and panted above him, stroking his hair.

"Come back to me," she whispered, reaching down to bring his face next to hers. Her free hand slipped his dick inside. Expelling a long, oozing sigh, she settled down upon it.

By the time they had finished, Shelby found himself more aroused than when they first began. His entire body throbbed with pleasure. His dick remained stiff, eager for another try. But Lemon had collapsed beside him.

"I'd love to. But it's too painful for my shoulder. Maybe a little later we could try again."

"It was fine. I loved every second of it." He moved closer now, to nuzzle against her breast.

"Will you still love me in the morning?" she jested.

"It is the morning. A brand new day."

"Then what shall we do with it?"

"I thought I'd wander over to the Lost Hope Saloon and check out the opposition."

Lemon sat up abruptly. "No, Shelby. You can't!"

"Why not?"

"They'll kill you. Ben doesn't take kindly to having his men shot out from under him. He'll kill you if he gets half the chance. You'd be crazy to go over there, just asking for it."

"I'm asking for nothing. Besides, I'll take Thunderbird with me."

Thunderbird Hawkins was out on the porch, rocking in his adopted chair. His belly was bloated with a gargantuan breakfast, and he seemed most contented in his easy slumber. Across his lap rested his shotgun. His revolver was tucked into his belt.

"Thunderbird? Thunderbird? Are you alive or dead?"

"A little of both," croaked Hawkins. "What do you have on your mind?"

"I thought we'd mosey over to the Lost Hope an' see what we're up against."

"A good idea," admitted Thunderbird, climbing slowly from his chair. He gazed longingly at the swinging rocker. "A good place for the present to become a memory," he said, nodding at the chair. "Oh, well, let's go take a look."

"Maybe I should go in first, and then you. I mean, if we go in together they might get ideas."

Thunderbird seemed impatient. "All right. If we must."

"What's the matter?"

"Just my senses acting up on me. I feel drawn by an unknown attraction. But soon enough I'll have the answer. Go ahead. When you're safely inside, I'll follow. If not, I'll give you cover while you try to escape."

"That would be awfully nice of you."

No one noticed Shelby when he entered the Lost Hope Saloon. Nor did they question the Indian, who was soon to follow. The few gunmen at the door were too intensely involved with their estimates of the women walking the street to be bothered with two more entries. Once inside, Shelby made for the bar, where he ordered a beer. Hawkins drew added attention when he neared the bar and wisely decided against it. Instead he made for the rear section of the saloon, where an entire wall was covered with different Indian artifacts and assorted memorabilia Big Ben had collected in order to attract the tourists. Paintings and blankets covered the walls. A glass showcase displayed different relics that Ben had collected. Pieces of silver, pottery shards mingled with arrowheads, tools and jewelry. Included among the display pieces was the Great Necklace.

"That's it, isn't it?" Lopez asked Hawkins, whose eyes were riveted to the Necklace. Shelby had ambled over to the exhibit when he sensed a change in Thunderbird. His eyes seeking danger, Lopez tugged at his companion's blanket. "C'mon. We'd better go."

Thunderbird refused to move. "All this time, it's been

held captive. Displayed to men who have lost their lives in false hopes and fantasies. It is a terrible fate for that which contains the wisdom of the world, the destiny of man."

"It is," agreed Shelby. "But it must stay here, until we can come back. They'd kill us for sure. Just for breaking the glass."

Thunderbird's voice raised its volume. "After all these years I've found it at last."

Ben's men were by now aroused. Through narrowed eyes they studied the cowboy and the Indian. "What the hell's he cryin' about?" asked one gunman.

"Some crazy Indian convulsion. He's had it for years. Comes out of nowhere. Nothing much. It passes with buttermilk." He dragged Hawkins toward the door. Just as he cleared it, one of Ben's men shouted after him.

"Hey! Hold on a minute. Hey!"

The companions took off, running for the Alaskan Queen. Bullets whizzed all around them. People scampered every which way. Shelby's lungs pounded as he ran for all he was worth. "C'mon, Thunderbird," he shouted to the slower man. "I'll cover ya." With his gun drawn, Lopez stood his ground and fired a couple of rounds. His first shot missed its target, but the second caught one gunman in the leg. The man spun around several times before falling. But others came on. Firing as they ran. From behind him, Belle, Shmuel and Jason opened fire from the Alaskan Queen. Shelby took advantage of the protective cover in order to dash inside. Bullets kicked up the dirt around him as he dove through the swinging doors.

"Let's give 'em what they came for," cried Belle Gluntz.

Lopez accepted a rifle from Hawkins and took his position by the window. "Oh shit!" he declared. "I really brought it down on us this time."

No one heard him. They fired at will, joined by their fellow Sno' Fuckers who fired from cover on the upstairs

308

floors. Ben's men dropped into the street. His private army was in full retreat, leaving its dead and wounded behind.

When the shooting ended, Belle Gluntz beamed with pride. "I'm tellin' you. We should only live through this."

"It is a good day to die," interjected Thunderbird.

"Not for me, it isn't," growled Shmuel Gluntz. "So don't give me any of your Indian clichés. Look at me . . . I'm a mess from this."

"Shmuel," Belle commanded. "Be still. What will happen will happen. It was set into motion long before Shelby arrived."

When the fighting ceased altogether, Thunderbird Hawkins dipped his pipe into a fresh pouch of smoke. He packed it tightly before lighting the contents. He then passed it around him. Shmuel refused at first, but Belle accepted for a few polite tokes. Shelby, Hawkins and Jason devoured the rest.

"Best shit I've known since they freed the slaves," smiled Jason, his eyes turning bloodshot.

Seeing the effect it had on his comrades, Shmuel stuck out his hand. "Here. Let me try some of that." He sucked in deeply, on several occasions, feeling better as the thought of gunfights faded from his mind. Shelby smiled at his uncle, before gazing out onto the street. It was empty now.

The gunfight had brought Star City to a grinding halt. The usual rippling visions of city sound in motion had vanished, replaced by a thick gray pallor combined from gunsmoke and foreboding disease. The sky and the ocean, which only hours before had sparkled like diamonds on a turquoise base, had been converted to gelatinous ash. A ghastly curtain of fog had rendered much of the town

309

invisible. Landmark buildings, thoroughfares and such receded into the milieu. Thick with its moisture, the fog undulated like a song from the damned. The streets were coated with its liquid angst. Iron benches, lampposts and empty wagons perspired with anticipation. Even the prodigious winos were gone from the streets, sequestered like magnified rodents in the abandoned livery stable. Here and there a sign creaked on its hinges, a horse whinnied, stamped its hooves against the earth. But there came no sound of human footsteps or the smell of the ladies pausing beneath a lamp. All was quiet, even in the Lost Hope Saloon.

"Hey, Chaz, where is everybody?" Shay Daniels quipped to one of the regular rummys. "Can't they stand a little gunplay?"

Chaz bowed his head with deep concern. He refused to answer Shay's question. Even the drink he was offered barely brought it out of him. "I dunno," he muttered beneath his acrid breath.

Shay was not well pleased. "Damn you! I asked, where are they?"

"Leav'm be, Shay," piped up Buzz La Crosse. "He's jes' 'n' ol' drunkard with nuthin' t' say. Can't git mor'n a belch 'n' a bad case from him."

"A bad case a what?" Shay wanted to know.

"It don't matter. The way things are t' day, it don't matter a-tall."

Shay turned his attention to Chaz. His pity forced him to smile. "Still. When push comes to shove, I guess I'd rather die in the streets than by any old bottle. But I best suppose I'd rather not die a-tall. I never liked the thought o' dyin'. Always climbed at me like a spider inside my windpipe. Did me no good t' picture myself dead. Just lyin' there, starin' up at nothin'."

"Hey, cut it out. Will ya?"

310

"What's a matter, Buzz? What are you talkin' about?"

"It's you, Shay. You've got sumthin' on yer min' 'n' I don't like it. Naw, not one bit. All day long, it's been clawin' at you. An' it ain't no spider you got caught in your windpipe, neither."

Shay fluttered his eyelashes. He managed a smile for Buzz La Crosse. "It's only a feelin'," he said, trying to pass it off as something minor.

"Yeah," scoffed La Crosse, "but ya ain't sayin' what kinda feelin'. An' 'at's what I don't like aboutcha. You got my skin a-crawlin', Shay, an' I don't like it a-tall."

"It's only a feeling," Shay repeated. "Years ago I learned never t' explain a feelin'. Hey, hey, that's all I have after fifty fuckin' years of fightin' 'n' whorin' 'n' whoopin' it up. Just a damn feelin'."

La Crosse traversed the Lost Hope to confront grizzly Shay Daniels. He slunk a chair beneath his ass, plopping down in reverse direction. With his arms draped across the back of the chair, La Crosse narrowed his eyes at Shay. "Sumthin's ailin' ya, ol' buddy. 'N' you' better tell me what it is."

Shay Daniels squinted his eye and downed two shots in succession. "I just ain't sure I'm a-fixin' t' die for some Goddamn't midget. It don't seem right ... me layin' face down in th' middle o' that turd-strewn street while Ben and the likes o' Chaz here stand over my vulgar corpse. Lacks justice."

"Jus' what are ya tryin' t' say, old man?" blurted out Red Biscayne, still not getting the point.

"I ain't tryin' t' say nothin'. Nothin' we don't know already. Even you, Red."

A stranglehold on his whiskey glass, Biscayne advanced toward Daniels. He and Kip Kearney were among the few gunslingers in Ben's employ who held little regard for Daniels. While others appeased him by listening to Shay's old jokes and gossip, Red Biscayne displayed contempt. "Ol' coot should be retired by now," he said whenever he had the chance. "Looks bad for our company."

But Shay Daniels was no man to back down from the likes of Red Biscayne. As old and as slow as he was, he could still outthink him. He squinted his eye in Red's direction and surmised what would unnerve him the quickest. He laughed beneath his breath. "I ain't sure it's my time. I've lived too good a life to die like a puppet, tangled in his strings."

"You're gettin' soft, Daniels."

"It's a right in life for men like me. Men who've lived this long."

"I think you're yeller! Jus' tryin' t' chicken out!"

After a second glance at Buzz La Crosse, Shay was certain he'd stand alone in any rising conflict. A glimpse of the other men, the twitch of an eye, the flick of a finger confirmed his suspicions. Pouring himself another belt of whiskey, Shay allowed for a brief review of his existence. He retreated through a long channel, enjoyed life's highlights, before arriving at his own demise. There he was dressed in white lace silk, a fabric to which he had always shown fondness. He then basked in the blue light of his own mortality, waiting patiently for the angels' songs. In response a muted chorus traversed the dimensions. Daniels smiled at his fortune. He slid his hand beneath the table and found his gun. Biscayne was edgy, moving closer to Daniels. Shay waited for him to make his move.

"Git on yer feet, ya ol' coot," bellowed Red. "Ya ain't got th' right t' talk th' way you've done."

Daniels smiled. "I'm surprised at you, Red. A hardened killer and all, lettin' a few words bend your shape. Some gunfighter. You keep actin' like this 'n' they'll be laughin' at 'cha down in purgatory."

Upon hearing the word purgatory, Red Biscayne was seized with fright. The Daniels seated before him changed briefly into the shape of his father, commanding him to obey the Lord. Harsh were the words of eternal damnation. It caused Red to delay for one second too many. For Shay had fired his pistol from beneath the table, killing Biscayne before his gun cleared its holster.

Buzz La Crosse laid clucking sounds over the bleeding corpse. "Deep down inside, he always felt poorly for the life he chose."

"He'll have eternity to think it over," interrupted Shay Daniels. "Now, bein' you gentlemen no longer have use for my company, I'd best be out th' door. No sense ya' tryin' t' follow, since I'll blast the first man that moves."

With that Shay Daniels backed from the Lost Hope Saloon. He mounted a nearby horse, his eyes still peeled for danger. With a doff of his hat he galloped away, slumping low on his saddle. Back inside the Lost Hope Saloon, Buzz La Crosse deliberated on chasing Daniels. He made more clucking noises before deciding he couldn't find it in his heart to do so. "Leave'm be," he ordered, and no one moved.

Once he was safely out of town, Shay Daniels slowed his horse to a canter. No one was in pursuit. And even if they were, they'd soon be lost from his trail. Around him the mist made the closest of objects seem nearly invisible. Branches and trees thrust out like tentacles. The distant mountains were shrouded by this humid mystery, like the pathway to limbo. The silence was damning. Shay's head swiveled, taking in all that he could. His breath turned cloudy in the wet, gray air. For no reason at all he broke into laughter. But soon his laughter abated and he spurred his horse onward, reaching a gallop as he climbed the foothills up ahead. Hunched across the animal's neck, his hat brim flipped backwards in the breeze, Shay Daniels considered the shrouded world around him. He wondered why some ride off in the sunset while others are lost in the fog.

*   *   *

313

The killing of Red Biscayne, and Shay Daniels' subsequent escape gave Big Ben reason to brood. Things were not proceeding as usual. Ben had perceived it all around him, in the dense fog which surrounded his empire, on the faces of his men. By his office window Ben stood, pounding his right fist into the palm of his left hand. A textured, mechanical toy, he appeared abandoned by his childish owner, left to repeat the same action for eternity. Slowly, sledgelike, the right fist continued to rise and fall, dropping with a slap into Ben's meaty little palm. All the while, Ben said nothing.

From across the room Crosly Finch observed his boss in silence. He too had perceived the foreboding. His throat was affected, and he tugged constantly at his tie knot and collar. Outside the office, Junior Arroyo and Lorenzo Stokes were arguing over who was the fastest gun, now that Kip Kearney was dead.

"Biscayne's been killed," came the news, a little more than an hour ago.

Ben had listened intensely. Unusual, since he cared little for the vulgar Red Biscayne. "How?" the midget wanted to know. "Why?"

"No one knows why, really," answered Buzz La Crosse. "It was just one o' those things that happened."

It struck Ben odd. Shay Daniels had been a brave man. It just wasn't like him to suddenly pick up and run off. A new swell of impending disaster impinged upon Ben's senses. He tried to suppress his latent desire to call the whole thing off, to allow Belle Gluntz free and open competition. No. He couldn't adjust to it, he decided. But how much easier it all would've been if he could have extended his warmest greetings to the Sno' Fuck Follies. If they all had shared a bottle at his request and formed a bond among themselves. It couldn't have happened. Times were changing, perhaps, but not that quickly. Not while Big Ben still had his nerve and his power behind him.

His tight little fist paused in midair, adding focus to the

space between his two hands. He turned to Crosly, studied his gigantic henchman, noting his huge eyes wide with excitement, the bottom lip overladen with drool.

"How many men have you killed in your life, Crosly?" asked Big Ben.

Finch shook his head. "I dunno."

"Does it ever bother you? That you pulverized so many?"

"Only some I pulverized. The rest I shot, stabbed or strangled."

Ben studied the giant's motions. A glance at his hands described the terror they wrought among mortals. With a quick snap of his wrists the behemoth Finch could snap off heads as if they were so many chickens. He could break backs like they were crayfish.

"Crosly? Are you afraid to die?"

Finch's jaw slackened, his eyes widened with surprise. He cocked his head to one side, staring at his midget boss. No one had ever before asked such a question of him. He was afraid to answer.

"I-I g-guess so," he stammered.

"Why?"

"Cuz I don't know what it's like."

"But you've killed so many men. You must have some idea."

"I never thought where they go when I leave 'em. I-I never . . ."

Ben waved off Crosly's attempt to answer him further. "Crosly, for years now you've been my most sincere admirer. Certainly there's much to be said for a man who still believes wholeheartedly in his superior. That's loyalty, Crosly. Loyalty is what we're speaking of. And you, as large and as gruesome as you are, remain a loyal and adoring man."

The giant's chest heaved a tremendous sigh. It was all he could do to brush back his tears. A dam-burst of snot washed down his nose. His lips quivered and his face turned red. "Ah, ahahah," he repeated over and over again, until the sounds took the shape and form of an ancient exotic chant. His voice was old hinges rusting with despair.

Ben was touched by Crosly's affectionate demonstration. He smiled at the giant before turning to his window, his eyes once again focused on the fog. Ben had always hated the fog. When he was a youth growing up in London, it near drove him mad with its impetuousness. A beautiful day could be spoiled instantaneously. He felt so isolated when lost in its mist. For the sunshine had faded from his eyes, abandoned him to a gutted warehouse where he had spent the night crying in his sleeve. He was so young then, hardly capable of making promises he thought he'd never keep. But he had kept them. Big Ben had become someone. He had left his impression against the world.

Ben turned from the window, once again glancing at Finch. "At dusk it'll happen," announced Ben. "Beneath a somber desert sky. Die we will amidst the fog. Or live, denied color, the solace of sunset's lovely patterns."

Finch began to cry. "What is it, boss? What is it?"

"Nothing. Nothing to be certain."

Chapter 18

The Alaskan Queen contrasted greatly with the tension inside Big Ben's office. In the rear section of the L-shaped complex the Sno' Fuckers were having a party. For hours their celebration penetrated the fog, stiffening the backs of the fearful who may have sidled by the Alaskan Queen. Assisted by Thunderbird Hawkins' contribution of smoke and an ample portion of whiskey and wine, the group of actors danced naked before the open fireplace. Or made love on blankets and pillows strewn about the floor. Mindless of the approaching conflict, they danced around like children, whooping it up for a very good time.

Inside the Alaskan Queen Saloon, Belle Gluntz ignored her troupe of actors. "Let 'em have their fun," she quipped, passing more wine to her brother Shmuel. Jason and Hawkins were also there, getting soused for all they were worth. Heads bobbed, eyes blinked and jaws slackened. Still, the whiskey and the smoke kept coming. A card deck had been dealt to all the players, yet no one knew the game they were supposed to be playing. Every so often, one tossed in a card or two, while another picked them up.

"You're supposed to discard now," Belle had corrected Hawkins earlier in the game. "Throw me a four."

"Here. Here's a four."

"Good. Now I have a set."

Shmuel was confused. "Hey, what type o' game is this, anyway?"

"A game with no contest," laughed Jason. "Your turn to throw cards, Shmuel."

Shmuel grumbled. "I'd rather be back there with the actors. Sounds like they're havin' themselves a damn good time. Looka there. Every now and then I can see bare ass, dashing through the firelight."

"No one's stopping you from going back there," Belle responded. "Jason, Thunderbird and I can keep it together if you want to scare the kids with that shriveled pisser of yours. They'd get to see what one looks like when it turns gray."

"Shmuel may be gettin' old, but not that old."

Thunderbird burped and took a long pull on his pipeload. He glanced at the shotgun he kept by his side, wondering if he'd be able to use it when the time came. His fingers were numb, his eyes saw double of everything. But he was too removed to worry. Time would tell, he considered, and then reminded himself of the Necklace. The Necklace. It was still in Big Ben's possession.

"Where's my Shelby?" asked Belle.

"Upstairs with Lemon. Where else? Seems he won't get off her, except to take a leak."

"They've been apart for quite a long time."

"Who are they? Adam an' Eve?"

"Shmuel, what were you like at that age?"

"What I was like at any age. Could never leave go of myself. I'd stretch it, just to keep the muscle tone."

Belle snorted and glanced toward the bar, taking in the magnificent portrait of an angel rising in flight above the liquor case. She smiled at the portrait, feeling suddenly tranquil. "It'll be all right," she stammered between snorts of whiskey. "He can't touch us now."

"Huh?"

"I was talking to my angel."

"Heheh. Were you asking forgiveness?"

"What? You wanta see it drop from the wall? Anyway, thank God Shelby's alive. Through him, through his children, which he'd most certainly have if he kept going with Lemon at this rate, Belle Gluntz, Shmuel, would live forever."

"Hey," cried Shmuel, looking at his watch. "It's getting dark outside. Think I should go rouse the troops."

"He'll be comin' t'night," opined Jason. "Dat's for damn sure."

Belle frowned. She was reluctant to stop the party. "It's been so long since the actors could enjoy themselves. I hate to ... but if you think he's coming. I'm tellin' you. I need this. Hey, isn't there any more wine left?"

Thunderbird grunted and closed his eyes. On the backs of his lids he saw Ben's army approaching. There were many gunmen, most of whom had been taken from the local bars and sleaze joints that fronted the coast. Only a few were as deadly as Crosly Finch, Junior Arroyo and Lorenzo Stokes. Still, by sheer numbers, Ben's army was most formidable. Hawkins could see them, stalking forward, hidden inside the shadows of the street. Coming they were, advancing with torches in their hands. Perhaps they would try to burn them out. But with torches they must reveal themselves. His eyes open again, Thunderbird stared out toward the street. It still was empty. Only the fog was present, thicker than it had ever been before. After a toke from his pipe, he announced his strategy.

319

"They'll be coming. Best if a few of us get outside, catch them from behind. They wouldn't expect it. We could thin them out before they even neared the building."

"Truly piratical," howled Belle Gluntz. "We'll catch them with their pants down and shove it up their ass."

"I'll rouse the troops from out back, yonder. Somebody best git d' honeymooners 'fore they too fucked out t' fight."

"I'll go," Shmuel volunteered. "I'm curious to see how they do it so long."

Belle hefted her rifle and took her position beside a window. Her eyes scanned the darkness for any odd movements. Nothing so far. She laughed, remarking to herself that it was indeed a long way from Poor Yussel's Home for the Insane Aged. Whatever became of her from this point, she'd always be thankful she hadn't died like a has-been garment, converted to rags before it was discarded. She had lived her life. True to the pirate spirit she believed was inside her. And she would die with friends, their banner waving above them. True pirates, their ship sinking, burning from stern to bow, they'd fight on through eternity, forever kicking ass. A grin on her face, Belle turned to Thunderbird Hawkins.

"So tell me? How long to the battle?"

"It's already begun," answered Hawkins, sensing movement at the far end of the block.

"Oooie, I'm so excited. I shouldn't pee in my dress."

Thunderbird flicked back the hammers of his shotgun. He sighed deeply, preparing himself for his best Indian trick. He would use his enemies' overconfidence to work against them. He'd sneak behind them, skulking about until his foes offered clear and easy targets. One by one he'd down them, making his way toward the Great Necklace. The Necklace. Soon it would hang from his neck, as it had done with his father. At least part of the truth would be restored to its rightful owner. How nice. He had not journeyed for

320

nothing. Some journey. The places it had taken him. Such a long, long way to travel. Such a long, long way to come.

Shelby had prepared himself for the first sound of gunfire. He was ready to leap to his feet and dash downstairs, drawing his gun along the way. But the chore was more than he had first imagined. He had just rolled from Lemon Lime, and was prepared to catch a short series of winks, when pistols and rifles reported below.

"C'mon," he shouted to Lemon. "Ben's attacking."

"Huh?" asked the weary Lemon. She hadn't had so much ass in an awfully long time. "What's a matter?"

"Ben's army. They're coming. Listen!"

Lemon cocked an ear to the window. "A catfight," she moaned, prepared to go back to sleep.

His legs aching, his balls sore to the touch, Shelby climbed out of bed and dressed himself. Before making for the door he checked his pistol, examining it for bullets. "Better get dressed."

Moody from being roused so suddenly, a sullen Lemon dressed herself. With great deliberation she adjusted her boots before strapping on her gunbelt and knife. "I hate this damn thing," she complained. "Always makes me look so thick around the waist. Did you see my other gun? The little one? The .32?"

"Dammit, Lemon, they're attacking the Alaskan Queen."

"Motherfuckers," she yawned. "I was having such pleasant dreams."

Shelby didn't listen. He had cracked open the door and looked out the window set in the hallway to the rear section of the compound. The Sno' Fuckers were drawing most of

321

the fire, offering easy targets to the attacking gunmen. Naked bodies dashed everywhere, attempted to avoid the flickering firelight that outlined their images. Glass and fixtures crashed all around them. The lounge's interior was ripped to pieces.

"We'd better help them," pointed Shelby, now that Lemon had joined him.

The couple crept through the hallway while bullets smashed all around them. Clocks, lamps and mirrors shattered from impact. Overhead lanterns swung madly above. They were nearing the rear sector, but drawing more fire with each cautious step.

"Let's make a run for it."

Lemon agreed. In a moment they were off, darting in and out of whatever cover they could find. Only the courtyard separated them from the rear building. Even from the distance they noted casualties. "It was too soon to have a party," moaned Lopez.

"Tomorrow could've been too late. Remember, we've been living with Ben for an awfully long time."

"I guess. Let's get over there and see what we can do."

While bullets kicked up the dirt around them, Shelby and Lemon raced for the converted hotel. They burst inside, greeted by the assorted screams of the Sno' Fuckers. Actors were everywhere, ants maddened by the first drops of water. By now those who had survived had armed themselves and had doused the remaining lights. Some were firing back against the assailants.

"Hold it for as long as you can," commanded Lemon, her head clearing with the action. "Don't let them get inside the compound. Fire from the windows, from behind the walls. Keep killing them."

A cheer rose from the surviving Sno' Fuckers. "We'll hold 'em," an actress shouted.

"Best see what's happening by the saloon," offered Shelby.

322

"Yeah. It seems your aunt's taking the brunt of the action."

Sure enough, most of the firing had been transferred to the Alaskan Queen. Bullets were pouring in from everywhere. The saloon was in shambles, its floor littered with splintered wood and shards of broken glass. The angel had fallen from the wall hanging, but was still intact somewhere behind the bar. That, too, was where Jason had taken position. He pumped bullets toward the street.

"What a mess," shouted Lemon.

"It's bad for business," retorted Shmuel.

"Where's Thunderbird?" asked Shelby.

Belle answered, her attention much occupied by the invading army. "He's trying to get behind them. For what, I don't know. But it's no time to fight with a crazy Indian."

His revolver reloaded, Shelby crept toward the side exit. "Cover me. I'm go'n after Thunderbird."

Before anyone could protest, Shelby had dashed outside. He raced up the side street, impervious to the surrounding dangers. Soon he was lost in the fog, headed up the street toward Big Ben's saloon.

In the distant shadows Lopez detected movement. He paused, listened again, then crept beneath a wagon. He waited, his pistol trained toward the fog. Seconds appeared like light-years, until the sound of footsteps reached his ears. More than one of the enemy was coming toward him. He cocked his pistol and waited for the men to fall into range.

Buzz La Crosse and his three men were not aware of Shelby when they stalked by the wagon. Nor did they expect danger as they talked among themselves. For they had taken a pool back at the Lost Hope and were now speculating on when the battle would end.

"Two hours," predicted one gunman, just as Lopez's first shot struck his back. La Crosse received the second blast, while the two others raced screaming down the block. Shelby crawled out from the wagon and continued toward the Lost Hope Saloon.

Hawkins had sensed someone was approaching the saloon. He cursed under his breath. He had just broken the glass over the showcase and was prepared to remove the Great Necklace when he heard approaching footsteps. He stepped back into the shadows, his shotgun pointed toward the door.

But Lopez wasn't stupid. He'd known all along that his companion was inside, retrieving the Necklace he deemed so precious. "Hawkins," called Lopez. "Are you in there?"

Thunderbird stepped from the shadows, pointed his gun away from Shelby. "I had to come get it," he apologized. "Before something else went wrong."

Lopez smiled at his crazy companion. "Now, I guess, we can take care of that fuckin' Big Ben."

"Yes," agreed Hawkins. He reached to his left and withdrew a large drum of kerosene he had found in the supply room. He smiled at Shelby. "I've not been idle all this time."

With Shelby's assistance, Hawkins proceeded to dump the contents all over the floor. He shook the drum so kerosene poured over the bar, a few wooden chairs and even the staircase. He then led Shelby toward the exit. "Watch this," he announced, and then struck a match. He tossed it into a puddle of kerosene and the Lost Hope exploded. "That'll fix his ass good n' proper," declared Hawkins, after he and Shelby had cleared the saloon. From the safety of the street the companions watched the flames rise from the building. Everything was engulfed in smoke. A yellowish haze mixed with the dark surroundings.

"Now," said Hawkins, "let's get back to the fighting."

On the way back the companions discovered several more men were coming toward them. These would be more difficult to overtake than the last, since they were aroused and expecting danger. Even from the distance Shelby could hear them cursing the fire, swearing Big Ben was finished once and for all. Their voices assured Lopez that he had gained the advantage. Morale among Ben's men was not as strong as it should be.

Suddenly the men disappeared inside the shadows. Not a sound came from their direction. For a moment Lopez assumed they had wandered off down a side street. He was about to step from hiding when Hawkins' arm cautioned him against it. "They're hiding, but not for long, since the darkness scares them."

Soon the gunmen appeared once more, surreptitiously making their way up the street. "Let 'em keep coming," advised Thunderbird.

When the gunmen appeared as easy targets, Lopez and Hawkins opened fire. Cries and screams combined with gunfire to ripple the fog. In a moment it was over. Five of Ben's men lay dead.

"What's going on here?" Ben demanded from further down the street. He had heard the sound of gunfire coming from up the block. The burning vision of the Lost Hope Saloon stood before him, portending ruination of all he had worked to build. It was all he could do to spur his men onward. For they had lost their initiative, and their impassioned advance had come to a halt. The return fire from the Alaskan Queen had found its victims. Dead men lay all over the street. The cries of the wounded dampened the others' desire for fighting. The army had retreated, seeking cover behind corners of buildings.

"We'll all be kil't," swore Junior Arroyo, who was standing between Big Ben and Crosly Finch. "The army's out of courage."

"The condemned don't need courage, but enterprise," came Ben's reply. "Tell them to continue fighting."

"But they're cutting us down like pigeons."

"It's all in your mind, fool. We're winning. Can't you see?"

"I can't see nothing in this damn fog," complained Arroyo. "Not rhyme or reason."

"Then go t' hell, coward," shrieked the midget Ben, his pistol raised to fire. An easy squeeze of the trigger and Junior Arroyo fell dead, a bullet between his eyes.

Finch looked on. "Teach him to get testy."

"Crosly," said Ben. "Why don't you take a few boys and try to storm the rear. We might have more luck there."

A childlike grin appeared on Crosly's face. "We'll git'm yet," he determined.

Inside the Alaskan Queen the defenders had taken heart. They had halted the first advance and now stood a chance to emerge victorious. By now the survivors had recovered from the party, and with each stitch in time their shooting had increased its accuracy.

"How ya holdin' up over there?" Shmuel Gluntz called to his sister.

"We shouldn't do this everyday. It's hard on the nerves."

"Jason, how they doin' in the rear sector?"

Jason hesitated. "We'll need more actors," he replied, not wanting to go into it further.

"Oh," Belle moaned, brushing the tears from her face. "That little sonofabitch. You'd ᐟthink he'd call it quits already. Where does he get the nerve, anyway?"

"God only knows."

Belle snorted. "Remind me to ask him when I get the chance."

Soon after Shelby had departed, Lemon had returned to the rear sector of the compound and organized the remaining actors. From inside the hotel they fought valiantly, despite their lack of combat expertise. Many had fallen in the first assault. Fortunately, some had not been seriously injured. Lemon's appearance had bolstered their morale. The actors adored the director of the Sno' Fuck Follies. With renewed vigor they had turned back Big Ben's private army. From behind makeshift protection, they returned the army's fire, dropping gunmen who scrambled for the gates.

And now they faced a second assault. For Crosly Finch had rounded up his men and was preparing to launch his desperate attack. Along with Lorenzo Stokes, Finch gave his survivors fair warning. Anyone who retreated would be personally destroyed by Crosly.

"After this heah, I guess we kin call it a day," sighed Lorenzo Stokes. Though he remained silent, he was not in favor of Crosly's plan.

"Not while I'm around," came Finch's answer. "I'm here to stick it out to th' end."

Reluctantly, Stokes drew himself upright. "Well, I'd guess we'd better git to it."

With a cry from Finch, the army advanced toward the rear gates. Many were nailed before they reached the center of the street. The rest charged onward, finding resistance was tougher when they neared the gates. From behind barrels and trashpiles the Sno' Fuckers maintained a steady barrage of fire.

"Don't let them enter the compound," cried Lemon Lime from her position on the balcony. But it was to no avail. The Sno' Fuckers were weary by now, and the army's final surge against the gates had broken through. Gunmen were scrambling everywhere, tusseling with actors in bitter hand-to-hand fighting.

"Oh shit," huffed the disappointed Lemon. With that she jumped from the balcony, just missing Crosly Finch, who had advanced toward the stairs. He was standing over her now, his rifle raised above his head. Just as he brought the butt down to her skull, Lemon rolled safely out of the way. She fired her pistol, catching Finch in the middle of his belly.

It took more than one bullet to drop the savage Crosly. He had the scars to prove his case. If anything, Lemon's last shot had only angered the giant. He rushed at her, howling like a wild beast. With the distance shortened, Crosly laughed maniacally. At long last, he would slaughter the enigmatic Lemon Lime. His eyes bulged and his mouth opened. Gluttonous drool spilled from between his teeth. He snarled, grasped for Lemon. She avoided his paw.

With her knife drawn, Lemon attempted to stay clear of Finch's apish limbs. The adversaries circled each other. Lemon crouched, her heart pounding, her veins surging with human electricity. She'd kill the giant, Godammit, or die trying.

Around the leaders all the fighting had stopped. Even the hardened professionals couldn't deny themselves the chance to witness the spectacle. Encouragement came from both sides.

"We've got 'em now," croaked the exhilarated Lorenzo Stokes. "Kill her an' you got'em all."

Finch grunted. He moved on Lemon, feinting one way and then the other. He swept his arm, barely nabbing her shoulder. When he charged by, Lemon hacked a piece from his forearm. As he paused to examine his fresh wound, Lemon dashed forward and slashed Crosly's face. The giant roared his disapproval. He backed out of range, retrieving a sledgehammer he had spied on the ground. He advanced again on Lemon Lime, swearing he'd kill her.

"You like this?" he asked of the Sno' Fuck director, the sledge waving menacingly all the while. "I'm a gonna mash your purty skull." He stepped forward, the hammer raised above his head. It fell with a whistle, missing Lemon but splitting the corpse of a fallen gunmen. The hammer landed with a sickening "plunk." The Sno' Fuckers revealed their disgust.

Again Finch swung the hammer. This time he destroyed an empty wine cask with his effort. The barrel shattered into countless fragments, while Lemon raced to the other end of the courtyard.

She well understood that it was only a matter of time before Crosly connected with his hammer. Lemon pictured herself reduced to the substance of fresh, wet cowshit. It didn't appeal to her at all. She searched her opponent, hoping to spot his fatal weakness. None was revealed to her. Only the blood spilling from the wounds she had delivered. They seemed to have had no effect at all. For Crosly was approaching once again, the menacing sledge raised above his head. He scuffed his boots like a mad bull, clearing them of mud and other impediments. He advanced slowly, certain victory was his.

Too exhausted to endure much longer, Lemon devised her desperate plan. She crouched, her knife brandished before her. Her back was to the wall, a boot pressed against its base. Crosly was giggling, but she had no intention of allowing it to affect her. She breathed heavily, awaiting his advance. He was sure he had her where she couldn't escape.

When the giant drew back his hammer, Lemon sprang from the wall, her boot pushing off for extra thrust. Her knife was extended to Finch's unguarded throat. His hammer was dropping atop her. It became a race to see who could strike the swiftest. Lemon won. Her knife pierced Crosly's throat, forcing him to drop the hammer harmlessly behind her. They toppled to the ground, Lemon on top of Crosly.

"Ragghaghgh," cried the giant, while Lemon twisted her knife in his Adam's apple. He gurgled for several more moments before he lay dead. Lemon roared triumphantly.

Taking their proper cue, the actors were imbued with a lust for blood. The remaining members of Ben's vagrant army were cut down in rapid succession. Lorenzo Stokes was the first to go. In moments the compound was cleared of any resistance. Only sporadic gunfire could be heard in front of the Alaskan Queen.

"I wish it was over already," admitted Shmuel.

"Tell me," Belle retorted. "I have to pee so bad. If there was only an intermission."

Before Belle could continue with her complaining, Lemon

Lime appeared before her. "It's over," said the director. "Crosly Finch is dead."

"And Ben ...?"

"He has nothing left to fight with. His army's been destroyed."

"Hallelujah!" cried Jason, leaping from behind the bar. "I knew it, I knew it. I jes' knew we could kick his ass."

Belle was not as ready to submit to victory. "And Shelby?"

"He's not back yet. But he will be."

Belle sniffed in speculation of her nephew's demise. It was too much to consider. Her head swiveling, Lady Gluntz took in the surrounding destruction. Everything was in shambles. Her actors, her longtime companions, had been killed and wounded. The entire compound was rampant with the efflux of slaughter. And now her Shelby could be missing or dead.

"Oh God," she moaned. "Don't let it happen."

As if in answer to her prayer, Shelby appeared in the doorway. Thunderbird followed behind. He was wearing the Necklace. "We're all right," Shelby insisted. "We had a fine time picking them off from behind."

"And Ben ...?"

"Dunno. I never saw him."

Belle turned her gaze to the window. "Then he still could be out there. It may not be over yet. Can you imagine?"

"I suppose we won't know until the fog clears," advised Lemon. "My guess is that Ben's either dead or long since gone from Star City. He's not the type to hang around and suffer the consequences."

"Well," said the weary Hawkins. "I suppose we best clear out the dead."

Once outside the companions were vaguely surprised to discover they had been relieved of their gruesome task. The undertaker had already arrived with several buckboards and

330

a handful of assistants and had piled most of the bodies onto the wagons. Stacked in grotesque formation was the pile of mutilated sinew that had once been living persons. The companions were sickened by the horrible vision.

"Not since the war have I seen it that bad," swore Lopez.

"Yes," nodded Hawkins. "Not since the war."

When the undertaker had departed, the companions turned to each other. Each in his own way vowed never again to be drawn into battle. Each in his own way prayed he could keep his word.

Daybreak had almost arrived when the battle finally ended. It had been a long night indeed. Through the darkened hours Ben's army continued their shooting. The vanquished paranoids fired wildly at anything that moved. But by dawn the shooting ceased. The surviving gunmen had either fled the city or returned to the beer joints and flophouses from whence they came. Big Ben, however, was nowhere in sight. Under cover of the last patch of fog, he had disappeared.

For the next week or so, the companions did little more than lie about the ruins of the Alaskan Queen complex. Everyone was much too weary or too grieved for celebration. A disturbing quiet encompassed Star City. No one knew what to make of it. Even the reputable citizens of the community had drawn no conclusions as to where Ben's demise would lead. They hadn't expected it and were by now much too confused to speculate on their city's future.

At the end of the week Shelby grew restless. On several occasions since the battle he had experienced his dream, the old man waiting on the porch for the wizened black man to appear. With each review of his dream Shelby became more attracted to its sensation. It even offered him an obscure sense of comfort. He questioned Thunderbird about it, but Hawkins had only scoffed at him.

"Soon enough we'll be off and travelling," said Thunderbird. "Meanwhile, enjoy yourself with Lemon Lime."

And now it was time to go. Lopez had sensed it the moment he had opened his eyes that morning. The sky loomed above him, hemispheric and pristine. He was startled by the lucid image of the mountains, winding north away from Star City. "It's time to go," he informed Hawkins, who was sleeping in his favorite rocking chair. The Indian appeared contented, his belly puffed more than usual from the enormous breakfast he had recently finished.

Hawkins opened half an eye. He took in Shelby while his friend was still unaware. Lopez's determination appealed to Hawkins. Thunderbird was sure his friend was ready. "And Lemon?" yawned Hawkins, rising from the chair.

"She said she'll come with us."

"For how long?" tested Thunderbird.

"For as long as it takes."

"Good," belched the Indian. "The Great Book. It's nearby. I can feel it in my bones."

"Where?"

"In your vision. Your dream has released the secret. North of here, along the coast, there should be a cliffhouse, an abandoned shack that resembles the one in your dream. I'm sure we'll find it."

After the travellers had covered several miles of their journey, Thunderbird pulled off to the side of the road. He removed several handfuls of mushrooms from his leather pouch and passed them around. "This will help us all share your vision," he explained to Shelby. "Then we will know what we are seeking."

Shelby refused to question Hawkins' wisdom. In the time since he had first come upon Thunderbird on the desert,

Shelby had learned to know better. As had Hawkins realized that Lopez was no mere novice, but had been experienced to some degree in the ways of the world. Even when Hawkins turned from the highway and began to climb a narrow pathway which seemed to lead directly toward the mountains, Lopez asked no questions. His only gesture was in consolation to the puzzled Lemon Lime. She smiled back at him.

"I didn't come along to be the odd man out," she quipped, and then turned her horse toward the narrow little trail.

Despite the precariousness of their ascent, Shelby remained calm. The green waves crashing against the rocks below him offered its own brand of tranquility. The sound was pleasing to his ears. He stared over the edge of the cliff, noting the random patchworks of blue and green, passing through hues of red, white and foamy yellow. He giggled, surprised to discover his nose was numb.

Upon their arrival on the crest of the first mountain, Thunderbird began to chant. He lifted their spirits with the sound of his voice, for much expression was given to his mutterings. Subtle emotions squirmed through Lopez. He closed his eyes, viewing the world as being very small. The entire globe shrank to a cinder's proportions. He was able to see it all very clearly. In the distance stood the abandoned shack, further along the narrow trail which snaked across the rim of the mountains, through canyons and gulches, rising and falling with the lay of the earth.

Then once again he became the old man. He felt much better now, less apprehensive toward the results of his sudden metamorphosis. The wind cooled the soles of his bare feet. His beard touched the middle of his chest. He rocked easily in the old man's rocking chair. His nose sniffed the salt in the air. Just out of range Mo Moriarity was approaching. He paused briefly to gaze toward the bottom of the cliff. He counted the waves splashing against the rocks below. Their sound and rhythm relieved Mo's fatigue. He had travelled a very long way, and he was exhausted.

"You don't remember me, do you?" smiled Moriarity when he neared the hermit's chair.

But the hermit refused to move. "Moses Moriarity," he chanted through his continued rocking. "Older and wiser at the end of his journey."

"How do you know I've come to stay?" effused the ancient gambler.

"Once here, there's nowhere else to go. Journeys begin and end at the front of my house. You should know that by now. Even I can't escape it. It turns around and begins again."

"It could just go on forever. With no beginning, or no end for that matter."

"Haha," laughed the hermit. "You and I are so old, so tired. Could we continue without an end? What can we expect from our dry bones and aching muscles? There must be a change. A time for reformation."

Moriarity laughed his infectious laugh. "I hope the change begins at my feet. These ol' dogs have hiked their last. From now on I'm jus' gonna prop them before me, so they frame the horizon for my tired old eyes."

With that Moriarity revealed the book he was carrying. Hawkins accepted it with his trembling hands. "It is it, isn't it?"

"Yeah," laughed old Moses. "At long last you've taken possession."

"Ha, t' think of the years I spent in search of this Book. And now it comes to me through the hands of a friend. I thank him for showing me what I for so long have hoped to see. With the ocean before me and the Book in my lap I can at last die a contented man."

Moriarity took two cigars from his jacket and stepped up

334

on the porch. "It's a pity we never had the Great Book an' the Great Necklace together, interacting like legend dictates. I would've loved to have seen it. Just once. Not that it would do me any good, mind ya. But just to know what I was missing ..."

"I'm afraid it's nothing you haven't seen already. In the end there's just a beginning. And where it leads we still have no idea. What the Book and the Necklace would answer for us, we have seen before. Only we've forgotten. The facts and the details have fallen from our instincts."

"Still. I wish I could see it all at once. Life's greater purpose laid before me. Me. Poor, black Mo Moriarity. But at this point, I guess it doesn't matter."

"It doesn't. The sea still meets the beaches and the air still shifts the breeze. Attention to much else is little more than a foolish habit."

Mo stared down at his cigar. Its ashes pursued his fingers. Too exhausted to flick them he allowed them to drop at their own discretion. Impassively he brushed the ashes from his trousers and regarded the hermit.

"I guess we'll soon know what death has in store for us. What the end will bring."

"Just the beginning. Just one more time around."

Before the companions had emerged from their trance, they had witnessed the deaths of Hawkins the Hermit and Mo Moriarity. They died peacefully, Hawkins a day after Moriarity. Since then their shack had deteriorated, its porch collapsing in the midst of a storm. A tired relic, on brief occasions it enjoyed the company of a passing traveller, who occupied its four walls before moving on. In time, hardly anyone ventured near the ramshackle cabin. Even the narrow, winding pathway had lost its usefulness. For now the greater number of travellers took to the highway instead of the precarious mountain trail.

On their third day out from Star City the companions discovered the cabin. As in the dream it appeared in ruin. The chimney protruded from the rubble, and the hermit's broken rocker lay on its side. Behind the house, a fractured bucket hung from the well. Window hinges creaked in the breeze. Thunderbird, Lemon and Shelby all rode forward, searching through the brush. They dismounted and advanced on the debris, lifting broken beams, chunks of roofing material. They sifted through old utensils and clothing that had been discarded by previous travellers. They found nothing.

"It has to be here," swore Shelby.

It was Hawkins who contested. "The Great Book has no obligations. It appears at its own convenience."

"It's here," insisted Lopez before making for the house itself. He stepped in, emerging anxious moments later with the Book in his hand. "I found it! I found it!" His face and hands were blackened with soot.

"Where?" asked Lemon.

"In the bed of the chimney. Beneath a loose brick." He flipped through the pages for all to examine. Though dusty, the Book seemed as good as new. The companions frowned at the foreign inscriptions, the alien symbols they found inside.

"What does it mean?" asked Lemon.

"We still must find its secret," Hawkins answered. "Until then, it's of little use to us."

So engrossed were the companions that they failed to notice a passing shadow, dodging from bush to bush. Taking great pains not to arouse their attention, the figure grew nearer, a pistol outlined in its hand. It was Big Ben. He had followed the travellers since they had first left Star City. Ben cackled to himself from behind a clump of bushes. Revenge would soon be his. Staring down at his ragged outfit, soiled, torn and barely recognizable as clothing, Ben was reminded of his humiliation. He brushed the coarse stubble that grew from his blackened face and rubbed at the grease which spotted his forehead. His legs ached and his belly was pained by hunger. Bloodshot, his eyes were ravaged by delirium. Only his lust for revenge compelled him forward, kept him from collapsing from exhaustion. He cackled again. Now they would see who they had fucked with.

"All right," he shrieked while stepping from his cover. "Don't move! I'll take that book if you don't mind."

"Just a minute," Shelby protested.

Ben would hear nothing of it. "Either you give me the book or your dear Lemon gets it through the head."

"Then we kill you," challenged Shelby.

"That's fine with me. What's inside that book you're holding? A treasure map, perhaps? C'mon now, don't be bashful. Tell Big Ben what you possess. After all, he made it possible, didn't he? His ruination became your gain. Tell me! What's in the book?"

"We never meant you no harm. All Belle ever wanted was to be left alone."

"Left alone?" shrieked the midget. "She was intruding on my ground. She and that ridiculous uncle of yours. And that rotten Follies. A terrible performance in any man's town. Except in my own. Where nothing I tried could match it. Now give me that book!"

"You still don't see that you are blind," said Lemon. "You still don't understand. Even now, you wish to go on with your evil ways. Beaten, threadbare, you still continue. What's wrong with you? Are you totally mad? Have you lost all your senses?"

"Yes, I was king once. I stood out from others. But thanks to you, bitch, and that lousy Indian, I've been ruined. No one can take me seriously. How can a midget stand among skeptics?"

337

"It depends on who he's standing," grunted Thunderbird.

Ben reacted bitterly to Thunderbird's insult. "I stood on my own for many years, thank you. It wasn't easy. But I schemed and planned and fought for power until there was no one left to face me. And then you took it all away. Fools that you are. You underestimated the ways of Big Ben. You scoffed at my claim that I was the cruelest one of all. You denied my evil instincts. And for that you'll suffer. Now give me that book!"

Lemon stepped forward. "For ages this man, Thunderbird, has searched for that Book. And now, at last, he's found it. Would you deny him the reward of his lifetime? Just for a lousy moment of vengeance?"

"Don't plead with me, bitch! With each step you take toward me, you become a better target. Now what is the secret of the book that caused you to come all this way?"

Thunderbird refused to answer. But Lemon did. "The wisdom of the world, the destiny of man lies inside the Great Book."

"Give it to me!" snarled Ben, cocking his pistol. "Give it to me, before you die."

In fear for Lemon's life, Shelby finally relinquished the Great Book. "Take it, asshole. Here."

Ben took the book and backed toward the edge of the cliff. He cackled wildly, too excited by his next action to even describe it beforehand. "This is what I think of the destiny of man," he hissed before flinging the Book over the side of the mountain.

In horror the three companions raced to the edge of the cliff. The Book had disappeared, swallowed from vision by a series of hungry waves.

.Shelby offered his condolences to Hawkins. "I'm sorry. Damn. How terrible. How fucking tragic."

"That's all right," interrupted Hawkins with unusual nonchalance. "It just wasn't meant to be our time. Somehow I always knew that."

With a shrug of his shoulders Thunderbird mounted his horse. He ignored all of Ben's pleas that they should kill him. "C'mon," he said. "It's time we were away from here."

Shelby and Lemon climbed on their horses. They regarded Ben with avid disgust. His blackened face and ragged clothes were more pathetic than sickening. Shelby relaxed his hatred for the screeching little man.

"Kill me!" Ben shouted behind them. "Damn you! Kill me!"

"Don't," said Lopez when Lemon drew her gun. "He's nothin' now. Just a dust speck beneath the light of the sun. He'll vanish in time."

"Or grow stronger," Lemon answered. "Big Ben could rise again, you know."

When their trail intersected with a fork leading eastward, Hawkins dismounted. Shelby and Lemon followed suit. Readily, Hawkins embraced them, kissed them on their cheeks and foreheads. "With the will of the spirits, you'll remain protected for the rest of your lives. It does me good to know that. For we met as strangers and part as friends. It was love that kept us together, long enough to know the difference between the two. For love is greater than wisdom, when it transcends the fashion of knowledge. Perhaps I was a fool for making this journey. Maybe we were all fools, and our union only compounds our stupidity. Even so. There is no sorrow within me. Only love. And satisfaction."

"Thunderbird, where are you going?" Shelby pleaded. "So much waits for you in Star City."

Hawkins disagreed. "I must be off now. I am summoned by the spirits who await my return to the desert. Somewhere, in some other lifetime, we will meet again. Of that you can be certain."

Shelby couldn't control his weeping. Nor could Lemon, who in the short time she had known him had been touched by the odd-looking Indian.

"B-but how will we ever find you?"

"You'll know me anywhere. By the journey I travel beyond the horizon. Look for me in the clouds, in the sea, among the grains of sand. Feel my warmth and sense my breezes. Touch my spirit, for I am with you. Honor me with the birth of your child."

"B-but, w-we could . . ."

Hawkins brushed it away. "Nonsense," he said. "This is how it must be. Leave me, to gather the reins in my hand."

Unashamed of their crying, Shelby and Lemon watched Hawkins' departure. He headed eastward along the trail, lost to their vision when the pass wound round the mountainside. Nothing but his hat was visible, that ridiculous high hat, and then it, too, faded from view.

"I guess we should be off now," sniffed Lopez, barely recovered from the shock.

"Maybe we should wait for him to change his mind."

It would've been to no avail. For Thunderbird Hawkins continued onward, fighting the tears that blurred his vision. Soon he'd return to the desert, where he had been born to die. Sometime he'd be born again, fated once more to reunite with Shelby Lopez and Lemon Lime. But for now his journey was over. He'd travel no more. As he had entered the life of Shelby Lopez, Thunderbird Hawkins walked away.